Cradle
to
Grave

ALSO BY ELEANOR KUHNS

Death of a Dyer
A Simple Murder

Cradle
to
Grave

ELEANOR KUHNS

MINOTAUR BOOKS
NEW YORK

CRADLE TO GRAVE. Copyright © 2014 by Eleanor Kuhns. All rights reserved. Printed in the United States of America. For information, address St. Martin's Press, 175 Fifth Avenue, New York, N.Y. 10010.

www.minotaurbooks.com

Designed by Steven Seighman

Library of Congress Cataloging-in-Publication Data

Kuhns, Eleanor.
    Cradle to grave / Eleanor Kuhns.—First edition.
        p. cm.
    ISBN 978-1-250-05000-7 (hardcover)
    ISBN 978-1-4668-5119-1 (e-book)
    1. Shakers—Fiction.   2. Kidnapping—Fiction.
    3. Murder—Investigation—Fiction   I. Title.
    PS3611.U396C73 2014
    813'.6—dc23
                                    2014008310

Minotaur books may be purchased for educational, business, or promotional use. For information on bulk purchases, please contact Macmillan Corporate and Premium Sales Department at 1-800-221-7945 extension 5442 or write specialmarkets@mac millan.com.

First Edition: June 2014

10 9 8 7 6 5 4 3 2 1

*To Laura, who wanted this book written
and who served as my first reader*

Acknowledgments

Thanks to my agent, Mitchell S. Waters, and to Elizabeth Lacks, my collaborators in the writing process. This would be a much poorer book without their help.

Cradle
to
Grave

Chapter One

When Rees heard the buggy rattle up the drive, he left his loom and went downstairs to meet his wife of two months in the kitchen. Lydia had thrown her cloak over a kitchen chair and was intent upon the letter in her hand. Her mouth was trembling. He hurried to her side and put his arm around her shoulders.

"What happened?" he asked. "Is it bad news?"

"Nothing like that," she said, brandishing the letter. "It's from the Elders at Zion."

Rees smiled. Zion was the Shaker community in Maine where they had first met. He'd been searching for his runaway son and she living on the outskirts of the Shaker community.

"Ahh, another offer to buy your farm?" Since she'd inherited it from her previous husband, the Zion Elders had expressed interest in purchasing the property several times. And Lydia was eager to sell. She felt that the farm was cursed.

"No." She shook her head. "I mean, yes, Elder Hitchens mentions it."

"We'll deal with that when the weather turns this spring." A traveling weaver by profession, Rees was also a wanderer by nature, and he took any excuse to return to the open road. He was especially eager to leave Dugard now, after he'd hit his brother-in-law Sam Prentiss and knocked him into a mounting block. Remembering the sound of Sam's head hitting the granite block and the red blood blooming from his head sent a shudder through Rees. And the resulting injury had left Sam touched. If it weren't winter, Rees would be eager to leave.

"But that's not the primary reason for this letter," Lydia rushed on. "Elder Hitchens encloses a letter from Mouse."

"Mouse?" Rees repeated, his voice lifting in surprise. Hannah Moore, also known as Mouse, was a Sister at Zion. Although the uncertain mail service meant they heard from her infrequently, both Rees and Lydia still considered her a good friend.

"Mouse is no longer at Zion," Lydia said, sliding an interior sheet from the outside page.

"No longer at Zion?" Rees asked. "Did something happen? Why did she leave?" He paused, thinking. He knew Mouse had been happy at Zion, and she had family living nearby. He added with a twinge of remorse, "Did the Elders transfer her? Is she in trouble for helping me last spring?"

"I don't know. Sometime last summer she was transferred to Mount Unity near Dover Springs, New York, and is now a member of the Second Family. Her note to the Elders in Zion begs for our aid."

"Our aid? For what?" Rees's heart sank. He would always help Mouse, of course, but he didn't favor a long trip in February.

"Mouse is accused of kidnapping." Lydia handed the letter to Rees.

Kidnapping? Mouse? Astonished, he skimmed the carefully printed lines. "I beg you," Mouse wrote to Elder Hitchens, "please locate Will Rees and Lydia Jane Farrell. I know they will help me with the charge of kidnapping." The note attached by Elder Herman of Dover Springs yielded some additional information. Mouse did not deny taking the children, but claimed their mother was unfit. The town officials of Dover Springs refused to intervene and Sister Hannah was now restricted to Mount Unity, forbidden to leave for any purpose, even to visit the distressed family.

Rees brought the letter to the fireside and held it closer to the yellow light of the leaping flames. Elder Herman had written crosswise over Mouse's lines and his elegant cursive was difficult to read.

"He says that Mouse is much distraught, unable to accomplish her tasks and eating poorly," Lydia said, moving to Rees's side. "And why would she be accused of kidnapping? We must help her." She tipped her face up to look into her husband's and put her hand upon his arm. "If this is true, and she broke a law, she may be expelled from the Shakers. Where would she go then?"

Rees looked down into his wife's upturned face, still startled sometimes by the mobcap of a married woman over her red hair instead of the Shakers' white linen square. Although no longer a Shaker when he met her, she'd lived near Zion and maintained the Shaker ways. "It's February, Lydia," he said. "The roads are near impassable and the weather chancy at best. The Shakers would not be so cruel." He was more concerned about the prospect of finding Mouse in jail. Or even worse, the target of a vigilante.

"But this is Mouse," Lydia said, looking up at Rees. He saw to his horror that her eyes were full of tears. "We must help her." She took the letter from him. "Mouse wrote this in December, before Christmas. She's been waiting for us for nearly two months. And," she added, "this document cost me nearly three dozen eggs. I went to Borden's for candles and Mr. Borden gave me the letter." Rees nodded. Although there was a postmaster general and miles of post roads, letters still went to taverns and general stores, and the proprietors charged whatever they wished.

"So we'll be short of both eggs and candles," Rees said with a sigh. Lydia nodded. The chickens laid fewer eggs in the winter and this one had seemed particularly severe to Rees. Maybe that was because he'd spent the winters of the previous few years further south, weaving for farmwives in Pennsylvania, Maryland, and Virginia. It felt strange to be home for so long; in fact, it would be unbearable if Lydia weren't here.

"Mouse doesn't even know we're married," Lydia said, looking up at Rees.

"I know," he said. He stroked her cheek gently. "If it were later in the spring . . ."

"Please, Will. David can handle the farm in our absence," Lydia said. "We can take the sleigh."

Rees shook his head. "You said New York, did you not? Perhaps it isn't cold and snowy in New York. We would be marooned in the sleigh." He paused, comparing the wagon and the buggy in his mind. The former, although heavier, had no covering, and he was loath to travel a distance with no protection from the elements.

"Then we must take the stage," Lydia said, her voice rising. "I don't want Mouse to think we've forgotten her."

"She's living in Mount Unity, not homeless and living on the road," Rees said, exasperated.

"What if that community expels her? She has no family in New York." Lydia's mouth trembled in distress.

"I doubt Mouse will be expelled," Rees replied, putting a

hand on her shoulder to calm her. "Especially not now. They would not be so cruel. The Elders in Zion allowed you to remain near the community."

"Elder White was kind," she agreed.

He hesitated and added tentatively, "The weather will surely break in six weeks or so. . . ." He would gladly make the journey then.

Frowning, Lydia shook her head. "She's waited long enough. Will, she's relying on us. We must help her. Please."

Rees heaved a sigh, but he couldn't bear seeing Lydia so upset. "The stage will take too long. And I would rather have my own vehicle. I'll speak with Mr. Wheeler at the livery stable and see what he might recommend." He glanced out the window. The bright sun glittered on the snow and sent melted water dripping from the icicles, promising an illusory balminess. The buggy still sat outside the weathered gray barn, waiting for David's attention. "There's several hours before dark," Rees said. "I'll drive into Dugard now and talk to Wheeler and be back in time for supper." Lydia nodded and tucked the letter behind the candlesticks on the mantel. Rees went out to saddle Bessie. He realized as he rode down the snow-packed drive that somehow, without even realizing it, he'd agreed to make this ill-advised journey.

"Mr. Wheeler strongly advised us not to travel until the weather breaks," Rees said when he sat down to supper a few hours later.

"What did you say?" Lydia demanded.

Rees shifted uncomfortably under her scrutiny. "That you were fixed upon this course." She did not often display an absolute inflexibility on a decision but when it struck, Rees knew better than to argue.

"Good. What else did he say?"

"He reminded me of the fights I jumped into as a boy," he said. He tried to pass it off as of no importance, but she knew him too well.

"The beast," she murmured, referring to the term Rees used for his temper. "Did he criticize you for striking Sam?"

"No. Congratulated me. Wheeler said Sam is a difficult man." Rees managed a faint smile, although his throat closed up with guilt and shame. Lydia patted his hand. She knew how much the fight and its aftermath troubled her husband. He would not have chosen to travel in the depths of winter, but he would be glad to escape the accusation that suffused every one of his conversations here in Dugard. "Wheeler recommended taking either the buggy or renting a gig from him. We will want a roof over our heads in the event of snow or, less likely, rain. He further suggested we follow the stage route, as the roads will likely be more passable. Some of the stages are equipped with rollers that flatten the snow and make a smooth hard-packed surface."

"Did he say how long such a journey might take?" Lydia asked, her brow creasing as she began to plan.

"Two weeks or so if nothing untoward happens. We'll have to change horses at the stagecoach stops, and I expect we'll have to spend several nights at the local inns."

"This is beginning to sound expensive," Lydia said.

"Indeed. Besides the aforementioned, we'll also have expenses for food and tolls. . . ." Rees paused, thinking of the strongbox upstairs and the coins inside, last summer's earnings. He'd spent very little of it.

"When I sell the Ellis farm to the Elders in Zion we'll recoup all we've spent and more," Lydia promised. "Will we take Bessie?"

"No," Rees said, shaking his head. "She is coming to the end of her working life. Soon I shall have to invest in another Bessie to pull my wagon." Bessie number four. "We won't take Amos either. I arranged to rent a horse from Mr. Wheeler. Since he engages in regular custom along the post roads, we can switch horses as needed, and his horses will be returned to him. I am not so sure that will happen if I take any of mine. Besides, David will need ours." He paused. He didn't look forward to sharing these plans with his son. Although their relationship had improved over the last six months or so, David still blamed his father for leaving him with his aunt and uncle after his mother's death. Rees had to travel; his weaving brought in the money that helped support the farm, but abandoning his son to the cruelty of his sister and brother-in-law had been a mistake. David's anger still surfaced every now and then, especially when his father left on another journey. Rees accepted it, understanding that it would take a long time for David to forgive him.

"I'll write a response to Mouse and Elder Herman," Lydia said. "With mail service being the way it is, we'll probably reach Dover Springs before the letters, but just in case we're held up along the way."

"Likely we will be," Rees said, envisioning snowstorms and icy roads. He gathered Lydia into his arms and kissed her forehead. "But we'll be together."

"Together where?" David asked, coming into the warm kitchen from the barns. "Where are you going?" Snow coated his hat and had frozen into ice particles in the scarf wound over his mouth. He stepped back, his face and neck coloring as he took in the embrace. Lydia and Rees broke apart, exchanging a glance.

"A friend of ours is in trouble," Rees said.

"A good friend," Lydia agreed, jumping in to forestall the scowl gathering upon David's face.

"She needs us . . . we'll only be away for a little while. . . ." Rees stumbled to a stop, silenced by his son's glare.

"It's winter," David objected. "I thought at least you'd stay home for the winter."

"You don't need me here, not right now," Rees said, realizing he'd thrown fuel on the fire as soon as he'd spoken.

"I do need you," David said. "Why won't you ever stay home?"

"I'm a traveling weaver; that's what I do," Rees said. He knew David could never understand the hunger for new experiences that kept his father on the road, weaving for a living, instead of toiling on the farm.

"This time I asked him," Lydia said, taking a step toward David.

"I'll wager he didn't say no," David said angrily. "You'll see. He'll never stay home. Not even for you."

Rees saw Lydia swallow, her distress evident, and he put an arm around her.

"He must travel," Lydia said softly. "Weaving is his livelihood. The money he earns supports us."

"He could weave here, in town." David glared at his father. "You're running away just like you did after Mother died." The words hung in the air. Although Rees opened his mouth, he could not argue. This time, David was right; Rees was running away. Sam's injury hung between him and his neighbors. He saw recrimination even in the glances of his friends. And from those who disliked him? There were the sudden silences when he approached, and sometimes people would even rise from their chairs and leave when he entered a room. David continued. "A lot of people in town blame you for Uncle Samuel, blame you because he's touched in the head now. You need to stay and fight for yourself."

Rees could think of nothing to say. His friend and attorney George Potter's sworn testimony, that Rees had hit Sam only in self-defense, had pulled Rees out of the fire. And Sam's injury could be construed as accidental; he'd fallen and hit his head on the mounting block. But Rees knew that many people *did* blame him and, worse, he blamed himself. How many nights had he woken up in a cold sweat wishing he'd pulled his punch or kicked Sam's feet out from under him. Something else, anything else. But the beast, his anger, had put power behind his punch and Sam had gone down like a felled tree, cracking his head on the granite mounting stone. "It's not that simple," Rees said. "People here think I'm one step removed from a murderer."

"So go ahead," David said. "Run away. Again." The implication that Rees was a coward stung and he spoke quickly.

"I'll return in time for spring planting." But David pulled on his old coat and stamped out the door without replying. Rees took a few steps after his son.

"He wants you home," Lydia said, putting her hand on her husband's sleeve. Rees looked down into her face. "He's had a lot of change lately," she said. "Our marriage was just the last of them." Rees nodded. Although David had said nothing, he hadn't liked it when Rees and Lydia moved into the large southwest-facing bedroom once shared by his parents. Lydia paused and added, "I wouldn't ask this of you, but Mouse, well, she's my sister in all but blood."

Rees nodded and touched her wrist. "I know. And I promise you, I'll be home as much as I can," he said. "I won't leave you alone more than necessary." He didn't want her to feel abandoned, as David did. And probably as Dolly had, although he had not thought about it like that before. But at least Dolly had grown up here, and when the fever took her, her mother and sisters had been at her bedside. Lydia was a stranger in Dugard.

"Go after him," she said. "Talk to him. He needs you right now."

"David?" Calling his son's name, Rees pursued him outside. He had to trot to catch up and his boots slipped on the icy ground. "David, wait." He followed the boy into the shadowy barn, redolent of hay and cattle.

"Leave me alone," David said, turning his angry face away.

"David, it's Mouse. This time we're going to help Mouse." Last spring Rees had tracked David, who had run away from his aunt and uncle, to Zion, where he had taken refuge. He knew Mouse. "She's in trouble."

David sat down upon a haycock and frowned at his father, not quite willing to surrender his anger. "Mouse? What happened?"

Rees sat down beside him. "We're not sure. But she was sent away from Zion and now lives in Mount Unity, New York. She's been accused of kidnapping."

"Kidnapping?" David repeated. He shook his head. "I don't believe it. She was so kind and gentle."

"Yes," agreed Rees, "I'm finding the accusation incredible myself."

"When will you be back?" David avoided looking at his father, staring instead at the straw on the barn floor.

"I don't know. As soon as I can be. . . ." Rees's voice trailed off. "I'm sorry, David. You were counting on me, at least for the winter."

"Yes. I expected you to ride away as soon as the weather turned warm." David's smiled was pinched. "But I understand. Of course you must go now. It's Mouse. And you speak for those who can't. You told me that." Rees nodded, touched and embarrassed that David remembered. "You'll save Mouse. I know that. You've a talent for unraveling such knots." They were both silent a moment, reflecting upon Rees's resolution of the murders in Zion and here in Dugard.

"I'm not . . . abandoning you," Rees said, struggling to find the right words. "I trust you to run the farm. You're a man now." David said nothing, but a smile tugged at the corners of his mouth. Rees impulsively reached over and put his hand on the back of his son's neck. David twitched and for a moment Rees feared his son would shake off the fond gesture.

But David let his father's hand remain. "You haven't done that since I was a child," he said.

Rees nodded. "I wasn't sure you would allow it," he said, self-conscious of the emotion in his voice. David's white teeth bit his lower lip and he looked away, toward the black-and-white spotted cow in the stall. Frowning, he turned his gaze back to his father.

"What do I do if Aunt Caroline comes over?" he asked, switching to a less emotional topic. "What do I do if she tries to move in?"

Rees sighed. Anger and frustration always infused his thoughts of his sister, especially now that she expected him to support her and her family. Even the return of the deed to the Prentiss farm, which Rees had acquired and given to her, did not satisfy her.

"I'll speak to George Potter and Constable Caldwell," he replied. "If you have any trouble you apply to them for aid. She has no business on this farm." Even though she felt entitled to it. "If necessary, ask Caldwell to speak to her." David grimaced, still uncertain, but did not respond. "If she gives you too much trouble, I'll deal with her when I come home." Rees shivered and stood up, pulling his son up with him. "Let's go inside. It's cold out here. And it's almost time for supper. I'm hungry. Are you?" David nodded and they returned to the kitchen together, not speaking but content with one another.

Chapter Two

After almost two weeks of icy roads, snowstorms, and dirty beds in different inns, Rees and Lydia reached Dover Springs, a small town to the west of Albany. Its main street boasted a church, a general store, and a sprawling inn called the Ram's Head. Rees drove to the inn and immediately arranged for a room. Since mid-February saw few travelers, the three rooms on the second floor of the Ram's Head were empty and he was able to secure a large private chamber at the back. This room was the warmest, with the heat rising from the kitchen below, and very clean. They would not need to use the sheets and quilts Lydia had brought from home. Rees hoped they might find lodging with the Shakers at Mount Unity when they arrived, but that wasn't certain.

The common room was crowded with other diners, mostly men, although a solitary woman sat by the fire. Rees thought most looked like regulars; the men engaged in easy conversation with one another as they tucked into their full plates with gusto. The food here must be passable, at least, although both he and Lydia were too knackered from their journey to care. Lurching over the rutted roads, the frozen surface hard as iron, had made Lydia nauseous and she looked white and pinched as a result. An elderly man with lank gray hair struggled to rise from his game of checkers. He motioned them to an empty table.

"Have you traveled far?" he asked.

"From Maine," Rees said. "What do you have to eat?"

"Mutton stew or venison. Ale or whiskey to drink. Bad time for traveling, winter." He inspected them curiously.

"Do you have tea?" Lydia asked, her voice faint. "And bread?" Rees looked at his wife, noting her pale face.

"Rough journey, I suppose," the innkeeper said. "My daughter baked bread this morning. And we have cider."

"No. Just tea, please," Rees said firmly. He took Lydia's hand in his. She offered him a weak smile.

"Very well."

"Mr. Randall." A man at another table hailed him.

"Just a moment." He turned back to Rees. "And to eat?"

"Stew," Rees said, guessing that the venison would be tough and stringy. "For both of us. And bread," he added, with a look at Lydia. "I'll take the cider."

With a nod, Mr. Randall turned to the customer who had summoned him.

"What's wrong?" Rees touched Lydia's gloved wrist.

"Just a little tired. I don't think I can manage cider." She leaned across the table and said in a low voice, "We should go to Mount Unity immediately after supper. Mouse is waiting."

"We need to rest," Rees objected. "And it will be dark soon." When her mouth took on a mutinous curve he added, "And Ares needs to rest as well. I think at the last posthouse they gave us an older gelding. If we want to use him here . . ." He allowed his words to trail away, knowing she would not treat any animal cruelly. Lydia's mouth relaxed and she nodded, although reluctantly.

"Of course you're correct. It's just that we've come so far and are now so close, and I know Mouse must be very anxious."

"We'll leave for Mount Unity first thing tomorrow morning," Rees promised. Although he tried to speak quietly, his resonant voice attracted the attention of a dark-haired gentleman at the next table. He leaned over, scowling.

"You connected with that group?" he asked.

"No," Rees said. "Visiting someone."

"It's a strange company. They get up to all manner of evil. Some say even witchcraft." His eyes lingered a moment upon Lydia, as though refraining from sharing specifics because of her presence.

"Now Caleb, they've been good neighbors," the innkeeper said, frowning the younger man into silence. "Please forgive my nephew for his thoughtless remarks." The old man offered Rees a polite smile.

Rees acknowledged the comment with a nod. He and Lydia exchanged a glance; both were familiar with the distrust the Shaker communities received. Then Mr. Randall brought their food. He hesitated by the table asking questions, but Rees resisted all attempts to be drawn into conversation and he and Lydia ate their supper in silence.

They arose at dawn the following morning. Rees ate a hearty breakfast, although Lydia contented herself solely with a slice of bread and a cup of weak tea. As soon as Rees obtained directions to Mount Unity from the innkeeper, they left. The main road quickly dropped behind them, but the smaller route onto which they turned appeared just as heavily traveled. The rutted snow shone with a glaze of ice as though rain had fallen upon it or warmer temperatures had caused melting, only to refreeze during the night. Lydia held on, her gloved hands grimly clutching the rail as they lurched from side to side, her face almost as white as the snow around them. Rees touched her shoulder anxiously and she managed to smile at him.

He suspected the extensive fields around them, lying fallow under their blankets of snow, belonged to the Shakers. Even in winter they looked neat and well kept. "Hearts to God, hands to work" was a Shaker motto; they believed in honoring God through their labor, so everything they turned a hand to was as perfect as they could make it. Rees admired them for that, but he knew he could be neither obedient nor celibate.

They passed an orchard on the right. A black man wearing a flat-brimmed Shaker hat walked through the aisles, inspecting the trees. He did not look up as the buggy sped past.

Barns appeared on the left, and as Rees drove into the village the white Meeting House suddenly came into view. Set back from the road and screened by the barns, it sat directly across from the brick Dwelling House. Except for the man walking the orchard, Rees had seen no one. Cold and the regimen of daily tasks kept everyone busy inside. Rees pulled to a stop in front of the Dwelling House and turned to Lydia. She was looking around her, her lips pressed together. Wondering if she felt nostalgic for her former life and regretting the life she'd made with him, he reached out and put his hand upon hers. She looked at him, her eyes full of tears.

"I'm sorry," she said. "I'm not sorry for our marriage but . . ." Her free hand made a slight motion toward the structures around them. "I was happy with the Shakers. They were my family for so many years."

"We'll have another family of our own," Rees said. He tried not to reveal his hurt, but she knew. Quickly wiping her eyes dry with her black-gloved fingers, she smiled at him.

"I know. And I chose you, over this. I just feel sentimental."

"Sir. And Madam." An elderly man with a white beard approached the buggy. He was clad in a much worn blue coat. His eyes rested a moment upon Rees's black greatcoat and beaver hat, a wedding gift from Lydia, and then glanced at her. "Are you lost?"

"No," Rees said with a shake of his head. "We received letters from Elder Herman and Mouse—ah, Hannah Moore, a Sister here."

"This is First Family. Elder Herman guides the Second Family. I will direct you." He started walking rapidly. Rees urged Ares into a slow walk so they could keep pace.

"Chancy weather for traveling," the Brother said. "I don't think the Elder expected you until April or after." If ever. Unspoken, the words hung in the air.

"We would never abandon Sister Hannah," Lydia said in a chilly voice.

"I see." He gestured at the turn ahead. "Go right here." He preceded them down a narrow twisty road. Buildings began to appear on both sides. He stopped in front of a large brick building. "Come into the Dwelling House while I fetch the Elder."

Rees jumped out of the buggy and went to the other side to steady Lydia. The heavy folds of her thick wool cloak twisted around her legs and feet and she clutched his arm while she twitched the burgundy-dyed fabric into order. The Brother gestured to the two entrances. "We have a door for Sisters and a door for Brothers. . . ." He paused and looked at Rees and Lydia questioningly.

"Don't worry," Lydia said. "I'll wait on the women's side." She smiled at Rees. "We'll meet soon." She disappeared through the left-hand door. Rees passed through the other entrance, frowning with displeasure at being left to pace the small hall alone.

All the doors along the hall were open and the Sisters on housekeeping duty scurried through them. Rees, who'd first met Mouse when she was cleaning the rooms of the Brethren at Zion, smiled at one young woman. Uttering a squeak of dismay, she fled toward the back. The Sisters rarely met strange men, especially when going about their daily chores.

"Mr. Rees?" A lanky man with a full beard appeared at the door. He removed his hat and revealed curly dark hair. Gray streaked his beard and glittered at his temples so Rees assumed the Elder was at least a few years older. "Come with me. I'm Elder Herman. One of the Eldresses will meet us in the office with your lady wife." As he spoke, he led Rees out of the Dwelling House toward the Meeting House across the street. "We're surprised to see you so soon, and in winter, too. I told Sister Hannah you were unlikely to arrive before spring, but she was convinced you would arrive sooner." Casting a thoughtful glance at Rees, Herman added, "I see her faith in you was not misplaced."

"I am very fond of Mouse," Rees said. "We both are, my wife and I."

They went up the narrow flight of steps to the second floor. The apartment in the Meeting House at Zion was arranged in a similar fashion, but this one was larger, with at least two additional rooms. And Lydia was already here, waiting in the hall, her cloak hanging from a peg on the wall. She turned to her husband with a relieved smile as he hung his garment beside hers.

"Eldress Agatha," Herman said, motioning toward the Sister behind Lydia. "The other Elders are busy at their work." With a gesture he invited them to enter the rearmost room. A large table occupied the center. Elder Herman took two chairs down from the pegs on the wall and put them in front of the table. "Please sit down, Mr. and Mrs. Rees."

"Will we see Sister Hannah?" Lydia asked, clutching at the back of the chair.

"Yes," the Elder said. He glanced at the Eldress standing next to him. She was older than he was, her wispy gray hair drawn back under her linen bonnet, but her face was smooth and unlined.

"I'll fetch her from the kitchen in a few moments," she said.

"We wanted to tell you what happened before you spoke with her," the Elder added. "Please, sit." Exchanging a glance, Rees and Lydia did as they were bid.

"Your letter said Mouse tried to kidnap some children?" Rees said. He hadn't meant to reveal his doubt but he could hear it in his voice.

The Elder nodded at Rees, his expression grave. "She did. She confessed to it, in fact, as I indicated in my letter." Lydia's eyebrows rose and Rees suspected he looked as astonished. "We always bring baskets of food to the needy before Christmas. And the Whitney family is very needy. Sister Hannah begged to be included. She'd only just arrived in August." His words trailed away.

"Only a little while after we left Zion," Lydia said remorsefully.

"We were asked to leave," Rees reminded her. All of the non-Shakers had been, while the new Elders and Eldresses reorganized the community. "Mouse was willing to brave the outside world?" Rees asked. Mouse was self-conscious of her harelip, even with those she knew, and had rarely set foot outside of Zion.

"Yes. But this was the celebration of the birth of Our Lord, who made the blind see and the lame walk. And we tried to restrict her to visits with some of our elderly widows. We thought they might be more tolerant of her"—he hesitated, appearing to consider several words before choosing one—"mark. And there were no problems with them."

"So what happened?" Rees asked.

"The Deaconess leading the group was accustomed to calling upon Maggie Whitney's aunt, Olive Tucker. She passed away a few years ago. Sister Hannah was willing to visit the children."

"Eager to," put in Eldress Agatha.

Lydia nodded. "She loves children," she said.

"The first visit went well. They returned a few days later with a second basket. But this time Mrs. Whitney was . . ." Again that hesitation, as the Elder struggled to find the appropriate word.

"She was drunk," the Eldress said, disapproval thickening her tone.

Herman nodded. "Mrs. Whitney is a wet nurse and has a foundling right now, a little boy. He was sick, so Sister Hannah asked to be left with the children, to care for them, and to tend the baby. She spent all night walking the cabin with that child in her arms. And he survived. But Sister Hannah made a complaint that Mrs. Whitney was unfit. The town fathers from Dover Springs looked into it." He paused and then added, carefully choosing every word, "They investigate Mrs. Whitney regularly. There is some question as to whether she should be warned out. I believe they are worried that she will apply for Poor Relief, although so far she has not."

"I see," Rees said, understanding the disapproval he heard in the Elder's voice. The selectmen enjoyed complete authority in determining who among the needy in their town deserved Poor Relief. Any poor soul not born in town, or sometimes those whose parents were not born in the jurisdiction, could be warned out. Warning out was a euphemism for expulsion and entire families, pregnant women, even young children could be seen wandering the roads in search of a home. "Mrs. Whitney was not born in Dover Springs?"

"She was, I am told, but not her mother. No one knows anything of her father. So, in the opinion of several selectmen,

Maggie is not a resident and so not deserving of a claim on the public coffers."

"But you said she hasn't even applied," Lydia said, her voice rising with sympathy.

"They must be afraid she will," Elder Herman said. "She has four children of her own besides the little boy." His expression combined both pity and anger.

"Would she have joined the Shakers?" Rees asked.

Elder Herman shrugged. "I don't know. Not everyone can live as we do. Celibacy and obedience can be difficult rules." He sighed. "Anyway, Maggie Whitney claimed she celebrated the season a little too enthusiastically and promised she would not fall into such a state again. So they left the children there. A few days later, Sister Hannah stole one of our buggies and drove to the farm. Although I don't know the particulars, she managed to gather up the children and put them in the buggy and drive them here. We were horrified, as you might imagine." He paused and added, "We worried that our entire community might be blamed. We are suspect for our beliefs as it is, and several of the town fathers still have not forgiven us for refusing to fight in the War for Independence."

Rees nodded. "Passions ran high during the war," he agreed.

"And haven't entirely faded now," said Herman, a line forming between his brows. "Anyway, a few hours later, Mrs. Whitney arrived to recover her children. Since she had not been declared unfit, we had to relinquish them to her care. Sister Hannah has been restricted to this community since."

"She has been in a state," said Sister Agatha with a frown. "She is in the kitchen right now, moping over the cut vegetables."

"Mouse has been a Sister a long time," Lydia said, shaking her head in disbelief, "and would not break her vow of obedience lightly. She must have been certain those children were in danger, to take that step."

Rees nodded in agreement. Mouse's goal had always been to become one of the Sisters charged with the care of the children adopted into the community. She might never attain that dream now.

"You say there are four children?" Lydia asked.

Herman looked at the Eldress. "Five, including the found-ling," she said. "But we'll let Sister Hannah disclose the remainder of this tale to you. We wanted you to know, however, that she has never denied taking those children. Indeed, she could not, since she brought them here. I don't know what she expects of you, or what you can do to help her."

"Be here, so she knows we support her," Lydia said. The sharpness in her voice created a short stillness. The Elder looked at Lydia but said nothing. Lydia did not lower her gaze. Then the Eldress rose to her feet and left the room.

The sound of footsteps upon the stairs interrupted the uncomfortable silence. But it was neither Mouse nor Sister Agatha who came through, but a young girl carrying a tray. The severe Shaker garb could not disguise her soft clear skin or the pink in her cheeks. She did not dare look at either of the visitors but slid the tray onto the table. "Sister Agatha sent me," she said in such a quiet voice Rees could barely hear her.

"Thank you," the Elder said. As the girl hurried from the room he gestured to the food. "Please," he said to Rees and Lydia, "refresh yourselves." He removed the lid from a tall pitcher and the fragrance of cinnamon and nutmeg wafted through the room. Rees sucked in his breath in delight; the Shakers were famous for their cider and this had been warmed and spiced. Both Rees and Lydia accepted mugs of the hot cider, but only he took a plate with a slice of apple cake. Lydia wrapped her hands around the mug but did not drink. Her knuckles turned white with the tightness of her grip and Rees realized she was nervous.

Well, he was, too, as he contemplated Mouse and the trouble she was in.

Rapid footsteps rattled up the stairs and Mouse appeared at the top of the steps. Tears of joy and relief filled her eyes and streamed down her cheeks. "I knew you'd come," she cried, and ran toward Lydia with her right arm outstretched.

Chapter Three

Lydia jumped up, releasing her mug so hurriedly it slopped cider on the table, and opened her arms. Mouse ran into Lydia's embrace. Elder Herman turned away from the naked display of emotion and joined Eldress Agatha by the door. Rees sensed their embarrassment and faint disapproval.

After more than a minute of hugging and loud exclamations, the excitement abated. Rees handed his handkerchief to Lydia. She mopped Mouse's wet face, drew her toward the table, and pressed her into a chair. Herman quickly took down another seat and placed it next to Mouse. Lydia sank into it and grasped Mouse's hand. "Oh my dear," she said. "What's happened to you?"

Rees pushed his chair forward so he could see the young woman's face, or what was visible above the hand that shielded her mouth from view. Dark circles ringed her eyes and her skin was pale and tired.

"Did the Elder tell you . . . ?" Mouse looked at Elder Herman.

"He told us a little," Rees said. "We know you took the children."

"I *rescued* the children," she declared. "I tried to tell the constable and the town council but they wouldn't listen. Maggie Whitney was born in Dover Springs, after all. And she's a property owner. She owns that little farm. But those men wouldn't listen."

"Tell us about the night you stayed with the children," Lydia said. "How many children are there?"

"Five. Four are that woman's, but the baby, Joseph, was put to nurse with her. He's a foundling." She clutched at Lydia's hand. "He was so sick. Coughing and struggling for breath. And that woman passed out in the other room." Rage twisted her features and for a moment she did not resemble the gentle girl Rees knew.

"So you stayed to care for the children," Lydia said.

"Yes. There was almost no food in the house, other than what we'd brought in the basket. So I made mush. Simon helps out at the dairy next door and he brought some milk."

"Simon?" Rees asked.

"Mrs. Whitney's oldest boy. He . . . I don't know what the arrangement is but he goes to the dairy every day. Like an apprentice. Fortunate for that family, else those children would starve. Anyway, after I fed them and washed up, they went to bed. And I walked with Joseph around and around. Every now and then I put a little rag on the end of a splint and swabbed out his nose so he could breathe. He hated that. But when I boiled water for tea, it seemed to help him; the steam seemed to help him. By morning he was better."

"But a child that young must still be nursing," Lydia objected. "How did you feed him?"

"Yes, Joseph is still nursing. Next morning I made more mush for the children. I thinned it with milk for Joseph and fed it to him with a pap spoon. His breathing was better so I put him in the cradle and he went to sleep. Then that woman finally left her bed." Her voice went shrill with fury.

"Then what happened?" Lydia asked, her voice low and calm. "Did the Deaconess return for you?"

Mouse nodded, angry tears exploding from her eyes. "Yes. And that woman, Maggie Whitney"—she spit out the name—"said she didn't need me anymore, unless I wanted to bring some more food."

"So you came home?" Rees asked.

"No, not directly. I went to the Ram's Head to look for the constable. I found him, too. He said he would speak to the town fathers. But a week later I heard they'd decided to do nothing. Mrs. Whitney was not a charge upon the town's Poor Relief, you see. Her aunt left her the little farm and Simon brought in some money and she seemed to be able to support the children on her earnings as a wet nurse, so they left her alone."

"So you took matters into your own hands," Lydia said.

Mouse nodded, sniffling. "I had to. I took one of the buggies and I drove to the Whitney farm. She was nowhere to be found, of course. So I packed up the four children at home—Simon was at the dairy, I believe—and drove them here."

Rees and Lydia exchanged a horrified glance. Rees could just imagine the mother's reaction to finding an empty house. "She must have been terrified," Lydia murmured.

"She went to the constable, I'll wager," Rees said. Mouse nodded. "And a few hours later the constable arrived here to recover the children?"

"Yes," Mouse said. "But why?" Raising her head, she stared at Lydia and Rees defiantly. "She can't possibly love them. Why would she want them returned to her?"

"And the children?" Lydia asked. "How did they feel about their visit here?"

Scarlet surged into Mouse's pallid cheeks and she looked away from Lydia.

"They were frightened," Elder Herman said, breaking into the conversation. "They ate a hearty meal, at least that was something they enjoyed. But the three youngest cried to go home and the oldest girl asked when they would be sent home to their mother. And when Mrs. Whitney and the constable arrived, they ran down to greet her."

"They didn't understand," Mouse cried. "Once they were used to us they would have loved it here."

"They would always miss their mother," Lydia said, her tone gentle. "I know. You love them and wanted to save them."

Mouse nodded. "The worst of it is, I've been forbidden to visit them again. I haven't seen them since. I don't even know if Joseph is still alive." Mouse broke down into sobs, terrible sobs that sounded as though they were being torn from her.

Lydia pushed her untouched mug of cider into Mouse's hands. "Drink some of this," she said. "You'll feel better."

Elder Herman rose to his feet and gestured to Rees. He stepped away from the two women and approached the older man. "Mrs. Whitney, of course," Herman said in a low voice, "did not want to chance losing her children again and the constable concurred. We, the other Elders, agreed it would be best not to refer to the children again in Mouse's presence." Rees glanced at Eldress Agatha, who nodded.

"We hoped she would put her memories of them aside."

"But her love and concern for them is tearing her to pieces," Rees said. He didn't care that he sounded accusing. "She knows she'll never have babies of her own. She cares for those children. Especially for the foundling."

Elder Herman turned to look at Eldress Agatha and they shared an unspoken thought. "Perhaps we were mistaken," he said, his tone stiff. "Perhaps we should have kept an eye on the Whitney family and shared our knowledge with Sister Hannah. Perhaps that would have been enough to ease her."

"We feared it would do more harm than good," Eldress Agatha

said. "Like taking a knife to her heart and inflicting a dozen little cuts. She would never have a chance to heal."

"Well, the method you chose certainly hasn't worked," Rees said, turning to look at the girl sobbing in Lydia's arms. He moved to stand behind his wife. "Mouse," he said sternly. "Stop crying. Tell us what you want us to do."

Mouse nodded. Rees and Lydia waited in silence as she fought to compose herself. "I want you . . . to look in on them. Is the baby all right? Talk to the constable and those town fathers." She looked directly at Rees. "You're a man. Maybe they'll listen to you."

"Very well," Rees said. He would do it even though he knew neither the constable nor the town selectmen would pay him any heed. Rees, too, was an outsider, not even connected to the Mount Unity Shakers. But at least he and Lydia could visit the family, check on the baby's health, and communicate their findings to Mouse. It would do no good to argue with her now. "Lydia and I'll drive out to the Whitney farm immediately," he promised. "And we'll return to report to you."

Mouse jumped to her feet and looked ready to throw herself into Rees's arms. "Thank you!" she exclaimed. "Thank you! I knew I could rely on you."

"It's time to return to your duties," Eldress Agatha said, eyeing Mouse with censure. "And I hope you perform them in the proper spirit, with a light heart as you honor God. Now, come with me. You must wash your face and order your clothing before returning to the other Sisters."

Mouse bowed her head obediently, but she shot a quick glance at Rees from blue eyes sparkling with hope.

As her footsteps receded down the stairs, Herman said, "Thank you both for coming. You have eased her heart."

"I don't know how much we will be able to achieve," Rees said, turning to look at the Elder. He nodded.

"We do not expect you to succeed in removing the children from their mother. That is a problem for the World outside. We invited you here to ease Sister Hannah, whose adjustment to Mount Unity has not been an easy one. And Elder Hitchens from Zion assured me you knew and understood some of our ways"— his gaze involuntarily touched Lydia—"and have acted on behalf of our community in the past."

"I didn't lie to Mouse," Rees said, annoyance sharpening his tone. "I will speak to the constable and to the selectmen for her, whether they listen or no."

"Of course," Herman said. "A promise is a bond." He gestured to the stairs, too polite to tell his guests to leave, but suggesting it just the same.

Rees helped Lydia into her cloak. They did not speak as they descended the stairs and went out into the cold air. "I had hoped they would invite us to stay," Rees said as they crossed the snowy road to the buggy.

"I'm glad they didn't," Lydia said. She took Rees's arm and turned her anxious face up to his. "Oh Will, I don't think Mouse is happy here."

Rees looked into Lydia's upturned face. He wished he could offer her comfort, but he couldn't. He thought the same.

They returned to the tavern for an early dinner. It was not quite noon but it had been a difficult morning. The bowl of hot stew and slice of fresh-baked bread put the color back into Lydia's cheeks. "Surely the town fathers would have taken those children away if Mrs. Whitney were truly unfit," she said for perhaps the third time.

Rees nodded and glanced pointedly at the crowded tables around them. The innkeeper sat at his checkerboard, well within earshot. Rees knew the old man was listening: there was something about his tense shoulders, despite his apparent focus on his game.

"Perhaps," he said. "Are you ready to leave?"

Lydia daintily ate her last bit of buttered bread and assented.

Rees put the rest of the loaf in his pocket with the last bit of cheese and a bottle of small beer, in case he felt hungry later. Then he approached Mr. Randall to ask for directions to the Whitney farm. The innkeeper straightened up and regarded Rees and Lydia.

"Are you kin to Maggie Whitney?" he asked.

"No," Rees said vaguely. "A friend of a friend. We just thought we'd look in on her." He didn't know how the town might feel about Mouse and her attempt to remove the Whitney children but found Mr. Randall's interest unsettling.

Mr. Randall nodded, looking around at the customers filing in, and said, "Come to the lobby." Rees grasped Lydia's arm and they followed the man out of the commons room.

The lobby was a small cramped box with a desk and stairs at the back leading to the upper floors. Mr. Randall could still see into the commons room but now had created some privacy. "Maggie could use a friend or two," he said, looking at Rees and Lydia with more warmth. "Go north on the road just outside. Follow it maybe ten miles out, turn right on the first road you come to. First drive on your right is the Tucker drive."

"Tucker?"

"Sorry. It's Maggie's. Old habits: the farm belonged to her aunt, Olive Tucker. If you reach a large farm, you've gone too far. And if you miss that first right, and reach a log church, you're on the wrong road."

"Thank you," Rees said, feeling faintly guilty. He was more a friend of Maggie's enemy than her friend. Lydia nodded politely at Mr. Randall before following Rees out to the stable yard. Ares resisted leaving his warm stall for the second time that day and the groom had to call for help from one of his fellows. The two men, with Rees's help, finally forced the gelding into the harness. Ares settled and the head groom handed the reins to Rees with a sigh of relief.

Rees waited until they were on the road before picking up the conversation exactly where they'd left it. "I hope the town fathers care about these children," he said, although he doubted they would take any action that might cost them money. "I know neither they nor the constable will take me any more seriously than they did Mouse."

"Maybe," Lydia said, throwing him an amused glance, "but when has that ever stopped you from doing what you think is right?" Rees laughed, a touch ruefully. Never, not even when it endangered his life. "That's what makes you such a good man," she added, and reached over to touch his arm. Rees felt a burst of happiness rise up inside of him. It was a new and unexpectedly wonderful experience to trust another person. He hadn't realized how alone he'd been. "But don't become prideful," she added, rolling her eyes toward him, and Rees laughed aloud.

"Yes, ma'am," he replied with mock contrition.

They soon left the main thoroughfare for a snowy secondary road. The going was slow and it took the better part of an hour to cover the ten miles outside of town. Lydia spotted the copse of trees marking the next turn and pointed it out. Rees groaned when he saw the lane. Although foot traffic had trodden down the snow somewhat, few horses and even fewer wheeled vehicles had passed this way. Ares struggled to pull the buggy but the snow caught at the wheels and held fast. Finally Rees jumped out and grasped the old horse's bridle. With his substantial weight gone, the buggy shot forward. Rees would have toppled facefirst into the snow but for his grasp upon the horse's leathers. They staggered forward the final one hundred feet to the drive.

Breathing hard, Rees stared up the slope to the weathered gray cabin at the top. Then he urged Ares forward the last twenty yards or so to the front door of the Whitney residence.

He looked around. This holding, although small, had once been cared for. The henhouse was out of the wind and well sited where it would catch the winter sun but sit in shade in summer. It was empty now. A battered scarecrow sat sentinel over an overgrown field and although a barn hinted at housing for larger livestock, Rees saw no cattle, pigs, horses, or even mules. He walked back to the buggy.

"Ready?"

Lydia nodded. Rees helped her down from the buggy and, arm in arm, they approached the cabin.

Chapter Four

❧

Rees knocked upon the weathered door. A baby was screaming inside. After a few moments a young girl opened the
door. Small and slight with tangled flaxen hair and a dirty face,
she wore a tow dress inexpertly cut down to fit her and overlarge
clogs. She could not have been older than nine, but her eyes were
red with exhaustion and her mouth was squeezed tight. She looked
at them without speaking.

"Sister Hannah sent us," Lydia said.

"Mouse?" The child broke into a smile. "Why hasn't she come
to visit us?" Rees, who'd expected her to be frightened or angry,
couldn't think of an immediate reply.

"She . . ." Lydia cast Rees a desperate glance. "She wants to,"
she said.

"She's been kept at Mount Unity," Rees said.

"That's why she sent us," Lydia said. "What's your name?"

"Jerusha," she replied, throwing the door open. "Come in."

The first thing Rees noticed was the smell, a pungent eye-
stinging ammonia odor of dirty diapers and the musky animal
aroma of unwashed children. Except for a table, five chairs lined
up in front of the fireplace, and a battered cradle, there was no
furniture. No beds, but for a small nest of blankets near the
hearth. And even in his stout boots and heavy greatcoat Rees

could feel the cold air seeping through the gaps between the bare wooden floorboards.

· Jerusha caught his overt inspection of the cabin. "We had to put the chairs there. Joe kept crawling toward the fire. I didn't want him to get burned."

Rees looked at the baby hauling himself to a standing position on one of the chairs. His dress was filthy and the long grubby tail of an unwinding diaper dragged behind him. He turned and offered the visitors a big grin, revealing three pearly little teeth. Unlike Jerusha and the small girl behind her, who were fair with bright blue eyes, he was dark with a fuzz of fine black hair and brown eyes.

"How old is he?" Lydia asked, her voice trembling. Rees glanced at her. Her face was so colorless it looked greenish.

"Ten months or so," Jerusha said. She gestured to the other two children staring at the visitors. "My brother and sister: Judah and Nancy."

Uncombed dark brown hair touched Judah's shoulders and his eyes were not blue but hazel. He still wore a dress but the front pleat that identified him as a boy was ripped almost to the waist. Judah put his hands over his eyes so he wouldn't see them. Nancy was older, five or six, Rees guessed, and quite dirty. Despite the cold, everyone but Jerusha was barefoot and, although not gaunt, none of them looked well nourished.

"Do you have any food?" Lydia asked, stripping off her cloak and bonnet. Then she looked around in bewilderment; there seemed no place to put them.

"Pegs by the door," Jerusha said with a nod, just like a little old woman. Without comment Lydia put her cloak next to the tattered shawl that probably served as Jerusha's coat and a woman's blue cloak with a long three-cornered tear at the bottom.

"I used the last of the cornmeal this morning," Jerusha said with a sigh. Rees recalled the bacon and eggs, the loaf of bread, and the oatmeal that had made up his breakfast and the hearty dinner he'd consumed not more than an hour ago and felt guilt sweep over him. Lydia glanced at him, her eyes moistening. She pressed her lips together.

"I have something," Rees said, putting his hand on the pocket of his greatcoat, then remembered he'd left the food in the buggy. "I'll fetch it." He darted outside and could not resist drawing in several deep lungfuls of fresh sweet air.

He broke the ice in the trough so Ares could drink and took the napkin-wrapped parcel from the buggy seat. When he entered the cottage, the ammonia stink from the diapers drying by the fire seemed even stronger.

Lydia had rolled her sleeves to the elbow and wrapped a rag around her waist to cover her gown. She was attempting to sweep the floor with an almost bald broom. "I'll need a kettle full of water," she said to Rees.

"I'll fill it with snow," he said with a nod.

"And drinking water . . . Is there a well?" Lydia turned to Jerusha.

"No. We fetch our water from a spring." She looked at Rees thoughtfully. "I'll show you. We can carry more if there's two of us."

"I'll fetch the wash water first," Rees said, grabbing up the copper. Old and much used, it was scratched and dented. But he suspected Lydia planned to wash diapers as well as the table and the floor, and he didn't want to use the kettle in which the food was cooked for that water. Not that it would matter; even the inside of the black kettle was crusty with the remains of several previous meals.

He went outside and found a drift of clean snow. He piled the snow into the pot, packing it in until it was almost too heavy to carry. He staggered back inside and put the kettle on the crane over the fire.

Lydia had already taken down the cloth squares from the line over the hearth and swept the table clean. Rees peered at the garment she had spread out upon the wood; it looked like her petticoat. As he watched she slashed the linen with a knife and ripped a long slit in the cloth. A slash across the top and down the other side, and she'd manufactured a large clean linen square. A fresh diaper. Folded into several thicknesses it would serve for a little while and perhaps the other clouts would be washed and dried by the time it required changing. She quickly cut several more. Under the guise of inspecting her work, Rees leaned over her.

"Where's the mother?" he whispered.

"In the other room. Sleeping. She's 'ill.'" Her mouth twisted with angry disgust.

Jerusha took her ragged shawl from the peg and wrapped it around her shoulders. "Watch the babies," she told Nancy. She picked up a small pot. "Ready?" Rees snatched up another pot and followed her from the cabin.

Rees watched her totter forward in the large clogs. The bare wood of her shoes rubbed angry red patches on her delicate skin. But she didn't complain and Rees wondered if her feet were so cold she didn't feel the scrapes.

They walked down to the lane and across to the woods on the other side. A well-trodden path looped through the trees and as they walked deeper into the forest Rees heard the sound of running water. They broke through the trees and Jerusha knelt on the bank of a fast-moving stream, the water whipped into a creamy froth by the jutting rocks and boulders. Rees looked at the ice coating the stones. "Does this stream ever freeze?" he asked.

"Sometimes. Not often. The water runs fast and it's deeper than it looks." She scooped up the icy water in the pot. She was careful and did not plunge her hand into the water. But Rees had a clear view of her feet, tinted blue by the cold.

He thought of his thick wool socks, hand-knitted for him by Lydia. After all, he wore stockings underneath them and stout leather boots so he didn't really need the socks, did he? He thought his wife would approve, something that had become increasingly important over the last few months. He sat down upon a boulder and began taking off his boots.

"What are you doing?" she asked.

"Giving you my socks. They'll be too big for you, of course, but they should keep your feet warm."

"Why would you do that?" Jerusha asked, her voice shrill with astonishment.

"I have stockings and boots," he said, peeling off the sock and handing it to her. "Put it on. I'll have the other one in a moment."

She took the sock, staring at it in disbelieving joy, and then quickly sat down and put it on. Rees peeled off the second sock and handed it over. He was so tall, and she so small, that the socks went up over her knees, the heels mid-calf. Stamping his feet back into his boots, which felt odd without the thickness of his socks, Rees picked up the pots of water.

"It is a long way to go for water," he said as they started back.

"Not really," Jerusha said. "It's better in the winter, though, than summer. Too many mosquitoes then. And we use more water, too," she added as an afterthought.

Lydia had scrubbed the table and laid out Rees's bread and cheese upon wooden plates. The other three children were seated at the table and even the baby was eating. Lydia had mashed the bread into crumbs and mixed it with something; Joseph's plump hands were clutching at the pottage and scooping it into his mouth. Rees peered in revulsion at the brownish mess. "Maple syrup," Lydia said, wiping her arm across her forehead. "I found a jug in the cupboard."

"Mama will be angry," Jerusha warned. "The syrup was a gift. We aren't supposed to eat it."

"Joseph must eat," Lydia said with a snap. When Jerusha, blinking anxiously, looked at Lydia, she clamped her mouth shut so she wouldn't express her opinions about Mama, all of them unkind.

"You must be hungry, too," Rees said, giving the child a little push toward the table. Tossing her shawl on the peg, she hurried forward. Lydia glanced at the child, noticing Rees's socks upon those small feet. When she looked up, he shrugged. "Her feet were bare."

"You are a good man, Will Rees," Lydia said, the approval in her smile warming him all the way through.

Bobbing his head self-consciously, Rees turned to pour the water into the oak bucket.

In a moment of quiet after the children had eaten, Lydia went to the copper boiling over the fire and stirred it. "I couldn't find soap," she said, "so I hope hot water will be enough." She swung the crane away so that the water in the copper could begin to cool.

She dipped a corner of a rag into the hot water and then into the cold. After testing it upon the soft skin inside her wrist and judging it the proper temperature, she brought it to the table and began wiping faces and hands. Rees watched her in amazement. Did women just instinctively know how to do these things?

All of the children fought the rag save Jerusha. Joseph screamed until Jerusha picked him up, her slight frame bowing with the effort. The baby relaxed into Jerusha's shoulder, snuffling wearily. "He's tired," she said. Lydia stretched out her arms to take the baby from the girl but suddenly paused.

"He'll settle with you," she said. "Why don't you lie down next to him and maybe he'll fall asleep. Judah, too." She looked at Nancy, who was rubbing her eyes. "And Nancy." She didn't comment on Jerusha but Rees knew Lydia saw the same exhaustion in the child's face as he did himself.

"I'm not tired," Nancy proclaimed.

Jerusha followed Lydia's gaze and nodded. "We'll all lie down for a moment," she said. "None of us slept well last night. Mama was . . . upset."

She shepherded the younger children to the pile of rags and arranged the tattered cover over them. Then, exhaling a weary sigh, she lay down in the middle, curving her body around the baby. Nancy and Judah rolled closer to Jerusha and in a few moments all was quiet. Lydia looked at the nest of children, huddled together under rags, and took her cloak down from the peg to spread over them.

"I suppose I'll have to wash my cloak immediately," she said, as though tears of pity did not shine in her eyes.

Rees smiled at her. "I know. I'll get some wood," he said.

Since the children had collected all the sticks nearby, he was forced to cross the road and collect the deadfalls. As he gathered as many of the downed branches as he could, he reflected that the gentler weather in New York was a blessing to these children. In Maine, or in a harsher winter, they might very well have frozen to death.

By the time he had made several trips for wood, hewn it into pieces, and stacked it outside the horse's lean-to, Lydia had gotten most of the diapers wrung out and hanging on the rope. The dripping water pattered on the hearth, hissing when it fell among the burning logs. She took the stick with which she was lifting the sodden cloths from the copper and laid it upon the floor. "I want to show you something," she said, breathing hard.

She crossed to the shelves and pulled down a large canister. "Empty." Another came down. "Empty." She pushed the lid off a barrel on the floor. "Empty. There is no food at all in this house. But I did find this." From the back corner of the topmost shelf, behind a large Bible with a worn leather cover, she pulled a small drawstring leather bag that clinked. She poured some of the coins into her hand. They were mostly coppers but there were a few English shillings in the mix. "Why isn't she buying food?" Lydia looked up at Rees, anger and outrage contorting her features. "I peeked into the bedroom. All whiskey bottles, Will."

Silently Rees took the bag and the coins from her and returned them to their hiding place. "Maybe she's forgotten this is there."

"These poor children. I agree with Mouse. She did the right thing and I will tell her so when next we meet."

"It certainly looks that way," Rees said more cautiously as he took down the Bible. He didn't want to judge until he understood the entire situation.

As Lydia returned to the diapers, burning off her emotion with the hard physical labor, Rees took the Bible to the table and sat down with it. Marriages, births, and deaths for the Baines family filled the unprinted front pages, inscribed in a variety of hands from a careful copperplate to crude block capitals. Rees searched for Olive Tucker, finally locating her married to Phineas Tucker but listed under her maiden name, Baines. A notation next to Phineas identified his brother Silas; they were the only survivors of thirteen Tucker children.

From the Baines family, a brother and a sister survived as well as Olive. Birth dates and marriage dates were inscribed. Rees noticed that Olive had had two sisters; a death date was noted for one. Someone, probably Olive, had written "gone west" next to the entries for her remaining siblings.

Olive and Phineas's three children were also included. Marriages were noted for all. Olive's son and his wife had followed his aunt and uncle west. There were no death dates. Rees wondered what had happened to Olive's daughters. Had they moved? Olive must not have known either; nothing was listed.

But where was Maggie Whitney's name? Wasn't she Olive's niece? Rees searched the page, finally finding a Margaret Tamar at the very bottom. There was no last name and no mother or father identified. Why, she was little better than a foundling. Rees felt a flash of sympathy for the girl. And what had Maggie used as a last name before she married? Tucker? Baines?

He turned forward one page. Maggie must have begun this page herself; her name was inscribed in tentative block capitals at the top. She'd noted her marriage and below that date was a list of her children: Jerusha, Simon, Nancy, and Judah. The months and years of the births were noted, but only Jerusha's entry bore a firm date: June 22, 1788. She wouldn't be nine for four more months. It did not require a mathematical genius to see that she was born a scant five months after her mother's wedding. Well, Maggie and her husband wouldn't be the first couple to jump the broom without benefit of clergy. The dates for the other three children were entered with pale hesitant strokes; Rees took that to mean Mrs. Whitney hadn't known the exact days and was certain only of month and year.

Rees closed the Bible and deposited it upon the shelf. "It's getting late," he said to Lydia. "I want to start back to Dover Springs before dark." And his stomach was beginning to growl.

"I still have some diapers to hang," she said, wiping the back of her hand across her forehead. "I think *she* must have used every single piece of cloth in the house."

Rees eyed his wife's pale, tired face. "I'll help you," he said, and crossed the floor to her. "I don't want you exhausting yourself."

"These children . . ." Lydia's voice suddenly broke. Rees put an arm around her shoulders. "It's not their fault," she said, her voice trembling. "That woman doesn't deserve them."

Rees gave her a squeeze. "I know." Someday he hoped they would have children of their own but this was not the time to say so. Nor did he want to remind her of the infant she'd lost before he'd met her. That was a wound he could not heal. Lydia freed herself from his arms and offered him a weak smile.

"They'll go through these in less than a week," she said. "With both Joseph and Judah . . ." He nodded and reached into the copper for the heavy cloth. He snatched his hand back with a gasp. The water in the copper was still plenty hot.

The front door opened suddenly, releasing a flood of cold air into the room. As Lydia and Rees looked up, a high treble voice piped, "What are you doing in my house?"

Chapter Five

Rees recovered from the surprise first. "You must be Simon," he said, inspecting the little boy on the stoop. He could not be more than seven. He wore shoes; a coat, too large and a little tattered around the sleeves, but still thick and warm; and a heavy cap. He carried a basket on one arm and a milk bucket stood on the step beside him.

"Come in before you let out the heat," Lydia said.

Simon obeyed, stepping through the door and depositing his burden on the floor with a huff of relief. He shut the door. "What are you doing here?" he asked as he shucked his coat and hat. Simon did not resemble his three siblings at all. A shock of black hair hung over his forehead and his eyes were an odd silvery gray, completely unlike either the lighter cerulean blue of his sisters or the hazel of his brother. Rees looked at the children, the differences in their coloring arguing for different fathers, and wondered what exactly Mrs. Whitney had been engaged in.

Simon removed his coat, revealing a very dirty one-piece suit of linsey-woolsey with ankle-length pantaloons and a row of buttons across the chest.

"They're friends with Mouse," came Jerusha's sleepy voice. The burgundy mound shuddered and after a moment she wriggled herself free. "They brought some food. What do you have?"

"Mr. Baker sent over milk," Simon replied. He looked around him, realizing with a start that the bucket was still outside. Rees opened the door and carried it in. "Not too much; the cows are going dry." Simon pointed to the basket and added, "And Mrs. Baker sent over a couple a pounds of cornmeal, some corn bread, and some apples."

Uttering a squeak of pleasure, Jerusha hauled the basket to the table and grabbed an apple. Lydia stared into the milk bucket. She took a spoon and stirred the frozen cream on top.

"It must have been a cold walk home," she said.

"Are you apprenticed to Mr. Baker?" Rees asked, examining the child dubiously. Seven was a little young for an apprenticeship; usually the children were sent out at twelve or thirteen.

The boy shook his head. "No. But I work for him. He has a dairy farm over the ridge there." He flapped his hand at the front door to indicate a general direction.

"Does he pay you?" Lydia asked, trying not to sound horrified and failing.

"Not in cash," Simon said. "In food. Like the milk and such." He sounded proud. "And he gave me these shoes and this coat."

"I'll have to meet Mr. Baker and express my gratitude," Rees said. Thank God some adult had been keeping an eye on these children.

With a wail, Joseph awoke and began thrashing around. Jerusha hurried to him, her clogs clattering. As she bent to pick him up, the door to the bedroom opened and Margaret Whitney appeared in the opening. She was fair and the hair hanging in uncombed tangles down her back was just a shade darker than Jerusha's. Her eyes were a clear blue, like her daughters'. She must have been very pretty once. But dressed in a stained and torn calico dress, her face bloated and reddened by drink, she looked far older than her years.

"Jerry, please keep the babies quiet. Mama has the most awful headache."

Then she saw Rees and Lydia. "Who are you? What are you doing here?"

"Taking care of your children," Lydia said, her anger boiling over. "Feeding them."

"And who asked you to?" Mrs. Whitney retorted, coming farther into the room. "I don't even know you. We're managing."

"By sending your little boy out to work? What's wrong with you? Don't you care about your children?" Lydia shouted. Rees turned to stare at her in shock. He had never seen her so furious. She was usually the most charitable of women. And even when angry she rarely raised her voice.

"Of course I do," Mrs. Whitney screamed in return. "Who are you to come in here and judge? You, a fine lady. Oh," Mrs. Whitney paused, staring at Lydia. "Now I understand. Where are your children? You don't have any, do you? So now you'll tell me how to raise mine. Well, you can just . . ."

Lydia slapped Maggie with all of her strength and burst into tears.

Mrs. Whitney staggered. "Get out. Get out of my house," she screeched. Nancy began wailing, quickly followed by Judah and Joseph.

Rees hustled the sobbing Lydia into the cold afternoon sunshine outside.

They stood in the snow outside the door for several minutes while Lydia wept. Rees held her and awkwardly patted her shoulder. The cold seeped through the leather of his boots and thin stockings and numbed his toes. He began to shiver and thought longingly of his greatcoat, hanging inside. He thought Lydia must be cold, too, in her dress and thin slippers, but in the depths of her grief she seemed not to feel it. "Lydia," he said, gently clutching her shoulder. "Lydia Jane. We can't remain out here much longer, not in the cold."

She nodded and tried to speak, the words erupting in spurts. "It's just that . . . my Polly . . . she was almost Joseph's age . . . when she died." Now Rees wrapped his arms around her. His pity was tangled up with jealousy, although he was ashamed to admit it. Before he'd met Lydia, while she was still living in a Shaker community, she had secretly married and borne a baby girl. The pregnancy meant she could no longer stay with the Shakers, and she hadn't returned even after the baby's death. Now, several years later, she still grieved. Rees always wondered if she thought of the child's father, for he'd been dead too when Rees and Lydia had met, when she remembered Polly. "That woman . . . doesn't deserve her babies," she said again in a passionate guttural tone. "She has four children. And I lost my darling girl."

"We'll speak to the constable," Rees promised, knowing how inadequate his promise sounded.

Lydia nodded and pressed her head into his shoulder. From the spasms racking her body, he knew how hard she was struggling to control her sobs. For several minutes he patted her back. He didn't want to promise her other children; well-meaning people said that all the time and instead of offering comfort it diminished the grief the bereaved felt. He couldn't do that to Lydia.

He turned around at the thud of horse hooves coming up the drive. A man in a heavy coat and beaver hat astride a rawboned chestnut trotted toward them. Rees released Lydia and turned to meet the new arrival. The stranger dismounted and walked toward them, his sharp eyes taking in their clothing and Lydia's tear-ravaged face. "Mr. Randall, the innkeeper, told me some of Maggie's friends were in town," he said. With his indeterminate brown hair and faded blue eyes, he was a man few would notice or remember.

Rees hesitated. Should he lie or not? Mouse must be known as a troublemaker. He opted for a partial truth. "Will Rees. My wife, Lydia. We were visiting the community at Mount Unity. And you are?"

"Constable Cooper." His eyes narrowed with suspicion. "I suppose the Shakers told you about the ruffians terrorizing the community. I told the Elder I was looking into it. In fact, I'll be standing watch tonight."

Rees shook his head in surprise. "No, they didn't mention it. What exactly is happening?" He heard his voice sharpen and tried to smile when Cooper glanced at him.

"We . . . well, there was some trouble between Maggie and one of the Shaker girls awhile back." Rees caught the automatic use of Mrs. Whitney's first name and examined the constable with increased interest. Was he a friend of Maggie's? "Since then," Cooper continued, "three or four boys have been riding through Mount Unity terrorizing the members. Probably kids. I haven't caught them at it yet. But I will."

The constable's quick defensiveness told Rees the situation was far more serious than Cooper wanted to admit. Rees determined right then he would drive to Mount Unity that night and keep watch.

"So, what did the Shakers tell you?" Cooper asked.

"Nothing about that. We are friendly with Sister Hannah, you see." Rees watched the constable's eyebrows rise.

"The Miss Moore that made the complaint against Maggie? She sent you to check up on the family? But that conflict was months ago."

"Yes. We received her letter recently. Our concern is not for Mrs. Whitney so much as Sister Hannah Moore."

"She is *very* concerned about these children," Lydia said, joining the conversation for the first time. Her voice was thick and hoarse from sobbing. Rees drew her close to his side, hoping she would draw some comfort from his presence.

"You can tell Miss Moore I was here," Cooper said. "When Randall said Maggie had company, I thought I'd check on her while I was checking up on you. The town fathers will want to know how she's doing anyway."

"You won't see much," Rees said. "My wife fed the children and cleaned the cabin."

Cooper shrugged and went into the shack. Rees turned back to Lydia. Although her eyes and nose were still a fiery red, she nodded at him. "I'm better now," she said. She didn't look restored but Rees refrained from comment.

"Then let's see what happens with the constable," he said, taking her arm and drawing her through the door.

Cooper had gone only a few steps inside and was looking around in disbelief. Maggie Whitney could not have staged the scene more effectively if she'd planned it. Although the cabin still smelled of steam and wet cloth, the pungent sting of ammonia was gone. She sat by the fire, nursing Joseph under a shawl. Children were typically nursed until two or longer; Rees wondered if the town fathers would agree to pay for Joseph that long. Judah was sitting on the floor at her feet, playing with a wooden cart and crudely carved horse. And Jerusha, Simon, and Nancy were lined up beside the table eating apples.

The constable threw a look back at Lydia and Rees. "How can I take any action when I have seen this?" He pointed at the charade of cozy domesticity before him.

"I told you my wife has been busy," Rees said, brusque with frustration.

Shrugging again, Cooper moved farther into the cabin. "Are you all right, Maggie?" he asked, his voice gentle.

"Yes," she said in a sweet voice. The marks of Lydia's fingers reddened her cheek. "I received some poor news; they caught me at an unfortunate time." She flashed Cooper a glance from under her lashes to see how he was responding. "We are faring just fine, although we have but little food." She paused.

"I'll bring something next time I come. And I'll apply to the town fathers on your behalf," Cooper said.

But Maggie shook her head. "Please don't." The artificial sweetness disappeared into genuine fear. "Applying for relief will give them just one more reason to evict us from this farm."

"Surely not," Cooper said. Even Rees heard that lie.

"You were there when Mr. Demming threatened to take away my children," she said. "He threatened to apprentice the older ones and put my babies in care all over town. I couldn't bear that."

"Well, apprenticeships . . ." Cooper began.

"What would happen to Jerusha and Simon?" Maggie cried. "And Judah is barely two and Nancy only five."

Cooper hesitated as though he wanted to argue, but he couldn't. Rees nodded reluctantly, a flicker of sympathy for Maggie Whitney springing to life in his chest. Twelve-year-olds were expected to work as hard as adults and Rees had seen more than one child worked to death. And, although twelve or thirteen was the typical age for apprenticeship, sometimes they were younger and the more vulnerable for it.

After a moment Cooper turned to Simon. "And how is Mr. Baker treating you?" Just as though the child was already a man.

"Well," said Simon, his light soprano at odds with the small and very dirty hand he extended, "I like him. Maybe next year he will take me on as an apprentice."

"Mr. Baker speaks well of you," Cooper said with a smile, gravely shaking the boy's hand, one gentleman to another.

"What about school?" Lydia burst out.

"Right now he's learning everything he needs to know to support himself," Cooper said, glancing at Lydia in annoyance. "If Mr. Baker takes him on formally, I'm certain he'll make provision for some schooling."

Lydia's mouth opened and Rees, fearing some scathing retort, pressed her arm warningly. They would get nowhere by antagonizing the man whose goodwill they most needed. Mrs. Whitney felt no such restraint.

"I wish that were true," she said. Rees heard an undercurrent of acid in her sweet voice. "As far as I can tell Simon spends all his time with the cattle." She eyed Cooper in sudden surmise. "What are you doing here anyway? Did Demming and his lackeys send you?"

"Can't I visit an old friend?" Cooper said, forcing a smile. "Besides, Mr. Randall told me you had company."

"Checking up on me?" She paused, staring at the ceiling as she thought. "I see. There's another meeting of the selectmen tomorrow. Isn't there?" Cooper's silence was answer enough. "I know my property taxes are late, but they'll get the money." Her voice rose, shrill with fear. "They always have, haven't they?" She pushed a weary hand through her tangled hair. "I have almost all of it." Rees's thoughts flew to the bag of coins.

"I'll tell them," Cooper promised.

"If you really want to help me, give me a few pennies," Mrs. Whitney told him. Her gaze moved to Lydia and then to Rees. "Do you . . . ?"

With a barely suppressed snort, Lydia stalked across the cabin and snatched up her burgundy cloak from the nest of rags.

"The selectmen are going to discuss Mrs. Whitney at their meeting?" Rees asked the constable.

"Probably. I'm required to attend the selectmen's meeting. I'll speak on her behalf." He paused, looking at Mrs. Whitney hopefully, but she turned her face away.

"I'd like to accompany you, if I may," Rees said.

Cooper looked at Rees in surprise. His mouth moved as though he would speak, but he did not. Instead, he motioned to the door with his head and stepped outside. Rees took his greatcoat from the peg and followed him.

Cooper walked a few steps away from the door and turned. "Why do you want to attend? I promise you, Mr. Rees, the town fathers are not going to pursue your friend. In fact, I suspect some of them would assist Sister Moore in removing these children from Dover Springs. They are a constant worry."

"Because they might become a charge upon the town coffers," Rees said sarcastically.

Cooper nodded. "That's the most passionately discussed topic."

"But weren't the children born here?" Rees asked. Usually that was the primary requirement for not being warned out. Then the selectmen would take some responsibility for offering aid. He had seen cases, however, where the parents were from another town and as the children were linked to the parents, the entire family was expelled.

"Yes. All but Jerusha. She was born in Boston. And Maggie was born here. But she was born to a mother from elsewhere, who left immediately after her daughter's birth." Cooper sighed. "Some of the town fathers want to rid the village of Maggie and her family and this is their best chance. I don't agree but I have no say. Fortunately, Maggie has a few supporters on the board, so they can't come to a unanimous decision. That Shaker girl almost saved us from the debate."

"I'd like to attend the meeting anyway," Rees repeated, although he knew better than to hope his presence would shame the selectmen into taking the moral path. Cooper regarded Rees and finally nodded.

"Very well. Stop at my workshop in town. The meeting begins at eight A.M." Cooper turned, his black coat flaring, and mounted his brown cob. Touching his hat in farewell, he urged his nag down the drive.

Chapter Six

Rees turned back to the cabin. Lydia was waiting for him outside the door, her burgundy cloak bright against the weathered wood. "I couldn't spend one more minute in that woman's company," she said. "Those poor children."

And poor Maggie, too, Rees thought. But he was wise enough not to speak. Instead he looked up at the sky. It would be dark within the hour but the sky was clear. "We are returning to Mount Unity," he said.

"We are?"

"Yes. I want to be there tonight, if Cooper's boys arrive to terrorize the Shakers."

Lydia looked at him and smiled. "I suppose you have your rifle in the back of the buggy." She gestured behind her. He nodded. Her smile faded. "Oh, Will, do you think they are trying to shoot Mouse?"

"Maybe," Rees admitted. "It could be just kids, as Cooper seems to think. But I fear their purpose is much worse."

Lydia clenched her gloved hands together. "Oh dear. The Shakers will not even try to protect themselves."

"I know," Rees said, and flicked the whip over Ares's haunches.

They reached the Second Family's central square just after nightfall. The last purple streaks of sunset were fading into black and the entire village was dark except for the ground floor windows of the Dwelling House. Rees guessed that the candles shone from the dining room windows; the community's kitchen was probably located in the basement below. All of the Shakers were making their way toward the dining room for supper. Rees called out to a young man and asked him to look after Ares. Then he and Lydia joined the throng. Rees hoped to find Elder Herman and speak to him before dinner began.

He and Lydia parted, each joining their own gender. Rees saw Lydia worming her way through the crowd and assumed she was looking for Mouse. Then he lost sight of her. Elder Herman was striding purposefully toward the dining room. "Elder Herman," Rees called, attracting several disapproving glances. But the Elder turned around, pausing long enough for Rees to reach him.

"Why didn't you tell me some of the townspeople were attacking your community?" Rees asked.

"I would not describe it as an attack," the Elder said, looking around at his fellows. He motioned Rees to one side, out of earshot of his Brethren. "Some young men have been riding through our community shouting threats."

"And you didn't think to tell me?" Rees said, his tone accusing. He took in a deep breath. "How often?"

"Once in a while." Elder Herman shifted his stance. Rees recognized an evasion of the truth.

"How often now?" he persisted.

"Almost every night," the Elder admitted. "It used to be a few times a week but it increased. . . ." His words trailed away. Rees nodded. The bullies interpreted the Shaker pacifism as weakness and now they wouldn't give up.

"Has anyone been hurt?"

"One of the Brethren suffered a broken arm. He was knocked down by a horse. But he's fine," Herman hastened to add.

"Huh," Rees grunted, unimpressed. The Shakers had been lucky so far. "Do they concentrate upon the Second Family or do they ride through the entire community indiscriminately?" Herman shuffled his feet and did not reply. "So, the ruffians concentrate their efforts upon the Second Family. They must know that Sister Hannah lives here." Rees knew he sounded both grim and angry and didn't care.

"What are you going to do?" Herman said, adding in warning, "Do not kill anyone."

"No. But I will stand watch the next few nights, until I catch one of them. I'll haul him off to Constable Cooper."

The Elder heaved a sigh. "Very well. Please, join us for dinner, you and your wife. We'll discuss this further after we've eaten."

Pressing his lips together, he turned and rejoined his Brethren. Rees followed more slowly. He just couldn't understand why Elder Herman was not more interested in protecting his Family.

There was little talk among the men waiting to enter the dining room, and once they entered, all conversation ceased completely. Since Rees had stayed with the Shaker community in Zion, he understood. Conversation was not permitted during meals. Herman pointed to a chair at his table; Rees joined him there and participated in the prayer. He saw Lydia, seated on the other side of the room, next to Mouse. Despite the lack of the square linen cap, Lydia looked completely at home and Rees experienced a pang. He hoped she did not miss her life among the Shakers. Sometimes he awoke at night, consumed by the fear that she might return to this community and he would lose her forever. The terror usually receded during the day but he felt it now, sharp and intense. Elder Herman cleared his throat, drawing Rees's attention away from the women's side of the hall.

When everyone was seated, the first kitchen Sister brought in bread and began distributing it to the tables. Slices of roast lamb, fragrant with rosemary, and green tomato preserves joined the bread on the table. Elder Herman picked up his fork. Upon that signal, the entire community began eating.

In the silence, Rees thought his hearing seemed even more acute. He listened for anything out of the ordinary, like shouts or hoofbeats in the road outside. Would the Shakers' tormenters come tonight? Or would Rees have to stand guard the next several nights?

The dishes were cleared and the Sisters were bringing in the dried apple pies with pitchers of cream when Rees heard the first thud of horse hooves. The Brethren around him tensed but no one spoke. The hands of the Sister carrying the pie to the table were trembling.

A gunshot cracked through the night. The Sister carrying the pie screamed and dropped it to the floor. Rees jumped to his feet and tore out of the dining room and through the Dwelling House to the road outside.

In the light of the risen moon he could see several mounted figures: three or maybe four. No, here came a fifth, a flaming torch held aloft. The face under the hat was dark and after a second of staring Rees decided the boy had a scarf wrapped around his mouth and chin. Shouting threats, the mob rode toward the Meeting House. In the break, Rees ran across the road to the barn. His rifle was in the back of the buggy, and although he did not intend to shoot anyone, he would fire it over the heads of the pack and hope it scared them off.

In the darkness of the barn, he could not immediately find his buggy and wasted precious seconds searching for it. But once he recognized the scraped side where David had brushed too close to a stand of trees, he was able to grab the rifle and the shot from the back. He loaded in the darkness, a skill he had obtained while fighting in the War for Independence, and ran to the barn door.

The gang had paused at the other end of the street, in front of the Meeting House. All of them carried lighted torches now, and as Rees watched, one of the boys tossed the flaming brand at the building. The torch hit the snow and guttered out.

Rees lifted his rifle and fired into the sky.

He could almost sense the shock; Shakers did not own guns. The horses jumped and twitched and, after a few seconds, the riders turned and rode toward Rees and the exit from the village. As they approached, the boys hurled their torches at the buildings.

Rees quickly leaned his rifle against the stable door and trotted into the road. If he could, he planned to leap at one of the riders and pull him down. Cooper would not be able to ignore this situation then. Rees chose the last to pass by. This horse was big, at least seventeen hands, and slow moving. Rees judged his distance and began to run. The rider did not see him coming. Rees leaped up and grabbed the young man, who was riding without benefit of saddle or stirrups, and jerked him right off the horse's back. The young man smacked into Rees and bore him to the ground. They hit the snow with a thud and lay there winded. The boy recovered first. Rees couldn't truly begin to breathe until the youth pulled himself to his feet. Gasping and choking, Rees sat up and attempted to grab the other fellow's legs. The young man turned and kicked Rees so hard his head snapped back and he fell prone into the snow. One of the other riders had turned back. He stretched out an arm and the boy grabbed it and jumped up behind his friend. They took off at a gallop, the snow flying out behind the horse's hooves. Distant shouting and the sound of approaching hoofbeats heralded another rider.

"Were you the fool firing the gun?" Constable Cooper's voice came out of the darkness. He dismounted and after a minute his hand reached down to help Rees up from the snow. "I was nearby. Heard gunshots."

"Second shot was mine," Rees said, struggling into a sitting position. His jaw and the back of his head hurt. "I fired over their heads. Wanted to scare them."

"You did that," Cooper said.

"But one of them had a gun." Rees cautiously levered himself upright. He brushed the melting snow from the back of his head. His hair was already soaked.

"Probably an old musket. Couldn't hit the side of a barn."

"Someone could still have been hurt or killed," Rees said, angry that Cooper should so easily brush off the shooting.

"I know." Cooper turned and looked around him. One of the torches had landed close enough to the barn to set a corner of it on fire. Some of the Brethren were tossing handfuls of snow at the flames but a more enterprising man had found a horse blanket and was beating at the fire with it. Sparks rose up like fireflies and the air smelled of wet ash and charred wood. "I recognized a few of the horses, especially that farmer's cob. I'll speak to that young scamp and find out who his friends were, although I have a pretty good guess. Then the boys' fathers and I will have a discussion. This"—he gestured around him at the cluster of buildings—"will not happen again." Rees wondered if he could trust the constable to keep his word. Without suspicion and distrust of the Shaker way from the adults of Dover Springs, those boys might not have felt comfortable attacking the community in Mount Unity. But, after all, Rees had no choice but to hope Cooper would resolve this problem.

The Shakers were clustered in front of the Dwelling House. Except for the men who shouted and cried out to one another as they beat out the flames, the people made almost no noise. Probably too terrified, Rees thought.

He followed the constable to Elder Herman and Eldress Agatha. She had buried her trembling hands in her apron. Cooper immediately repeated the same promise he'd made Rees. "Thank you," said Herman, sounding so shocked Rees wondered if the Elder had even understood what Cooper had said.

"I'll return to town now," Cooper said, nodding at Rees. "Remember, first thing tomorrow."

Rees and the two Shakers watched Cooper trudge back to his horse. He mounted and rode away.

"Come inside," Herman said to Rees. "It's cold out here."

Rees nodded. Now that the excitement and activity of the last twenty minutes was over, he was shivering. He ached all over. "Very well. I'll be just a minute." He returned to the stable and stowed his rifle back inside the buggy. He would clean it tomorrow.

Rees joined the people streaming back to the dining room. A low mutter of whispered comments and exclamations accompanied them as they turned to their neighbors to share their horror.

But everyone lapsed into silence as they entered the dining room; the force of the prohibition against talking was too strong to ignore. When everyone was seated once again, Elder Herman, who had remained standing, began to speak. "Constable Cooper has assured me this . . . tonight's event will not happen again," Herman said. "We must thank the Lord that no one was hurt. The fire was quickly extinguished and did no real damage." He paused and added, with a certain reluctance, Rees thought, "We must also thank our guest, Mr. Rees, who scared away those men. . . ." The eyes of everyone in the room turned his way. Unexpectedly embarrassed, Rees stared at the fat congealing on his used plate. "Finish your dinners," Herman said. He looked at Rees. "Please accompany me to my office, Mr. Rees."

Feeling like a guilty schoolboy summoned to the front of the class for a whipping, Rees rose to his feet and followed Elder Herman from the room.

Lydia was already seated in the Elder's office, Eldress Agatha by her side. The two Elders disappeared again and Lydia turned to Rees. "Oh, Will, Mouse is so distraught. She blames herself." Lydia's eyes were red-rimmed, as though she'd been crying.

Rees nodded, not trusting himself to speak. By taking the Whitney children two months ago, Mouse had provided the spark that started the attacks.

The door opened and the four Elders entered. The second Elder was younger than Herman, with dark brown skin. They each took a chair from a peg and sat across from Rees and Lydia. "First, we want to tell you how very grateful we are to you for your assistance tonight," Herman said. "Although I do wish you hadn't brought a gun to the community."

Rees grunted.

"It is late," Herman continued. "Please spend the night before returning to town tomorrow."

"What about Mouse?" Lydia asked suddenly.

"She will go on as before," Eldress Agatha said. "Perhaps now we can all put her foolish behavior behind us." Disapproval weighted her voice. The other Elders nodded in agreement.

"Beds are being prepared for you," Herman said after a brief silence. "But please finish your suppers first. There is no Union tonight. And, after today's excitement, I would suppose most of our Family will retire early."

Rees and Lydia shared an affectionate look, the only conduct of a married couple they would be permitted here at Mount Unity. They knew from Lydia's past as a Shaker, and Rees's brief sojourn in Zion, that they would be separated for the night. Lydia would stay with the Sisters and Rees with the Brethren.

"You will share a room with Sister Hannah, Mrs. Rees," Agatha said to Lydia. "Perhaps you can calm her." She heaved a sigh, as though her patience had been much tried and was now at an end.

"You must know," Lydia replied, springing to Mouse's defense, "how much she wants to care for children. It is her greatest wish."

"Stealing someone else's babies is hardly the way to obtain her desire," Herman said, his tone dry.

"Quite the opposite, I believe," Eldress Agatha said in a wintry tone.

"Perhaps we should all retire," Rees said, his gaze on Lydia. A vein throbbed in her forehead and it appeared she was holding her tongue by an effort of will.

"We will return to these matters tomorrow, after a good night's rest," Herman said, sounding relieved.

Rees did not think Lydia would be any less quick to protect her friend in the morning but did not say so.

Chapter Seven

Rees slept poorly that night, but not because of the evening's excitement. He found it hard to settle. The gentleman in the next bed snuffled and wheezed all night. And Rees missed the comforting weight of Lydia's body next to his. How many years had he slept alone? Eight or nine? And now, after only two months of marriage, he couldn't rest without his wife beside him.

He finally fell into a light doze in the early morning. It seemed only a few minutes had passed when he was awakened by the Brother from the other bed. The sky outside the uncurtained window was black and Rees guessed that the hour was no later than four. But the cows would need milking, and the rest of the livestock needed feeding. Rees remained in the luxuriant warmth of the bed a few more minutes, until his roommate left to start his chores, before reluctantly hauling himself out from under the quilt. He ached all over and bruises dappled his left thigh and flank. Since the fire in the stove had been banked the previous night, the room was so cold the water in the ewer was frozen. Rees dressed hurriedly and went downstairs as quickly as he could.

The door to the dining room wasn't open yet, but the small

waiting room was much warmer than the bedroom. Rees took up a post by the wall and waited. Gradually, the Brothers, their early chores complete, began arriving. Rees received a few curious looks but most of the men recognized him. Several of the Brothers acknowledged him with nods.

The aroma of frying bacon leaked around the door and into the cramped chamber. Water rushed into Rees's mouth, and he saw several of the young men sniffing the air like hounds on a scent. Finally the doors opened and they stepped into the dining room. Candles flickered upon the tables, bathing them in a golden light.

Rees experienced a sudden dislocation; everything seemed identical to the night before. But he did not join Elder Herman at his table, instead choosing to sit with three striplings who could barely be described as men. And the Sisters brought in platters of flapjacks and bacon and pitchers of syrup, not lamb. The moment passed and Rees settled to his breakfast with enjoyment, secure in the certainty that there would be no gunfire this time.

By dawn Rees and Lydia were in the buggy and heading for Dover Springs. Although one of the Shaker lads had harnessed Ares to the buggy and drawn it up outside the Dwelling House, no one, not even Mouse, had come to see them off. Lydia had taken her leave from her friend earlier, but Rees had seen Mouse only from a distance, in the dining room. The Shakers had scattered to their various chores. If it were not for the charred streak creeping up the side of the barn, Rees could almost pretend nothing unusual had happened the night before.

"Mouse is praying you are able to persuade the selectmen to take Mrs. Whitney's children from her," Lydia said abruptly, her breath misting in the frosty air. "It is partially my fault. I told her about our visit to the cabin." Rees took his hand from the reins to pat her wrist.

"It is not your fault. Mouse was determined to take those children before we arrived."

"I added fuel to the fire though," Lydia said, "and I'm sorry. I made things worse. Mouse is more determined than ever to take those children from their mother."

"I am not at all positive I will succeed," Rees said, frowning. "I am an outsider, after all. Why should the town fathers listen to me?"

"I know," Lydia said with a nod. "I reminded Mouse that Mrs. Whitney, for all that the selectmen would prefer to expel her from the town, is still a local girl. She has at least some friends here. We saw that last night. I do not believe she will lose her children that easily. But Mouse won't listen to me. And, if you don't succeed, she will be devastated."

Rees exhaled in frustration. "Her passion for those children could have cost one of her fellow Shakers his life. Or at least their barn. Doesn't she see that?"

"Maybe. I suspect she thinks if the children are sent to Mount Unity, everything will be worth it." Lydia hesitated and then continued in a rush. "She will never marry and bear her own children, and her father, who was a drunkard, reminded her of that every day. When she sees Maggie, Mouse sees a drunkard like her father who has something precious that she herself can never have." Lydia shook her head, her mouth twisted with regret. "Mouse is beyond reason on this, Will. I tried to talk to her but she won't listen."

Rees sighed. Mouse's passion was an example of the old aphorism about good intentions: they could be dangerous without good sense.

Rees drove into the yard of the Ram's Head and allowed the stable boy to take Ares. Lydia, complaining of fatigue, went into the inn to lie down. Rees elected not to wait for Cooper but set off down the street to find him.

Dover Springs, Rees soon realized, was a village even smaller than his hometown of Dugard. But then with the proximity of Albany, by all accounts a large and bustling city, maybe the residents in this town felt they needed no more than a meetinghouse, a blacksmith, and a general store. There was no printer and no chandler, although when he peered into the store he saw candles for sale. He was quite surprised to find Constable Cooper and his shop a short distance outside of the village center. Although located on the main road, the shop fronted a stream or river; Rees could hear the rushing water. A path ran around the edge of the shop to a house in the back. Rees peered through the window. Cooper was surrounded by his apprentices and lecturing them on something. Cooper seemed a kindly master. When he threatened one of the boys with a stave, everyone laughed. Glimpsing Rees outside, Cooper ended his lecture and sent the boys off to have their breakfasts. The boys, the oldest not more than sixteen or so, burst from the shop in a mob. Although quiet at first, once they crossed the street they began yelling and whooping as they headed to their homes. Then Cooper emerged.

"Mr. Rees," he said.

"You are appropriately named," Rees responded with a grin.

"My father had a sense of humor," Cooper replied. "But coopering provides a good living. I sell my barrels in Albany." He glanced through the window of his shop.

"As opposed to serving as a constable," Rees said.

"Poorly paid at best," Cooper agreed. "What are you doing here now?"

"Just walking around," Rees said. "Looking at the town."

Cooper nodded, hesitated a moment, and then said, "Don't worry. I'll keep an eye on those children. I'll do my best to ensure they come to no harm."

"Thank you," Rees said. He hoped he could trust the constable to keep his word. Cooper did not need to promise even that much, but he had already displayed some concern for the Whitney family.

"Daddy." A little girl in a blue cloak ran up the path and straight to Cooper. He picked her up, dislodging her hood and revealing a mass of blond curls. "Mama says breakfast is ready." She eyed Rees curiously with round blue eyes. A young woman paused at the top of the path. Her eyes lighted upon Rees with interest.

"I'll eat later, Genevieve," Cooper said to his wife as he put the child down. "After the meeting. I don't have time now."

"Not even a cup of coffee to warm you?" Mrs. Cooper asked. The constable shook his head.

"No."

"Come sweetie," said Mrs. Cooper, extending a hand. The little girl hurried to her mother's side.

"How old is your daughter?" Rees asked. He could not help contrasting this pampered child, surely almost of an age with Nancy, to that neglected little girl.

"Just four." Cooper smiled. "I also have an eight-year-old son and a little boy of one year. Do you have children?"

"A son. Just one. So far." Rees didn't want to try to explain his complicated family.

"Let's go." Cooper gestured toward the town center. "You'll

be happy to know that I rode out to the Cooke farm early this morning and spoke to Mr. Cooke about his son. That young scamp will not be teasing the Shakers again."

Rees turned to stare at the constable. Teasing? "Someone might have been killed," he said, keeping his voice calm with an effort. "And what about the other boys?"

"Don't worry," said Cooper with a smile. "I'll take care of them, too."

"By speaking to their fathers?" Rees thought something more was called for.

"None of the boys will misbehave again. I promise you that," said Cooper. Rees bit his lip but didn't say anything further.

As they climbed the slope, they joined a steady stream of men, all crossing the icy town center.

"Yes, most of these men will attend the meeting," Cooper said, catching Rees's quick exclamation. "I pray to God it won't go on forever. Some people just can't stop talking."

The parade of men crossed the road to the meetinghouse on the other side. "We're meeting in the church?" Rees asked.

"Only place big enough besides the inn. We, I mean this area, was separated from Albany County a few years ago and re-named Schoharie County. And so far even the county seat has no courthouse, although there are plans to build one. So"—he swung his hand at the fine gray stone building with its tall bell tower—"we meet here."

Rees followed Cooper to the benches at the front and sat behind him. A table and chairs had been set up facing the hard benches, and several men were already in their seats rustling papers and whispering. The ubiquitous whiskey jug was making the rounds and at least one of the men drank off his first glass in one draft and helped himself immediately to a second. As Rees watched the sly whispers and inside jokes pass from one selectman to another, he wondered how many of the cases on the docket had already been decided.

Hoofbeats clattered to a stop outside. A few minutes later Mr. Randall limped into the meetinghouse. He listed to the left and the cane in his right hand rapped a staccato rhythm on the floor as he crossed to the final empty seat at the table. He was dressed all in gray and wore his lank gray hair loose to his shoulders. He carefully lowered himself into his chair, put on a pair of round spectacles, and hooked his fingers in his waistcoat pockets.

The meeting was called to order and the chairman, a man with brown hair and a tired lined face, rose to his feet. "First order of business: Poor Relief for Mr. Peleg Thompson. Most of us remember his parents." He looked at the men sitting on either side of him at the table. Nods all around. "Pel was born here in Dover Springs and worked as a wheelwright until last fall when a wagon fell upon him. His shoulder and hip were so severely injured he could no longer work and now he and his wife have fallen into the most dire extremity. There being no one who can take him in, his children having moved west, we have decided to give him two pounds for his care. We'll revisit his case in May.

"Second case: Joanna McNally. An elderly widow, she was put in the care of Widow Jackson and has since died. We will pay for her burial.

"Third case: Widow Leah Axston and her three dependent children. Since she was born in Albany, she is the responsibility of that city and will be warned out of Dover Springs."

Rees's attention began to wander. This scene, he knew, must be playing out in towns and villages all over the northeast. In late winter, when all the resources of the poor must be exhausted, especially for women and children, the requests for Poor Relief surged. But Maggie Whitney, for all her obvious poverty, owned property, and so should be considered in a different category.

"Now, we take up the case of Margaret Whitney, widow."

Rees's attention focused upon the selectmen.

A wiry man in a dark blue coat, seated at the opposite end of the table from Mr. Randall, rose shakily to his feet. "I say no—" he began.

"Wait, Mr. Demming," Cooper interrupted. "She has not applied for relief."

"She is late, again, with her property taxes," Demming snapped. "And she has requested relief before. . . ."

"Only once," Cooper burst into speech. "And that was soon after the death of her aunt, Olive Tucker."

"Mr. Cooper," the chairman said, "if you interrupt again I will be forced to remove you from this meeting."

Cooper sat down with a thud and muttered something under his breath.

"She is insolent, a woman of intemperate habits and well known to be a thief," Demming said, swaying slightly where he stood. "She demands relief as her right."

The chairman looked at Demming. "We've discussed this previously. Mrs. Whitney was born here. She grew up here. And Phineas and Olive Tucker adopted her and left her their farm."

"But Maggie Whitney was born to Olive Tucker's sister, who was neither born here nor lived here. Maggie Whitney should have no claim upon the taxpayers of this town."

Rees turned to Cooper. "So Maggie really is Olive Tucker's niece?"

Cooper nodded. "So Olive always said."

"Maggie Whitney and her children should be warned out," Demming continued. Rees eyed Demming's superfine jacket with its silver buttons and wondered why such an affluent man should balk at paying a few pennies for the care of a woman and her children. Demming must not believe Mark 10:25: "It is easier for a camel to go through the eye of a needle, than for a rich man to enter into the kingdom of God."

"And she and those bastard children of hers are living upon land that should be mine," a man exclaimed as he surged upright on the other side of the meetinghouse. Rees had to shift forward and crane his neck to see the scrawny man of about fifty years. His graying hair was neatly tied back and he'd shaved recently. Although his jacket was of good-quality linen, it was much patched.

"Silas Tucker," Cooper whispered to Rees. "Phineas's brother. And Maggie's uncle, although you wouldn't believe it from his behavior."

"I accepted the right of my brother's widow to continue to live in her home," Silas continued. "I was generous. But Maggie? She's not my brother's child, and none of my kin. So that property belongs to me."

"I've said it before and I'll say it again," Demming said. "That offensive rubbish should be warned out."

"To where?" For the first time Mr. Randall spoke. Slowly, painfully, he rose to his feet. No one spoke while he did so, the silence revealing the respect in which this gentleman was held. "We know only that Olive helped her sister bear this baby, Maggie, in the very cabin where she now resides. Olive and Phineas, your brother," he added, fixing Silas with a steely gaze, "adopted Maggie as their own."

"Phinney was on his deathbed," Silas argued. "Everyone knows that. He didn't understand what his wife was asking."

"He understood more than you believe and he agreed that Maggie should bear his name," Mr. Randall said. "And Olive left that property to Maggie at her death. Her children, all but Jerusha, were born in Dover Springs."

"To different fathers," Demming sneered. "I say those bastards should be removed from her care and given as orphans to families who can raise them properly."

Where, as apprentices, they might be worked to death. Rees's jaw began to ache with the effort of keeping his mouth shut. He wanted to argue with Silas Tucker and Demming and expose them as the coldhearted bastards they were. Cooper's hands were so tightly knotted together his knuckles were white.

"I say, as I have done before, that Mrs. Whitney fulfills all requirements for relief. She was born here and she owns property. The need for relief is temporary. And she and her children strive to maintain themselves with their own labor, she by wet nursing foundlings and her son by working on Mr. Baker's farm." Mr. Randall stared at Demming. "And she has always paid her taxes, eventually."

"At least once with a silver dollar that she surely stole," Demming shouted, spittle flying from his mouth. "We should have let that Mount Unity woman keep the brats."

"I also must add that this discussion is premature," Mr. Randall said, his low calm tones sounding even more reasonable juxtaposed against the shrill passion in Mr. Demming's voice. "Mrs. Whitney has not applied for relief. And Constable Cooper, who has been making regular visits to investigate the situation, reports that so far the family is managing." He glanced at Cooper.

With an apologetic glance at Rees the constable rose to his

feet. "I was just there yesterday. There was food in the cabin. The laundry had just been done. And Mrs. Whitney was nursing the baby."

Cooper's statement was certainly true, but not the complete tale. Still, Rees found himself reluctant to stand up and tell the plain truth: that he and his wife had accomplished all that Cooper saw while Maggie Whitney lay passed out in a drunken stupor in the other room. It seemed that this family might just as easily be tossed into the road as taken care of. Rees decided he must make Jerusha aware that the Shakers would accept them, if they were able to make it to the community themselves. They'd have to be quick, though, before Silas signed the oldest children into apprenticeships and farmed out the babies to families all over town.

"With all respect to my esteemed colleague, Mr. Demming," said Mr. Randall as he sketched a bow at the other man, "I suggest we stop wasting our time discussing Mrs. Whitney, who has not applied to us for relief, when we have other cases that are unresolved."

"I agree," said the chairman with alacrity. "Let's continue on to the case of Mr. Obadiah Claremont."

"Why does Mr. Demming bear Mrs. Whitney such animosity?" Rees asked under cover of the discussion.

Cooper shrugged. "I don't know. I don't believe they have ever met, and yet he seems to resent her very existence. And this argument is played out again and again at every meeting."

"And Mr. Randall?" Rees asked, turning to look at the old man curiously.

"Phineas Tucker was his best friend from boyhood." Cooper's mouth quirked up into a mirthless smile. "Owen Randall, the innkeeper; Phineas Tucker, Maggie's adopted father; and Elias Gray, the gentleman who lives by the log church, were as close as peas in a pod. Mr. Randall and Judge Jacob Gray, Elias's father, looked after Olive Tucker on the strength of that friendship. The judge is dead, so I suppose Randall is doing the looking after now."

"I throw myself upon your mercy, kind sirs." A woman's voice cut through the low-pitched grumble of male conversation: every head turned toward the speaker, a woman dressed in an assortment of grimy, ragged clothing hesitating in the doorway. She was of swarthy complexion and the hair under her tattered bonnet was as black as night. Rees guessed she was of mixed blood.

"Mary Pettit," said the chair with weary exasperation. "You know this is no place for a woman."

"But when I applied for relief before I was denied. . . ." Mrs. Pettit began.

"Constable, please remove her from the room." The Chair thought better of his terseness and added in a more kindly tone, "We'll discuss your request immediately, I promise."

With a sigh, Cooper stood up and approached the woman. Rees took the disruption as an opportunity to escape and hurried out through the church door. But he had just descended the stairs to the street and started back to the tavern when Cooper pushed Mary Pettit out of the church. He slammed the door behind him. Mary staggered unsteadily down the three steps to the road and toppled face-first into the snow.

Rees hurried back to her and extended a hand to help her up. She was not as young as she'd appeared from a distance. Her hair was only lightly threaded with white, but what he had taken for well-nourished fat was bloating. Her ankles were swollen and she limped, uttering regular gasps of pain. He offered her his arm and helped her across the street to the tavern. Close up she smelled of wood smoke and whiskey.

"Thank you kindly, sir," she said. "I midwifed most of them men into life. But now they dismiss old Mary as worthless."

"Were you born here?" Rees asked.

"That I was. But my father was French and Seneca and I suppose that makes me undeserving of Poor Relief." She sounded bitter and Rees nodded in sympathetic understanding.

"But Mr. Demming," he said, trying to cheer her, "wouldn't pay a farthing to see his Lord Jesus Christ ride down the street upon a white horse."

An involuntary snicker escaped from Mrs. Pettit. "He wouldn't," she agreed, and chuckled the remaining few steps to the tavern. "You are correct about that, Mr. . . . ."

"Rees. Will Rees."

Once inside he offered her a couple of farthings so she might sit by the fire and have something to eat and a glass of ale. But when she stepped into the common room, a young woman bustled over. "My father says no more credit, Mary." She sounded sympathetic but unbending. "Go home." Mary opened her grubby hand to show the coins and the girl, Mr. Randall's daughter Rees assumed, stepped back and allowed Mary a seat in the corner. Rees hoped her personal appeal might succeed with the selectmen when the more formal plea had not, but he knew better than to expect it. Some of the town fathers had flint for hearts.

He soon left and went upstairs and into the bedchamber. Lydia, seated in a chair by the window, was knitting. She'd eaten: a teacup and an empty plate sat by her elbow. When she saw him, she jumped up and hurried forward to greet him. He was glad to see she was smiling and that color had returned to her cheeks. After she kissed him she asked, "What happened in the meeting? You were gone a long time. Will they remove the children from Mrs. Whitney?"

Rees looked at her, knowing he looked guilty. "No," he said. He couldn't lie to her and with a sigh he continued. "Removing the children was mentioned, primarily as a way to save money," he said. "And I didn't insist. Cooper is keeping watch upon that family."

Lydia glared at him. "Didn't you even try?" Her voice rose.

"I did try," he said. He thought of Mr. Demming. Shaking off his guilty feelings, Rees went on. "I know you're angry, but I couldn't insist. There is little mercy in these town fathers. Those children would be apprenticed out or worse."

"They can go to Mount Unity," Lydia said.

"I suppose. If Mrs. Whitney agrees. And if the selectmen agree." He thought of Demming's speech and Silas Tucker's anger. "It would be risky. I wouldn't be surprised if Mrs. Whitney and her children were required to pay back the funds already given them. And some of the selectmen seem vindictive. They might try to punish the Mount Unity community for interfering."

"Mouse will be disappointed," Lydia said. To Rees's ears, she sounded accusing.

"I know," Rees said remorsefully. "And I would spare her this sadness if I could. But those children are better off with their mother, I promise you. As imperfect as we know her to be, she loves them."

Lydia shot him a look of utter disbelief and said stiffly, "I daresay you would prefer we eat dinner before we go to Mount Unity and give Mouse this sad news."

Rees shook his head. "Let's go now." He always preferred to finish the difficult chores first, and get them behind him.

As they passed through the common room, he looked for Mary Pettit. She was still by the fire, a plate of bread and cheese and a mug of small beer before her. She raised a hand to Rees and he inclined his head in response.

"Who is that?" Lydia asked.

"Mary Pettit. One of the petitioners for Poor Relief," Rees said. "I fear she will be disappointed in her appeal. Again," he added in disgust.

Chapter Eight

This time, upon their arrival at the Second Family court-yard, they were shown immediately to the second floor in the Meeting House. Elder Herman met them there, his expression anxious, but he asked no questions. Several minutes later one of the Sisters accompanied Mouse into the room. This Sister was young, with soft smooth skin and large brown eyes. She watched Mouse steadily, fluttering around her like a large moth.

"What happened?" Mouse cried, rushing to Rees's side. Although flushed and excited, her eyes were clear and showed no evidence of tears. "Did you speak to the constable?" Rees did not reply immediately, distracted by the Sister. Instead of behaving with the proper disinterest in someone of the World, she kept sneaking curious glances at Lydia. "Rees?"

"Yes, I spoke to him. He promised he would monitor the situation and keep those children from harm."

"And the town fathers? Did you apply to them to have those children removed?"

"I attended a meeting," Rees said, choosing his words carefully, "and the matter was discussed. The children will remain with their mother for now."

"How could you let that happen?" Mouse whispered, accusing

Rees with the eyes of the betrayed. "As long as they remain with that woman they are in harm's way."

"It's not that simple," Rees said.

"Yes, it is. That woman already lost one baby she was wet-nursing—"

"That was a fever," Elder Herman tried to interrupt. "Several babies died. . . ."

"He would not have perished if she were a better mother," Mouse shouted. Rees saw his own shock mirrored upon Lydia's face. Mouse raising her voice?

"Sister Hannah," Elder Herman remonstrated. "Please."

"Strive for peace and harmony," said the Sister, putting a hand upon Mouse's shoulder. Mouse shook it off.

"Do all those children have to suffer and die before someone does something?" Mouse burst into sobs. Rees stepped back, at a loss.

"Cooper seems a good man," Lydia said in a calm voice, putting her hand on Mouse's back. "He'll watch over the children." Rees knew Lydia did not agree with him about that, but she managed to sound convincing as she comforted Mouse.

"He'll do nothing," Mouse said, consigning Cooper to the company of the wicked.

"I agree with you. Mrs. Whitney is not a fit mother," Lydia said. "But you won't be permitted to take those children. Not yet, anyway. I'm sorry." She glared at Rees when Mouse put her hands over her face and wept.

Rees retreated to the top of the stairs. He knew Mouse had expected him to succeed in removing those children from their mother and, although the situation was more complicated than she knew, he still felt guilty.

Elder Herman stood and crossed the floor to join him. "Sister Hannah has been out of the World most of her life; she doesn't understand what it's like. Especially after the events of last night. I don't want to quarrel with our neighbors."

Rees looked at the Elder. "Have you had experiences with the selectmen of Dover Springs?"

"I prefer to say this is for the best." The Elder nodded at Rees. "Thank you for all your assistance," he said. "You've done more than anyone could expect. I suppose you'll be leaving for home soon?"

Rees jerked his head in a cautious nod.

"Don't worry about Sister Hannah. We'll watch over her."

"If anything changes, will you write?" Rees asked, watching Mouse wipe her eyes on her apron and pull herself erect. The Elder nodded.

"Of course."

Mouse jerked away from the Sister. "Thank you for trying to help," she said to Lydia. Glancing at Rees and then back to Lydia, Mouse said, "I appreciate your friendship and I understand what you have done for me." She straightened up, her shoulders stiff and her spine straight.

"This is God's Will," Herman said, watching Mouse with approval. "We must accept that which we cannot change."

Mouse nodded at everyone in turn and started for the stairs.

But Rees didn't think the sudden determination expressed by Mouse's posture meant acceptance. "Mouse," he called after her in worried concern. "Don't do anything foolish, Mouse."

"Of course not," she promised, hiding her mouth behind her hand. "Good day to you all." She clattered down the stairs. They heard the door slam below.

"She will be obedient to God's Will," Elder Herman said. He spoke with total confidence. Rees shared an anxious glance with Lydia; they knew Mouse too well to believe she would meekly submit.

They followed the Shakers down to the snowy street. Herman waved a farewell and hurried back to his chores. But the Sister lingered a moment longer. "Is it true," she asked Lydia in a soft voice, "that you were once a Shaker Sister?"

"Yes," Lydia said. "I was. I lived in Zion."

The Sister's gaze went to Rees and for a moment she inspected him, as though she could not understand how he had enticed Lydia away from the community. Then she, too, turned and walked quickly away.

Rees and Lydia climbed into the buggy. Lydia's forehead was furrowed, and when she was settled she said, "I'm worried. I'd like to stay an extra day, if we can? Just in case Mouse behaves rashly."

"I agree," Rees said, far more alarmed than he cared to admit to his wife. "We can spare a day. David will be surprised to see us return so soon—less than a month gone."

Lydia smiled, although the anxious pinching around her eyes did not ease.

The night passed with no alarms, and Rees began to believe he was worrying needlessly. And he was happy to see that Lydia ate a good breakfast, so he was hopeful that she, too, regretted her anxiety.

After breakfast they purchased a substantial quantity of cornmeal and molasses at the store and set out again for the Whitney farm. A fresh layer of snow cloaked everything and more was falling from the gray sky. Although it stopped before they reached their destination, the pearly opalescent sky promised another shower. Rees looked at the sagging clouds and frowned, worried that a heavy snowfall would delay their departure.

This fresh white coat made even this shack pretty, lending an austere purity to the battered dwelling and frosting the pines standing sentinel over the outhouse. The scarecrow's rags flapped gaily at them in the cold breeze. As Ares struggled to pull the buggy up the snowy drive, Rees noticed fresh wheel tracks in the powder. They were not the first visitors this morning.

Rees threw a heavy horse blanket over Ares and he and Lydia crossed the drive to the cabin.

Jerusha opened the door, greeting them with a smile. "Come in," she invited. "I never thanked you properly the day before yesterday."

"You're very welcome," Lydia said. Rees looked around the cabin. Mrs. Whitney had produced a small spinning wheel and it was drawn up to the hearth waiting for her attention. She was rocking by the fire, nursing Joseph, who appeared to be half asleep. Nancy sat on the floor carding wool while Judah played beside her. And the handful of baskets heaped upon the table proved that Maggie still had friends in Dover Springs. Someone had brought soup in a pail and now the stew bubbled over the fire. Rees recognized the wheel of cheese as coming from the inn, and Mr. Randall had included a freshly baked loaf of bread as well. Maggie had hung a chunk of fly-specked ham on a hook in the ceiling. Rees would wager that was from Cooper. Rees put the cornmeal and the molasses next to the cheese.

Jerusha clapped her hands. "We shall have enough food for a month and more," she cried.

Rees looked at it. He did not think the food would last even a week with all these hungry mouths.

"I'll put Joseph in the cradle," Maggie said abruptly, carefully detaching Joseph and standing up. "I must go out, Jerry." She ignored both Rees and Lydia as though they were not there.

As she carried the baby into the back room, there was a knock. Rees, who stood closest, flung the door open. There were two visitors on the step: a man and a woman. The gentleman wore black, of plain cut although excellent broadcloth. He carried a heavy basket on one arm. His companion was a gentlewoman, garbed in a fashionable riding costume with a dark purple velvet jacket. The rich color did not flatter her sallow skin. A velvet purple hat completed her ensemble. With the addition of two more, the cabin felt even smaller and more cramped than previously.

"I am Reverend Vermette," the man said to Rees, eyeing him curiously. "And this is my betrothed, Miss Pike. We thought we would pay a pastoral call and offer Mrs. Whitney whatever succor she requires." He spoke in a rush, with a febrile intensity that Rees found unsettling. Reverend Vermette was all long lines: tall and lanky with a high white forehead, gaunt cheeks, and a long chin. A narrow blond mustache decorated his upper lip over a pronounced overbite. He looked desperately in need of a square meal. Maggie popped out of the back bedroom. She frowned at her new visitors but did not speak.

"So many children," Miss Pike said, her smile revealing jagged teeth. "We heard they needed food." She was a homely woman, her features irregular, but Rees thought her concern was genuine, although a little condescending.

Maggie shot her an angry look. "We're managing," she said stiffly, to Rees's surprise. Why was this young woman refusing aid, especially with five hungry children to feed?

Vermette swung the large heavy basket up to the table. "These foodstuffs should sustain you for a few days or so," he said. "Especially with the provisions Simon earns." The boy drew himself up proudly.

Maggie crossed the cabin and lifted her shabby blue cloak from the peg. Rees noted with surprise that her blue eyes were full of tears. Her expression reminded Rees of a puppy, kicked once too often, and hiding behind her basket so no one would hurt her again. Unwillingly, pity threaded Rees's distaste for the woman. "I'm so sorry I can't stay and visit," Maggie said, her tone indicating just the opposite, "but I have several errands."

"Please," said Reverend Vermette. "Please," he said again, softening his voice, "allow me to take you into town."

"No," she said. "Thank you, no."

"Allow me to at least take you to the main road in the buggy," Rees said. Maggie turned to look at him. Although her hair had been combed and twisted into a knot, her eyes were still red rimmed and tired in her pale face. She nodded.

"Very well," she agreed, to Rees's surprise. "But just to the main road."

Now why, Rees thought, would Mrs. Whitney prefer to ride with him, a total stranger, instead of a man she must have at least met previously? But he didn't ask. Instead, he put on his coat and followed Maggie from the cabin, trying to ignore Lydia's horrified expression.

Maggie climbed up into the buggy, limber as a boy despite her long skirts. Rees glanced at the two horses tied up next to Ares while removing the heavy horse blanket. Since the Reverend had ridden up to the cabin on a rangy black gelding, Rees wondered how Vermette had planned to ferry Mrs. Whitney anywhere. Riding double? Surely not on Miss Pike's mount. Smaller, and saddled with a fine red leather sidesaddle, the mare shouted money in the shape of her head and her elegant carriage. Miss Pike would certainly object, and besides, Maggie probably didn't ride.

She did not speak until they reached the main road into town. "Let me off here," she said. "Please." As soon as Rees pulled up, she jumped down into the snow. "Thank you." And she turned and trudged away without another word. Rees, if asked, would have described Maggie's behavior as oddly ungracious.

He turned Ares around and retraced his path. Ten or so minutes later, he pulled up to the cabin once again. After re-covering the horse with his blanket, and tying him next to the other animals, Rees went inside.

Lydia looked at Rees in undisguised relief. She had taken the rocking chair by the hearth and was leaning over Jerusha. The girl was seated at the spinning wheel and Rees realized the wheel was for the child, not for Maggie, as he'd assumed.

"Your mare is a beautiful animal," Rees said to Miss Pike.

"Yes, thank you," she said with a flash of her teeth. "My father interests himself in horse breeding."

"Miss Pike is a far better rider than I am," Reverend Vermette said, directing a fond glance at her. "And a better marksman as well."

"My father had no son," Miss Pike said, brushing away the compliment with one gloved hand. "So I enjoyed the benefits of his complete attention."

"Have you sisters?" Rees asked, returning his greatcoat to the hook.

"No. My dear Mama passed on soon after my birth and my father has not remarried."

Rees cast a glance of cynical understanding at Vermette. Miss Pike, and her husband, would likely inherit a sizable estate.

Miss Pike rose to her feet. "Please call on me as soon as you're able, Mrs. Rees," she said. "I hope we shall become great friends." She stretched out a hand. Lydia took it but dropped it almost immediately.

"Of course," she said with insincere politeness. Concealing his surprise at Lydia's abruptness, Rees shook hands with Reverend Vermette and saw them out the door.

"Are you ready?" Rees asked his wife.

"In a minute." Lydia knelt beside Jerusha. "Let me show you how." She twisted the yarn from the spindle between her fingers until it formed a long uniform strand. "Feel this. Do you see how it is?" Placing her hand over the child's, she guided Jerusha's fingers gently over the yarn. "Now, press the treadle with your foot. Yes, like that. The roving comes puffy into your hand. Your fingers smooth it and twist it into yarn."

Rees peered into the bedroom. Joseph, snoring faintly, turned over in the cradle. It was already too small for him. In an attempt to tidy the room, Maggie had lined the whiskey jugs up against the wall. But there were a lot of them, and Rees would wager most were empty. The pity he'd felt for her just the moment before shifted again to contempt. When he withdrew he left the door open slightly. The air inside the bedroom smelled fusty and stale, heavy with the sharp sweet pungency of the alcohol.

Lydia stood up when he reentered the room and reached for her cloak.

"Mouse didn't come by yesterday, did she?" Rees asked Jerusha. She shook her head.

"Or last night?" Lydia added. Jerusha shook her head again.

"Was she supposed to?" she asked. "I wish she would. She was kind to us."

"No, she wasn't supposed to," Lydia said. "We were just wondering." The look she shot at Rees accused them both of unjust suspicions.

"If the selectmen warn you out of Dover Springs," Rees said to Jerusha, "remember you can always go to Mouse and the Shakers." He stared into Jerusha's face until she nodded. "Now we will say good-bye."

"Will you visit us again?" Jerusha asked.

"Of course," Lydia said, hugging each one in turn.

Rees put on his coat and wrapped Lydia in her cloak. They returned to the buggy in silence.

In unspoken agreement, they drove to Mount Unity. "To take our leave of Mouse," Lydia said. Rees nodded, ashamed of his suspicions. And Mouse, when she came out of the kitchen to speak with them, seemed composed. But although she wished Lydia and Rees farewell and safe journey and promised to write, Rees felt a certain reserve in Mouse's manner. He didn't think her coolness was due to the presence of a Sister standing a short distance away, either. After those few short sentences, Mouse turned abruptly and disappeared into the kitchen once again. Lydia stared after her in dismay and then turned to Rees with an unhappy frown.

"I suppose Mouse is still angry at us," he said as he drew her back to the buggy.

"I hate to leave it like this," Lydia said with a sigh, looking back over her shoulder. But the door to the kitchen was firmly shut.

"There's nothing further we can do," Rees said. He glanced at his wife. Her mouth was drawn closed and her forehead wrinkled. He drew her to him and kissed her cheek. "Don't worry," he said. "Everything will be fine."

"I hope you're right," she replied, and forced a smile. "I hope you're right."

Chapter Nine

They started out at daybreak the following morning. The fiery sunset of the evening before had promised a fair day and as the sun rose into the sky the clouds vanished and the sun came out. Although barely an inch of snow had fallen, the wet stuff clung to the buggy wheels. Rees allowed Ares to maintain a slow but steady trot, knowing this would be a long journey.

As the morning wore on, other vehicles and some horsemen joined them on the post road. When Rees heard the rapid galloping thud of horse hooves behind him he thought nothing of it, until he heard Elder Herman's voice calling his name. He pulled the buggy to the side. Elder Herman and the black Brother pulled up beside him.

"What happened?" Rees asked, his heart sinking at the sight of Herman's anxious face.

"There's been a murder," the Elder blurted.

All the blood drained from Lydia's cheeks and she clutched the side of the buggy. "Not Mouse?"

Rees, whose thoughts paralleled Lydia's, said, "Did one of those young ruffians kill her?"

"No. They have not returned. Thank God. But it is almost as serious. Sister Hannah has been accused of murdering Maggie Whitney," Herman said. While Rees struggled to understand that impossible statement, the Elder continued. "She took a buggy last night without permission and drove to Dover Springs. She says she was trying to rescue the Whitney children. In any event I caught up to her before she reached the Whitney farm. Sister Hannah insists she is innocent of the murder, and that only you can prove it."

"Where is Mouse now?" Rees asked, struggling to separate the terrible fear aching in his chest from the actions he must take to save her.

"At Mount Unity." The Elder made a helpless gesture. "Locked in her room. The constable agreed she could stay home on my personal guarantee she wouldn't flee." He swallowed, and added in a shaky voice, "At least for now."

"She is safe until public opinion rises against her," Herman's companion said, his world-weary tone speaking to his own distrust of the law.

Lydia reached out for Rees. "Oh, Will. We must go to her." He clasped her hand and nodded.

"I know." He turned the buggy around and started back to Dover Springs.

They reached the Ram's Head shortly after noon. Rees had pushed the horse hard and they'd made the trip in little more than half the time the journey out took. Mr. Randall was unsurprised to see them, but not very welcoming.

"Yes, you can have the room," he said. He sighed. "But I doubt you'll save that Shaker girl. People are saying she'll hang."

"Are you so sure she's guilty?" Rees asked.

"Well, she went after those children once, didn't she? Maybe this time Maggie fought back. Anyway, there's no one else that would kill Maggie. We've all known her since she was a baby."

"Uh huh," Rees said. And where were all her friends and neighbors when Maggie needed them most? Before her murder, *she* was the outsider. Now she was one of them. "In that case, we won't be required to remain here very long." He knew he would hear many variations on Mr. Randall's theme throughout his investigation. The Shakers, too, a separate group, would be suspect. But although Rees didn't argue, he could already name a few outside of the Shaker community who wanted Maggie Whitney gone.

He and Lydia moved their things back into the room. Rees could not persuade her to stay behind when he accompanied Elder Herman to the body, and she followed her husband downstairs. As soon as they entered the common room, crowded with men at this dinner hour, all talk ceased. Almost all the customers turned to look at them with expressions that ranged from overt hostility to the naked distress on Mr. Randall's face. Rees hurried Lydia toward the door and she uncharacteristically held his arm as they raced through the silent room.

But before they reached the door it opened. Jerusha and the other children huddled together on the stoop, blinking at the sudden dimness after the bright sunshine outside. Jerusha carried Joseph, both of them wrapped in her ragged shawl. At least she wore her clogs and Rees's socks. Nancy and Judah wore nothing on their feet but rags, now sodden with melting snow. Simon, in his hat and coat and stout shoes, looked like the lord of the manor in a group of orphans. Mr. Randall started forward, his face working.

"I'm sorry, Mr. Rees, Miss Lydia," Jerusha said, her gaze going straight to them. "I hoped you would still be here." The marks of tears scored her dirty face. With a muttered epithet, Lydia ran forward and lifted the baby from her. Jerusha gasped as the weight disappeared from her aching arms.

"Why didn't you stay at the farm?" Rees asked, also stepping forward. "Surely you didn't walk all the way into town."

Jerusha shook her head. "No. We went to Mr. Baker's dairy farm first. Uncle Silas—well, he said he wasn't really our uncle—he came to our farm and told us he owned it now and we had to leave. He said Mama was dead." A strangled sob broke through her control. "I know it's not true. But he said we couldn't stay there."

"It's not true, is it?" Simon said, looking at Rees. "He's lying, right? Mama isn't dead. Right?"

Rees didn't know what to say. He looked at Jerusha.

"I couldn't even take Joseph's teething stick," she wailed.

Lydia, whose cheeks were shiny with her unchecked tears, pulled the child close to her.

Rees recalled the scrawny bantam rooster of a man who'd stood up at the meeting. Once Maggie was gone, Silas hadn't wasted a minute before snatching at those pitiful few acres. And telling the children about their mother in the cruelest way possible. "That . . . !" Rees was so furious words failed him.

At that moment a heavyset man with crimson cheeks came into the tavern. He looked at Rees kneeling on the floor and Lydia holding Joseph and sighed in relief. "I'm Tom Baker," he said. "Jerusha and the other children walked to my farm."

"I'll take them upstairs," Lydia said. She wiped her arm across her face.

"Make sure they have something to eat, too," Rees said, not just for Lydia's benefit but for Mr. Randall's as well.

She nodded. "We can talk later." She meant, Rees understood, that they would confirm the death of their mother after the children were fed and warm and better able to handle the terrible news.

Forcing a smile for the children's benefit, Lydia gathered them together and herded them toward the stairs. "Why didn't they remain with you?" Rees demanded of Mr. Baker. "My wife and I were on our way."

"My wife. She . . . Well, they couldn't." Mr. Baker fumbled for words. "And they were already all in. Jerusha carried that baby the entire distance. Thank the Good Lord, today is not terribly cold, else they probably would have frozen to death."

"Thank the Good Lord, indeed," Rees said, his voice trembling with anger and sarcasm. He turned and glared at every man sitting behind him. Mr. Baker had, at least, tried to help. Most looked away from him. Rees hoped they felt guilty and ashamed.

"When my wife said they couldn't stay . . ." Mr. Baker's eyes slid away from Rees's. "She's afraid, you know, that the town fathers might simply leave them with us. But I could see these children could walk no farther. So I told them I'd take them to town. We stopped first at the log church but Reverend Vermette wasn't there. He left today on circuit. Then Jerusha remembered how kind you and your wife were to them."

"Thank you," Rees said, although the words choked him. He turned to the door, intending to speak to the Elders waiting for him outside. It looked like Mouse would get her dearest wish and the children would come to live with the Shakers after all. "Silas was certainly quick to evict these children from their home," he said, his voice laden with disgust. "Is there any way to prevent this?"

"Olive and Silas never got along," Mr. Randall said, moving forward a few steps to converse quietly with Rees. "He despised her. But she"—he shook his head admiringly—"she was as intelligent as they come. She had a will. Quite uncommon for a woman. I don't believe Silas has the right to take the farm."

"Of course not," Rees said. "But Mr. Demming will probably

agree with Silas and give him that little farm. Then where will the children go?" Rees wondered if Mr. Randall would speak up for them with the selectmen. Would the town fathers even notify Elder Herman of the desperate circumstances of the Whitney children, or simply wash their hands of the family and turn them out to starve on the road? Rees realized he was shaking with rage.

"We need to find Olive's will," Mr. Randall said.

"I've got to return home," Mr. Baker said, throwing a nervous look at Rees's expression. "I have chores. . . ."

"Of course," Rees said. "Thank you, Mr. Baker." The farmer, with another squint at Rees's furious face, quickly disappeared through the door.

Rees glanced at Mr. Randall but couldn't spare the time to question the old man further right now. He needed to see Maggie's body before too many people tramped around, destroying all signs of the killer. In his past experience he'd seen how quickly evidence of the murderer could disappear: the murder weapon carried away, boot prints obliterated by the tracks of the curious.

He directed one final glance at the men in the common room, raking them with his contempt, and went outside to meet the Elders waiting for him.

Chapter Ten

Elder Herman handed the bridle for his horse to the other Brother with him and came across the yard. "Are the children all right?" he asked in concern. "We saw Mr. Baker driving them here."

"For the time being," Rees said. "My wife will watch them for a while." He paused, startled at how odd and yet how natural it seemed to refer to Lydia as his wife. "And now?"

"I'll guide you to the body," Elder Herman said, nodding at his companion. He acknowledged the wordless instruction and offered the bridle of his horse to Rees.

"Your horse is all in. Take mine."

"What will you ride?" Rees asked.

"I'll start walking toward Mount Unity," the Brother said. "Someone will stop. If not, well, the community isn't very far away."

"Take him," Herman said to Rees. "We're wasting time."

So Rees mounted and, after spending a few minutes adjusting his stirrups to fit his long legs, followed Herman out of the yard. They rode west, maybe ten or so miles out from the center of town, until they reached a log church. The logs, most still sheathed in their bark, were chinked with fresh white clay, and the large cross over the door had the unstained pallor of freshly peeled wood.

"Is this Reverend Vermette's meetinghouse?" Rees called out, recalling the circuit minister mentioning his church.

The Elder nodded. "He insisted on building his church this way, as unspoiled and natural as possible."

Rees, who thought this grandiose log cabin was simply a different form of ostentation, said nothing.

They rode past the church to the yard behind it. A few simple tombstones marked the snowy meadow as a graveyard. There were still plenty of spaces left for the faithful. Herman stopped at the back, just before the thicket of winter-bare forest began. Constable Cooper and a crowd of men were gathered around an open grave at the extreme edge of the cleared land. Rees jumped down and tramped through the snow toward them.

Maggie Whitney lay at the bottom of the grave. Her limbs were askew, as though she had been tipped in and left where she fell, and the skin around the reddish swollen eye and the bruises left by someone's fist was as white as the thin layer of snow that covered her.

"What am I supposed to do for Mr. Gray?" a grizzled old man was demanding of Cooper. "That's his grave."

"We'll remove her from the grave," the constable shouted, wiping his sleeve across his damp eyes. He sounded as though he'd repeated this same statement several times and had run out of patience.

"I sent someone after Reverend Vermette," Cooper said, keeping his eyes fixed upon the body. "He'll want to officiate at the funeral on Sunday." He sighed. "He'll be horrified by this . . . this tragedy. The meetinghouse, all of this"—he swung his arm around to include the cemetery—"was his dream."

"How was Mrs. Whitney killed?" Rees asked. That poor young woman.

"Look at her face," Cooper said, his voice breaking. "I think someone beat her to death."

She was little more than a girl, really, Rees thought, looking at the bruises and the black blood trailing across her marble cheek. "The wounds aren't severe enough," he muttered. "Unless there are more where I can't see them." He knelt at the hole's frozen edge. Was that bruising around her throat or simply shadow? "I'd like to go into the grave," he said. "Take a closer look."

"I'm sure that's sacrilege or blasphemy or something," Cooper said with a shake of his head.

"You need to take her out anyway," Rees said. "I'll lift her up to you after I've finished my examination."

Cooper regarded Rees thoughtfully. "Have you done this before? Investigated sudden death?"

"Many times," Rees admitted. "More times than I wish to remember."

"Ahh. Now I understand why Miss Moore asked you to help her."

"When Mouse and I first met I was looking into the murder of a young Shaker girl," Rees said.

After a few moments of silent thought, Cooper nodded. "Very well," he said. "If you're sure. Call me when you're ready to climb out."

Rees carefully lowered himself into the deep hole. Dug for a coffin with a man inside, the grave was more than large enough for the short slender woman. The dirt on the sides of the pit was white with frost. Rees bent and straightened Maggie's legs and adjusted her skirts over them. Although her limbs were stiff they were not rigid. She'd lain here for some time, long enough for the rigor that came with death to pass off. Her flesh had begun to freeze.

He squeezed in to kneel by her head. She should have been wearing either a cap or bonnet, but her dirty blond hair lay unbound across the dirt. And where was her cloak? Rees turned her head slightly, so he could better see her face. As Cooper had said, someone had administered a severe beating; bruises purpled the left side of her cheek and her split lip dribbled blood down to her collar. The darkness circling her throat proved to be bruises left by fingers. But her eyes exhibited none of the red spots Rees had noted in other strangled victims, and her expression was peaceful. When he slid his hand under her head he felt something. A cold frozen clot. He jerked his hand free. Some of the icy particles came with his fingers. Already melting, they left red smears on his skin.

Rees flashed back to his brother-in-law, lying on the mounting stone with blood pouring from his head. Sam had come after Rees, as he had done many times before; Rees had tried to talk sense into Sam but had lost his temper and hit him. The beast had infused the blow with all of Rees's strength, and Sam had fallen. For a brief moment Rees smelled the metallic odor of blood and a shudder began in the pit of his belly, spreading outward until he was trembling uncontrollably. He wished he hadn't hit Sam so hard. Cooper looked at him.

"Are you all right, Mr. Rees?" he asked in concern.

"I'm fine," Rees said, forcing the words through his chattering teeth. "I'm fine." Taking in a deep breath, he pushed away the memory and focused on the young woman lying upon the frosty ground.

"She's been struck on the back of her head." Rees bent over once again and wormed his hand under her. He struggled for a moment to lift her torso; there was scant room and despite her slenderness she felt almost too heavy to lift. But once he maneuvered her into a sitting position, her torso flopped over to her knees. Her hands were scratched and bloody, the nails broken. Maggie hadn't gone tamely to her death.

And the wound on the back of her head was a mass of frozen blood spangled with ice crystals. The dark stain had run down the back of her dress and when Rees looked at the dirt where she'd lain, he saw a pool of blood. A sizable pool, so deep some of it was still sticky. A large stone, dark with blood, protruded from the hollow where her head had fallen and Rees realized that if he dropped the body again, the stone and the wound at the back of her skull would line up exactly.

"Are you ready to send her up?" Cooper asked.

"Mr. Gray will not like sharing his final resting place," said the old sexton, his leathery countenance suddenly appearing over the side.

"The ground is frozen," Rees said, slowly rising from his squat. "When did you dig this grave?"

"October," the old man replied promptly. "Mr. Gray was failing then. We all thought he would soon meet his Maker. Mr. Randall ordered the grave. But Mr. Gray rallied. I left the grave for him, figuring we might need it this winter."

"And what, Mr. Rees," Cooper asked with a mocking smile, "do you deduce from all of this?" Rees looked at the constable, recognizing Cooper's uncertainty in his jeering.

"She knew her killer. But I'm sure you knew that before I told you."

"Of course. Your friend, the young Shaker girl."

"Maggie wouldn't fear Mouse, that's true. But the killer had to be someone who knew this grave was here. And he had to be strong enough to drop her into it." Rees thought about Mouse. "She's a small woman, too," he said. "Do you really believe she could carry Maggie through the graveyard?"

Cooper scowled. "Maybe she had a cart," he persisted.

Rees resolved to look for wheel tracks, if he could spot anything in the trodden mess around the grave. "And, whoever beat her had to be fairly strong. Look at the bruises. This was no spat. What about one of those boys that were attacking Mount Unity?"

Cooper shook his head. "If it had been your friend Sister Hannah who died, maybe. But not Maggie. Why would they terrorize Mount Unity and then turn on Maggie?"

"Her death may have been an accident." Rees held up the stone. "She fell on this and smacked her head."

"That shouldn't be in there. I tried to take out all the rocks so Mr. Gray's coffin would lay true," said the gravedigger. "It's not my fault."

"Maybe it worked its way up," said Cooper, throwing the old man a glance. "No one is blaming you."

"She was still alive when she was thrown in here," Rees said. "Maybe unconscious, but alive and bleeding. Look at the blood. She bled for a long time, but I don't think she bled to death; there isn't enough blood for that. She froze to death. It was the cold that killed her."

Cooper blanched. "She froze to death?"

Rees nodded. "I think she went into this hole yesterday, probably yesterday afternoon while it was still fairly warm. She was alive then and bleeding. She might still have been saved. But whoever threw her in here just left her. He let the cold finish this murder for him. When the temperature dropped at nightfall she had no chance, not unconscious and without a cloak." He paused. Horror kept the other two men silent. Cooper's jaw worked and he looked away from the grave, not trusting himself to look at the remains of the young woman. "And she wasn't beaten here," Rees added. "Where are her cloak and bonnet? When we find them, we may know more."

The sexton glanced at Cooper. "Lift her up, Mr. Rees," he said, "I'll take her to the cabinet maker to be fitted for a proper coffin."

Rees put his right arm under the body's knees and, using his powerful legs, lifted her straight up. When he stood upright, his height allowed him to see over the grave but he still had to raise his arms and the burden in them above his head. Together, Cooper and the sexton took the body and carried it to the wagon. Rees looked around the hole once more before scrambling up to the bank.

As the wagon pulled out of the graveyard, Rees blocked Cooper from running after it. "I want to look around a bit more, for those cartwheel tracks," he said with a sour grin, "and then we need to stop at the Whitney farm. Now it's time to focus on the living."

"What do you mean?"

"Maggie's children were thrown off the farm by Silas Tucker." As he spoke he watched Cooper's face change.

"I wondered where he was going when I saw him hare off from the churchyard. He's wanted that farm since his brother passed, but it does not belong to him. Olive was very clear on that."

Rees grunted and started walking the lane back to the road, dropping to his knees every now and then to inspect the ground. But too many horses and men and vehicles had passed this way, and he could see nothing that might point to the killer.

"What were you doing?" Cooper asked, his eyebrows rising.

"Sometimes a murderer will leave traces of himself. Footprints or something. But there's been too much activity here." Rees stood and looked around the snowy yard. When he caught Cooper's surprised stare, he added, "I learned a few things from an Indian guide during the war."

"So I see," Cooper said.

Rees looked all around him. But the log meetinghouse had been built outside the village and except for a roof dimly seen through the trees at the back of the church there was nothing here.

"That's Mr. Gray's house," Cooper said, following the direction of Rees's gaze. "But you can't suspect him of any involvement," he added. "He's past sixty, infirm, and as deaf as a post."

"Maybe so," Rees said. "Still, I think a visit to that gentleman will be in order. He might have seen something." He mounted his borrowed horse. "But the Whitney children are of more immediate concern."

With a nod, Cooper swung up into his saddle. He took the lead, riding west a distance before turning southeast. They approached the Whitney farm from a direction unfamiliar to Rees, riding past the Baker dairy farm on the way. This affluent property sprawled over several acres. Despite the snow, a herd of black spotted cows clustered around a haystack in the center of a pasture near the road. Behind the house and barn, the land sloped up into a steep hill and Rees, visualizing the lay of the land, realized that the Whitney farm was positioned directly over that hill.

"Those children had to walk a long way," Rees said, furious all over again.

"Yes," Cooper agreed. "It would be several miles by way of the road. But they probably took the shortcut over the hill. That would have cut off a mile or two."

"Judah and Nancy were barefoot and Jerusha was carrying the baby," Rees said angrily.

"I know," Cooper said. "Calm down. I'm only saying it would have been worse for them on the road." Rees refused to apologize, still enraged.

When they rode up the drive they found a wagon pulled up to the front and the door to the cabin wide open. As Cooper and Rees dismounted, Silas Tucker came out of the cottage carrying the spinning wheel. Two of the chairs were already in the wagon. Cooper dismounted.

"Just what do you think you're doing?" he shouted, running up the slope to the shack.

"Taking what's mine," Silas said. He pursed his thin-lipped mouth. Rees wondered if the man ever smiled. "I'm the nearest male relative; this is my property now. It should have been mine years ago, but everyone was soft on that harlot and her bastard children."

In two strides Cooper reached him. "You put those children out in the snow. They might have died." Rees, joining him on the step, nodded.

"Ah, I would've let them back in eventually. They could live here until the town fathers make a decision." He grinned. "And we know what that will be; the farm will finally be mine. Finally. From true Christian charity I allowed Olive to stay here after my brother's death. And then I permitted Maggie to live here. But Maggie is dead now, so the farm is mine."

"Huh," snorted Cooper. "Christian charity? You tried to force her off, too, and when that failed, you offered to buy the place for a pittance."

"This is my land. And she's behind on her taxes anyway. Or was behind. Now that she's dead I have a right to claim the farm."

"Not until you know it's yours," Cooper said. "Olive did not want you to have this property. I know that. Her will left it to Maggie Whitney, free and clear." He nodded at Rees, who snatched the chairs from the wagon and put them beside the spinning wheel in the snow.

"This property should have come to me upon the death of my brother." Silas's voice rose. "But Phinney left it to his widow.

A woman! And then Olive left it to a bastard niece? It's against everything right and normal. But Maggie is dead now so everything should come to me."

"You will return everything to the house," Cooper said through his teeth. "And you will not set foot upon this property again until we have had time to sort this out." Silas frowned and pinched his lips even more tightly together. "Do you hear me?"

Silas spit into the snow and did not move. "Everyone knows this land should belong to me," he repeated. "And it will."

"If I find you on this property again," Cooper said, "I swear I'll put you in jail."

"You wouldn't dare," Silas said, stepping forward to crowd Cooper, daring him to react. Rees stared at the bantam rooster of a man, dumbfounded by his insolence. Cooper folded his arms and stared at the other man over them. Silas dropped his gaze first. "You'll be sorry," he said, stamping to his wagon. "I'll go to the town fathers. You'll lose your job."

"Good. I need to spend more time at coopering."

With a ferocious scowl, Silas jumped into the seat of his wagon and cracked the whip over his horse's flanks.

"Is that likely?" Rees asked as they watched the man ride away. "That you'll lose your position as constable?" He appreciated Cooper's help; Rees knew how easily the children could lose their home, and right now the constable was the best friend they had.

Cooper shrugged. "Maybe. He does have friends in town, although not everyone likes him. But as I told you, I make most of my living from my business, not from this . . . this constabling."

"They'd lose a good constable," Rees said.

Cooper nodded his thanks.

"So, if Olive has a will, where is it? Do you think Maggie had the document? And would she have a will, too?"

Cooper sighed. "Maybe, but I would bet not. Olive Tucker

was a force in her own right. She was as practical as a man. Maggie is—was—a much softer woman. Silas was obviously counting on that." He paused and rubbed his forefinger down his nose. "I'll find out who helped Olive with her will. Maybe he'll know something about Maggie as well."

"Why did Maggie inherit this farm?" Rees asked as he picked up the spinning wheel and a chair to return to the cabin. "Olive had children of her own."

"They all moved away." Clutching the remaining chair, Cooper followed Rees into the cottage. "When Olive needed care in the last few years, she promised Maggie the farm if she came home from Boston to help."

"So Maggie came home with Jerusha. What about Jerusha's father?"

"He had died by then. Maggie returned with no husband in tow, and she was big with bastard child: Simon. No one knows who his father is."

"Or Nancy's or Judah's," Rees said. "Any guesses?" He turned just in time to see an indefinable expression cross the constable's face.

"No. Maggie never said." He sighed. "We might never know. Closemouthed, that was Maggie, like her aunt Olive before her."

"And Joseph? He isn't Maggie's child, is he? He's a foundling that she was wet-nursing?"

Cooper nodded.

"So who will care for him?"

"I don't know. Not many women want to wet-nurse foundlings. But Maggie was always willing."

Rees understood. With no mother or father of her own, Maggie saw an echo of her situation in these unwanted babies. A flicker of respect for this young woman stirred in Rees's breast and he crossed the cabin to the shelves. His fingers sought the leather bag and found it, undiscovered by Silas Tucker. "Maggie was saving up for the taxes, just as she said. Here." He handed the sack to the constable. "Maybe we can keep this little farm from falling into Silas's hands, at least for a little while."

"I'll keep watch," Cooper promised. "Slimy little cur that Silas is."

Rees's belly rumbled. Cooper laughed. "Am I keeping you from your dinner?" He looked around once again. "I think we're done here, at least for the time being. I'm hungry, too. Let's return to town."

Chapter Eleven

❧

Half an hour later Rees walked into the Ram's Head. With dinnertime long past, the common room had emptied and most of the tables were scrubbed clean. Mr. Randall limped forward, his expression sorrowful.

"No one is talking of anything but Maggie Whitney," he said.

Rees paused. "Her death may have been an accident," he said, choosing his words with care. He didn't want to reveal his suspicions to anyone at this point. "Last night was cold."

"No doubt the drink got her," Mr. Randall said with a sigh. "What will you tell *them*?" He rolled his eyes toward the ceiling.

"I don't know," Rees said. "Is there anything left from dinner?" He needed time to decide on what exactly he was going to say to the Whitney children.

"Oh. Of course. There's mutton stew?"

"That'll do," Rees said, and sat down at the nearest table. Mr. Randall shouted for his daughter and turned back. He studied Rees for a moment.

"May I join you?"

"Of course." Rees paused and then went on. "It was kind of you to speak for Maggie Whitney at the selectmen's meeting," he said. A variety of emotions flickered across Mr. Randall's face, too rapidly for Rees to identify more than a few. Grief dominated, but Rees also thought he caught shame.

"Phinney was my greatest friend," the old man said, lowering himself into his chair. He sighed. "He and Elias and myself . . . well, we got into no end of trouble as boys. As adults we helped one another, through bad times and good. Phinney asked me to watch over Olive, and I took that to mean their adopted daughter and her children as well. In fact, that's what I wished to speak to you about."

Rees waited. The old man seemed oddly nervous and that made Rees wonder what Mr. Randall had in mind.

"Those children will need care," Mr. Randall said. "They seem attached to you and your wife. Would you consider looking after them until a more permanent solution can be found?"

Rees stared at the other man. "Why us? We're strangers. What will your fellow selectmen say?"

"Most of them won't care, as long as the Whitney children are not a charge upon the public coffers."

"And Demming?"

"I can handle him."

Rees hesitated a moment. "We can't remain in Dover Springs for very long."

"I know," Mr. Randall said with a nod. "But maybe the religious community will take them after you leave."

"Maybe," Rees said. Zion, the community he was most familiar with, accepted children, foundlings and orphans, as well as runaways like his son. "But I don't want to speak for the Elders at Mount Unity. And there is the matter of Sister Hannah."

"If she's found guilty, you mean. But you just told me Maggie's death might be an accident." Mr. Randall paused and rubbed his nose thoughtfully. "I suggest we worry about that when—if—her guilt is determined." He glanced at his daughter, hesitating in the kitchen door. Mr. Randall leaned forward and continued in a low tone. "I can fight for the farm. I know Olive wanted Maggie to have it. But if there is no one to care for the children, Silas will take them, as their nearest living relative, and so gain possession of the farm in that manner. The eldest will be apprenticed out. The youngest, well, they will be in Silas's care. I leave the quality of that care to your imagination."

Rees shuddered. Judah and Nancy would be lucky to survive. "And the foundling?"

"Sent to someone else. Perhaps." Mr. Randall rose slowly to his feet, leaning upon his cane. He rubbed his right knee. "No one will care you are a stranger. Please think about it." He turned and limped back to his checkerboard.

Rees's first emotions were frustration and anger. How dare the old man hand the responsibility for those children over! But his next thought was about the children. Could he be so callous as to just walk away from them, knowing what their future would hold? Lydia certainly would not be so indifferent to their plight.

Mr. Randall's daughter hurried over to place the stew in front of Rees. He tasted it. It needed salt but it was hot. The bread brought out a moment later was still warm from the oven, with a crisp buttery crust. Rees dived in, eating with hungry speed.

And he still had to tell those children about their mother's death. What should he say? Death, of both parents and children, was common, but this was something altogether different. He still hadn't decided what to tell them when he finally pushed his empty bowl away and left the table.

Rees went upstairs. Since he heard nothing, no crying or sounds of conversation, he knocked quietly on the door before entering. Three of the four children were asleep in the bed; Nancy's blond head nestled next to the two dark ones. Jerusha and Lydia were sitting together, Jerusha awkwardly holding knitting needles and Lydia bending over her to offer instruction. "Wrap the yarn around this needle, like so. . . ." She paused and looked up at Rees.

"Where's Simon?" he asked.

"He found a ride to Baker's farm," Lydia said. "He didn't want to risk losing his job." She raised her arm to wipe her forehead and Rees noticed the dark wet patch on her sleeve.

"I gave them all baths," she said, catching his glance. "And they ate dinner."

"Did you?" Rees asked in concern. "I don't want you exhausting yourself—" He stopped short. He had meant to say "exhausting yourself for these children," but he couldn't say it with Jerusha's bright eyes fixed upon him. Lydia dropped her gaze and did not reply.

"Where's my mother?" Jerusha asked, dropping the needles and the lumpy strip to her lap. Her mouth was already trembling with the expectation of bad news.

"No one told us anything," Lydia said, her eyes sparking with anger.

"She is dead, isn't she?" Tears spurted out of Jerusha's eyes. "Tell me."

Rees nodded.

"What happened?"

Rees hesitated, considering and discarding one explanation after another. "We don't know," he said finally.

"Did someone hurt her?"

Jolted, Rees stared at her. "Why would you say that?"

"She said, before she left, that he wouldn't be happy to see her. That he would be angry even though he should love her. And she was crying and laughing both."

Rees contemplated the child in mingled pity and regret. "Who is he? Did she mention a name?"

"She must have been joking," Lydia said, frowning at her husband.

He ignored her. "Did she give you any idea who she might be meeting?" he persisted, looking at Jerusha.

She shook her head. "Just that she needed to get the rest of the money for the taxes." Raising tear-filled eyes to him, she added, "Did someone kill her?"

"Maybe not," Rees replied. "It's possible she froze to death. It was cold last night and she was without her cloak."

"She was wearing it when she left," Jerusha said, tears rolling down her cheeks. "And her best bonnet. You saw."

"Enough," Lydia said, putting her arm protectively around the child. "This is a sad time. These questions can wait." The child wept quietly and Rees, who would have expected a child's noisy uncontrolled sobs, was moved by the little girl's resigned control.

"Don't worry," he said, offering her what comfort he could, "if someone hurt her, I'll find him." He paused. Although Mouse seemed to be the only suspect so far, she could not be the "he" to whom Jerusha referred.

"What happens to us now? Can we go home?"

"I think it might be better if you went to the Shakers," Lydia said. "They'll take care of you."

"We don't need anyone to take care of us," Jerusha said fiercely. "Simon and I can do that." Rees and Lydia exchanged a glance.

"There won't be enough money," Lydia said, her voice gentle. "Your Mama earned money wet-nursing Joseph. Of course you and Simon helped a great deal." Rees, who knew how much it must cost her to praise Maggie Whitney, put a hand upon her shoulder.

"We'll sort it out tomorrow," he said, glancing at the darkening sky outside the window. "We need to stop at the farm anyway;

I'm sure your brothers and sister need some of their things."
And he needed to discuss the proposal made by Mr. Randall with
Lydia before any decision was reached.

Jerusha nodded and, twitching her shoulders away from
Lydia's arm, withdrew into her grief.

Squeezing five children, for Simon had slept at the tavern that
night also, into the buggy made for a tight fit. Lydia was heavy-
eyed with fatigue and Rees suspected he looked as drained. Telling
Simon the previous night about his mother had been emotional
and exhausting. The scene had culminated with Simon launch-
ing himself at Rees, fists flying, blaming him for not preventing
Maggie's death. And Rees had let it happen, believing in some
corner of his mind that Simon was right. Then he had sat up
most of the night listening to the boy weep. Rees hated feeling
so helpless.

The three younger children cried, too, not understanding
why Simon and Jerusha were so upset, but scared by it. Today
the two oldest were trying to put on a good show for their
younger siblings. Nancy and Judah did not miss Maggie yet; she
had not been much of a presence in their lives. Joseph erupted
into screaming cries every now and then and clutched at Lydia's
chest. "He misses nursing," she said, adding, "Thank the Lord
he is able to manage soft food, otherwise I don't know how we
would feed him."

Rees recalled the child stuffing oatmeal into his mouth with
his pudgy hands and winced. He barely remembered David
progressing through that phase, but surely he had not been so
messy. But then, Rees had been away so much. He recalled David as a baby, maybe four or five months old, and then as a child
Joseph's age, on the cusp of walking. Rees had gone away, look-

ing for work as a traveling weaver, and when he returned David was a toddler. The regret that had long shadowed Rees suddenly caught up to him. He had missed so much, and only now did he realize it. His gaze rested upon Lydia, cuddling Joseph to her and crooning, and he wondered if he would someday have another chance.

Ares struggled to pull the buggy with its additional weight, and by the time they reached the farm he was blowing hard. Rees jumped out of the buggy and took the gelding's bridle to encourage him the last few steps to the door. Simon was next out; he fetched some hay from the lean-to. As Jerusha ran to the cabin door, Rees held out a hand to stop her. "Let me go first." He opened the door and peered inside. He would not have been surprised to find half the furniture missing, but apparently Silas Tucker had taken Cooper's warning seriously. The cottage looked as Rees had left it the previous day, although with no fire in the fireplace, the room was cold and unwelcoming.

He stepped aside to allow Simon entry. The boy took a pail outside and filled it with snow. Then he stopped, realizing there was no fire inside to melt the snow into water. Rees took pity on him. As Lydia and Jerusha carried the younger children into the cottage, he retrieved his tinderbox and spent a few moments fussing over kindling. He finally got a small blaze going, and although the fire didn't put much warmth into the air, just the sight of it made the cabin feel more habitable.

Nancy ran from a chair to the nest of rags exclaiming, "My chair! My bed!"

Jerusha began collecting a pitifully small pile of belongings: the dry diapers, the one change of clothing each child owned, and a few trinkets. Lydia picked up the teething stick from the tiny heap. "Will," she said, "look at this." He peered over her shoulder. The metal wand, although tarnished and dented by teeth marks, was clearly made of silver. The handle was a dark pinkish stone, unfamiliar to Rees. Lydia looked up at him and said in a soft voice, "This seems a trifle expensive for Maggie."

Rees nodded. "Where did this come from?" he asked Jerusha. She spared a quick glance at the object. "Simon," she said promptly. "Someone gave it to Mama for Simon. But the younger kids have used it."

Rees picked it up and turned it over, examining it carefully. A *G* in a circle was incised into the handle. A clue to Simon's father, he'd be bound. He returned it to the pile. Maybe there were other traces in the cabin that hinted at the fathers of these children. Rees looked around but saw nothing other than the poor sticks of furniture and the large Baines Bible. He crossed the floor and went into Maggie's bedroom.

Other than the rope bed with its mattress of old husks and a rickety table beside it, there was no furniture. There wasn't room: the end of the bed almost touched the back wall. On the other side of the bed, on the front wall, several nails pounded into the wood held a few pieces of ragged clothing. A candle sat upon the table. Rees dropped to his hands and knees and peered under the bed but saw nothing but dust and a thick layer of mouse droppings. He squeezed past the bed, knocking over several whiskey bottles as he did so, and sorted through the articles hanging on the nails. Save for a linen scarf, yellowed with age and worn to holes, and a man's old black coat, Maggie had owned nothing but the clothing she stood up in. Rees turned away but then, on second thought, went back to examine the pockets of the jacket. Save for a small pocket Bible, they were empty.

Frustrated, he tossed the grubby pillow and ragged quilt to the floor. There was a box under the pillow, a small beautifully carved wooden box. Rees eagerly snatched it up and opened it.

Inside he found two bags: one of leather and the other velvet. Velvet? Where would Maggie Whitney obtain velvet? Underneath was a small scrap of paper. Rees inspected it first. Written in a strong hand were the words "Giroux" and "Boston." Instantly Rees's thoughts flew to the incised G upon the teething stick. Surely someone in Dover Springs would know the significance of the name Giroux.

Then Rees opened the leather bag. Heavy, and with an enticing clink, the bag clearly held money. But the silver dollars he turned into his palm stunned him. "There must be eighty or ninety silver dollars here," he whispered in astonishment.

So why was Maggie struggling to pay her taxes? And living on the thin edge of poverty? Rees thought he knew the answer to that. He'd already heard someone accuse her of theft simply on the basis of having one silver dollar in her possession. But from whom could she have stolen these dollars? Not from anyone in Dover Springs. Rees doubted anyone in this town could lay claim to such a sum, and anyway Maggie would already have been hung for it, were that the case.

The smaller velvet bag held a necklace with a cross at the end. Although of silver, it was poor quality and old. The chain was damaged in several places, one of the links broken clear through. It did not look like a love gift, more like something a parent would give a child, but Rees reserved judgment.

He pressed the box into his pocket. The money and the necklace belonged to these children and he would do everything in his power to prevent Silas, or anyone else, from stealing them.

He examined the bed more carefully and then looked around once again. He saw nothing, and although he planned to search again, he was sure he'd found everything.

Suddenly aware of the steady buzz of whispers in the other

room, he went through the door. Everyone except Judah and Joseph turned toward him. Lydia was holding the baby. "What?" he asked warily.

"If we can't stay here alone and our only other choice is to move to Mount Unity," Jerusha said, lifting her chin and facing Rees directly, "why don't you and Miss Lydia stay with us?"

"What? Absolutely not." He frowned at Lydia. He'd managed to communicate Mr. Randall's suggestion to his wife the night before and now immediately assumed she'd told the children. "There's nowhere to sleep, for one thing." He was not sleeping in that noisome bed in the fetid little bedroom. "Besides, we won't be here very long. A few days at the most." He thought longingly of the warm clean bedchamber in the tavern and the plain but plentiful food in the common room.

"Then we'll remove to the Shakers," said Jerusha, folding her arms across her chest. "But we won't stay."

"I have to get to my job," Simon said. "It is too long for me to walk from Mount Unity or from Dover Springs."

"You won't have to work for Mr. Baker if you go to the Shakers," Rees said. "You'll have food and clothing, and they'll school you both. They'll take good care of the babies."

"I can take care of the babies," Jerusha said. "I know how."

"I know you do," Rees said. He sighed and raised his eyes to Lydia's. "What do you think?"

She brushed her lips over the baby's dark silky hair. He found himself wondering what his and Lydia's children might look like. Would they be red-haired, the soft baby fuzz the color of peaches instead of dark like Joseph's? "We should talk to the Elders before we decide anything," she said. But Rees knew he'd lost the argument. She'd already decided to care for these children. He clicked his tongue in exasperation.

"I need to hurry," Simon said suddenly. "I'm late already."

"I'll drive you," Rees said. He wanted to speak with both Mr. and Mrs. Baker about Maggie anyway. Throwing a quick glance at Lydia he added, "I'll return soon. And then we'll drive to Mount Unity. I have a few questions for Mouse." He followed Simon out to the buggy. It was barely colder outside than in, despite the fire burning on the hearth.

"Hurry, hurry," Simon said, running to the buggy and throwing himself into the seat. "Mr. Baker started milking hours ago." His face was white with worry.

"I'll explain that I kept you," Rees said. "What do you do for Mr. Baker?"

"I help milk," Simon said proudly. "And I put hay in the stalls. Next summer Mr. Baker said I could help take the herd to the meadow. And maybe," his voice dropped to hushed amazement, "if I'm good, Mr. Baker might give me a heifer. I can start my own herd."

"Mr. Baker is generous," Rees said. He wondered if Mrs. Baker felt as kindly toward these children. Or was she one of the many who despised both the children and their mother? Rees would find out.

Chapter Twelve

Rees pushed Ares into a trot. Still, it took them the better part of twenty minutes to reach the drive into the Baker farm. Even before he pulled the horse to a stop, Simon jumped out of the buggy and ran toward the barns. Rees followed at a walk. When he peered into the shadowy space he saw several boys, of varying ages, working with Simon, but no Mr. Baker.

Rees turned his steps toward the house, following the icy, well-trodden path to the back door into the kitchen. He could see a plump woman and a young girl whose resemblance marked them as mother and daughter through the window. He knocked. Wiping her hands upon her apron, Mrs. Baker came to the door. She looked at Rees with a cautious expression.

"I'm Will Rees." He realized with a start that he usually presented his loom as his reason for visiting. What could he say today to disguise his curiosity? "I brought Simon over."

Mrs. Baker's suspicious expression changed into reserved friendliness. "Ah, the gentleman the children spoke of." She glanced behind him. "Your wife isn't with you?" Mrs. Baker eyed him quizzically and he rushed into speech.

"She's at the farm with the children. We'll be staying with them until other arrangements can be made."

"Well, come in then and have a bite of cake." She held the

door wide open. "This is my eldest daughter." Rees nodded at the girl, who looked to be a few years older than Jerusha. She promptly reddened under his regard.

Rees sat down and allowed Mrs. Baker to serve him an excellent cake redolent of cinnamon, and a cup of cider. "This tastes like the Shaker cider," he said.

Mrs. Baker nodded. "I bought several hogsheads last fall. Now, Mr. Rees, what is it you're wanting to know?" She sat down across the table and clasped her hands together.

"What makes you . . . why do you think . . . ?" Rees heard himself stammering and closed his mouth.

"Please, Mr. Rees," she said with a scornful frown. "We are not completely isolated out here."

"Of course not. You heard then about the . . ." He glanced at Mrs. Baker's daughter. "About Maggie."

Mrs. Baker nodded. "Pru, go finish the beds upstairs." Both adults waited until the girl disappeared out of earshot. "I heard Maggie was dead."

"I'm working with the constable," Rees said, exaggerating slightly. "I wondered, since you were Maggie's neighbor, what you could tell me about her."

Mrs. Baker sighed. "I've known her all my life."

"You must be about her age," Rees said with polite flattery.

Mrs. Baker snorted. "I'm her elder by almost ten years, as I'm sure you can guess. I knew her aunt well; Olive and I were friendly. But Maggie—a flighty girl. Rather too pretty for her own good, I always thought."

Rees could imagine Mrs. Baker as a girl watching the younger and prettier Maggie dance away with all the young men.

"She grew up here?"

"Yes. Born here."

"Did you know Olive's sisters?"

"You mean Maggie's mother? Saw her once or twice when Olive first married Phinney. They were born and grew up in one of the neighboring towns around here. But once Rose married, she and her husband moved west. Maggie resembles her: blond and blue-eyed. Olive was darker. But," she added, "when Olive took sick, it was Maggie that came home to care for her. As was right and proper seeing as how Olive took Maggie in when she was born. And times were not easy for Olive then, I can tell you. Phinney had been sick for months. I don't know how Olive managed. No money and the farm going untended, and, of course, she needed medicine for Phinney."

"Mr. Cooper told me Maggie married Roger Whitney and moved to Boston." Rees brought the conversation back to the topic. When a grimace passed over Mrs. Baker's face, Rees paused. Mrs. Baker did not speak. "Yes, Mrs. Baker?"

"I won't speak gossip," she said. "But Mr. Whitney was an older man. A sailor. From what Maggie told me, he shipped out as soon as they arrived in Boston. His ship was lost at sea and there she was, a widow. Jerusha was born only a few months after the wedding. She could be Whitney's, I'm not saying she's not, but I wondered."

"Hmmm. And she was pregnant with Simon when she came home?" Rees said.

"Indeed. Well, he couldn't be Whitney's boy, that's for sure. And, to tell the truth, I wasn't surprised. Maggie was . . . well, I won't speak ill of the dead."

"Is Simon a good worker?" Rees knew the answer to that; the boy was conscientious to a fault.

Mrs. Baker's expression softened. "Yes, he's a good boy."

"When Mr. Whitney died, how did Maggie survive?"

"Wet-nursing. Same as she did here."

Rees nodded thoughtfully. "Do you know the name of the family?"

Mrs. Baker shook her head. "In Boston? No. But Reverend Vermette might know. The circuit minister. Have you met him?"

"Yes. Briefly. Did he know Maggie well?"

Mrs. Baker looked startled. "No, certainly not. He arrived in town after Maggie. But he knew Olive Tucker. He paid many a pastoral call upon her in her last weeks. She might have said something about Maggie. Probably did. I know the fate of that girl weighed heavily upon Olive. And although she was closemouthed in her prime, her mind was beginning to wander at the end."

"Thank you," Rees said. "I'll ask him."

"When he returns," she said. "He's on circuit now. I'm guessing he'll come home for the funeral. Will you still be here?"

"Most likely," Rees said. He hoped he wouldn't be kept here for much longer than that.

"You're fortunate this is winter; Abner Vermette is away most of the summer."

"So, Jerusha may be Mr. Whitney's, and Simon's father is someone in Boston," Rees said, circling back to the topic that interested him. "What about Nancy and Judah? Who might their fathers be?"

"I don't know," Mrs. Baker said. "And don't ask me to guess. In my mind, it's Maggie who was at fault. All the men who helped her were good and generous men. Although I didn't know Mr. Whitney well, I'm certain he was a good man also." She rose to her feet, purposely putting an end to the conversation. "I can't waste any more time chatting; I hear the boys coming in for a snack. I don't know anything more anyway. Maggie and I were not friendly."

Rees stood up, too, unsurprised by her obvious dislike for Maggie but sorry for it. He had hoped another woman might be more generous to the girl. Moreover, Mrs. Baker had just lied to him; she did know something about the men Maggie knew, and she probably suspected who among them had fathered those children. Her assertion, that they were good and generous men, had come from personal knowledge, not from guesses. But he also knew she would confide nothing to him. Perhaps she'd be more comfortable with Lydia. "I'm sure my wife would enjoy meeting you," he said. "I'll return later this afternoon to fetch Simon."

Mrs. Baker nodded. As Rees stepped toward the door she called him, "Mr. Rees." He turned. "Maggie wet-nursed for a few families, not just foundlings. One baby came from Albany. . . . I don't know the name of that family. The baby was here for about ten months, until her mother came to take her home. But the other family was local. Name of Griffin. Their little girl died under Maggie's care. A fever, I believe. You might want to speak with Mrs. Griffin."

"Thank you," Rees said. "Where does she live?"

"Outside of Dover Springs," she said, frowning in thought. "Maybe I've said too much; I don't like to be gossiping about my neighbors."

"I would have learned about the Griffin family eventually," Rees said. He fixed her with a stern glare. "Murder is never right, never permissible, and everything is important in the search for a killer. You did the right thing telling me." She did not look comforted but she had no time to argue. A crowd of boys, including Simon, and young men came through the door, jostling one another and talking. Mrs. Baker began putting out cups and plates.

Rees spent a few minutes searching for Mr. Baker. No one knew where he'd gone, and it seemed to Rees as though the man had disappeared off the farm. Finally deciding to question the farmer another time, Rees climbed into his buggy and drove home.

When Rees reached the cabin, an unfamiliar horse was tied up outside. Although a farm horse, not an expensive mare, it was clearly well cared for: plump with a glossy brown coat. Instead of a saddle, a blanket was thrown across the back. Puzzled and very curious, Rees unhitched Ares, put him into the lean-to, and hurried inside.

Mouse was sitting on the hearth with the children around her and Joseph in her lap. Lydia, smiling but with a furrow between her brows, was clearing the table of cups and plates and scrubbing away crumbs.

"What are you doing here?" Rees asked Mouse. Did the Elders know she'd run away? Did Cooper know she'd left Mount Unity?

"I had to see the children," Mouse said, raising her head. Although her left hand covered her harelip, Rees knew she was beaming by her rounded cheeks and the wrinkles at the corners of her eyes. "I had to make sure they were all right. I heard about their mother." She stopped and stroked Joseph's head, shooting Jerusha an anxious glance. "But I see they are safe now, with you two, my dear friends, until they come to Mount Unity."

Rees turned to Lydia. She shrugged helplessly. "Does Elder Herman know you're here?" he asked.

Mouse shook her head, keeping her eyes lowered. "No."

"He gave his word to the constable that you would stay in Mount Unity after you took the children," Rees said. Mouse did not reply. Rees sighed and moved a few steps forward. "What happened last night? Elder Herman told us you took a buggy."

"No one would do anything to save these children." She looked down at Joseph. Using her arm for support, he had pulled himself to his feet and was swaying unsteadily. "So I had to come. I know how it feels to be unloved and unwanted. Called names and slapped . . . always at the mercy of a drunken parent."

Rees turned to look at Lydia.

"And after you took the buggy?" Lydia asked in a sympathetic voice. Mouse looked up, startled.

"Oh, well, I never made it to the farm. Elder Herman caught up to me first."

Lydia eyed Jerusha, who was clearly listening intently, and gestured both Mouse and Rees to the table. "Little pitchers," she said. "Jerusha, mind Nancy and the boys while the adults talk." Jerusha frowned and sat down beside her brothers with an angry thump.

"Where were you when the Elder caught up to you?" Rees asked.

"Past the log church. Driving south toward Dover Springs."

"And when was that?"

"About eight, I believe. It had been dark for hours."

"Did you see anything? Any lights?"

Mouse shook her head. "I heard singing."

"Singing? What was being sung?"

Mouse screwed up her face in thought. "Hymns, I think. I couldn't hear all of the words." She shuddered. "Every now and then the person would stop singing and shout. Words like 'harlot' and 'Jezebel.' I heard those."

"Man or woman?" Lydia asked, leaning forward.

"Woman, I believe," Mouse said uncertainly. "High voice? But I wasn't paying attention." She clutched Lydia's hand. "You don't think I killed . . . ." Her eyes cut left to the children and she paused. "I wouldn't. I swear it on Mother Ann Lee." Since Mother

Ann Lee was the founder of the Shakers in the United States, and almost a goddess to some, Rees knew how serious Mouse's affirmation was.

"Did you see anyone, anyone at all?" Rees asked.

"No. I told you. It was too dark, anyway."

Rees sat back, thinking. The constable had been quite sure of Mouse's guilt, and for the first time Rees found that certainty odd. "You did not stop the buggy or get out?"

Mouse turned a look of impatience upon Rees. "No. Why would I? I was driving as fast as I could to this cabin. I thought Maggie would probably be passed out in the bedroom and I—" She stopped suddenly, her head snapping around toward the door. "Someone's coming," she gasped, her face going white. "What if it's Constable Cooper?" Rees heard the buggy wheels also and jumped to his feet. He did not know how he would explain Mouse's presence to the constable, if he was the new arrival.

Chapter Thirteen

s Rees crossed to the window, Mouse fled into the bedroom to hide. But when he peered out, he saw not Cooper,
but Elders Herman and Agatha approaching. Rees opened the
door.

"Did Sister Hannah come here?" Herman asked. Rees looked
at Lydia for direction. With a sigh, she pointed at the bedroom
door. Agatha started for it, but paused, staring at the five children
seated by the fire. Rees saw her eyes widen but she did not speak.

Before the Elders reached the bedroom door, it opened and
Mouse appeared, her eyes downcast.

"We have been searching for you," Herman said.

"We've been so worried," Agatha added.

"You made a liar of me," Herman said. "I promised the constable we could keep you at Mount Unity."

"I had to assure myself of the safety of these children," Mouse
said, her voice soft but determined. "Now can they come to us?"

"It's not that simple," Herman said.

"Of course it is. They're orphans now." For all her low tone,
Mouse sounded uncompromising.

"Sister Hannah," Herman said with a sigh, "the constable
suspects you of killing Mrs. Whitney. Leaving the community
twice will only serve to confirm that opinion."

"And you put all of us in danger," Agatha said. "Next time the ruffians who ride through the community will not be boys but men, determined to destroy us."

Mouse bit her lip.

"The constable has every right to confine you to jail." Rees added his voice to the chorus. "I didn't see one in Dover Springs. That means Cooper would take you to the nearest jail, probably located in the county seat. Besides all the discomfort of imprisonment, you'd be separated from everyone. Is that what you want? Cooper gave you a gift when he allowed you to stay home." Mouse's eyes filled with tears. Lydia frowned at Rees. He himself felt guilty at the harshness of his speech. "I'm sorry if I sound cruel," he went on. "But I want you to understand why you need to stay at Mount Unity. Promise me, you won't leave again."

Mouse sniffled and wiped her eyes. "Will you come visit me?"

"Yes," Lydia said. "Of course."

"I'll have questions for you anyway," Rees said.

"Will you bring the children?" Mouse turned to look at them. Jerusha's eyes were huge as she watched the scene being played out before her.

"Maybe," Rees began. But Herman shook his head, looking across the room to Rees.

"You must remember what it was like during the war?"

"I was a boy then, but I remember it well," Rees said.

"We, the Millennial Church, did not arrive here until 1776. Feelings ran very high. Loyalists, and those suspected of supporting the British, saw their homes and businesses burned. Some were dragged out of their homes at night and beaten or tarred and feathered." He paused and added quietly, "It was frightening."

Rees nodded. He recalled participating in such actions as a boy in Dugard, including piling live coals in front of the doors of suspected Loyalists. One of Rees's father's friends hung suspected

Tories without benefit of trial, and he was by no means the only one who did so. And the Tories treated those they thought of as traitors in the same manner. King Carleton, the largest landowner in Dugard and a known British sympathizer, had faced down a mob armed with nothing but a musket. Unwilling to lose his property and possibly face expulsion from his home, he'd turned his coat shortly thereafter, becoming a Patriot, at least in name. "It was an emotional time," Rees agreed.

"We had just purchased this property," Herman said. "I was a young man then, simply a Brother. I remember those times well. We do not believe in fighting, Mr. Rees. We are a peaceful community. So we were suspect. Some of our fields were burned, because people were afraid we were offering support to the British. Elder Johannes was hauled off to jail, humiliated." His voice trailed away and his face worked. "We did not dare leave our lands for any reason. We feared attack, you see. And sometimes bands of drunken men would ride through our village. They would beat the Brethren, and sometimes the Sisters." He turned his somber gaze upon Mouse. "It was much, much worse than the harassment we saw this winter." He looked back at Rees. "So, perhaps you understand that although we will be happy to adopt these children, we cannot, at least not until Sister Hannah's innocence is confirmed. Doing so may bring another storm down upon our heads."

"Surely the townspeople will be glad to have you accept the children," Lydia said.

"Perhaps," Herman agreed. "And perhaps, even though they are happy to surrender these children to us, some will use it as an excuse to turn against us." Rees nodded in unhappy agreement. Sometimes any excuse would do.

No one spoke for several seconds. Joseph said, "Da-da-da-da," and Mouse swept him up into her arms. She hugged him hard and then put him down again.

"We will take you home now, Sister Hannah," Herman said. She nodded, holding her head up so the tears in her eyes would not fall. Agatha whispered something to Lydia before turning and grasping Mouse's wrist.

"I have a few questions for you, Elder Herman," Rees said. "If you don't mind."

Herman turned to Agatha. "Take Sister Hannah to the buggy. I'll be out shortly."

Agatha swept Mouse out the door.

Rees gestured Elder Herman to a seat at the table while Lydia went over to speak to the children. Rees couldn't hear what she said, but Jerusha nodded and rose to her feet. She picked up Joseph and drew Judah and Nancy into the bedroom. "Naps," Lydia explained as she swung the coffeepot nearer the fire.

"When did the constable arrive at Mount Unity and accuse Mouse?" Rees asked.

"First thing that morning," Elder Herman said. "It must have been seven thirty or eight."

"Did anyone from your community talk to the constable before that?"

"Of course not." Herman managed a faint smile. "That is how we knew Mouse had been accused. We set off after you as soon as the constable told us."

Rees sat back, thinking. Besides the obvious question—who was singing in the dark on a winter's night—how had Constable Cooper known of Mouse's proximity? Rees called to mind the log meetinghouse. Except for Mr. Gray's house, he recalled seeing no other habitation. A thick stand of woods lay across from the church and the graveyard and fields sprawled north and south. Mouse had said she saw nobody that night. So who had seen Mouse?

"Did the constable give you the name of the person who accused her?"

"No," said the Elder.

"It is possible Mrs. Whitney's murder was accidental," Rees said. "If she'd been conscious, she could have climbed out of the grave." He did not believe it. The presence of the stone, and the absence of Maggie's cloak and bonnet, spoke to a purposeful crime.

"Mrs. Whitney was found in an open grave, with a severe wound on her head," Herman said now, as though he'd heard Rees's thoughts. "Of course she was murdered."

"Mouse is not strong enough to lift another woman, carry her a distance, and drop her," Lydia said, an edge to her voice. Rees knew she was as frightened for Mouse as he was.

"Constable Cooper said she could have used a cart to carry the body." Herman sighed. "He said that Sister Hannah had more reason to wish Maggie dead than anyone. I believe we would all agree, despite the affection in which we hold her. And she was there, near at the graveyard, last night, about the time that poor unfortunate woman was murdered."

"If he were completely convinced, Mouse would be in jail already," Rees said. "I saw no sign of cart wheels, and only a man would be strong enough to carry Maggie's body. When you recovered the buggy, did you find her cloak?"

"No. Nor blood either. I examined the buggy myself." He paused and then, focusing his gaze upon Lydia, he added, "Mouse is in danger of expulsion from our community. The Elders from the First Family are insisting upon it, in fact."

"But Mouse is innocent," Lydia protested, her voice rising.

She threw a quick frightened glance at Rees. "She has nowhere else to go."

"She may be innocent," the Elder agreed. "But she has been disobedient. She was forbidden to see those children, but she stole a buggy with the express purpose of taking them from their mother a second time. Now, because of her unwillingness to obey direction, the entire community is in danger." He stopped speaking abruptly, shaking his head in distress.

"Please give me a chance to at least resolve the question of Mouse's guilt or innocence," Rees said. "The situation may not be as terrible as you fear. I believe some of the townsfolk would be happy to see you take on responsibility for the Whitney children." Rees recalled Mr. Demming's statements. "I know it, in fact."

"But would they all?" Elder Herman asked.

"Maybe not. But perhaps they could be brought around," he said.

"I doubt that," Herman said instantly.

"Please, please don't expel Mouse," Lydia begged. "Please."

"We pleaded for mercy and the Elders from First Family agreed she should be confined to her room instead."

"Oh dear," Lydia said involuntarily. Rees nodded in understanding. The enforced solitude would destroy Mouse.

"At least she will not be in jail," Herman said. He fixed Lydia with a stern gaze. "But she will not be permitted visitors either."

"I am not a visitor," Rees said, feeling himself stiffen. "I am trying to prove her innocence. And in my efforts to discover the actual killer, I may need to speak to her several times."

The Elder inclined his head.

"One other thing," Rees said. "We must all agree to keep this from Constable Cooper. Thus far, he has been fairly impartial and willing to at least give Mouse a chance. We don't want to encourage him to change his mind."

Both Lydia and the Elder nodded solemnly. He rose to his feet and extended a hand. Rees grasped it.

"I'll ride out and inform you of everything I learn," he promised. The Elder's worried expression did not fade but he tried to smile.

"Thank you," he said. He went out the door and a few minutes later Rees heard the thud of horse hooves and the creak of carriage wheels disappearing down the drive.

"I'd give my farm to know the name of the witness who talked to Constable Cooper," Rees said. "I'm going to press him." Since Mouse had seen no one, Rees thought the very convenient arrival of a witness was suspicious. And where could a witness have been, to see the road? In the church? Standing in the woods? "This afternoon I may take a drive to the log church and look around," Rees said. And he would call on Mr. Gray, the only one whose house adjoined the graveyard where Maggie's body was found.

"Sister Agatha told me they'll gather up clothes and shoes for the children," Lydia said, breaking into his thoughts. "We can either collect them when we visit Mouse or one of the Shakers will deliver them." She added sourly, "I'm grateful but I can't help thinking they must not have believed Mouse when she told them of the dire circumstances of these children. Otherwise, that clothing would already be here."

With a little click, the bedroom door opened and Jerusha came through. Rees knew instantly she had been listening, She looked frightened. "You aren't going to take us to the Shakers, are you?" she asked.

"Don't you like them?" Lydia asked.

"They seem . . . nice. But I would rather live with you."

"Did your Mama have friends who visited her?" Rees asked.

Maggie and her family seemed so isolated, and yet someone had hated her enough to kill her. And since she was a young and pretty woman, Rees's first thought was that it might have been a lover.

"Well, Constable Cooper. We've seen him the most. I don't think Mama liked him very much. She called him the rod of the town council. Reverend Vermette used to visit often, but that was when Aunt Olive was dying. He doesn't come much now. Mrs. Baker, once in a while. And not in a long time. She and Mama argued. She did bring us a big basket, though, right after Aunt Olive went to Heaven. With cheese and cake. And Mrs. Pettit used to visit, especially when Mama was expecting Nancy and then Judah."

"Mrs. Pettit?" Rees repeated. "The midwife?"

Jerusha nodded.

"Anyone else?"

The child shook her head.

Since no man seemed to particularly stand out in Jerusha's memory, Rees abandoned that line of questioning. Maggie must have taken her activities away from home, and for that he respected her.

The afternoon evaporated in preparations for the night. Rees firmly refused to sleep in Maggie Whitney's bed, so Lydia prepared it for the children. She found a few linen sheets, only slightly mouse chewed, in a chest, and then spread out the tattered blankets Judah and Nancy couldn't sleep without. Maggie's worn quilts went over all. Lydia had brought some of her own sheets and blankets from the farm in Maine in case they stopped at an ill-equipped inn along their journey, and with these she made pallets on the floor before the fire for herself and Rees.

By the time they completed this activity, the last rays of sunset were disappearing behind the trees across the road. When

Rees stepped outside his feet almost went out from under him. Ice filmed every surface with a hard slippery glitter as snow that had melted during the day refroze. And when he looked up the hill he saw Simon's small figure tramping down the slope toward home.

Chapter Fourteen

During the night the floor grated hard on Rees's hipbones and elbows, and he began to regret his fastidiousness. But he finally fell asleep, only to wake up again when a small body wedged itself tightly against him. When he awoke the following morning, he found Nancy snuggled up against his chest and Judah behind him, so spread out half of Lydia lay off the pallet uncovered by a blanket. Groaning, Rees levered himself to his feet. It was still dark but the faint gray in the sky promised sunrise. He peeked into the bedroom. Jerusha and Joseph lay together in the bed, the baby's dark hair next to Jerusha's blond. Simon was gone. When Rees looked at the pegs by the door the boy's hat and coat were missing; he'd already left for work. Rees hoped Mrs. Baker would be kind enough to give the boy some breakfast before sending him home.

He twitched the blanket over Lydia, who was beginning to rouse, and stirred up the fire. A sudden rush of warmth billowed out into the cold room. Rees pushed the kettle over the blaze, knowing his wife would want tea, and then busied himself with the coffeepot. That's when he discovered there was no coffee. Damn! He put a pot of oatmeal over the fire. The children would want to eat.

Lydia rolled out from under the quilts and wrapped her cloak around her. Her red hair, usually neatly combed and confined under a cap, hung down her back in a long and untidy braid.

"There's no coffee," Rees said, an angry snap to his voice.

Lydia caught his tone and offered him a quick pat on the wrist. "I know. We'll have to stop at the shop today. I'll see if they carry coffee beans. Although I expect they will cost."

Rees, who regretted snapping at her, said in a conciliatory tone, "I'm sorry for my ill temper. I slept poorly." Lydia smiled at him.

"I know how cross you can be first thing in the morning. Anyway, I understand. I did not sleep that well either; the floor is hard."

Rees looked at the cereal, beginning to bubble over the fire. "The oatmeal won't be done for another twenty minutes. While you and the children are eating, I'm going to visit Mr. Gray. His house is just behind the log church. Perhaps he saw something the night Maggie was murdered."

"But you haven't eaten," Lydia objected.

"I'll eat when I come back."

"Very well. We'll drive into town together after you return," Lydia said.

The children were stirring. As Jerusha appeared at the bedroom door, Rees put on his coat and went outside to harness the buggy. Ares had weathered the night's cold without injury, but he seemed eager to move. They set off at a rapid pace down the slippery drive, skidding around the corner of the track. Consistent traffic on the main road had crushed the ice into a more passable surface and Rees made slightly better time. He soon approached the left turn onto the lane. He could see the log church through the trees on his right.

The road curved, first to the right. Rees wondered if someone in the Gray house could see a buggy traveling past on the main road. But when he drove down the track a few feet and looked back over his shoulder, he couldn't even see the road. It was blocked by the curve in the lane. So, who could have seen Mouse driving the buggy? Someone in the meetinghouse? The front doors did provide a clear and unobstructed view of the road.

Thoughtfully, Rees followed the lane around to the left and then to the right again, toward a stone house nestled in a hollow and surrounded by evergreens. A buggy was drawn up beside a familiar bay mare, but Rees didn't remember where he'd seen her last. He pulled up next to her and jumped down. He thought the house might be sited on the opposite side of the trees from the graveyard, but the strip of trees and shrubs was so thick he couldn't see through it. So thick the residents would not have seen the killer discarding Maggie's body in the grave. Would they have seen lamplight? If the killer even carried a lamp; Rees couldn't know that for sure. But surely someone in this house could have heard the singing Mouse described.

Rees started up the path. Ashes had been sprinkled upon the packed snow to provide safer footing. As he put his foot upon the first step up to the porch, the front door opened. He couldn't see who stood inside the shadowy hall, but he was startled to see Miss Pike, the pastor's wealthy fiancée, who was on her way out.

"I know Reverend Vermette would be delighted to see you at the meeting tomorrow," she said over her shoulder. The woman inside made some polite response, of which Rees only heard "thank you," and then Miss Pike turned and started down the stairs.

"Why, Mr. Rees," she said, sounding pleased. "How nice to see you again." She paused to offer him her hand before continuing to her mount.

Rees went up to the open door and the pregnant woman

waiting there. She looked at Rees from eyes drooping with fatigue. The hair hanging in wisps from under her mobcap was neither brown nor blond, but an indeterminate color that was lighter than the former and darker than the latter.

"Three callers in one morning," she remarked. "And this early as well."

"Is Mr. Gray home?" Rees asked.

"You aren't from around here," she said, in a voice brittle with weariness. She did not immediately invite him inside and Rees had a clear view of the welter of cloaks and boots lining the wall behind her.

"No." He looked down into her face. "I'm working with the constable on the recent death of Mrs. Whitney. Do you live here?"

"No. I come in twice a day to care for my uncle." She pulled a face.

From the back of the house came a bellow of masculine laughter and a voice crying, "Maartje. Maartje."

"I suppose you'd better come in," she said with sour reluctance.

"Is that Mr. Gray? "

"Of course," she said. "His old friend Mr. Randall stopped by and now my uncle . . ." She stopped and started again. "Please, come this way." She preceded him down the hall, past the rack of cloaks and shoes and one pair of pattens, through the inside door into the kitchen beyond. As they passed the table, she dropped a small pocket Bible upon it. That must have been the reason for Miss Pike's visit.

A very old man, warmly wrapped in a blanket, sat between the fireplace and the window. His white hair was so fine and thin Rees could see the pink scalp underneath. He'd probably spent most of his life wearing a wig. Mr. Randall, the innkeeper, sat across the table. He looked at Rees in surprise. Mr. Gray turned and his faded blue eyes examined Rees with attention. "Who are you?" he asked in a surprisingly strong voice.

"Will Rees. I wondered if you knew, I mean, has anyone told you Maggie Whitney was found in the graveyard?"

"Speak up," Mr. Gray said. "I can't hear you."

"He's hard of hearing," Mr. Randall said. He pushed himself upright and gathered his hat and cane. "Farewell, my old friend," he said, squeezing Mr. Gray's shoulder affectionately. "See you tomorrow." He addressed his comment to both Maartje and Mr. Gray as he brushed past Rees.

"Who are you?" Mr. Gray shouted at Rees.

"I'm Will Rees," he said in a louder voice.

"Louder."

"I'm Will Rees," he bawled, now quite sure Mr. Gray had neither seen nor heard anything of Maggie's killer.

"You don't need to shout. Who are you? I don't know you."

Rees gave up and turned to look for the woman. Although seemingly entirely occupied cutting bread into tiny cubes, she was smiling. "Did you see or hear anything the other night?" he asked.

"You mean the evening Mrs. Whitney died?" A fleeting expression of triumph crossed her face. She held up a finger. "Wait a moment."

Since she did not seem unwilling to talk, Rees retreated to the door to wait while she served her uncle. Maartje brought the plate of chopped bread to Mr. Gray. She poured a cup of cider, the aroma inspiring a growl of hunger in Rees's belly, and put it beside the old man's hand. Although good manners required her to offer refreshment to a guest, she did not, instead urging Rees toward the front door.

"As I was leaving here I saw a buggy. I recognized the driver as that Shaker woman." She looked up at him with guileless blue eyes and Rees knew she was lying.

"You can't see the road from here."

"No. I know. I meant when I went around the curve." Catching herself, she added, "I mean the second curve."

"And what time was that?"

"Just before sunset. After I'd given my uncle his dinner and cleaned up."

"How could you see and recognize the driver?" Rees asked. "Wasn't the road dark by then?" Rees visualized the shape of the land and shook his head doubtfully. Surely the setting sun would have been behind the trees, behind someone facing the road. Mouse and her buggy would have been in shadow.

"It was light enough." She leaned forward and added emphatically, "I'm telling you what I saw."

"You didn't hear any singing or any talking from the log church?"

"No. And I wouldn't pay any attention if I did. We always hear pieces of the services whenever Reverend Vermette is here." Rees heard disapproval.

"You don't care for the minister?"

"Not much but then I scarcely know him. I usually go to the Dutch Reformed Church in town."

"The stone one?"

"Yes. But Mr. Gray likes him very well. He gave Reverend Vermette the land for his meetinghouse. And Miss Pike regularly attempts to persuade me to attend the Reverend's services. Well, she would, wouldn't she? She wants to befriend me. If the pastor does not succeed in squeezing more land out of my uncle, he will apply to me, as the only heir." From her tone Rees understood she would not give Vermette so much as an additional foot of land. "I'll attend the service tomorrow though, for the memorial." She flashed Rees a look that he couldn't interpret.

On cue, the old man began shouting from the other room: "Maartje. Maartje."

"My uncle will attend as well. As he does whenever Reverend Vermette is in residence. My uncle—"

"Maartje!" She turned and hastened back into the kitchen. "Help me into my chair," Mr. Gray commanded. Maartje, standing beside her uncle, slid her young shoulder under his arm. Leaning upon her, the old man levered himself upright. She half-supported him, half-carried him to a chair by the window. Rees took a few steps in their direction but hesitated, fearing they would not appreciate his help.

"You still here," Mr. Gray shouted, turning to Rees. "That girl was a wanton, a harlot, and a liar." His cheeks flushed a mottled red with anger.

"What girl? Maggie Whitney?"

"She was a liar," Maartje agreed. She glanced at her uncle in concern. "Don't distress yourself, Uncle Elias. We won't speak of her again." Putting a hand protectively on Mr. Gray's shoulder, she frowned at Rees.

"Please show yourself out, Mr. Rees. As you see, my uncle could not have heard anything. And any talk of Maggie upsets him."

Rees said nothing. Mr. Gray clearly heard and understood more than he wished known, and he shared what seemed to be a common view of Maggie. Rees was beginning to feel defensive of this young woman, who was so alone and so scorned by the townsfolk.

He found his way to the narrow dark hall and out to the brightening morning outside. Mr. Randall's buggy was gone and a different one had been drawn up in its place. A farmer, by the looks of his clothing, was standing by the horse's head and smoking a long Dutch pipe. The man looked at Rees from eyes so dark a brown they appeared almost black. He seemed familiar, and Rees wondered if he had seen him in the tavern. "You called on Mr. Gray?"

"Yes," Rees said, startled by the other man's hostility.

"My wife ready to go?"

"If your wife is Maartje, almost. She's just getting her uncle settled for the day."

The man turned away and knocked his pipe upon the wagon, releasing a ball of burnt tobacco.

Rees climbed up into the seat. "You see the Shaker buggy the other night?" he asked.

"Shaker buggy?" repeated the farmer.

"You wife saw a Shaker buggy after leaving here the night Mrs. Whitney died."

"That woman! I told her not to involve herself. But she never listens . . . always sticks her nose in where it isn't wanted. I saw nothing, no buggy or anything else. And my wife didn't either." He turned away, putting an end to the conversation. Rees couldn't tell whether this gentleman had lied to him or whether Maartje had, although he was inclined to believe it was her husband who had told the truth. Rees just didn't understand why Maartje would manufacture such a tale.

"I'm ready to go, Caleb," Maartje said as she came down the walk. He gestured toward the buggy, assisting her into the seat with rough attention. As he whipped his mare into movement, Caleb's words floated clearly through the cold still air.

"Why did you tell the constable you saw the Shaker buggy?" Her reply, if she had one, was lost in the clatter of hoof beats and the squeak of buggy wheels skidding over the icy ground.

Later that day, although Lydia expressed a certain reluctance to leave the three young children in Jerusha's care, Rees and his wife set out for Dover Springs by themselves. He deposited her at the general store and drove on to Cooper's workshop. One of the lads opened the door to Rees and welcomed him inside.

The workshop smelled pleasantly of wood and the Franklin stove in the back wall emitted enough heat to allow the apprentices to work in vests and shirtsleeves. Through the windows on the back wall, Rees could see down the slope to the small house and a red painted barn. Behind the latter ran a rapid river, probably one of the several bodies of water from which the village took its name. The water was gray and chips of ice rimmed the boulders with collars of white, but the water itself was too deep and fast-moving to freeze completely.

Since Cooper was talking to another man, Rees positioned himself at the back of the shop, out of the way of the activity. A young apprentice was struggling to fit a group of staves, soaked in water and curved, into the iron band. After the wood strips clattered to the floor for the fourth time, one of the older boys took pity on his younger fellow and held the band. When the staves were in position and steady, he slid the iron ring over the wood and pushed it as far down as he could. He spun the future barrel over and reached for another iron ring.

Rees noticed the barrel of imperfect and broken staves, destined for the fire. Some of the wooden pieces were shattered but many were large enough to nail over the gaps in the cottage's walls and floor. He delved into the barrel and collected an armful of wooden pieces.

"Planning to try your hand at coopering?" the constable asked from behind him.

Rees laughed. "No," he said. "Planning to stop up some of the holes in the cabin walls. How much for these staves?"

"Take what you want," Cooper said, adding with an inviting gesture, "Come into my office." As he led the way to the small room attached at the opposite side of the shop, he said over his shoulder, "I thought I might be seeing you." Unbuttoning his coat, Rees followed him through the workshop. "Still working on a defense of that Shaker girl?"

"She didn't murder anyone," Rees said. "We talked about this. Why did you go to Mount Unity to accuse her?"

Cooper sighed.

Rees stared at the constable, seeing in his slumped shoulders a suggestion of defeat, and answered his own question. "You're desperate."

"There's a witness who saw Miss Moore driving a Shaker buggy near the graveyard the night Maggie was murdered," Cooper said.

"So I've been told, and I would question Maartje's account if I were you. Mouse has already admitted her intention to rescue the Whitney children so her presence near the log church is purely circumstantial. Anyway, she claims the Elders caught up to her just as she reached the meetinghouse." Again Cooper remained silent. "Maartje's own husband refuted her story."

"He would. Caleb Griffin is a surly bastard."

"Griffin?" Recalling his conversation with Mrs. Baker, Rees said, "Is Maartje the Griffin woman whose baby died while Maggie was wet-nursing her?"

"Yes." Cooper smiled slightly at the expression upon Rees's face. "You didn't know?"

"No. I would have questioned her more thoroughly if I had. Did she blame Maggie?"

"She certainly did at the time."

"I need to talk to her again." Recalling Mr. Gray's constant interruptions, he asked, "Where does she live?"

"She lives west of the log church, about five miles out. Take the first left turn after the Baker farm. But she isn't your murderer. All of the arguments against your Shaker friend apply to Maartje Griffin as well. She's not big or strong enough to wrestle Maggie into the ground. Besides, she's pregnant."

Maartje had certainly seemed strong enough caring for her uncle. "I'd still like to speak to her. And the other nursling?"

"Let's see." Cooper furrowed his brow. "Maggie took on that baby when Simon was but two or three months old. The family was from Albany . . . what was their name? Van something. But I never heard of any complaints from them, and the baby was recovered before she was a year old."

"Then what about the men in Maggie's life?" Rees asked. "Jerusha may be Roger Whitney's child, and Simon from someone in Boston. But who fathered Nancy and Judah?"

Cooper shrugged, his eyes sliding away from Rees's. "I don't know. Maggie never said. And the men themselves never came forward."

"Was there anyone who seemed especially close to her?" When Cooper didn't immediately reply, Rees added, "You've known her all your life. Surely you can make a few suggestions."

Cooper shrugged. "I knew her when she was just a girl in school. I was a few years ahead of her and was already betrothed when she turned sixteen. And no, I can't guess. She was a beauty. All the lads liked her."

"And since she came home from Boston?"

"I've visited only a few times. When Olive passed on, the town fathers gave me the unenviable task of investigating Maggie and ensuring she could care for herself and her children. She began hating me then. Of course, Mrs. Tucker had willed the farm to her."

"You haven't found Maggie's will?" Rees interrupted.

Cooper shook his head. "I don't think she made one. She never approached Mr. Schuyler. I asked him and he was adamant on that point."

"What about Olive's will?"

"Mr. Schuyler remembers drawing up that document and says he recorded it at the Albany courthouse about a month later. We were still part of Albany County then. He gave her a copy. But that's a dead end," Cooper objected. "We know what Olive's will says."

"I think I'd like to see it myself," Rees said. "Every time I've read a will I've been surprised. Mr. Schuyler didn't keep a copy?"

"He's barely a lawyer, more of a knowledgeable copyist," Cooper said with a grimace. "He doesn't work from an office but makes his living riding around helping people like Olive write wills."

For a moment the two men remained silent. Then Cooper said, "Maybe you should consider coopering. Or carpentry at least." He nodded at Rees's hands, stroking the smooth wood pieces without conscious volition.

"I thought of carpentry," Rees admitted. "I like wood. But I preferred weaving." He wanted to travel, and carpentry would have tied him to Dugard.

"What did your father do?"

"He was a printer." In response to Cooper's interested expression, Rees added, "I didn't want to get my hands dirty." An image of his father's hands, so stained with ink no amount of scrubbing could clean them, flashed into his head. As a boy, he'd hated his father. A volatile fellow, he was as likely to punch his son as hug him. Rees hadn't wanted to resemble his father in any way at all. With age, his feelings had moderated. He no longer loathed his father with the furious passion of a boy, but he still didn't want to be like him either. He'd vowed to be an entirely different father—and he had become one. But he wondered now if David might have preferred a man like his grandfather—unpredictable, perhaps, but always present.

"That must have disappointed him," Cooper said.

Rees shook his head, unwilling to continue that discussion. "How far is Albany from here?" he asked.

"Half a day's travel." Cooper paused. "Blau," he said suddenly. "Van Blau: that's the name of the family that put their baby out to nurse with Maggie."

Rees nodded his thanks. He foresaw a trip to Albany to obtain a copy of Olive's will, and he might as well visit the Van Blau home while there.

Cooper paused, his expression both angry and resigned. "I think you should know that Silas, now that Maggie is dead, is planning to appeal the town council's decision. His argument is that they agreed to allow Maggie to continue residing in the cottage, not her children."

"So, he'll throw them out on the road." Rees felt anger building in his chest.

"Maybe he assumes they'll go to the Shakers," Cooper said. "I hope he possesses enough charity for that. We have a month before the selectmen meet again. After that . . ." He shrugged. "I suspect they'll side with Silas this time. And, by the way . . ." He handed Maggie's little leather bag of coins back to Rees. "I went to pay her taxes, but someone had already paid them in their entirety."

"Who?"

"No idea. But they were paid, so for the next month those children have a home." He forced a grin. "You can use this now for food. It must be costing you a fortune to feed five hungry children."

Rees nodded and said absently, "Lydia is buying more food

now." He paused and added, "Did Silas want that tiny farm enough to kill his niece?"

"I hope not," Cooper said.

"I think I'll have a few words with him," Rees said.

"He's in the Ram's Head," Cooper said, rising to his feet. "Let's go."

Chapter Fifteen

Silas stopped eating and pushed his plate away when he saw Rees crossing the floor toward him. "What do you want?" he asked, wiping his greasy mouth on his napkin.

"I want you to leave the Whitney farm alone," Rees said.

"That farm should have been mine years ago," Silas snapped. "My fool brother—"

"Spare me," Rees said, seeing that the other man was mounting his favorite hobbyhorse again. "I've heard this tale before."

"They're no family of mine," Silas grumbled. "That whore Maggie was Olive's niece, so her bastard children are none of mine. But I was kind. I allowed them to stay while their mother lived."

More like as long as Maggie had a legal right to the farm, Rees thought. "What about the children? Will you take them, as their closest relative?" Rees asked.

Silas frowned but then looked thoughtful. "The two oldest, maybe. They're big enough to earn their keep." Rees's heart began pounding with anger. "But the foundling brat can go back to the town and the two youngest will have to make their own way." Rees's temper snapped at Silas's casual dismissal of the younger children, and he grabbed the old man by the collar. His words ended in a surprised gurgle as Rees hauled him to his feet by his shirt. "You miserable, selfish . . ." Chairs clattered to the floor as several of the other diners leaped up. As two of the men detached Rees's hands from Silas's throat, Cooper inserted himself between the combatants. His head barely cleared the taller man's chin but his fierce gaze, confident with his authority as constable, drove Rees back a few steps.

"Calm down, Mr. Rees." Cooper put his hand on Rees's arm.

Silas wrapped his hands protectively around his throat. "Anyone'd think they were your brats," he snapped, his voice rough. He hawked and spit upon the floor. "I'm not a cruel man. You got a month. I won't take the farm until April first, after the selectmen's meeting. Everything should be settled by then."

Cursing himself for a fool—he should have better control of the beast—Rees shook off the constable's hand and swept his gaze around the room. "Is this how you treat children in this town?" he asked, biting off each word with scorn. "Putting five-year-olds out to fend for themselves?"

"Silas does not speak for either the selectmen or the town, Mr. Rees," Mr. Randall said, shoving himself painfully to his feet. "We will not abandon those children, I promise you that."

"Dammed outsiders, telling us what to do," Silas said, leaning forward and glaring belligerently at Rees. Rees made as if to lunge forward and the man jumped back, sprawling into the men behind him.

"Come on, Will," Cooper said, grasping Rees's arm again and urging him toward the door. "I thought you wanted to talk to him, not brawl with him."

"A selfish bastard like that should be shot."

"I know you want to protect those children. I do, too. But right now the law is on Silas's side. And you do yourself, and them, no favors threatening him."

Rees wrenched his arm from Cooper's grasp and stamped down the street toward his buggy.

"You're fortunate Silas Tucker is not a popular man hereabouts," Cooper called after him. "Else we might have had a riot. And even a big man like you couldn't beat off all the men inside."

Now that Rees's anger was cooling, he knew he'd behaved foolishly. He climbed into the buggy but did not drive away immediately. Instead, he sat for a few moments waiting for the pounding of his heart and the buzzing in his head to subside. Usually he maintained better control of his temper, but something about Silas Tucker rubbed him into fury. Given the chance, that selfish old man would cast the youngest children onto the town's mercy and work Simon and Jerusha to death. Of course, if the children lost their home, they would go to live with the Shakers; Rees would see to it. But Silas didn't know that.

After several moments, in which he attracted several curious stares from passersby, Rees picked up the reins and slapped them down upon Ares's back. The gelding leaped forward and the buggy wheels slid across the icy surface before jolting back into line. Rees guided the horse in a circle and headed for the general store to collect Lydia.

"All right, what's wrong?" Lydia asked as they headed back to the farm. "You've said barely a word since we left Dover Springs."

Rees stopped worrying his lower lip with his teeth. His lip was already sore. "Maggie left no will, that anyone knows about anyway. And now that she's dead Silas is applying to the selectmen once again to take the farm."

"The children will have to go to the Shakers then. Elder Herman would be forced to take them in." Lydia said.

"Not yet. Cooper thinks we have a month's grace. Tomorrow is Sunday, and Maggie's memorial. I want to search the cabin and the outbuildings. Thoroughly. I doubt Maggie left anything. She didn't seem bright enough to realize she might need a will. But Olive had a copy of her will, and depending upon the wording, it may give Maggie's children some standing. If we can't find anything, I'll drive to Albany next week and search out Olive's document."

"Why does Silas even want the farm?" Lydia asked. "I doubt it includes more than eight or ten acres, and it hasn't been taken care of in years."

"He says that land should have been his all along. I think he wants it just to have it." Rees shook his head in amazement. "The other thing . . ." He turned to look at his wife. "I discovered that several years ago Maggie was wet-nursing a baby who died. I want to speak to the mother, Maartje Griffin, as soon as I can. Monday, maybe. Will you join me? I hope she will be more forthcoming in the presence of another woman."

Lydia favored him with a radiant smile. "Of course. I'll gladly accompany you. It will be like Zion." Rees smiled back. Assigned to assist him while he investigated a death at the Zion Shaker community in Maine, Lydia had proven invaluable. And it was there that they had grown to know and then to love one another. Inarticulate in the presence of his feelings for her, Rees could only pull the buggy to the side of the road and draw her into his arms.

While Lydia prepared the noon dinner, Rees began his search for Olive's will. First he riffled through the pages of the large family Bible. Olive must have been a regular reader of the Bible; she'd inscribed comments in her firm script next to many of the stories. All the blank pages, fore and aft, had been used: the front for records of births and deaths, notes at the back. Rees examined them, but it looked like a record of expenses. "Sal volatile—2 cents, pennyroyal—1 cent, 1 ounce of tinct of op"—what ever that was—"25 cents." On the other side he recognized her abbreviations for chickens, a mule, and a hog, with prices attached. Income. Slamming the book shut, Rees returned it to the shelf.

Then he turned his attention to the bedroom. Since he'd searched this small, barely furnished room only the day before, he was fairly sure he would find nothing. And, although he took up the mattress and pried up loose floorboards, he was correct.

He returned to the main room. The enticing aroma of bacon had drawn the four children (Simon was still at the Baker farm), to the fireside, where they watched Lydia with hungry attention. She continually pushed them back, away from the fire, finally instructing Jerusha to take them to the other side of the cabin. Rees marveled at her patience. He did not remember Dolly struggling so with David, but then David had been the only child. Lydia was caring for five.

"We never eat bacon, never," Jerusha said, reluctantly obeying Lydia's command. "Mama said it was too dear."

"Well, you'll have it today," Lydia said, leaving the hearth so that she might make a little cage around the children with the chairs. Jerusha grabbed Judah and Nancy and held them so they wouldn't escape. Joseph hauled himself upright and grinned at Rees, displaying his gums and teeth. Rees grinned back, wondering again what a child of his and Lydia's would look like. Not dark like Joseph. Maybe they would someday have a little girl, but Rees would not want to see her afflicted with the coppery hair and freckles he shared with David. Maybe she would have Lydia's dark red hair and blue eyes.

"Ha-ha-ha," cried Joseph. "Da-da-da-da-da-da." He looked at Rees expectantly.

"Da-da yourself," Rees said. He went to the shelves and began running his hands over them, top to bottom. All the food in the house, including the supplies he and Lydia had just purchased, barely filled the bottom level. Olive must have stored her pickles and other preserved foods on the upper levels. But that started him thinking about a basement. "Jerusha," he said, turning to the little girl. "Is there a cellar here?"

She nodded. "There's a door in the back. But nothing's down there."

"I'll just take a look," he said, putting on his coat. He went out and walked around the small cottage. On the opposite side from the door he found a snow-covered wooden plank. Underneath it, steps, cut into the dirt and shored up by logs, dropped into the darkness. He descended into a small hole, a basement under the bedroom. Barrels supported on rocks to keep them above the soil filled the small space. But when he looked inside he found them all empty. Olive may have preserved food for the winter, but since her illness and death it had all been eaten. And there were no shelves, no boxes, no paper of any kind.

Sighing with disappointment, Rees climbed the makeshift stairs and re-covered the hole. He paused at the lean-to, startling Ares from his rhythmic chewing, but realized at a glance that nothing could be hidden inside that small space.

When he returned inside, he saw that Lydia had arranged the children around the table and was distributing bacon and stirred eggs onto the wooden plates. Joseph picked up his plate and began banging it loudly upon the table. Judah's pudgy hand crept toward his plate. "No, Judah," Lydia said, removing the dish from Joseph. She spread crumbled bacon and egg in front of him. "Eat like a big boy," she told Judah, handing him a spoon. He immediately abandoned it in favor of his hands, but at least he did not pick up his plate and begin slamming it upon the table. Both Nancy and Jerusha were using their spoons to shovel food into their mouths as fast as possible.

With everything quiet and the children occupied for the moment, Lydia scraped the back of her hand across her forehead and looked at her husband. "Anything?"

"No. And I wouldn't put it past Maggie . . ." He stopped abruptly, as Jerusha's eyes swung in his direction. "You haven't seen any papers around, have you?" She shook her head.

"Just the Bible."

"I may have to travel to Albany," Rees said to Lydia. "I want to make sure these children will be safe after we leave. And that they hold onto everything that should belong to them."

"It's outrageous that man thinks he should own this property just because he's male," Lydia said.

"He's got the law behind him," Rees said. "Women don't inherit, except in unusual circumstances." He smiled at his wife. "The world doesn't operate as the Shaker communities do, with equality of men and women."

"Well, it ought to," she said, turning to the fireplace. She scraped out eggs onto a plate, added a thick wedge of bacon, and brought it to Rees. He ate in silence, thinking hard, as his wife shushed the children into quiet and then shooed them away from the table when they were done. With a towel dipped into the warm dishwater, she washed faces and hands. Then the two youngest went into the bedroom for naps. Lydia set Nancy to churning butter. She enjoyed slamming the dasher up and down, but Rees suspected she would soon tire. As Jerusha began washing the dishes, Lydia finally sat down to eat her own dinner.

Rees looked at the heel of bread on Lydia's plate and then at her face. Fatigue darkened the delicate skin under her eyes. "Maybe you'd better lie down with the children," he said. "I'll help Jerusha."

"No," said Lydia with a smile. "Jerusha and I can manage. While the younger children are asleep, I'll begin teaching Jerusha and Nancy their letters." She glanced over at Nancy. The thud-thud of the dasher was becoming erratic. "I doubt the butter will be done in time for a nap."

Rees worried his lip with his teeth. "I think Silas murdered Maggie. Murdered her to obtain this poor little farm and these few paltry sticks of furniture."

Lydia nodded. "He seems the most likely."

Now Rees just had to prove it.

Chapter Sixteen

Rees awoke before dawn, the tip of his nose a spot of cold on his face. The cabin was even colder than before, and the air felt damp with approaching snow. He put on his coat to stir up the fire and brought in several armfuls of wood. Then he put the kettle over the flames and set out a basin and his shaving knife.

"What are you doing?" Lydia asked from the nest of quilts on the floor. She made no effort to arise; they'd been awake long into the night discussing Silas and the children.

Rees rubbed his hand over the ginger stubble on his chin. "Haven't shaved since we stayed in town at the inn. And it's the memorial service today . . . for Maggie." His voice roughened and he turned his eyes away from Lydia in embarrassment. Now that he'd seen how isolated Maggie had been, and not only isolated but actively disliked, his feelings had changed to pity. Yes, and some shame that he'd been so quick to judge. More than most, he understood how it felt to be the outsider.

"I know," said Lydia, her voice warm with sympathy. "She must have been so desperate."

Rees smiled at her, pleased to see they were of like minds. By now the kettle was gently steaming. He poured some hot water into a basin on the table and washed his face, using a fragment of soap on the bristles fringing his chin and cheeks. Then he took his leather strap to the window over the sink and began stropping the blade of his Perrit Strength razor. From behind him, Judah began speaking his own untranslatable language. Rees heard Lydia say something as she arose from the bed but he couldn't make out the words against the loud snap-snap of the stropping. Every now and then he tested his razor edge against a moistened thumb.

When he turned around Judah had not only come into the main room but also climbed into the nearest chair. He had dipped his right hand into the water and now stared at the drops rolling off his fingers in fascination. Rees dropped his razor and strap into the sink and took three giant steps to the table to lift Judah away. His piercing squeal spun Lydia from the fireplace and brought Jerusha to the bedroom door.

"What's the matter?" Lydia gasped.

But Judah had already stopped squealing, distracted by the soap whitening the lower half of Rees's face. The child touched the soap and brought his hand toward his mouth. "No," Rees said.

"Oh dear," Lydia said, whisking Judah out of Rees's arms. His shriek of frustration turned to gurgles of delight when she plunged his hands into the shaving basin and washed away the soap. "Better shave soon," she said. "The water is cooling."

Rees looked at his shaving water spraying across the table as Judah slapped it. "I'll start over," he said in amusement. "At least his hands are clean now."

Working mostly by touch, since the mirror shard was so small he could see only a corner of his face at a time, he began scraping away his whiskers. He'd begun to grow fond of these irritating children. Was this how Mouse felt? Thinking of Mouse brought his thoughts to Mount Unity. He wondered if they had made it through Saturday night without incident. He must ask Elder Herman.

"Better hurry, Will," Lydia reminded him. "We're running late already." He brought the razor to his chin and rubbed a long furrow in the white suds. Haste made him careless. Although the wooden guard kept him from slicing off an ear, he did nick his chin, and Lydia had to rush over with a piece of rag.

Lydia dumped the basin of shaving water, now pink with Rees's blood, outside in the snow. She added fresh warm water and began washing the faces and hands of the children. Rees slapped bread and cheese on the table. They were late, he was sure of it, although the gray sky outside made it hard to tell the time. As Lydia finished washing one child, Rees pushed him into a chair to eat breakfast. When all but Joseph sat at the table, Lydia thrust the child into Rees's arms and darted into Maggie's small bedroom to change. Rees held the baby awkwardly, away from his body. Joseph stood on Rees's thighs and leaned forward to put his hands on either side of Rees's face. For a moment Rees was transported to the past. David had been six months or so, and Rees held him just as he held Joseph now. David had leaned forward, his mouth open, and before Rees could react the boy had latched onto his nose. Rees had let out a yell and Dolly had snatched the baby away. Rees had left the next day on a weaving journey. When he'd returned, David had been almost a year old and walking. Rees sighed in involuntary regret and pulled Joseph to him. "It's all right," he said. "No one will ever hurt you." Lydia came out, the door banging behind her, dressed in her best, a simple indigo wool gown. Rees thought she was the most beautiful woman he'd ever seen, and he made a vow to himself that if he and Lydia ever had children, this time he would do better.

Lydia looked surprised but glad, too, to see him cuddling Joseph, but she said only, "Better change to a clean shirt. Simon is just coming down the hill from Mr. Baker's." Rees handed Joseph to her and quickly darted into the bedroom for his clean shirt and jacket. Then he put on his coat and went outside to hitch Ares to the buggy.

Twenty minutes later they pulled into the churchyard. Rees looked around. The number of horses and buggies tied up outside and parked on the road confirmed they were late. The double doors fronting the road were closed but not locked. Rees and Lydia hustled the children through the vestibule, marked off by a wooden half wall. Several people, seated upon the logs that served as the rear benches, turned to stare.

Hot with embarrassment, Rees hurried his foster family to the rearmost log pew. Once they were settled, with the children behaving for the moment, Rees took a breath and looked around.

Maggie had drawn a good crowd. Owen Randall and his daughter sat upon a beautifully polished wooden pew several rows in front of Rees. Constable Cooper, accompanied by his wife, sat behind them. Miss Pike, her proud eyes fixed upon the pulpit, sat in the front, across the aisle from the Randalls. The Bakers and the Griffins occupied pews across the aisle, with a scattering of unfamiliar faces among them, and way in the back, seated upon the very last log, was Mary Pettit. She wiped her sleeve across her eyes.

Rees scanned the crowd again. What he found interesting were the absences: none of the selectmen, except for Mr. Randall, was in attendance, and certainly not Demming. He should have shown up, just for form's sake, Rees said to himself, a bubble of anger tightening in his chest. Poor Maggie. She'd lived among these people and deserved more than their disdain. And she'd fought hard for her little family. For that alone, she deserved some respect.

Heads began to turn right but Rees couldn't see why. Then Reverend Vermette appeared, his black robes sweeping behind him like the wings of a bird. He climbed into the chalice-shaped pulpit and opened the Bible before him.

"Before I call you all to worship," Reverend Vermette said, his voice hoarse, "let us take a moment to remember our sister, Margaret Tucker Whitney." His voice broke and he turned away momentarily. At least Vermette grieved; Rees was glad to see it. When the pastor turned back to the congregation, he had composed himself. "Many of us remember Maggie fondly. Some of us grew up with her while others met her as an adult. She experienced many tests in her life and did not pass them all with grace, but despite that she remained cheerful and determined to provide a home for her children."

Rees lost the next few words; he turned to scold Nancy, who was squirming on the hard bench. He settled her with a hand upon her shoulder. When he turned his attention back to Vermette, the pastor had moved into Psalm 23.

The Lord is my shepherd; I shall not want.
He maketh me to lie down in green pastures.

The congregation echoed the pastor in a ragged chorus, and Rees found himself joining in, almost involuntarily—his mother had dragged him to church for his first twelve years of life.

Lydia, holding Joseph tightly upon her lap, leaned across to scold Judah. Biting her lip in frustration, she moved the little boy to her other side, pinning him to the seat with a stern glare.

"Let us raise our voices in song," the Reverend said, extending his hands in supplication. "Dust to dust, the mortal dies, both the foolish and the wise. . . ." His clear golden tenor soared through the church and the sudden lump in Rees's throat startled him.

The congregation shuffled noisily to their feet, their less than angelic voices rising into the hymn. Rees, who would cheerfully confess that he couldn't carry a tune in a bucket, listened to the singers around him. Caleb Griffin, the owner of a pleasant tenor of his own, and his wife, who sang with more enthusiasm than melody. Mr. Baker bellowed the words rather than singing them, but Rees was glad to see the fervor; here was another who mourned the young woman.

All of the children remained quiet during the hymn, even Joseph. But when the singing stopped and Vermette announced his text for his sermon, Judah made a break for freedom. Tearing himself from Lydia's side, the little boy began running down the aisle toward the pulpit. Rees jumped to his feet. With the restraint of his looming presence gone, Nancy promptly climbed down from the bench and went after her brother. Joseph began shrieking at the top of his lungs, twisting his body in Lydia's grasp as he stretched his pudgy hands after the other children. Simon and Jerusha abandoned their seats and hastened after their younger siblings. Rees looked around at the horrified expressions surrounding him. With his cheeks burning, he pursued the children.

He caught up to Jerusha first. "Return to Miss Lydia," he said. "Now. Go."

"But Judah and Nancy . . ."

"I will deal with them," Rees said. Jerusha peered into his face and then, without speaking another word, she turned around and went back to her seat.

Rees turned. In two long steps, he caught up to Nancy and grasped her skirt, jerking her backward. "Stop. Now." The commands snapped out. Gulping and beginning to cry, Nancy halted. Rees took her hand and, spinning her around, pushed her toward Jerusha. "Go to your sister."

"Disrespectful!" someone muttered. It must have been someone close to Rees, otherwise he would not have been able to hear it over Joseph's wails.

"Remove these children," Vermette shouted. His lanky arms shrouded in his black robes flapped helplessly. Lydia, her face white except for two spots of scarlet burning on her cheekbones, stood up. With Jerusha and Nancy before her, and Joseph in her arms, she swept toward the door.

Rees started toward the pulpit, veering left as Simon went right, with Judah in between them. Judah's shrill giggles rang through the hall.

"This is a place of worship!" Vermette shouted.

With a gasp of relief, Rees scooped up Judah and carried him, kicking and screaming, toward the back door. Very conscious of the condemning glares from the congregation, Rees did not dare look to either side. He was dimly conscious of Simon running after him.

They burst through the doors and out into the gray morning light. The air was already much colder and smelled of snow. Rees put Judah down and turned to Simon. "Take him to the buggy. We're going home." The girls were already inside but Lydia had paused by the wheel. Her shoulders were shaking, and Rees put on a burst of speed to reach her. "Lydia. What's wrong?" He put his arms around her. "It's all right."

She turned a face streaked with tears and a mouth trembling with emotion toward him. "I'm sorry. I know it's wrong." She erupted into helpless laughter. Rees stared. "It's so disrespectful.

But when Judah ran around that pulpit . . ." Gusts of hilarity overtook her once again.

Rees smiled. "Yes, it was very funny."

"The expressions on their faces." Lydia's words disappeared in a burst of helpless laughter. "Judah's skirts flapping." She fluttered her fingers.

As the image unrolled in Rees's head, he began laughing, too. "Judah's break for freedom," he said.

"My mother's death isn't funny." Jerusha's small voice barely penetrated the laughter but both Rees and Lydia heard her. They sobered instantly.

"Oh, sweetheart," Lydia said, turning and touching the child's arm. "We aren't laughing at your mother."

"No," Rees said. How did you explain to a child that sometimes the most awful tragedies elicit laughter as a way of softening the blow? "Your mother would have found the scene funny, too, to see all of those sitting in judgment upon her confounded by Judah."

Jerusha shook her head.

Rees held out his hand to Lydia. "Let me help you into the buggy. I think it's time to leave."

She nodded. "I feel so sorry for your mother," she told Jerusha in a trembling voice. Since Lydia's laughter seemed ready to evolve into tears, Rees put his hand upon her shoulder and gave a brief squeeze.

"It has been a very emotional time. And you are overtired." He glanced at the children sitting in the buggy, all staring in rapt attention. He jerked his head in their direction. Lydia wiped her eyes and smiled at them all. Jerusha responded with a tremulous grin.

"Time to go home," Lydia said.

"I have to go back to the Baker farm," Simon said. "I prom-ised I would help the Bakers."

"But it's Sunday," Lydia objected.

"The livestock still have to be fed and watered," Simon said, "and the cows milked. I have to go. I promised." Rees understood; hard work was how the boy coped with emotions he couldn't comprehend.

Lydia turned to continue the argument. Rees put a hand upon her wrist. "He must go." She shook her head without un-derstanding but said no more.

So Rees stopped by the Baker farm and watched Simon climb the drive. He looked so small and so determined struggling over the slippery snow; Rees was unprepared for the wave of protec-tiveness that swept through him.

Thick gray clouds continued to stream in from the west. All the melt was freezing, although it was almost noon and usually the warmest part of the day. When they reached the cabin, Rees was careful to put Ares into the lean-to and close the ill-fitting door before he went inside. He suspected the horse would need protection from the weather tonight.

And they would probably need more firewood, he thought, for tonight as well as for the few days he would be away. He went around the lean-to to the woodpile. He chopped the larger of the branches into logs and then split them. Most of the firewood he stacked outside the cabin door but when he went inside he carried a large armful.

Because of the fire blazing on the hearth, the small cabin felt fairly warm. Rees dropped the freshly split wood by the fire and shucked his greatcoat. He could feel the icy air streaming in around the door and up through the floorboards, but at least the walls were tighter against the cold, he thought, surveying the amber-colored barrel staves he'd nailed up. Lydia had put beans in a bake kettle and thrust it into the embers to cook. The churn had been abandoned; Nancy carded wool while Jerusha struggled to spin an even strand of yarn. Judah staggered busily around the cottage on some toddler errand. "Joseph?" Rees asked.

"Napping." She came forward to greet him.

"I chopped enough wood for several days. It should last while I'm in Albany." Lydia nodded, clenching her hands involuntarily together. "Will you be all right?"

"Yes." Lydia forced a smile. "It will be lonely."

Rees touched her shoulder gently. "What happened to the butter?"

A crease formed between her brows. "I can't get it to come."

"Ah. I think it may be too cold in here. My mother used to pour a little hot water down the dasher. That may help."

With a doubtful expression, Lydia went to the churn. She pulled out the dasher and poured a thin stream of hot water from the teakettle upon it. Dropping the dasher back into the churn, she began the rhythmic pounding, up and down. Joseph's soprano babbling floated through the bedroom door into the cabin.

With a sigh, Lydia abandoned the churn and went to fetch him. Rees went to the churn and peeked inside. The butter would form soon; he pounded the dasher down with such force he felt the vibration through his boots.

Jerusha rose from the chair and peered through the small window by the door. "It's snowing harder," she said. Rees joined her, looking over her shoulder to the whirling white outside. In just those few minutes since he'd been outside, the weather had gotten much worse. The wind had picked up, and it whipped the snow into a blinding curtain. Rees could feel the change in temperature; it felt very cold standing by the window. "Will Simon be able to make it home?" Jerusha asked, her voice trembling.

"Of course," Rees said. "Don't worry." He urged her back to the fire. But he threw an anxious glance through the window at the blizzard outside.

The weather worsened throughout the afternoon. Not only Jerusha but Rees and Lydia spent many minutes staring through the window, cleaning away the frost patterns as they developed. Darkness fell in mid-afternoon, and then they could see nothing at all.

"Where is that boy?" Rees muttered, trying in vain to see through the whirling white outside. "Mr. Baker must have gotten home from the funeral hours ago."

"Mr. Baker probably kept Simon," Lydia said, joining him at the glass. Using her apron, she scrubbed a large circle in the frost but it did not provide any additional visibility.

"Simon should be home soon," Jerusha said, squeezing in front of Rees to lean her forehead on the cold glass.

"Little while," he said, trying to see through the unbroken wall of gray outside.

"Supper is almost ready," Lydia said.

Rees nodded and pulled up a chair to the table. As he sat down, Jerusha fetched an oddly shaped object shrouded in a linen towel from the counter. She watched breathlessly as Rees unfolded the linen from a lumpy loaf of bread, slightly burnt on one side. "Did you make this?" he asked. Jerusha nodded, pride and anxiety mingled in her expression.

"Her first attempt at baking," Lydia said as she placed bowls and spoons around the table. Her tone warned him to be kind.

"It looks wonderful," Rees said, sawing a slice off at the end with his pocketknife. He took a bite. It was chewier than it should have been and Rees could feel his jaws working. Still, it would be edible once he dunked it into his beans. "Great," he said, through the sticky mass in his mouth. "Wonderful flavor." Lydia took pity upon him and scooped a large spoonful of beans into his bowl. He took several large bites. With a smile Lydia poured him a mug of cider. Rees swallowed the whole of it in one draft. He could still feel the bread lodged somewhere under his breastbone. Sliding the remainder of the ragged piece into his bowl, he added, "I'll enjoy eating the rest of it with my supper." Jerusha beamed.

Lydia called all the children to the table and served them. For Joseph, she soaked some of the bread in milk and a little of the molasses syrup from the beans. He seemed to like the soggy brownish mass. Rees couldn't watch.

Simon still had not returned by the time they finished supper. Rees wondered that the parade of feet, as he, Lydia, and Jerusha went back and forth from the window, did not wear a path in the floor.

"Maybe I'd better go and fetch him," Rees said, rising to his feet.

"He might be coming over the hill by now," Lydia said anxiously.

Rees put on his coat and lit the candle in the lantern. "I'll start walking over the hill toward the Baker farm; maybe I'll meet him," he said. He knew Lydia would not rest until the boy was safely home, and anyway Rees was worried, too.

The cold air outside took his breath away. Rees left the snowy rutted drive behind and began ascending the slope. The untouched snow was deeper than it looked and every footfall snapped through the icy crust like a shot. At least the snow scattered the light so Rees could see his way.

As he reached the crest he saw a dark blot a distance away, slowly lumbering through the snow. "Simon. Simon," Rees shouted, breaking into a stiff trot forward.

"Mr. Rees," the boy said as they came within earshot of one another.

"We were worried," Rees said.

"Mr. Baker kept me after." Simon's words dissolved in a fit of coughing and he stumbled. Rees caught his arm. "I'm so tired."

Rees looked down at Simon, so little he did not even reach Rees's waist. He carried a milk pail and although it was only half-full, it seemed too heavy for the boy to lift. Rees took the pail and put it down into the snow. "We're almost home," he said, bending down and lifting the boy into his arms. "Don't worry anymore. We're almost home." When he next saw Mr. Baker he planned to say a few harsh words to him.

"I'm not a baby," Simon protested. "I'm the man of the family."

"I know you are," Rees said. "But I'm taller and this is faster."

He lengthened his stride, half-sliding down the slope to the shack below. He was close enough now to see Lydia limned against the candlelight. And by the time he reached the cabin, she had the door open and her arms outstretched for the boy.

"Food on the table," she said to Simon as Rees deposited him inside. She helped the boy off with his coat and hat.

"Mr. Baker kept me after," Simon said again, his words slow with fatigue. He sat down at the table and took up his spoon. But he ate no more than a few bites before his eyes began to droop and his head nodded over the bowl. Lydia shook his shoulder. When Simon looked up at her, his eyes heavy with sleep, and she saw his scarlet cheeks, she put a hand on his forehead.

"He's burning up. Help me get him into the bed, Will."

Rees picked up Simon, who roused sufficiently to say again, "I'm not a baby."

It suddenly hit Rees that Simon was almost the age David had been when Rees left him with his aunt and uncle after his mother's death. This could have been David in his arms, unloved and worked half to death. Sudden moisture burned in Rees's eyes. This time he wouldn't allow that to happen. This time he would make it right. Simon, in fact none of these children, would be abandoned to such harsh care, he'd make sure of that. "It's all right," he told Simon. "It's all right."

He didn't want to think of that now, did not want to feel tears burning his eyes. Dumping Simon in the bed, he fled to the outer room. But he couldn't sit. He picked up the poker and stirred up the fire with such unnecessary vigor that a swarm of sparks rose into the chimney. The milk: recalling the pail Simon had been carrying, Rees jerked on his coat and went back outside. Although it was much darker now, his tracks were deep and black, like ink stains, and he was able to follow them to the pail.

That night, after all the children were in bed and Rees was finally alone with his wife, he said, "Do you know that Simon is the same age as David when I left him with my sister?" His voice broke on the last word and Lydia moved forward to put her arms around him.

"This situation is not the same," she said. "You left David with family. And you brought money home, to support him and secure his future. These children here, they have no one but us."

"David only had me," he said. "He was my responsibility. I failed him."

"You didn't fail him," Lydia said. "You went back home for him. You followed him to the Shaker community at Zion. You didn't abandon him."

"No one wants these children," Rees said, looking up at her.

"Only Maggie cared for them. It must have been so hard for her."

"They have us," Lydia repeated. "They're our responsibility now."

"I know." Rees said. Suddenly recalling Judah's mad dash down the church aisle, to the horror of the congregation, he burst into laughter. "No one will ever forget us. Or Maggie Whitney's memorial service."

Chapter Seventeen

When Rees awoke Monday morning he found the fire half extinguished from snow sifting down the chimney and the cabin frigidly cold. Jumping to his feet, he quickly stirred up the embers, until flames hissed and crackled with the fury of its blaze. Rees glanced at the wood stacked in the corner; they would burn through it very quickly in this weather. Fortunately the pile outside was almost as tall as he was and ran half the length of the lean-to. He put his boots on and tiptoed to the door. Snow had drifted in around the windows and the door and ice coated the inside of the windowpanes. He scraped a hole and squinted through the frost into a white world. Even the lean-to that housed Ares was almost invisible; snow plastered the walls and the roof and wedged the door tight shut.

When Rees craned his neck and looked at the front, he could see that snow buried the cabin door almost halfway up. He could see no sign of the drive and suspected the road at the foot was as impassable.

"What's the matter?" Lydia sounded groggy with sleep. "Oh my, I overslept."

"No one is going anywhere today," Rees said, nodding at the window. "I wouldn't allow Simon out in this weather even if he weren't ill."

Lydia jumped to her feet and threw her cloak around her to run into the bedroom. She returned a moment later, shaking her head. "He still feels feverish to me." She dressed quickly and put the kettle on. "I'll make tea for him. Mush for breakfast and a hearty soup for dinner." She stopped talking very suddenly, her face going pale. She went for the bread, already hardening, and sawed off a chunk. She cut it into small pieces and carefully ate each morsel, one by one.

"What's the matter?" Rees asked.

"Nothing. I'm fine. Just very hungry."

"I'll see to Ares," Rees said, with an anxious look at his wife. Putting on his coat, he jerked the door open. A drift of fine white snow tumbled into the cabin. He took the broom and began sweeping, making a path to the lean-to and the woodpile beside it. The air felt solid with the cold and by the time he reached the lean-to he was shivering despite his heavy coat. Pulling open the lean-to door was an added struggle. After he fed and watered Ares, he gathered up another armful of wood and hurried back to the warm cabin.

Simon spent most of the day in bed. Lydia made tea with some of her Shaker herbs, but the boy was too ill to drink very much. The other children ran around the main room, quarreling and screaming until Rees thought he would go mad. He would have sent all but the baby into the snow to play if they'd owned boots and coats. Lydia settled them down with tasks but as soon as she left to check on Simon, they were up and running around again. Rees finally gathered them together, compelling obedience with bellowed threats, and started a story. "Once upon a time . . ."

With Monday's heavy snowfall, a journey to Albany would not have been possible, even if Rees had not planned to question

Maartje Griffin again. Since he knew she spent a few hours every morning and afternoon with her elderly uncle, Rees and Lydia intended to leave just after daybreak on Tuesday and catch the woman before she left home. Rees expected the journey to be a long one.

After hitching Ares to the buggy, they set out through the deep snow. The drive was slow and even the short distance to the Baker farm took over an hour.

When Rees told Mr. Baker Simon would not be working for the second day in a row, the farmer said in annoyance, "I need him here. Several of my hands and my own sons are down with the fever."

"Simon is still quite ill," Lydia said in a frosty voice. "I don't want him outside in this weather."

Mr. Baker frowned.

"You rely on the child, don't you?" Rees asked.

"I took him on to help out Maggie, at the constable's suggestion," the farmer said. "My wife didn't like it, though. She's a bit jealous, I suppose." He smiled and Rees saw how much the thought of two women quarreling over him pleased him. "But she's glad of Simon now. And fond of the boy as well. He's a hard little worker."

"He is only seven," Lydia said, even more coldly.

"His mother agreed to it," Mr. Baker said with a shrug.

"Because she was desperate," Rees said. Mr. Baker did not respond. He turned and marched back to the barn. Lydia seemed ready to follow, but Rees took her arm and urged her back to the buggy. He doubted they would gain anything by continuing the argument. And besides, Mr. Baker had been kinder to the children than most.

They drove around the log church and headed northwest. Rees found the drive described by Cooper, and they soon approached the farmhouse squatting in the center of a patchwork of empty fields. As Lydia jumped down, Rees took the horse blanket from the back and draped it over Ares. They went up to the porch and knocked. Rees hoped Maartje was still home.

A slender maid with olive skin and dark brown eyes opened the door. Rees's eyes rested upon the smooth black hair revealed by her cap and wondered if she were part Indian.

"We're here to speak with Mrs. Griffin," he said. The maid glanced over her shoulder.

"I don't know . . . She'll be leaving soon."

"Who is it?" Mrs. Griffin came up behind the maid. "Mr. Rees." Her gaze shifted curiously to Lydia.

"My wife, Lydia," Rees said.

Mrs. Griffin frowned at her visitors but stepped away from the door and pointed them to the parlor on the left. "I can't visit long," she said. "My uncle will be waiting for me."

"Just a question or two," Rees said with a smile.

The scream of a young child punctuated the air. With a muttered apology, Mrs. Griffin turned to the maid. "Go to Sarah." The girl obediently disappeared toward the back of the house. "Please sit down," Mrs. Griffin said, gesturing them to the wooden bench. With a groan she lowered herself into the rocking chair. "I expect you're here to talk about Maggie Whitney. Everyone knows she killed my baby."

Left breathless by Mrs. Griffin's venomous accusation, Rees took a moment to reply. "I was told you sent a baby to her for wet-nursing."

"My little girl, my Beatrice." To Rees's horror, tears flooded into Mrs. Griffin's eyes. Worse, sympathetic emotion sent water streaming down Lydia's cheeks, as well. She moved forward on the bench and grasped Mrs. Griffin's hands.

"I know," Lydia said. "I lost a baby girl." For several minutes, while Rees shifted uncomfortably upon his seat, the two women wept together.

"Even though I bore Sarah after that and I'm expecting again, I miss Beatrice no less," Mrs. Griffin said.

"I know," Lydia whispered. "I know. The grief never disappears. What happened?"

Mrs. Griffin freed her hand from Lydia's and wiped her eyes with a corner of her apron. "I was ill after Beatrice's birth, very ill. And Maggie had just had Nancy and was nursing her. And she'd already wet-nursed a baby for a family in Albany. So my husband hired Maggie to nurse Beatrice. A few months later she died." She tried to stifle her involuntary sob.

"I was given to understand the baby died from a fever," Rees said, speaking for the first time. Mrs. Griffin glanced at him as though she'd forgotten he was there.

"All of those brats came down with the fever. But Nancy lived. I think Maggie fed her baby at the expense of mine. And of course in that horrible little shack . . . and who knows the identity of Nancy's father? He could have been anyone. Maggie was a whore. And a thief. Did you know she tried to pay me back with a silver dollar? Where would she even get a silver dollar? She must have stolen it."

"Maybe Nancy's father gave it to her," Rees suggested, unsettled by her vitriol. "And the money? She was doing her best to make amends." Lydia put her hand on his sleeve.

"No amount of money could make up for the loss of my daughter," Maartje said, glaring at him.

"What happened after your daughter's death?" Lydia asked.

"No one would hire Maggie to wet-nurse, of course." Her face contorted with triumph and fury. "She paid for my baby's death. After that she nursed foundlings, and only when the town fathers could find no one else."

"Joseph seems to be thriving," Rees said. Of course, Mouse had assisted with the baby at a critical time, but he saw no point in mentioning that.

"No one else would take him. Look how dark he is. No doubt a mixed blood, although Mrs. Pettit, the midwife, claims ignorance of his parents."

"Mary Pettit?" Rees asked. "I've met her."

"She was a well-regarded midwife until the drink got her. The baby just turned up one day on the church steps." Maartje shifted uncomfortably. "And now I must find my husband. My uncle will be looking for me soon."

"Would you like us to drive you?" Lydia asked, throwing a quick glance at Rees. "We're driving in that direction anyway."

Mrs. Griffin hesitated and then nodded. "Yes, thank you. My husband is out doing chores. I hate to disturb him."

"How will you return home?" Rees asked.

"He'll come for me in two hours or so." She sighed. "And then I'll go back in the evening to offer my uncle his dinner."

"It sounds difficult," Lydia murmured.

"He wants me to move in," Mrs. Griffin said, turning to Lydia. "Leave my husband and children." She shook her head in disbelief. "And he refuses to have anyone else in the house, otherwise I'd be willing to offer him my maid. I am the favored niece." Her mouth twisted.

"And how is his health?" Lydia inquired delicately.

"Perfect. Except for the deafness. He might live another ten years." Mrs. Griffin sighed again.

"And what will you do when you are confined with . . . ?" Lydia gestured to Mrs. Griffin's swelling belly.

"My cousin will come for a few weeks to help him." She frowned unhappily. "But my uncle doesn't like her; he says she isn't biddable, so I'll be back with him as soon as I can be."

After she left a message for her husband, Maartje swathed herself in her gray cloak and followed Rees and Lydia from the house. The two women squeezed in together and Rees, feeling rather like a coachman, whipped Ares up into a trot.

They all could hear Mr. Gray bellowing for Maartje as soon as they approached his house. Maartje sighed again. Rees jumped down and went around to help her alight. He allowed the women to precede him down the path. Their cloaks, one the color of a ripe cranberry, the other a bright gray, made vivid spots of color against the white of the snow.

"Maartje," Mr. Gray bawled from the kitchen. "Maartje." She quickly threw her cloak onto a peg and hurried in to her uncle. He was sitting in almost the same position as he had been at Rees's last visit. "Where have you been?" the old man shouted. "I'm hungry."

"We kept her late," Rees shouted in reply. Mr. Gray looked at him.

"Lights. Lights in the church," Mr. Gray bellowed. "Those boys are sneaking inside and smoking again. The damn building will burn." Rees turned to Maartje for clarification.

"Some of the local boys, those Baker boys mostly, sneak into the church when Reverend Vermette is away on his circuit," she explained.

"I'll take a look," Rees said.

"What's upstairs?" Lydia asked as Rees headed for the front door.

"Bedrooms. My uncle's bedroom. Of course, he hasn't been up there in several years."

Even from the front hall Rees heard Maartje's sigh and Lydia's quick expression of sympathy. Then he closed the door behind him, shutting off all but a murmur of the conversation inside.

He walked around the house and started for the line of evergreens separating the two properties and the break between the trees that marked a path. He soon had cause to regret his decision; the fresh untrodden snow reached past his knees. But he floundered through it, almost falling when he staggered into the ditch separating the two properties, and fighting his way through the shrubbery at the back of the church. To his surprise, a small lean-to was nestled into the pines at the corner and Vermette's rawboned gray munched hay inside. Rees looked at the horse thoughtfully a moment before putting his feet upon the icy footpath leading up to the back door.

When he entered through the back door, he found himself standing on one side of the church. Reverend Vermette was in the pulpit. The main door was behind the pews on Rees's right. "Reverend Vermette," he said. "I thought you were riding the circuit." The man jumped and screamed like a girl, dropping the candlestick to the floor with a crash.

"Mr. Rees," Vermette said, clutching at his chest. "What are you doing here?"

"Mr. Gray said he's been seeing lights in the church. I came to investigate. Was it you?" Rees walked forward so he could better see Vermette's face in the gloom. The pastor was unshaven, his linen neck cloth grubby and carelessly tied.

"Not me. I just arrived about an hour ago. I haven't even visited Miss Pike or gone home yet." He descended the few steps to the floor. "Those Baker boys could benefit from a good whipping!" He looked at Rees. "They hole up in the church and smoke and drink and generally carry on. I've spoken to Mr. Baker more than once." His lips tightened and he threw back the hair hanging over his forehead with an impatient gesture.

"I'll reassure Mr. Gray," Rees said.

"No need. I'll stop by before I go home."

"Will?" Lydia came through the double doors at the front. "I brought the buggy around." She stopped when she saw Vermette.

"Mrs. Rees," he said, moving toward her. "How nice to see you again. And without the children." He smiled. "Please forgive me for scolding them at services." He hurried toward her, his hands outstretched. "Have you had an opportunity to call upon Miss Pike? I know she would truly enjoy speaking with you." Reaching her, he grasped her hands.

"No," said Lydia, nonplussed. "I've been very busy." She carefully removed her gloved fingers from his grasp. Rees, who'd followed the preacher through the church to the door, walked around him and stood shoulder to shoulder with his wife. In the light streaming in through the front doors, Rees saw cigar butts scattered upon the floor and a number of ugly black burns on the floor by the front door. Reverend Vermette followed his gaze and scowled with frustration.

"I must talk to Mr. Baker immediately," he said. Turning back to Lydia, he said, "I'll suggest Miss Pike call on you."

"No, no," Lydia said hastily. Rees knew she was thinking, as he was, of the chaotic cabin in which they now lived. "When is she at home?"

"Usually every afternoon."

"I will make calling upon her an immediate priority," Lydia said. Rees stared at her. He had never heard that professionally polite tone of voice from her before. "And now." Lydia extended her gloved hand to Reverend Vermette. He had no more touched her fingers when she withdrew her hand and turned to her husband. Recognizing his cue, he took her arm and escorted her from the church to the buggy she had drawn up to the gate.

As he assisted her over the high step, he said, "I see you do not like Reverend Vermette."

"No, not him. It is Miss Pike I do not care for," Lydia replied. "But I see I have no choice." She sighed. "I shall be forced to call upon Miss Pike upon your return with the buggy from Albany."

Chapter Eighteen

Although the morning was rapidly disappearing, Lydia insisted they drive to Mount Unity to visit Mouse. "We're already out. And she will want to know you're still working to prove her innocence."

"If you think it necessary," Rees said. "I'll be gone for only a few days."

"She'll want to know," Lydia repeated. So Rees yielded.

This time, although they drove directly to the Second Family courtyard and introduced themselves to a Brother immediately, they waited a long time before one of the younger Sisters arrived to guide them to the apartment on the second floor of the Meeting House. Then they waited in the small front hall for another twenty or so minutes, until Elder Herman finally appeared.

"I apologize," Herman said. "I was in the cow barn."

"I'm sorry," Rees said. "My wife and I thought we should tell Mouse I'll be away for a few days. In Albany, as part of my search for Mrs. Whitney's murderer." Herman inclined his head but did not speak.

"How is she?" Lydia asked. "Mouse, I mean."

"Resigned, I suppose. She spends most of her time alone in her room. Spinning and weaving." He paused. "I daresay she'll be glad to see you."

"I expect she will," Lydia said, not very civilly.

"Mouse is not accustomed to being alone," Rees said.

"I know." Herman met Rees's gaze. "But this isn't jail, either." His gentle reproof silenced both Rees and Lydia.

After a pause, Rees said, "Have you had any additional trouble here?"

Herman shook his head. "On Saturday night a group of drunken men rode by our community. But they didn't come past the fence. So far, we are not being blamed." He sounded surprised. "And since then the weather has been so harsh." He stopped and looked toward the stairs.

In the sudden quiet, Rees heard footsteps. A Sister with fair hair and a demure expression arrived first. She stood aside with her eyes lowered while Mouse ran up behind her. "Good news?" she cried. Her eyes were clear and her expression was calm. She smiled at Rees and Lydia.

Rees, surprised to see Mouse so serene, glanced at Lydia.

"Will is going to Albany to research Olive Tucker's will," she told Mouse.

"Why? Maggie was confident her aunt Olive had left the farm to her."

"I want to confirm the— Wait. What? You spoke with Maggie during your visit? I thought you said she was passed out in the other room?"

"No, no, I spoke to her. When the Sister and I delivered the basket, Maggie was sober and we talked briefly. And when we went to visit the second time, well, she was . . ." She paused and Rees could see her struggling for an appropriate word. "Tipsy. But we spoke for a little while."

Lydia took one look at Rees's expression and asked quickly, "What did you talk about?"

"About a man she expected to marry her."

"Did she tell you his name?" Rees didn't care that he sounded abrupt. "Was he married? Or important in the town? He might then have a very good reason to kill Maggie."

Mouse shook her head in dismay. "No. And I tried not to listen."

"Did she talk about anything else?"

"She was planning to apply to some of her friends and her brother for the tax money," Mouse said, staring over Rees's head as she cast her mind back. "I felt sorry for her. She was so afraid the selectmen would turn her and her children out of the cabin if she couldn't pay her taxes." Her mouth turned down in sympathy. "But mostly she talked about that man."

"And there was no hint as to his identity?" Rees persisted.

Mouse shook her head and then paused, thinking. "She may have been talking about two men. I don't know. She referred to the one she had always loved. But then she talked about her last chance at marriage. Maybe it was one man."

Rees regarded Mouse in frustration. "You have no idea who that man, or men, might be?" He paused and suggested carefully, "Perhaps the local pastor?"

Mouse shrugged. "I'm not sure."

"How long will you remain in Albany?" asked Elder Herman.

"Just a day or so," Rees said. "I should return to Dover Springs on Thursday."

"Will you visit me again?" Mouse spoke in a low voice, but she turned an anxious face toward Rees.

"Yes," he said, adding for the Elder's benefit, "I'll probably have more questions for you."

"If you must," Herman said without enthusiasm.

"We know we are interrupting your work," Lydia said, leaning forward. "But we need Mouse's help."

The Elder said nothing.

"Will you bring the children with you the next time you come?" Mouse asked.

Rees looked at Elder Herman's expression. "I doubt it."

"We took them to the log church," Lydia said. Rees recounted the tale of the memorial service. Mouse laughed until she hiccoughed and even Herman smiled.

"So inappropriate in a church," Mouse said. "Oh, I miss them so much."

"They miss you, too," Lydia said, laying her hand upon Mouse's. Mouse turned her hand over and clutched at Lydia.

"I am so grateful," Mouse said, her voice breaking. "Thank you."

"We are happy to help you," Lydia said.

They passed the last few minutes of their visit talking about the children and the cabin, and then Lydia and Rees took their leave. On their way out, the Sister handed over a large brown paper parcel tied with cord. "For the children," she said. While Lydia tore the package open to look inside, Rees drove back to Dover Springs in silence, pondering Mouse's surprising revelation. He would have to speak to her again, and press her to remember everything she could about the identity of that man—or men.

By daybreak on Wednesday morning, Rees was on his way to Albany. Within an hour or so he reached the post road. He saw less traffic than he expected, and he recalled Cooper telling him that most transportation went by way of the frozen river during the winter. The snowy surface had been smoothed and flattened by a roller so, although the road was icy and somewhat rutted, the traveling went faster than Rees anticipated. He approached the outskirts of the city within a few hours, and by mid-morning he was within sight of the city limits.

The first task: finding a tavern or inn. Rees planned to spend the night before heading back to Dover Springs the following day. He didn't want to leave Lydia alone for too long. And a tavern keeper would most likely know the directions to both the courthouse and to the Van Blau family.

He stopped at the first post house he saw. A handsome stone building on the southern side of Market Street, it looked like it had been there for forty or fifty years. The wooden sign was probably as old, and although it now read THE KING'S HEAD, with a bloody severed head pictured, Rees could still read the word ARMS underneath the newer paint. The thrifty tavern keeper had reused the original sign.

The yard around the building was already busy with horses and a variety of vehicles. Wondering if he would find room here, Rees tied Ares to the post and went inside.

The aromas of bacon and coffee tantalized his nose as he entered the large common room. A corpulent man, his shuddering belly swathed by a stained apron, hurried to Rees's side. "I am Mr. Witherspoon. Breakfast?"

"Yes. I think so." Although Rees had eaten breakfast at home, the meal seemed many hours ago. "Do you have any room for the night?"

The tavern keeper hesitated for a moment, thinking. "I believe so. Several of the gentlemen are leaving today. But you will have to share."

Rees's heart sank to his boots. He did not care to share his bed with a stranger. Still, this would be only for one night, or two at the most, so he nodded in agreement.

"Breakfast first," Mr. Witherspoon said, gesturing to the tables behind him. Rees spotted a vacant seat and squeezed himself into it. A mug of coffee, so strong it looked like ink, appeared before him. He dropped in a sliver of the sugar and a long pull of cream and took a gulp. Now that was coffee. Most men drank ale or whiskey, but Rees disliked the latter and considered the former more of a dinner beverage.

He had arrived late for breakfast. While he tucked into his plate of steak and bacon with a slice of bread to soak up the grease, the chairs around him began emptying. The men were leaving for their day's toil. By the time he wiped his plate clean, he was almost alone.

A young girl, the tavern keeper's daughter if her plumpness and brown eyes were any indication, directed Rees to a room upstairs. He brought his canvas valise to the room and was thankful he carried very little with him when he saw the boots, horse leathers, and clothing strewn over most of the chamber.

He stowed his roll under the bed, hoping that no one would help themselves to his one change of clothing, and went back downstairs. Mr. Witherspoon knew the location of the county clerk and gave Rees directions to the Stadt Huys, the city hall just a block or two north on Market, but of the Van Blau family he knew nothing. Rees applied to another guest, a tall burly man in the rough clothing of a driver. A fringe of blond hair stuck out from under his hat like pieces of straw, and he looked at Rees from blue eyes as round as marbles.

"Saai van Brugh," he said, sticking out his hand.

"Saai?" Rees repeated, clasping the other's moist palm.

"Henry really, but everyone calls me Saai." He smiled, revealing gapped teeth. "It means 'dull.'" He laughed uproariously at the joke. "Will you ride or walk?"

"I have a buggy," Rees said.

"I think you can walk; it isn't far. Follow Market Street to

Hudson and Hudson to Washington. Gray gabled house." Saai paused, eyeing Rees thoughtfully. "Are you a merchant?"

"No," Rees said. "A weaver." As he'd hoped, Van Brugh accepted that reply and lost interest.

The two men left the post house together, parting in the yard. As Van Brugh hurried to his wagon, anxiously examining the pewter-colored sky, Rees took himself off to the Stadt Huys. Although the English had moved into Albany many years ago, the name Stadt Huys remained, a remnant from an earlier Dutch building also constructed at the corner of Market and Hudson streets. This new structure was a fine three-story brick house that functioned as the city hall, with a court and a jail. It also boasted a weather vane and belfry, and a gallows in the backyard. Despite the cold, the appropriately named Market Street was thronged with women engaged in their daily shopping. Servants carrying baskets trailed the more affluent. Rees noted that the shops boasted a wide range of goods, some from as far away as China. But the half-wild pigs so common in New York and Philadelphia ran freely here as well, scavenging the garbage in the middle of the street. A cabriolet, forced to stop short so as not to run over the swine, flipped over to its side with a great screaming of the occupants. Rees ran over to offer what assistance he could and helped pry an older gentleman from the wreckage. The man thanked Rees profusely while trying to staunch the blood from a head wound. No one seemed seriously injured and Rees, thankful he'd chosen to walk to the Stadt Huys instead of driving, set out again.

He applied himself to the county clerk, who presided over several large wooden document cases with large flat drawers, and paid him a few pennies for his trouble. Even when the clerk stood up, he was so short Rees could look down upon the bald spot in the middle of his dark hair. The clerk handed Rees not one document, but three, and directed him to a small table. Rees quickly skimmed through them. One was a copy of the deed to the small Whitney farm with a description appended. Rees put that aside. But he read the will from Mr. Phineas Tucker leaving his property to his wife, Olive, in the event of his death. Although simple, this will made his wishes clear; his wife was his heir, not his brother Silas. Rees noted with interest that Owen Randall, the innkeeper in Dover Springs, had served as witness.

Rees put that paper aside. Legally, as a widow, Olive should have been her brother-in-law's ward, but her husband had ensured her independence. Rees suspected Silas had tried to take possession of the farm anyway, but the final document, Olive Tucker's will, explicitly left the small property to Margaret Whitney. Just as Rees expected. He felt he knew something of Olive now. She was a very forceful personality. She hadn't relinquished ownership of the farm to Silas and if he'd tried to control her, as a man over a woman, he hadn't succeeded.

It was the will's second paragraph that took Rees completely by surprise. Should Margaret Whitney predecease her children, the farm would pass to first her eldest son, and second, to Jerusha Whitney, Margaret's eldest daughter. Mrs. Tucker had signed at the bottom with a large and very determined signature. The Reverend Abner Vermette had witnessed this document.

Rees read the will again. Olive Tucker really had not wanted to surrender the property to her brother-in-law—there must have been some history there—and had taken what steps she could to prevent it. This will was an unusual action for a woman. Rees could recall no other women he knew who'd written their own wills. Rees stared into space, thinking. Seven years ago Maggie had just returned home from Boston, pregnant, with Jerusha in tow. No one knew then that she carried a boy.

So Simon owned the farm. Rees could hardly wait to tell Silas and see his expression.

"Could you make me a copy of this?" Rees asked the clerk.

He pursed his lips and said sourly, "Usually the testator keeps a copy."

"Olive Tucker is dead and her copy is missing," Rees said, approaching the clerk and looming over him. Rees understood the effect of his height upon shorter men.

"Very well. But I won't have it until this afternoon. And it will cost you a shilling." Rees hesitated; this investigation was beginning to prove unexpectedly expensive, and the tax money returned to him by Cooper was running low. Finally he nodded. With a copy of the will, and Reverend Vermette's testimony, Silas surely would not be able to take the farm.

But, as Rees walked west to Washington Street to call upon the Van Blaus, he realized he didn't know if Reverend Vermette *would* testify to Simon's inheritance. Rees couldn't at that moment conceive of a reason why not, but without speaking to Vermette he couldn't be sure. And then there was again a suggestion of a different Maggie than the one Rees had met. Olive Tucker must have had some confidence in her niece; she had left her everything. The intervening seven years had changed Maggie, and not for the better. What had happened to her?

By the time Rees reached Washington Street his feet and hands were numb from the cold wind sweeping off the river. A thin snow had begun to fall, veiling the houses huddled together in white lace. Most of the buildings were gabled, after the Dutch fashion, but only one was gray. Rees knocked on the door.

"I wish to speak to Mr. van Blau," he said to the young girl who opened it. She could not be more than fourteen, barely old enough to pin up her hair.

"He isn't here at the moment," she replied.

"Then Mrs. van Blau? The family hired a wet nurse a few years ago and I wanted to speak to someone about her."

The girl hesitated a moment and then said, "Come in then, out of the cold. I'll ask the mistress." She drew Rees into a narrow hall and closed the door behind him. Abandoning him there, she hurried away to the back of the house. A few minutes later a woman of about thirty appeared. Her glance raked over him and Rees was instantly conscious of the fine greatcoat he wore over his much worn wool jacket and breeches.

"Dear me, I am sorry. You should not have been left here; that child is still in training. Please come into the morning room." She spoke with a very slight accent. She directed Rees to the left, into a small sitting room. Rees suspected she now met with him in the same room she used for shopkeepers and recalcitrant staff. When both were settled, and Mrs. van Blau had called for coffee and *koekjes*, she said, "Now, how can I help you? Mary said you were inquiring about a wet nurse?"

"Yes. Margaret Whitney."

"Ah. Your wife isn't with you?"

"No. She stayed home with the children." He spoke only the truth, and she jumped immediately to the obvious conclusion. Rees opened his mouth to correct her assumption but thought better of it. She had given him a perfect reason to inquire into Maggie's background. The young servant brought coffee and a plate of small but delicious cakes, redolent of cinnamon and ginger and thickly frosted with sugar. Rees wrapped his hands around the cup and felt himself beginning to warm up.

"I put my youngest daughter out to wet-nurse with Mrs. Whitney," Mrs. van Blau said. "I was ill after my daughter's birth and I wanted her to stay in the country. We were going into summer and I thought it would be a healthier environment for her."

Rees nodded, trying to keep his face blank. Perhaps Maggie's shack looked more charming in the summer. "And Mrs. Whitney was acceptable?"

"Oh yes. A lovely woman. My daughter thrived."

"And how long did Mrs. Whitney work for you?"

"Let me think. Katrina was born at the end of April. I nursed her for a few weeks before I became too ill to continue. Maggie delivered her son in May. That's one reason why I was so eager to employ her: her milk was fresh. Far healthier for an infant. My husband actually found her advertisement in the newspaper but we both drove out to Dover Springs to meet her. I retrieved Katrina from Maggie in November. I know, seven months is young to wean a baby, but I didn't want to leave her there over winter. Would you like to meet my daughter?"

"I would," Rees said.

Mrs. van Blau rose to her feet and preceded him from the room.

They went upstairs to a small room on the upper floor. While a small boy, of about Nancy's age, Rees thought, played on the floor, a slightly older girl recited her ABCs. "Katrina," said her mother. "Come here a moment."

The child immediately abandoned her lesson and ran over. Pink-cheeked, blue-eyed, and with two pale blond plaits hanging over her shoulders, she smiled confidently up at Rees. Since her fond Mama seemed to be expecting some comment, Rees said, "What a beautiful child!"

Mrs. van Blau nodded complacently. "Indeed. Everyone comments upon my daughter's beauty. And my son is not far behind."

Rees glanced at the little boy. He could not be more than a year and a half younger than his sister. As fair as his sister, he spared Rees no more than a fleeting glance before returning to the lead horse that he galloped over the floor. "Beautiful children,"

Rees said, although they seemed bland to him, without the snapping personalities of Jerusha and Simon.

"So you can assure your wife that Mrs. Whitney would be an excellent wet nurse," said Mrs. van Blau, turning to Rees.

"I will," he said. "Thank you."

"It was no trouble. One wants the best."

Rees left soon after. From a thin veil, the snow had developed into a blinding curtain. As he walked back to the inn by way of the Stadt Huys, he pondered Mrs. van Blau's recommendation. Her praise of Maggie only served to reinforce Rees's impression of two different women. Had the relentless hostility from the townsfolk and Silas changed her into the slovenly creature he'd met? If so, Rees could not entirely blame her.

Chapter Nineteen

Rees reached the King's Head after two in the afternoon. Although late for dinner, most of the men, who would usually have left for an afternoon of work, were still sitting in front of their plates, using the snow as an excuse for sloth. Rees found an empty table and sat down.

"Of course we should become the permanent capital," insisted a gentleman at the next table.

"But New York City is already of greater importance," argued his companion, a gentleman in a jacket of blue superfine and riding boots. The other men wore sturdy shoes or clogs. "Besides, Albany was under British control and . . ."

"You are both ignoring Kingston," said a third man, leaning over from his seat by the fire.

"What do you think, sir?" the first speaker asked Rees.

"I am a stranger in these parts," Rees said. "I have no knowledge of the issue at hand."

"The capital of New York State has rotated among Albany, New York City, and Kingston these last few years," explained the fashionable gentleman.

"The legislators tired of the travel and passed a bill setting the permanent capital as the last location visited. That will be Albany. As it should be." The first speaker glared at his friend.

"But New York City is an important and rapidly growing city," the other man persisted.

Seeing that the argument would continue for some time, Rees spread his copies of the documents upon the table and turned his attention to them. The clerk had copied all three, including Phineas's will, initialing each of the signatures and stamping the documents with a red wax seal. But the seal was not the official Albany seal, and since these were not the originals, with authentic signatures, Rees suspected Silas would try to dismiss them out of hand. He would not succeed. Anyone could travel to Albany and confirm the information. For Rees, they provided incontrovertible proof of Simon's right to the cottage, and so he would argue.

Mr. Witherspoon's arrival with Rees's hearty dinner, a slab of beef swimming in gravy with a mound of fried potatoes—he could not accuse Mr. Witherspoon of stinting upon portions—forced him to put the papers to his pocket but not to cease his deliberations.

Of course Silas would protest that since his sister-in-law and her niece were women, they should never have been permitted to own or maintain their occupation of the farm. As the town fathers had turned a blind eye to that transgression in the first place, Rees felt cautiously optimistic that that particular argument would not prosper.

Of more concern was Maggie's status as a nonresident. Would her children now suffer a warning out? Or would the selectmen accept Simon's right to the farm as proof of residency and allow them to remain?

Shaking his head, for Rees could not guess which the town fathers would choose, he carried the documents upstairs to tuck into his valise. Tomorrow he would set out before first light and hope to arrive in Dover Springs mid-morning.

His roommate was already in residence; Rees recognized

Saai van Brugh immediately. "Ah, Mr. Rees," said the driver, smiling his gap-toothed smile at the other man. "Did you find Mr. van Blau?"

"I did," Rees said. "Thank you."

Saai nodded incuriously and lay down in the bed. A big man, he soon sprawled across the entire surface. Sighing, Rees sat down in a chair by the window. The heavy curtain of snow falling from the sky produced a curious half-light that made it hard to tell the time of day. Rees thought it could not be past three thirty or four, but he couldn't be sure. After a few more minutes sitting in the cold room listening to Saai's soft grunting, Rees recovered his documents and went downstairs to the common room to study them. The clock in the hall read four thirty.

Rees returned to the bedroom a few hours later. Laying his handkerchief across the grubby pillow, he squeezed in beside his roommate. Physical discomfort held slumber at bay for a long while, but he finally dropped into sleep thinking of Lydia. When he awoke, the Whitney children were on his mind. He thought of them nestling close, their feverish bodies seeking comfort and security. Thoughts of those kids brought him straight to David. Although he still wasn't sure what he could have done differently, after all he had had to support them both, he realized that his regret at abandoning his son to his sister's neglect would haunt him for the remainder of his days.

Rees got out of bed. With a snort, Saai flopped over into the vacated space. Rees put on his boots, collected his valise and his coat, and went downstairs to pay the bill.

By daybreak he had reached the road west with its new thick blanket of snow. The going was very slow, especially since Rees and his buggy were one of the first vehicles on the road. Ares strained between the traces and Rees climbed out several times to help the horse and buggy through a particularly deep or icy spot. Snow melted into his shoes and soaked his stockings and breeches. He revised his estimated time of arrival in Dover Springs to dinnertime, finally pulling into the yard at the Ram's Head past noon. The ostler came out for Ares, and Rees, shivering and hungry, tramped into the tavern.

All conversation ceased and everyone gaped at him in various degrees of shock and disbelief. When Mr. Randall's daughter looked at him with wide eyes, Rees said, "Stew. And coffee, please." She hesitated but at a gesture from her father disappeared into the kitchen. Rees glanced around him; all of the other diners hastily looked away. Puzzled, Rees turned to Mr. Randall. He gestured to a chair by the fire. The two other occupants quickly abandoned their seats, leaving an empty table behind them. Rees sat down, staring around him in bewilderment. But he forgot the other diners when the girl placed a bowl of steaming stew upon the table.

Rees's proximity to the fire and the hot food quickly warmed him. He was scraping the bottom of his bowl when the front door opened with a bang. "Mr. Rees," the constable said. The unusual grimness of his voice brought Rees's head up. Cooper paused a few feet away. Four other men, one holding an old musket, one a rifle, and the other a flintlock pistol, stood behind him.

"Yes?" Rees said. "What the . . . ?"

"Where have you been the past two days?"

"In Albany. I wanted to show you." He began to bend toward his valise but the sudden sound of a trigger's movement froze him in place. Lifting his hands, he turned slowly toward Cooper. A man behind the constable had lifted a rifle to his shoulder and trained the gun upon Rees. "What's the matter?" Rees could barely get the words out past his chattering teeth.

"Silas Tucker was shot and killed yesterday."

"He was? Are you sure?" Rees struggled to understand what he was hearing. "Do you think I did it?" A quick glance at Cooper's expression told Rees the constable suspected him. "It wasn't me. I was in Albany. I have proof." He nodded his head to the canvas roll at his feet. "Look in there. You'll see." His heart thudded in his chest.

Cooper approached the table and bent to retrieve the bundle. With a sharp glance at Rees, the constable untied the straps and extracted the rolled documents. "Where did you get these?"

"I told you. I went to Albany first thing yesterday morning. The clerk copied the originals for me."

"Where did you stay?"

"At the King's Head, formerly the King's Arms."

"Hmmm," Cooper eyed Rees. "You could have shot Silas Tuesday and left Wednesday. He lived close enough to you."

"I don't know where he lived."

"His farm connects to the Whitney farm; lies right behind it, in fact."

"I didn't know that," Rees said. Cooper's suspicious expression didn't change. "Think, man. I'm not from here. How would I know?"

Although Cooper didn't reply, his expression shifted subtly.

"Besides, first thing Tuesday morning, my wife and I visited Maartje Griffin. Then we drove to Mount Unity. Mrs. Griffin and Elder Herman will confirm we visited them. In fact," he added with sudden inspiration, "he told me a group of drunken men rode past Mount Unity on Saturday but didn't go in. You wouldn't know anything about that, would you?"

In the sudden silence the snapping from the burning logs sounded like a fusillade of shots. One of the posse shifted position and his shoe scraped the wooden floor. Cooper, his cheeks coloring, stared at Rees for a long moment and then almost imperceptibly relaxed.

"All right, I'm listening," he said, waving the posse back. Rees inhaled what felt like his first breath in several minutes.

"Look at Olive's will. She left the farm to Simon. This is proof." His words tailed off as he realized that, with Silas Tucker's death, the will ceased to be important in proving Silas had good reason to want Maggie dead. Cooper shot him a sharp glance.

"You thought Silas killed Maggie?"

"Yes. It still makes sense. Silas Tucker wanted that property. But then, who killed him?" Rees paused. "What happened to him?"

"He was shot to death while he sat at his desk. Mr. Baker discovered the body when several of Silas's cows wandered down to his farm and he went up to the farm to complain. Something that's happened regularly," Cooper added with a wry twist of his lips. "I can't tell you how many complaints I've received from Tom Baker."

"Where was the body?" Rees asked in confusion. "I thought you said Silas was shot while sitting at his desk."

"He was. Mr. Baker didn't go in, but he could see the body through the broken window."

"I need to see Silas's farm," Rees said. "I must see where the shooter stood and I can't visualize the scene from here."

Cooper contemplated Rees. "Very well," he said at last. Something about the set of his shoulders assured Rees that the constable was now willing to offer him a chance to prove his innocence. "Have you been home yet?"

"No," Rees said. "I stopped here first."

"Very well. I won't remand you to the sheriff quite yet. But don't leave Dover Springs, especially without speaking to me. And tomorrow I'll escort you to Silas's farm."

"I agree," Rees said. Picking up his spoon, he stirred the last drops of stew but found he'd lost his appetite. "I also spoke to Mrs. van Blau about Maggie while I was in Albany."

"And?"

"She praised the girl. So, I wonder, what happened to change Maggie Whitney into the woman I met?"

Shrugging, Cooper rose to his feet. "I don't know. Maybe the death of her aunt? Grief changes people." With a gesture to his men, and to their obvious disappointment, he departed. Rees sat for a few minutes longer, but he was fed and warm now, so he paid his bill and followed the constable from the tavern.

An hour later he walked through the cabin door. Lydia greeted him effusively although a worried crease drew her brows together. "The constable came here several times looking for you," she said. "I told him you had gone to Albany, but he behaved as though he didn't believe me."

Rees turned his eyes at the children, all staring at him and listening. "I saw him in town," he said. She bobbed her head to indicate she understood; they would discuss this later. "I see you've been busy." Although diapers still festooned the fireplace in banners of white, the cottage was clean and the children tidy.

She nodded. "Mr. Baker also came to the door, looking for Simon. I said he would go back to work tomorrow." Her mouth curled. "I didn't want to permit it but Simon insisted. He wants to go back to work. He is very conscious of his responsibilities."

Rees turned to the boy and searched his face carefully. The color had returned to Simon's cheeks, and when he saw Rees looking at him he nodded emphatically.

"Very well," Rees said to him. "But if you tire, I want you to come home immediately."

"I promise," Simon said. Rees doubted he could trust that assurance and decided to visit the Baker farm early to fetch the boy home.

He waited until the children's noisy scuffling in bed faded before sitting down by the fire with Lydia, and then he kept his voice low. "Silas Tucker is dead, murdered."

"Murdered . . ." Lydia's repetition of the ugly word faded into a gasp. "The constable didn't tell me." She dropped the mending into her lap.

"No, I daresay he wouldn't."

As Lydia's initial shock diminished, she said, "Revenge? Or was Silas murdered by the same man who killed Maggie?"

Rees spread his hands to express his uncertainty. "Tomorrow I will visit Silas's house. Maybe then . . ."

"How was he . . . ?"

"Shot."

Lydia hesitated, unconsciously kneading the dress she held in her lap. One of Judah's, Rees thought. That child was so hard on his clothes.

"I think we need to consider the possibility that one of the fathers of these children murdered Maggie," she said.

"I'm ahead of you," Rees said. An old and common story: a pretty girl, a man, and the inevitable result. "But her youngest is two. If she were pressing someone to marry her or trying to black-mail him, wouldn't he have killed her before this?"

"She needed money for the taxes, remember? What if she applied to him for money and threatened him with exposure?"

"That means questioning every man in the entire village," Rees objected, his voice rising with frustration.

"No. She was confined to this farm most of the time with few opportunities to escape. What men did she see? Whom did she speak to?"

"Reverend Vermette," Rees said, recalling his name on Olive Tucker's will. "He was a regular visitor when Maggie's aunt was ill."

"Yes, he may be a possibility. But he's single and his betrothal to Miss Pike is recent. Reverend Vermette was available to wed Maggie. But he didn't." Lydia paused and then added with unwilling sympathy, "She would have wanted to marry him. People aren't kind to women with illegitimate children." Rees, who knew Lydia was thinking of her previous husband and the baby she'd borne and lost, reached across the table and took her work-worn hand in his. "I think the man who murdered her is married."

"Mr. Baker?" Rees said, recalling Mrs. Baker's barely disguised jealousy.

"Constable Cooper," Lydia said. "He visited frequently. I know Jerusha said her mother didn't care for him much, but there could be many reasons for that."

Rees sighed. "I don't relish the chore of tracking down the father of every one of these children."

"Well, not Jerusha or Joseph," Lydia said.

"We can't be certain Roger Whitney fathered Jerusha," Rees pointed out, remembering the difference between the wedding date and Jerusha's birthday. "And we know Simon's father is in Boston."

"I doubt he would make the journey to Dover Springs to murder Maggie," Lydia said.

"Especially since Simon is almost seven," Rees agreed.

"We should look for Judah's father," Lydia said, a yawn breaking the words apart. Rees looked at the smudges of exhaustion under her eyes.

"Don't worry about it now," he said, giving her hand a shake. "Time for bed. These children are wearing you out."

"I have been more tired than usual of late," she admitted, loosening her hair. Rees helped her plait the red mass and change into her nightgown. He kissed her goodnight, and then the kisses became more urgent, and soon neither of them was thinking about the murder of Maggie Whitney at all.

Chapter Twenty

By the time the constable arrived the following morning to accompany Rees to Silas's farm, the sun had been up for hours and Rees had worn a path to the cottage window looking for him. Cooper rode over on his gelding. But Rees had no saddle and so was forced to hitch Ares to the buggy so he could follow the constable. As he fell in behind Cooper, Rees revisited his conversation with Lydia from the night before. He began wondering about Cooper and Maggie. But the constable seemed untroubled by any secret knowledge, and finally Rees put his suspicions aside.

Cooper turned just past the Baker farm onto an infrequently traveled lane. Although Rees steered his vehicle down the center of the road, where horses had tramped down the snow somewhat, the deep snow caught at the buggy wheels and held it. The journey became a series of sudden stops and lurches forward, and by the time they turned onto a drive, both Rees and Ares were tired. Steam streamed off the horse's neck into the cold air. When they stopped some distance from the house, Rees threw a blanket over the animal to protect him. Cooper tied his horse up and together the two men walked toward the house.

It was a fine two-story with many windows. Shutters covered all of them on the second floor, but even from the line of trees across the yard where they'd tied up the horses, Rees could see the broken window. On the first floor, it lay to the left of the front door. Before crossing the twenty feet of open ground, he paused and looked around him. Many horses and men had tramped through here, their prints resulting in a confusion of churned snow. Rees would not be able to identify one set from another. He turned and walked into the trees, finding a scattering of black powder where the murderer had loaded his gun. Again, no help. Rees guessed every man hereabouts owned either a musket or a rifle or both. The shooter was an accurate shot, but again, that was a skill that would be possessed by many.

He turned and followed Cooper through the door into a small central hall, dominated by a flight of stairs rising to the second floor. An open door on the right led into a kitchen. As Cooper went up the steps, Rees turned left, pushing open the door into an office/living area. The room was very cold. Drifting snow blew through the broken window, forming a white coat over the turkey red carpet. A narrow bed dressed with one grubby pillow and a ragged quilt was drawn up to the hearth. But Rees suspected from the small amount of old ashes in the grate that this room had always been kept cold. And, from what he'd seen of Silas, it was most likely to save fuel.

He turned his attention to the desk pulled up to the window, probably to catch all of the natural light. Snow, broken glass, and blood sprinkled the top. "Silas was found lying across his desk," Cooper said as he stepped into the room.

Rees turned around. "So Silas inherited the bulk of his father's farm?"

Cooper nodded. "He was the eldest and the one who looked most likely to succeed." He sighed. "Phinney and Silas were as different as chalk and cheese. Phinney was a tearaway who spent most of his time in the tavern. But he was funny and good humored and popular with everyone. And after he wed Olive he settled. Silas was a different man entirely. Sour disposition, something of a miser. He never married. Some think he wanted Olive, but she chose his brother."

"What do you think?"

Cooper considered the question a few seconds before speaking. "Maybe. By all accounts, she was the prettiest girl around. Like Maggie in that. Certainly Silas never surrendered an opportunity to boast about his worth in comparison to his brother. When their parents carved out the ten acres or so from their farm and gave it to Phinney, well, Silas never forgave them, and after they passed on, he made it his mission to try and recover the land."

Rees felt a sudden surge of recognition. Did not his sister Caroline feel the same about Rees's farm, that she should own it? "I'll wager the relationship between the brothers was poor?"

"Very," Cooper said with a nod. "Why do you think Phinney left a will? He wanted to be sure his brother didn't acquire those ten acres. And Olive felt the same, especially after Phinney's death. Silas hounded her. By the time Phinney made his will, besides being well liked, he was part of the town council, so no one was disposed to support Silas."

"I suppose, if Phinney and Olive and Maggie were still alive, we would have a surfeit of suspects in Silas Tucker's death," Rees said dryly.

Cooper grinned. "Indeed. Silas was liked by very few."

Rees turned to the desk and very carefully began pushing the thick broken glass to one side. Blood had dried to a dark maroon brown, spangled with sparkling ice crystals. But not all the red was blood. Taking his handkerchief from his pocket, he began dusting away the snow and the smaller glass chips. "What the . . . ?" Rees picked up the document. It was the original of Olive Tucker's will, with signatures and a red wax seal. "That dirty bastard!" Rees exclaimed. Cooper looked at him in surprise. "Silas had Olive's original will," Rees said, brandishing the parchment at the constable. "He knew those ten acres belonged to Simon. He stole this, probably from the cabin after he threw those children into the snow. He knew. I guess he thought no one would ever find out. The man was no better than a thief."

"Well, in the long run," Cooper said, "it did him no good. And Simon, as the nearest and eldest male relative, now inherits all of this as well." He gestured around him at the house. Rees nodded. Both law and custom dictated such a result.

"Silas would be furious," Rees said.

"The mills of God do grind exceedingly fine," Cooper said with a grin.

"Indeed they do," Rees agreed. In life, Silas Tucker had been unwilling to allow those children even the shack in which they lived. Now Simon inherited not only the shack and the ten acres of Phinney's land, but also the large and affluent farm of his uncle. Poetic justice.

"That greedy old man knew all along that property didn't belong to him," Rees told Lydia early the next morning. He heard his voice rise and closed his mouth with a snap. None of the children were awake yet. But the fire was beginning to burn well; by the time they rose the cabin would be warm. Lydia turned from the fireplace, where she'd just put the kettle on to boil.

"He had a very empty life," she said. She sounded as though she pitied him. "No family, no friends, no . . ."

"By his own actions," Rees interrupted.

Lydia frowned at him. "Don't judge, Will."

"I was so sure he murdered Maggie," Rees said. "I wanted him to be guilty."

Lydia smiled at his glum tone and put her hand over his. "He may have done it. But then who killed him? And why?"

"Exactly what I wonder. I heard . . ." Rees stopped. He'd heard very little to the credit of either Silas Tucker or Maggie Whitney and had assumed they were enemies. "I don't know," he said. Raising his head to look at her, he admitted, "I don't feel I understand Maggie very well. Mrs. van Blau had nothing but praise for the girl and yet, well, we saw someone very different."

Lydia stared at him. "You're right. God forgive me, I, too, rushed to judgment."

"We both did." Rees took her hand in his. "I missed you in Albany, you know." He paused and said, more embarrassed than lover-like, "I am so grateful you married me, Mrs. Rees."

"Someone had to civilize you." She smiled and Rees pulled her into his arms.

Then Joseph began babbling in the other room and Rees heard someone's feet hit the floor. With an irritated sigh, he released Lydia just as Nancy and Jerusha appeared at the door. Jerusha's gaze flicked from Rees's and Lydia's hands on the table and went anxiously to their self-conscious expressions.

"You're not going away again, are you?" she asked. "Please don't take Lydia—"

A sharp knock upon the cabin door interrupted her. Rees glanced through the window.

"Oh dear God!" he exclaimed. "It's that Reverend Vermette and Miss Pike."

"Don't take the Lord's name in vain," Lydia said involuntarily. And then, as Rees's words penetrated, she said, "Are you sure? But we're not dressed. Oh no." She grimaced, looking like she wanted to swear, too.

Another onslaught rattled the door. Rees and Lydia exchanged angry but resigned glances, and he opened the door.

Reverend Vermette followed his fiancée inside. He was dressed in much-worn black trousers and a jacket but she, when divested of her dark green cloak, was revealed a fashion plate. Since she was garbed in a morning gown, long sleeves covered her arms to her wrists, and lace, rising up to a collar at the neck, occluded her chest. A pale blue ribbon just above her waist provided the only color in that expanse of white fine muslin, too fine for a cold cabin on a winter's day in upstate New York.

She smiled at Lydia. "I am so happy to renew our acquaintance."

"I planned to call upon you," Lydia began, sounding stiff.

"But I know you're busy. It is so Christian of you to take charge of these children. Was Miss Whitney a relative?"

"No," Lydia said, glancing around her at the messy cabin. "I'm so sorry but you catch us at sixes and sevens."

"We wanted to call on you before Reverend Vermette left again," Miss Pike said. "Please don't worry."

"Jerusha, clear the table," Rees said, moving to the hearth to stir up the fire. "Tea?" He looked at the two unwanted visitors.

"That would be wonderful," Reverend Vermette said. "We brought a basket. . . . I'll fetch it from the buggy." As he disappeared through the door, Rees offered Miss Pike a chair. She eyed it, her hand touching the lacy handkerchief tucked into her sleeve, but finally sat.

Working together, Jerusha, Rees, and Lydia soon had the table cleared and the dirty dishes in the dishpan. Lydia set the tea to steep and scrubbed the table. By then, Vermette had struggled inside with the large basket. Lydia selected a cake and sliced it. The Reverend accepted both a slice of the cake and a cup of tea but Miss Pike, examining the plates as though she suspected they might be dirty, accepted only tea and then she put the cup aside and never touched it.

"It is so unusual to see such selfless devotion to the poor," Miss Pike said, leaning confidingly toward Lydia.

"I believe in helping those less fortunate," Lydia said, her tone cool.

"I spoke to Mr. Gray and assured him I would take steps in future to secure the meetinghouse so those boys couldn't get inside," Vermette said to Rees, stepping away from the table and the ladies sitting there. "I very much appreciate your concern and your willingness to investigate."

Rees inclined his head. "You're close to Mr. Gray?"

"Indeed I am. He donated the land for the church and the graveyard. After my marriage, I intend to give up my post as circuit preacher and remain here, in Dover Springs. I'll offer services at the log church every Sunday."

"I'm sure Miss Pike will much prefer that when you're wed," Rees said, acknowledging the woman with a bow. She smiled in return.

"Indeed. I could not afford to marry as a circuit preacher. We earn too little to support a family and the traveling means long months away. But with this church and . . ." He stopped suddenly as a scream erupted from one of the children. Without speaking, Rees crossed the room to separate Nancy and Judah, who were quarreling over a toy. Miss Pike's horrified expression was a study.

"What will happen to these children?" she asked. "Surely you don't intend to adopt them?" Lydia smiled but did not reply. Rees wondered why she did not explain they planned to leave the children with the Shakers. After a moment of silence, Miss Pike said, "Well, I can see how very busy you are." She began to gather herself up. Reverend Vermette collected her cloak and helped her into it.

"Please call upon me," Miss Pike said to Lydia. "I'm sure we will become fast friends."

"I will," Lydia said. Her words came out with difficulty, as though she'd stitched her lips together.

Politely Rees held the door open. Reverend Vermette and Miss Pike could not ignore the hint and quickly departed.

"That's the very worst kind of charity," Lydia said, turning to face Rees. "Not with an open and loving heart but from a sense of her own self-importance. I knew so many women like her growing up in Boston. They say they want to help the poor but flaunt their wealth and good breeding so that those they assist appreciate the wonderful generosity of their benefactors. We should be grateful that someone of Miss Pike's elevated status pays attention to us. Well, gratitude to such condescension makes for a cold and unsatisfying meal."

Rees put his hand upon Lydia's shoulder. "I know," he said, gesturing at the children with a jerk of his head. "Miss Pike wants to help. Maybe her manner will moderate once she is involved in regular pastoral duties, as Reverend Vermette's wife and helpmeet."

"I doubt it," Lydia said. Turning to Jerusha she asked, "Has Miss Pike ever visited you before?"

"Yes," Jerusha said. "You were here, the first time. Remember? I don't think Mama liked her very much."

"I understand," Lydia said. "Your Mama probably didn't like such charity either."

"But you know Reverend Vermette, don't you?" Rees asked, his thoughts converging upon the pastor. After all, Maggie had been found in the graveyard of his church. And Mouse had heard someone singing there.

"Yes. He visited Aunt Olive often. He doesn't come anymore, though."

Rees leaned over the table to help himself to a large slab of cake. "I'll drive into town now and speak with the constable. I wonder if he's thought of Vermette as a suspect in all of this. When I return, we'll fetch Simon from the Baker farm."

Rees went outside to hitch up Ares. Although the sun shone brightly, and the icicles hanging down from the eaves dripped, the air was cold. Still, March had finally arrived and that meant April and May were galloping down the track. Spring would be here soon.

Chapter Twenty-one

Rees drove into town, pulling up in front of Cooper's shop. The snow was packed down by traffic and icy, and Rees slipped and half-fell knee deep into the snow before making it to the shop.

The stove was roaring. Today, the apprentices were sanding and smoothing barrel staves in preparation for soaking. The workroom smelled pleasantly of fresh wood, and pink- and white-hued oak shavings carpeted the floor. Cooper sat in his office, sorting through the papers piled upon his desk. The appreciable distance from the stove meant Cooper needed to wear a jacket.

"Mr. Rees." Cooper pushed aside the papers with an expression of relief. "What brings you into town? Any news?"

Rees thought he should ease into the true reason for his visit. "You know Reverend Vermette is back?"

"Yes." Cooper raised his eyebrows. "Surely you don't suspect him of the murders?"

"Maybe. He spent a significant amount of time at the farm."

"When Olive was alive."

"He knew Maggie before he knew Miss Pike," Rees persisted.

"I never saw any connection between Reverend Vermette and

Maggie," Cooper said. "And now he is betrothed to Miss Pike. She was quite a catch for him: a sizable dowry and wealthy father with a successful business in Albany."

"Maggie was found in the graveyard of his church," Rees said. "Vermette's church."

"An already prepared grave," Cooper argued. "And that church is close to Maggie's farm."

"Mouse heard singing."

"Hmmm. Don't let your friendship with Miss Moore blind you," Cooper said. "No one else heard anything."

"Mouse will always tell me the truth," Rees said. But he understood Cooper's hesitation. Like most constables and sheriffs, and like Rees himself, Cooper expected everyone to lie. Rees discounted half of what he heard. So, although Cooper did not argue, his expression indicated disbelief in Rees's assertion.

"Reverend Vermette may be as poor as a church mouse now but he has a shining future," Cooper said. "Why would he take on a woman with four children by different fathers? Maggie had nothing to offer him."

"She was a beautiful girl," Rees said. "I'm not saying Vermette intended marriage. In fact, he had good reason to want her gone, if she pressed him."

"Reverend Vermette is a pastor," Cooper interrupted. "I never heard any scandal about him." The constable leveled his finger at Rees. "You'd better stop barking up the wrong tree. First Silas Tucker and now Reverend Vermette. I see a desperate man putting his own self in danger."

"I can't believe you would suspect Sister Hannah," Rees began. His words trailed away as he regarded Cooper in dawning comprehension. "The selectmen want *me* to be guilty, don't they?" Cooper could not meet Rees's gaze. "I see. But even if I murdered

Tucker, somehow making it back from Albany to do so, I had no reason to hurt Maggie. And I am persuaded the two deaths are related."

"You don't know that."

But the faintness of his protest told Rees Cooper thought exactly the same. "Most certainly I do. Two people connected to this farm, and in this small community—of course the deaths are related."

"Now that Silas has been murdered, interest in Maggie has evaporated," Cooper said. "You know what people say about her? That she's a whore. Some of our leading citizens say good riddance. All attention is focused upon her uncle, the good businessman." Cooper made an indefinable sound in his throat.

"That poor young woman," Rees said. "Maggie must have felt so alone."

Cooper nodded. "Indeed. No one cares about Maggie. Except me. I want *her* murderer found."

"What was your relationship with Maggie Whitney?" Given an opening, Rees jumped in with the question.

Cooper smiled. "When we were children we talked of marriage. She was the prettiest girl . . . But at fifteen she married Roger Whitney and left for Boston. I daresay he could offer her more than I could. And then I wed Genevieve Shaw."

Rees thought Cooper's reply a little too quick and too rehearsed. "What about after Maggie's return from Boston?"

"I was still married. And when I was assigned to keep an eye on her for the town fathers . . ." He spread his hands wide in resignation. "She barely speaks . . . She barely spoke to me after that." His mouth twitched and he jumped to his feet and faced the window. When Cooper recovered his composure and turned back, his eyes still glittered with moisture.

Rees didn't know what to say. Cooper's grief, at least, was genuine. "Any ideas about Silas's murderer?"

"Not one." Cooper sighed. "He fought with just about every-one. No one stands out." Wiping his eyes with his handkerchief he reclaimed his seat. "And just about all of his adversaries were here, in Dover Springs, under the eyes of their fellows or at home with their families."

Rees grunted. He knew no one would tell him anything; he was the outsider. "If I identify Maggie's murderer," he said, "I promise you he'll lead me to the man who shot Silas Tucker."

"Good fortune," Cooper said, adding bitterly, "Mr. Demming wants me to concentrate upon Silas."

Rees started for the door but paused with his hand on the knob. "Was Maggie's cloak ever found?"

Cooper shook his head. "Not yet. We've searched all the land around the church, across the road, everywhere I can think of. No cloak."

"Hmmm," Rees said. What had happened to that garment? "The murderer attacked her somewhere else. He must have."

"But where? And how did he bring her to the cemetery? We didn't see any wagon tracks," Cooper objected.

"I don't know. But I'll find out, I promise you that," Rees said with determination.

Cooper rose to his feet and clapped Rees on the shoulder. "My mouth is dry after all this chatter. Let's go to the Ram's Head for a drink."

Rees agreed and they walked up the slope together.

Since it was Saturday, the common room was thronged with customers. The hubbub caused by many conversations could be heard outside the door and was almost deafening inside. Cooper found two empty seats at Demming's table. Rees almost elected to leave then; he disliked the selectman and did not want to spend time in his company. But once Cooper had sat down and Demming had seen Rees, it was too late to make a graceful exit. As he sat down, Demming turned his eyes toward him but made no other acknowledgment.

Mr. Randall's daughter and another young girl were running around the room, serving whiskey. Rees declined whiskey and asked for ale. When no one returned, Cooper muttered an epithet and rose from the table to collar one of the servers. Rees found himself alone with Demming.

"Why did you dislike Maggie Whitney?" he asked, the words sliding out of his mouth before he knew he was going to speak.

Demming turned to look at him, startled. "How can you ask that? You saw how she lived. Four children from different fathers. Always just one step removed from requiring Poor Relief. If we had been generous, she and her children—and who knows how many she would have had—would have been a drain on the town for years to come."

"But she was born here, wasn't she?" Rees asked.

"To a mother who promptly abandoned her and returned to her own home. If I knew where that was, Maggie and her brats would have been sent away years ago." He paused, taking a deep draft of his whiskey. "We have a nice town here. Peaceful. Pleasant. Well regulated. Women like Maggie would take advantage."

So many arguments occurred to Rees that he couldn't decide which to begin with. Christian charity alone would seem a forceful answer, especially to a churchgoer like Demming, but as Rees opened his mouth, Cooper returned with a flagon of ale in his hand. As Rees extended his thanks to the constable, Demming drained his glass and reeled from the room. He apparently had no wish to continue the conversation.

Mr. Randall paused by the table. "Did you learn anything of

import from my friend Elias Gray?" he asked. Rees shook his head.

Mr. Randall sighed. "He has gotten very deaf, my old friend. And quite frail. He used to come to the inn every day. We played draughts for hours."

"He made it through the winter," Cooper said.

"Thank the Lord," Mr. Randall said fervently. "I doubt I will ever recover from losing Phinney. I don't want to lose Elias, too. That's old age; it takes everything you love."

Rees and Cooper looked at one another, neither one knowing quite what to say. Rees drained his ale and bade both gentlemen good-bye.

Rees paused by the cabin to collect Lydia and then continued on to the Baker farm. When they pulled in, no one came out to greet them save a skinny mutt who shied from Rees's foot. Exchanging anxious glances, they jumped down from the buggy. It was now just after noon; the yard should have been noisy with hands finishing up morning chores in preparation for dinner. As Lydia went to the front door Rees turned to the barn. He heard persistent ragged coughing before he jerked the door open and stepped into the hay- and cow-scented interior. He did not at first see Simon, only the Bakers' daughter milking with her back to the door. She glanced at Rees but did not pause. Simon was in the next stall, forking hay to the front for all he was worth. Rees followed the coughing to the rear, and found Mr. Baker, collapsed against the cow's flank.

"You aren't taking the boy, are you?" he asked, his voice hoarse and thick. "I need him. Everyone's down with this damn fever."

Rees examined the other man's face. Dark shadows ringed

Mr. Baker's eyes and, despite the cold, his forehead was slick with sweat. Mr. Baker should be in bed, too, but Rees did not say that. The livestock had to be cared for, no matter what.

"Don't worry," he said, grabbing a pail and heading into the next stall.

Only a few of the cows were producing, and their milk was scanty, so they completed the milking quickly. Rees shouldered Simon aside and finished throwing down the hay. Then he helped Mr. Baker to the house, the two children at their heels, and into the warm kitchen. Mrs. Baker was coughing but on her feet. She came forward and grasped her husband's arm. Lydia glanced at Rees and went back to stirring the soup bubbling on the fire.

"Thanks . . . Thank you." Coughing punctuated Mr. Baker's words.

"Don't talk," Rees said, helping the other man into a seat at the table. "How long have you all been sick?" he asked Mrs. Baker.

"My oldest son came down with it about one week ago. Simon recovered the most rapidly," she added, smiling at the boy. "I don't know what we would have done without him. Everyone else has been bedridden for days." She suddenly pressed one hand to her back and the other to her forehead. Rees urged her into a seat by her husband.

Lydia filled two bowls of soup and placed them in front of Mr. and Mrs. Baker. "Eat something," she said. "You'll feel better."

As Mr. Baker coughed fitfully, one of the boys plodded into the kitchen. His white face protruded from the top of a thick blanket, wrapped around him as a shawl. Lydia filled a bowl for him as well. He sat down and dragged the spoon up to his mouth as though it weighed a hundred pounds.

"We'll take Simon home now," Rees said, looking at Mr. and Mrs. Baker in turn. Mr. Baker frowned in dismay.

"But he'll return tomorrow?" he said, coughing. "I need him."

"Tomorrow, for a little while," Rees said. "He was just recently ill himself. I don't want him relapsing."

"Mr. Baker is counting on me," Simon shouted. "They need me here." He began coughing.

"See?" Lydia said, putting one hand on the nape of his neck and pressing his head down. "Shouting makes you cough. Breathe quietly." She held him there for a moment until his coughing eased.

"In future," Rees said, "I don't want him to work all day. Even if there is an emergency. And I want him paid in cash money." Mr. Baker eyed Rees, clearly considering the advisability of an argument. Rees stared him down.

"Morning and evening milking, as before," Mr. Baker said, surrendering without a fight. "And we'll give him breakfast."

Rees looked down into Simon's face. Simon nodded, his expression anxious. With a sigh, Rees said, "All right. But he comes home in between and also as soon as the evening milking is finished."

He and Mr. Baker dickered over the pay and settled on three pennies for the week. "But you're taking advantage of a sick man," Mr. Baker said.

Rees just stopped himself from snorting. "Maybe you won't need Simon quite so much when your boys feel better."

"They are recovering," he said, looking at the boy eating soup.

"Soon you'll be getting back in trouble at the log church with your friends," Rees said to him. He delivered his message in a jocular tone but the boy understood it nonetheless and he dropped his spoon with a clatter.

"It has been several months since I visited that church," he said. "Not since the Reverend spoke to my father and he told me never to go there again."

"Neither he nor his brother could sit down for a week," Mrs. Baker put in.

"We saw a burned patch on the floor, in the front lobby," Rees said. "Reverend Vermette said he had to sweep out ashes."

"Well, I had nothing to do with that."

"Maybe your friends?" Lydia suggested.

"They live even farther out from town than we do. I doubt they've had a chance to come out this way since the snow started." He lowered his eyes sulkily.

Rees said, "I hope you and your brother were not involved in the gang terrorizing Mount Unity." A tide of scarlet swept up into the boy's cheeks.

"I had better not hear you were," Mr. Baker said, fierce despite his hoarseness. "The constable will whip you and then I'll whip you. Those people may be different but they're good neighbors."

"No. I was already sick," the boy said, sounding slightly sullen.

Mr. Baker directed a stern look at his son. "You knew about it and didn't say?" he shouted. His son stared down at his plate. "I don't want anyone coming to me about you boys," Mr. Baker said. "And if I find out you were drinking and smoking in the meetinghouse again . . ."

"We weren't. Anyway," the boy added, "we always went upstairs in the church. More private. The Reverend never locks the door, so anyone could go in."

Although the lad spoke with vehement earnestness, Rees regarded him doubtfully. He was probably fifteen or sixteen, itching to break free of his parents, like his friends, eager to raise some hell. And the church was within walking distance. But Rees didn't prolong the argument. Instead he asked after the health of those who'd been ill with the fever, and after Mrs. Baker pronounced them all on the road to recovery, he turned and looked at Lydia.

"Please call upon me again," Mrs. Baker said, coughing intermittently. "We will have a proper visit when I've recovered my health."

"Of course," Lydia said, putting on her cloak. "I hope everyone feels better soon."

Very conscious of Simon's listening ears, Rees did not ask any questions. They turned onto the main road, the buggy wheels slipping across the ice. The weight in the buggy kept the vehicle grounded but Rees pulled gently on the reins, slowing Ares even further. When he glanced over his shoulder, he saw that Simon had fallen asleep. His lashes shadowed his cheeks and he looked very young and very tired. Rees regretted the agreement he'd made with Mr. Baker, but he knew Simon wouldn't allow him to renege.

"I'm glad you weren't there to listen to Mrs. Baker," Lydia said. "She really did not like Maggie."

"Did Mr. Baker demonstrate some attraction to the girl?" Rees asked.

Lydia was silent a moment, thinking. "Perhaps. I rather got the impression he was partial to Maggie, despite their age difference, before he married Mrs. Baker. Of course, she married Mr. Whitney and left town, but Mrs. Baker hasn't forgotten."

"Mr. Baker can't be more than a few years younger than I

am," Rees said. "Maggie must have been little more than a child."

"She was fourteen. Ah, you're wondering about Mr. Baker's sons. They aren't his natural sons. They are from Mrs. Baker's earlier marriage. She is, I believe, slightly older than he is. And when her first husband died she set her cap for Mr. Baker. He had already inherited this productive farm, you see."

Rees saw. If Maggie had wed Mr. Baker, she and her children might now be living a comfortable life, not Mrs. Baker.

"I think he still nurses feelings for Maggie," Lydia said. "He tried to help them."

"Simon's job."

"Yes. I doubt Mr. Baker fathered any of Maggie's children, though. He's been married now these ten years and even Mrs. Baker admitted she never allows him out of her sight."

"Does she have any ideas about who might have, then?" Rees asked.

Lydia shook her head. "Mrs. Baker was most emphatic that she never saw any men visiting the cabin."

"Maybe they slipped in after dark?" Rees suggested.

"Maybe," Lydia said doubtfully. "But how? When Maggie returned from Boston she had Jerusha and was already pregnant with Simon. And her aunt was still alive. After Olive's death, Maggie cared for not only her children but the nurslings."

Rees thought that through and nodded. "So, where did she meet her lovers?"

"Somewhere inside," Lydia said. "Had to be. Nancy was born in early October so she was conceived in February: the depths of the winter. And Judah was born in September, conceived in January."

What had the Baker boy said? He and his friends used to

sneak onto the second floor of the log meetinghouse? "I need to pay a visit to Reverend Vermette," Rees said. "And thoroughly search his church. Maybe this time Maggie was meeting the man there."

Chapter Twenty-two

Rees continued to ponder Maggie and the fathers of her children throughout the day. After the children were in bed, he raised the topic once again with Lydia. "Although it's possible none of the fathers of these children are guilty of murder, I won't be happy until I've proven their innocence to my own satisfaction."

"Or guilt," Lydia said. "It would be such a common story."

"Someone must know, or at least be able to guess, who fathered Maggie's children," Rees said, thinking aloud.

"Mrs. Baker was pretty definite that Roger Whitney, for all that he gave Jerusha his name, wasn't her father."

"I don't know how much credibility I'd give Mrs. Baker's opinion," Rees said, remembering the woman's hostility.

"I suspect she is correct," Lydia said with a touch of acid. "Look at Jerusha and Nancy. They look so much alike I suspect the same man fathered them both."

Rees nodded, his mind racing. Jerusha and Nancy also strongly resembled Constable Cooper's little girl. "I need to talk to the constable again. Mouse remembered Maggie saying something about the man she'd always loved. Cooper?"

Lydia nodded. "That connection would have been a long-standing one, considering the age difference between the two girls."

"They knew each other from childhood. But any relationship ended, eventually," Rees said. "Judah does not resemble his sisters at all."

"Maggie realized Nancy's father couldn't, or wouldn't, ever marry her." The sympathy in her voice drew Rees's attention. Lydia looked up and met his gaze. "I understand. When I was engaged to marry in Boston, I knew, before Edward told me, that he wanted to break the engagement. I saw him speaking to my best friend and I knew. Oh, Edward would still have gone through with the wedding had I insisted. He was too afraid of my father to refuse. But he would have hungered after Nell and that I couldn't accept." Rees reached over to clasp her hand. He hated seeing the sadness in her eyes. And sometimes, although he fought the impulse, he wondered if she missed the affluent Boston life Edward would have given her.

Lydia turned with a smile. "It is much better to marry someone I can trust," she said, exactly as though she could read his mind. "Anyway, if something similar happened to Maggie, well maybe that's why she wed Roger Whitney."

"And then Judah's father did not marry her either," Rees said. Lydia nodded sadly. "I feel for her."

"I do, too," Rees admitted. The more he learned of her situation, the more he pitied her and admired her courage. "I'll drive into town tomorrow; I now have several gentlemen with whom I must speak," he said, thinking aloud.

"Tomorrow is Sunday," Lydia reminded him. Yawning, she reached up and loosened her hair.

"The Reverend Vermette will not be available until the afternoon, if then," agreed Rees. "But Cooper and Randall should be around." He knelt on the hearth to bank the fire for the night.

"I'll do my part and call upon Miss Pike sometime next week," Lydia said. She did not sound enthusiastic.

"Quiz her about her betrothed," Rees said.

"Of course," Lydia agreed. But she added, flashing him a derisive glance, "You're foolish if you're hoping she'll confide the secret of any relationship between Reverend Vermette and Maggie to me. Even if Miss Pike knew of a connection, she would pretend it did not exist. And she'll express only scorn for Maggie, the fallen woman."

Rees sighed and nodded in agreement.

Before driving into town the next morning, Rees went by the log church. Reverend Vermette was home and preaching. The yard outside was crowded with wagons and buggies. Rees pulled Ares to a stop and listened. He heard the sound of hymn singing and guessed the service would continue for at least another hour. He slapped the reins down on Ares's flanks; he would stop again on his way home.

The cooper's shop was closed when he arrived, and the proprietor was nowhere to be seen. But Rees spotted movement in the yard behind the shop, and as he descended the path he saw Mrs. Cooper loading canvas-wrapped parcels into the back of her buggy. She turned in a swirl of her fustic yellow cloak when she saw him approaching and looked at him quizzically with red-rimmed eyes. Rees thought she'd been crying, and crying hard. "I'm just looking for your husband," he said.

"If he isn't in the shop then I don't know where he is." She pushed one of the bundles into the buggy with unnecessary force.

"He isn't."

"Well, he's around town somewhere. Probably in the tavern."

Rees inclined his head in silent acknowledgment and turned. But he spun back around. "Did you know Maggie Whitney?" he asked.

"Of course." She scowled. Oh, she had known Maggie all right, and hadn't liked her. "Not well. I didn't grow up in town. But I knew her by sight. And I spoke to her a few times." She looked up at him from her velvety brown eyes. "Why do you ask?"

"I thought I might obtain a woman's perspective on her character," Rees lied, with a casual motion of his hand.

Mrs. Cooper paused for a moment, her eyes shifting away from his. "I felt sorry for her," she said at last. "She was an orphan, you know?"

"Yes, I did hear that," Rees said.

"Her aunt Olive treated her lovingly, that's true. But it isn't the same, is it? Not having a mother. She had no father to protect her and her uncle—"

"Phineas Tucker?"

"No, no. I never met him. His brother, Silas, did not treat Maggie as an uncle should."

Rees thought of Silas ejecting Maggie's children from their home and nodded in agreement.

"I would have avoided him. Sometimes the way he looked at her . . ." She shuddered delicately. "But Maggie liked attention."

Rees regarded Mrs. Cooper thoughtfully. "Hmmm. I would have thought two young women of an age would seek one another out," he said. "Befriended one another."

Genevieve shrugged. "Maybe we might have, in the future," she said, leaving Rees with the exact opposite impression. "But I just moved to Dover Springs two years ago to be closer to my husband. Before that, I lived with my parents. And Maggie and I were both busy."

"And you're moving again?" Rees asked, pointing at the bundles thrust into the backseat.

"I stayed on my father's farm for the first five years of my marriage and now I'm returning." She tossed her head angrily. Oh, now Rees understood. She and her husband had quarreled, as any man and wife did, and she was running home to her parents.

"I'm sure Cooper will miss you," Rees said, feeling sorry for both of them.

"I'm sure he won't," she retorted.

Abruptly the door to the little house flew open. "Mama?" A young boy of about nine came out upon the top step, his arms heaped high with sacks and boxes. His fair hair had darkened to brown and like his mother his eyes were brown, but for all that he resembled Cooper.

"Go help your mother," said a deeper male voice from inside. "Don't worry about packing everything, Genevieve," the man continued as he stepped through the door. He was white-haired, and his face was familiar to Rees. "I'll return with the wagon." He followed his grandson out upon the porch.

Mrs. Cooper said, "My son, Mr. Rees. And have you met my father?" Shaking his head, Rees stepped over the icy expanse of ground to the porch and reached up to grasp the other man's hand. The man stared at Rees with hard brown eyes.

"Are you one of Malachi's friends?"

"No," Rees said, dropping his hand. Malachi? No wonder Cooper went by his last name.

Cooper's father-in-law stared at Rees for another hostile moment and then pulled his grandson into the house.

"My father is angry with my husband just now," Mrs. Cooper said in half-apology.

"So I see," Rees said, nodding his farewell at Mrs. Cooper.

Rees went up the path to the road and climbed into his buggy. He drove the few yards to the tavern and handed off his horse and buggy to the ostler. Cooper must surely be inside. But when Rees went in and looked around he saw no sign of the constable. "Breakfast?" asked Mr. Randall.

"Not today," Rees said. "Is Mr. Cooper here?"

"Haven't seen him," Mr. Randall said. "Not at all today." He turned and limped away. Rees stared after the older man. Mr. Randall, an older gentleman, would not know the answers to the questions about Maggie that Rees wanted to ask.

But he knew someone who might: Mr. Randall's downtrodden daughter. When the innkeeper's back was turned Rees quickly darted into the kitchen. Mr. Randall's daughter was standing at the large wooden table rolling pastry. She looked at Rees in surprise.

"Did you know Maggie Whitney?" Rees asked.

"Not really." But her eyes slid to a point somewhere over Rees's right shoulder.

"You are a poor liar," Rees said. "You must have gone to school with her."

"That was fifteen and more years ago," the girl objected. "I know no more than what everyone else knows." Rees eyed the girl thoughtfully until she began to squirm. She banged her rolling pin on the table and rolled the pastry with fierce attention.

"I suspect you know who fathered at least one of her children."

"How would I know something like that?" But she did not look at him.

"You hear people talk. And the tavern would be a good place for Maggie to meet a man."

The girl uttered a bark of laughter. "Past my father? Surely even you cannot believe that."

Rees acknowledged the truth of that. "I suppose you rarely saw Maggie?"

"That's true." The girl nodded, her shoulders relaxing. "Only when . . ." She stopped abruptly.

"Only when you sold her liquor?" Rees said. Her cheeks went white and her eyes flicked back and forth. "Somebody sold her whiskey," Rees persisted. "I think it was you."

"I never sold her whiskey," she replied. But her tense body betrayed her.

"Did you give it to her? I suppose you felt sorry for her. Or maybe she tempted you with a silver dollar." He knew at once he'd struck a nerve. She gasped and began to breathe heavily.

"You don't understand," the young woman hissed. "She came to me sobbing, threatening to kill herself. I thought the whiskey would give her some comfort. It only happened twice."

"Why was she threatening to kill herself?" Rees asked, leaning forward.

"It was over a man. It was always about a man. I could barely understand her, she was crying so hard, but she kept saying nobody ever loved her." She paused and then, sensing Rees's condemnation, she burst out, "Once the jug was empty, Maggie would stop. I knew that. It had happened before."

Rees, recalling the whiskey jugs lining the wall in Maggie's bedroom, asked, "How many times did it happen?"

"I told you. Twice." She hesitated and then added, "She offered me a silver dollar and I took it. She knew I wanted to leave Dover Springs. But we weren't friendly. She was too pretty for the likes of me. Even my brother buzzed around her . . . but my father soon put a stop to that."

"And where is your brother?" Rees asked, glancing around him as though this fellow would spring up.

"Gone. He and my father had a falling out many years ago. That's why Father dotes on cousin Caleb." For a moment no one spoke. Rees watched the girl, who was still carefully not meeting his eyes.

"You must know who fathered Jerusha?" Rees said.

"Roger Whitney." Her face cleared.

"I doubt that," Rees said.

"Of course he did. They married very hurriedly."

"Who else buzzed around her? Cooper?"

She nodded once, a quick jerk of her head. "I thought she'd wed Cooper. But he married Genevieve Shaw, and suddenly she married Roger Whitney and moved away."

Rees leaned back, thinking about Mrs. Cooper and her father. "Was it possible Maggie was already pregnant when she married Mr. Whitney?"

"My mother thought so. Cooper was so handsome." She sighed. "Four months before Cooper was married, everyone in town was invited to Mr. and Mrs. Baker's wedding. Mr. Baker did not stint on the whiskey. By the time Cooper wed Miss Shaw, Maggie was . . . gaining weight. Some of the women in town thought she was expecting, was maybe five or six months gone. She married Whitney a week later and left town."

Rees sat back. And Jerusha and Cooper's boy were about the same age, within months of one another if Rees had to guess. Cooper had told him his son was almost nine. If Jerusha was a month or two older, well, that would explain everything. "I wonder, did the constable and Maggie renew their friendship when she returned to town?" Again, nothing but quiet on the other side of the wooden table. Rees let the silence lengthen.

Mr. Randall's daughter fidgeted, lifting her hand to her mouth and tearing savagely at a piece of loose skin. A drop of bright red blood ballooned at the side of the nail and dropped upon the table.

"Maybe," she blurted at last. "Cooper's wife lived with her parents for a few years after her son's birth. Although she lived in town afterwards, she returned to her parents after Maggie came home."

Not just Jerusha then, but Nancy also might be Cooper's, Rees thought. Lydia's guess was correct.

"And then Genevieve moved back into Cooper's house, behind the shop. After Cooper had to call Maggie before the selectmen a few times they weren't so friendly anymore."

"Maggie expected Cooper to shield her," Rees guessed. "And did he?"

"Probably. She got to stay in that shack with her children, didn't she?" She sighed. "If they were together, well, I don't blame Maggie. Life is hard without a husband."

"So who fathered Judah?" Rees asked.

"I don't know." She shook her head.

"Besides Cooper, did Maggie have any friends?"

"Men friends, you mean." She grimaced. "I don't think so. I know she had no woman friends, unless you count her aunt Olive and Mary Pettit. The midwife who delivered Maggie's children, you know."

"Mr. Rees?" Mr. Randall stepped into the kitchen. "What are you doing here?" His words were mild but the expression he directed at Rees was arctic. "Speaking to my daughter?"

"Just asking a few questions about Maggie," Rees said in his most disarming tone. "I thought, as another young woman, your daughter might have some information." He stopped, catching the girl's wide-eyed expression of fear. "Sad to say, she could not help me," he added quickly. The girl ducked her head, not quite masking her relief.

"Next time," Mr. Randall said, his jovial tone not disguising his anger, "you must speak to her in my presence." Rees nodded, startled by Mr. Randall's hostility. But of course the old man would want to protect his daughter.

Deep in thought, Rees left the inn and began walking down the street. He walked past his wagon and found himself at the general store. Of course, since it was Sunday, the store was closed. Rees rattled the door a few times in frustration and was just turning away when the shopkeeper threw up the window and leaned out.

"Ah, Mr. Rees," he said. "What do you want? Did you run out of cornmeal?" He chuckled at his own joke; he had seen Rees several times already as he purchased food for the hungry children.

"No," Rees said. "I wanted to ask you . . . did you know Maggie Whitney at all?" he asked.

"Of course. She was behind me in school. A very pretty girl."

"Did she come in here much?"

"Sometimes. Mostly for cornmeal. She always seemed to be struggling for money." He sounded genuine and when Rees looked up the man's expression was a mixture of sadness and regret. "It's a shame; a young woman shouldn't pass away, especially like that."

Rees nodded. "Did she ever purchase whiskey?"

"No." The friendliness in his voice and expression faded. "She didn't have the money. Why do you want to know?"

Rees thought of the line of whiskey jugs but said, "No reason. I heard a rumor."

"No," said the shopkeeper and slammed down the window.

"Thank you," Rees said to empty air. The mystery of the whiskey jugs was probably not important, but it was a loose end and Rees hated loose ends.

Chapter Twenty-three

B y now the sun was high in the sky and Rees thought morning services might be done. Instead of going straight home, he drove to the log church. He knew he might not see Vermette if he had already left again on circuit, but as Rees had been told the meetinghouse was always open, he was determined to see the second floor. As promised, the front doors were unlocked and Rees went directly inside. The air was as cold inside as out and the nave was dark; no candles were burning. Rees walked down the center aisle between the benches, his feet echoing upon the bare boards. He intended to pause at the pulpit and look all around. He did not remember seeing stairs on his first visit.

As he approached the altar, Reverend Vermette appeared at a side door, a whiskey jug in one hand. "Oh, Mr. Rees," he said in surprise. "What are you doing here?"

"I spoke with one of the Baker boys," Rees said. "He claims he and his friends have not come in here to smoke for several months."

"Of course he would say that," Vermette said, with a sniff. "Surely you don't believe him."

"And when they came inside, he said they congregated on the second floor. I thought I might take a look," Rees said. "I want to see if I can find out who might have been in here."

"Ah," said Vermette. "You suspect something illicit occurred there. Come with me. I'll gladly show you." He put the jug down and then held the door behind him open for Rees to pass through. In the light from the open door Rees saw a narrow twisting stairwell rising into the darkness. When Vermette allowed the door to swing shut behind him, the darkness was so complete the stairs were invisible. Rees felt forward with his foot, finally locating the first step. Slowly he climbed, placing his right hand on the wall to anchor him. He went around several bends, climbing until he saw pale daylight leaking down the last of the stairs and finally stepped up into a large, low-ceilinged room. A few chairs were the only furnishings. A narrow opening in one wall allowed a view of the pews and, if Rees craned his neck and looked straight down, he could see the pulpit below.

Vermette panted up behind him. "I did find ashes and an empty whiskey bottle or two up here," he said.

"What is this room for?" Rees asked.

"It was to be my quarters, when I began presiding over this flock," Vermette said. "But you see how low the ceiling is? The roof was not built to the proper height or the ceiling of the meetinghouse below was constructed higher than planned; I don't know which. In any event, a mistake was made. Now the church fathers are discussing the future use of this room. Storage, perhaps? I rent a room at the Ram's Head when I visit Dover Springs. Of course, after my marriage, I'll live with my wife in her house." His words trailed away as he watched Rees inspect every corner.

Rees saw only cobwebs and mouse droppings, and although this would be perfect for those rowdy boys, there was no sign anybody had been up here for a very long time. He would have to look elsewhere for a meeting place.

"I'm all turned around," he said. "The window, which way does it face?"

"Toward the road," Vermette said.

In that case, Mr. Gray could not possibly have seen any light from the second floor. "Thank you," Rees said to Vermette. "Perhaps you should lock the doors. Someday one of those young scamps will set the entire building on fire."

"I know. I'm waiting on a locksmith now; in fact I thought you were that gentleman when I heard you enter. I'll arrange to chain and lock the front doors shut and offer the key to Mr. Gray. So that," he added, "someone with a legitimate need to enter the building can do so."

"A wise plan," Rees agreed, beginning to descend the narrow staircase. Vermette fell into step behind him.

"I'm late in leaving for another few days away ministering to those poor souls in need of spiritual guidance."

"And where will you be?"

"Ohio this time, I believe. I went to the Pennsylvania frontier the last time." His reply was cut short by a grunt. He fell heavily against Rees's back. Rees felt himself losing his balance but threw out his arm to brace himself against the wall, and just stopped himself from tumbling down to injury or death in the darkness. "Oh dear, I am sorry," Vermette said. "My foot slipped and I lost my balance. This is why I come up here so infrequently."

Rees moved forward a little more rapidly, putting some space between himself and the pastor. Vermette was an enthusiastic whiskey drinker and stank powerfully of alcohol now, but of more importance, he could be the father of one of Maggie's children and a possible killer. He certainly knew the woman, and the possibility that Vermette's loss of footing was not accidental occurred to Rees. He considered that for a moment, stepping off the final stair with a surprised thud and reeling into the wall. He fumbled around for a moment until he found the knob and pushed the door open. Welcome light, which seemed so bright after the darkness in the stairwell, greeted him.

"Thank you, Reverend Vermette," he said, speaking over his shoulder. The minister limped down the remaining few steps and into the light.

"I'm glad to be of assistance," he said, holding onto the door-frame with a grimace of pain. Rees made an involuntary movement toward him but Vermette waved him away. "I just twisted my ankle. I was not so quick to catch myself as you were. I'm certain I'll recover in a few moments."

"Very well," Rees said. He started for the front doors, passing a dark-haired gentleman coming up the central aisle.

"And here's the locksmith," Vermette said. Then Rees was through the doors and descending the path outside. He would be glad to reach the cabin.

Rees did not find an opportunity to confide to Lydia all that he'd learned until later that night, after the children had been put to bed in the other room. They weren't all asleep: muted giggles burst through the door every now and then, but at least Rees could sit down across the table from Lydia and talk without constant interruption.

They shared the last of the coffee in the pot, black as tar and so bitter Rees's tongue curled. He folded his hands around his mug and began recounting the gist of his conversations with the Randall girl and Reverend Vermette. But he barely made it through the first few sentences before a thunderous knocking on the door interrupted him.

"Now what?" he muttered. He rose to his feet and went to

the door. A blast of icy air accompanied Constable Cooper into the room.

"I understand you saw my wife," Cooper said. "I came home and the house was empty." Unshaven and disheveled, he looked half-mad with worry. "No one seems to know what happened to my wife and children. Mr. Randall thought you might."

Rees eyed Cooper in concern. He motioned to the table. "Would you like something to drink?" Lydia asked, rising from the table. "We've no whiskey but I can put a fresh pot of coffee upon the fire. Or tea, if you'd prefer."

"No, thank you," he said, bowing to her. He turned immediately to Rees. "Did you see her? Do you know anything?"

"Let's talk, shall we?" Rees said, gesturing Cooper into one of the chairs. Lydia dumped the grounds in the barrel by the fireplace and began grinding fresh coffee. "Yes, I saw your wife. Your father-in-law was at your house."

Red fury boiled up into Cooper's cheeks and his blue eyes bulged. "That bastard! He's done everything in his power to turn my wife against me. What did he want this time?"

"I don't know what *he* wanted," Rees said. "I didn't speak with him. And your wife said little. But she'd been crying. And she was packing the buggy."

"She left me?" Cooper shook his head. "We quarreled . . . she is exceedingly jealous."

"I was told you liked the girls," Rees said. And he added after a beat, "Where were you today?"

"That was my reputation as a boy," Cooper said angrily. "I was at Mount Unity. I went there last night to make sure those rowdy boys took my warning seriously. I was prepared to arrest them if not, and throw them in jail."

"So, what did happen?" Rees asked.

"My wife accused me of sleeping with another woman. And

I have thought about it. But yesterday I went to the Shaker village."

"I see." Rees unwillingly entertained the possibility that Cooper had visited the other woman before riding to Mount Unity. But he had no proof. "Well, your wife suspects the worst. And her father seemed very angry."

"Oh, he's always angry. Especially at me. He didn't want his daughter to marry me. I wasn't good enough, you know. But she was expecting."

"Your son?"

"Yes."

"And Maggie? What of her? You told me yourself you had planned to marry her."

"It was a child's dream."

"No, it wasn't." Rees glared at the other man, furious on Maggie's behalf. "You'd already asked Maggie to marry you, hadn't you? But you didn't marry her after all."

"Genevieve said she was carrying my child." Cooper paused. When Rees said nothing, Cooper cried, "There was nothing I could do. Her father had already forced my hand. I was as good as married."

"Maggie kept the necklace you gave her all these years." Rees wanted Cooper to understand what he had done.

Cooper looked stunned. "She did? Are you sure? A silver chain?"

Rees nodded. "Maggie loved you," he said in a low voice. "And she was also carrying your child. Jerusha."

"I loved her, too." Cooper's face contorted. "But Genevieve's father is important in this town."

"Well, Maggie solved that problem for you. She married Mr. Whitney and left for Boston."

Cooper nodded.

"You knew Jerusha was your child, didn't you?" Rees leaned forward, shaking his finger at Cooper. "And when she returned from Boston you took up with her again. Maggie gave birth to two additional children, Nancy and Judah."

"The boy can't be mine. Goddamn, he doesn't even look like me."

"Please, Mr. Cooper," Lydia said. "Language."

"But Nancy is?" Rees fixed his fierce eyes upon the constable.

Cooper met his gaze for a moment and then his weary blue eyes dropped. "It's possible," he admitted.

"Of course she's yours," Rees said, not bothering to soften the harshness in his voice. "The resemblance between Jerusha, Nancy, and your legal daughter is very strong. What happened that time?"

"I'd come by a few times to check on Olive," Cooper admitted in a low voice. "Genevieve lived with her parents on the farm then. Another quarrel and she went home. Maggie and I took up where we left off. It was just . . . pleasure. But Maggie wanted something more." His voice took on an aggrieved edge. "She thought I could live with her, desert my family, you know, and she would become my wife in all but name."

"But you didn't want that?"

"I already had a wife," Cooper said, scowling. "I didn't want another. Anyway, there was Simon, her son by another man. God knows how many men she took into her bed."

Lydia slapped the coffee mug down upon the table with such force the hot liquid sprayed out of the cup and upon Cooper's arm. He yelled and jumped upright.

Rees looked at him in disgust. "I see. And what happened the night she died? Did she ask you for help? Ask for money for the taxes? Threaten to tell the town Jerusha and Nancy were yours?"

Cooper stared at Rees, and as his words sank in, the constable leaned across the table and pounded his fist upon the wood. "I didn't kill Maggie. I would never do that. I knew her from childhood. I loved her. And I wouldn't orphan my children by her."

Rees stared at Cooper in scorn. "You loved her but wouldn't marry her. Of course, that didn't stop you from fathering two children with her. Did she threaten to tell everyone your secret?"

"Maybe I'm a coward," Cooper said. "I couldn't antagonize Genevieve's father. But I tried to keep Maggie safe, as safe as I could. I didn't kill her, Rees. I swear it. I've been searching for her killer as hard as you have."

"I think you'd better go after your wife now," Rees said in a soft voice. "Maybe she'll come back to you. I don't know, though. She seemed pretty angry to me, and her father was as well."

Cooper glared at Rees a moment longer before jumping up and striding out of the door.

"That . . . that hypocrite," Lydia snapped.

Rees sighed.

"Do you believe him? About not murdering Maggie?"

"I don't know," Rees admitted.

"He had two, maybe three reasons, for wishing Maggie out of the way," Lydia said. "Jerusha and Nancy, and maybe Judah. Of course Mrs. Cooper would be furious if she found out."

"Maybe, although I think she already suspected," Rees said. Cooper's secret wasn't all that secret. He stared into space. "I wonder if Cooper's attachment to Maggie wasn't one of the reasons she was constantly under the threat of being warned out and possibly losing her children. Mr. Shaw, Cooper's father-in-law, probably tried to get Maggie out of Dover Springs for the sake of his daughter's marriage."

"So why didn't he?" Lydia asked. "Maggie was still here."

"She had her defenders. And I'll bet he never admitted to the town selectmen that his son-in-law had fathered at least two, maybe three, of Maggie's children. His daughter would have been shamed in front of the entire village. And Cooper's income would have been affected. The selectmen probably would have sacked him and would have also pressured him to take some financial responsibility for his children." He paused. Lydia nodded.

"So not just Mr. Cooper, but also Genevieve and her father had good reason to want Maggie out of the way," she said.

Rees nodded. "Maggie kept Cooper's name to herself, but she could have broadcast it any time she chose. She was dangerous."

"I have no sympathy for Mr. Cooper at all," Lydia said with unusual sharpness. "He should support his children. His problems are entirely of his own making." She turned her back to Rees and, moving very quickly, changed into her long nightgown. She loosened her hair and plaited it into a long rope down her back. Although her auburn hair looked dark in the dim light, the firelight sent flashes of red and gold through it. She blew out her candle and lay down upon the pallet, curling her arms protectively around her. Not once did she look at Rees; it was almost as though she blamed him for Cooper's behavior.

Rees sat for another moment at the table in the pool of light from the one remaining lighted candle. He wished he could wholeheartedly believe in Cooper's innocence, but he couldn't. The constable's reasons for wanting Maggie out of the way were too many and too plausible. And Rees knew he could share nothing of his own investigation with Cooper until he could be positive the constable was innocent.

"And he might be," he said aloud. "Cooper might be innocent. If he did not father Judah, and I am inclined to believe he did not, then the same reasons he might have for murdering Maggie might also apply to Judah's father."

Lydia did not answer and Rees saw no movement.

"Fathering two of Maggie's children doesn't mean he is guilty of murder."

Still Lydia made no response.

Suddenly recalling Mr. Randall's comment about Mr. Gray, that he'd known Maggie's Aunt Olive well, Rees thought he would visit the old man again the next morning. Rees didn't relish trying to carry on a conversation with him, but maybe Mr. Gray knew something more of Maggie's history and it would shed some light on her murder.

With a sharp determined nod, Rees blew out his own candle and by the light of the banked fire made his way to the pallet. Lydia did not roll to face him, and when he looked over he saw she was already asleep.

Chapter Twenty-four

Rees left immediately after breakfast the next morning to call on Mr. Gray. "Please come home by dinner," Lydia said. Rees looked at her in surprise. She smiled faintly. "I plan to call upon Miss Pike. Get it over with."

"Jerusha can watch her brothers and sisters," Rees said. "It will only be for a few hours."

"Yes, but we have but one buggy and one horse. If I'm visiting Miss Pike what will you do? Wait outside for me?"

Rees almost offered to drive her and pick her up again, but reconsidered. He didn't want to be held to a set time, especially if he were involved in an especially productive conversation.

"I don't want her to come here again and I suspect she will if I don't prevent her," Lydia said. She looked around at the battered cabin. "I don't expect to stay very long. Please. We will never be friends, and I know she invited me only because she's lonely."

"You are almost certainly the only other woman in this town with some pretensions of gentility," Rees said.

"You're forgetting Maartje Griffin," Lydia said with a smile. "Perhaps Miss Pike sees me as a peer. But I am not my sister or Nell. I've no doubt Miss Pike will find me greatly disappointing." She sighed. "I can't imagine what we shall discuss."

Chuckling, and very relieved Lydia had recovered from last night's ill humor, Rees agreed to return promptly.

He was soon on the main road and heading for Mr. Gray's home. As he passed the log church, Rees noticed that new shiny chains and a large padlock secured the front doors. The local lads wouldn't be creeping into the church to escape adult supervision again.

Maartje opened the door to Rees. She looked even more pregnant than ever and the slightest exertion sent her into a paroxysm of rapid panting. Rees suspected the birth was not far away. "Mr. Rees," she said.

"I wanted to speak to your uncle," he said.

"He is with Mr. Randall." She cast a glance over her shoulder.

"I was just leaving," Mr. Randall said, coming up behind her. "Please, permit me to drive you home. It will save your husband a trip." Nodding, Maartje stood back to allow Rees to enter. Then she put on her cloak. The shabby blue garment did not meet over her belly.

"How much longer do you have?" Rees nodded at the round bulge protruding through the gap in the cloak.

"I guess not more than a week, if that," she replied, breathing between each word. "My cousin is on her way."

"Let me help you," Mr. Randall said, taking the basket from her.

Rees watched as Mr. Randall helped Maartje down the steps and over the icy path. She struggled to climb the high step and fell panting and perspiring into the seat. A flap of the cloak hung down from the seat, a small tear in the hem. Gasping for breath, she flipped the cloak inside the buggy. Mr. Randall waved farewell. Rees lifted a hand in acknowledgment and turned back to the house. He had come out without his greatcoat, and although already into March, the air felt cold and wintery. He hurried inside, shutting the door firmly behind him, and found his way through the darkness to the bright kitchen. Mr. Gray looked up with a broad smile, but when he saw it was Rees, his smile disappeared.

"What do you want?" he shouted.

"To ask a few questions," Rees shouted in return.

"Questions? Questions about what? Not that wretched girl again."

"Yes, Maggie Whitney. I thought you might know something of her history. Maybe about her mother? Owen Randall said you were friendly with Phineas Tucker."

"With Phinney, yes. With Owen, too." He sighed. "A long time ago. Knew Olive some too, from school." Shaking his shaggy white head, he said emphatically, "Phinney was ill and died twenty or so years back. I was about your age. Had my own family. Besides . . ." He paused and then asked, "How much do you remember of that time?"

"I was a boy then," Rees bawled at the top of his lungs. "I remember."

"Phinney, and of course Olive, and Owen Randall were passionate Patriots. I had to behave more circumspectly. My father was a judge."

Rees understood what Elias Gray did not say. His father was, at least, a moderate if not a Loyalist sympathizer.

"But you did see Olive and Phinneas?"

"Of course. Phinney, Owen, and I were like brothers. My father visited Olive and Phinney regularly. I daresay he suspected Phinney of some of the anonymous pranks on the local Tories. You remember? Fires set on doorsteps, hanged dummies, that sort of thing."

Rees nodded. He'd participated in such mischief himself.

Mr. Gray smiled at the memory. "Phinney was always thinking up new ways to irritate the British."

"But I thought he was dying," Rees objected.

Mr. Gray nodded. "Yes." Sudden tears moistened his eyes.
"Sorry. So many years and I still miss him. He had such vigor,
such life."

Rees thought of his good friend Nate, who had died before
his time last year. Murdered. As boys, they'd been like brothers,
and Rees would always regret the estrangement that later came
between them. "I understand."

"Probably Phinney suggested and Owen performed. Owen
would have followed Phinney to world's end. Loyal, that's Owen
Randall."

"Hmm. Did you know Olive's sisters?"

"I met them, of course, when I was a boy. But Olive was the
youngest. Her sisters married and moved west and I never saw
them again."

"And Olive's brothers?"

"They moved away too and, as far as I know, haven't come
back since."

Another dead end. Rees chewed his lip. "Why didn't Olive
remarry?" he asked. "It's uncommon for a widow to remain single. And she had young children to care for. And then her sister's child, as well. Was she ill-favored?"

Mr. Gray chuckled. "Ill-favored? No." Without Maartje's presence, he seemed softer, more willing to help. "Go upstairs. Bedroom on the left. Take the silhouette from the wall by the door.
Second row from the bottom. Um, three, no four in."

Rees eyed the old man in perplexity. "Why?"

"Go on. Do it."

So Rees returned to the hall and went up the steps to the
second floor. Mr. Gray's former bedroom lay directly across the

landing, with windows that overlooked the street outside. Although very tidy, the floor and the bedside table bore a thick coat of dust. Maartje had been unable to climb the stairs for some time.

Another bedroom occupied the corner of the second floor, and when Rees peered through the open door, he saw an entire wall of silhouettes, all of young women. He counted up from the bottom and in from the door; the silhouette resembled Maggie. He lifted it from the nail and turned to go downstairs.

But before he did so, he walked to the last door on the landing. Unlike the other two this door was closed, and Rees could not resist his curiosity. He opened the door and went inside.

Located at the back of the house, the windows in this room overlooked the log church. From this vantage point Rees could see only the small window on the wall over the altar and under the loft above. A small old-fashioned rope mattress bed was positioned underneath the window and covered by a quilt worked in shades of blue and pink. At the foot of the cot was a worn canvas valise, unrolled, and with men's shirts and other linens hanging out. But this room had been decorated for a baby. A crate of toys was pushed into one corner and a rocking horse stood opposite. Whose room had this been? For the first time he wondered about Mr. Gray. Maybe this room explained why his nieces cared for him instead of one of his own children.

Rees quietly withdrew from this monument to an old grief and closed the door behind him. Then he went down the stairs and into the kitchen. Mr. Gray, intent on some inner world, stared blindly through the window. His mouth turned down in an unhappy curve and Rees wondered what thoughts disturbed him so. "Mr. Gray?" Rees said loudly.

The old man turned and wiped his sleeve across his eyes. "I

reflect upon the past more as I age," he said. "Reverend Vermette and I are planning to add stained glass windows," the elderly man added, gesturing toward the log structure on the other side of the greening shrubs. "It was a dream of mine. I wanted to see them before I died." Rees followed his gaze to the two large windows on the northwestern side of the meetinghouse. "But now I wonder if I concentrate too much upon my selfish legacy rather than the people around me."

"What do you mean?" Rees asked, startled by the old man's cryptic utterance.

"Nothing. Nothing. Just an old man's wandering thoughts. Did you bring the picture?"

Rees held out the silhouette.

"And who do you think this is?"

"Maggie?" Rees guessed, looking at the black paper profile. It was clearly a young girl and the artist had managed to suggest Maggie's wispy curls at the nape of her slender neck.

"Olive Baines Tucker." Mr. Gray chuckled. "Yes. Maggie resembled her. Cutting silhouettes was a hobby of my father's."

Rees barely heard him. As he worked through the conversation, he experienced a flash of inspiration.

"Olive was Maggie's mother," he said.

Mr. Gray hesitated, frowning and nodding in turn. "I don't know. Maybe. It is true that throughout that winter Olive never came to town. When I saw her for the first time in many months the following April, she had Maggie. We were all so intent upon the British then."

"Why keep the pregnancy a secret? Unless . . ." Rees followed his thought to the logical conclusion. "Maggie wasn't Phinney's child. Who was her father?"

"I don't know. Ask Owen Randall. He always seems to know

everything." He sighed. "It was a long time ago and yet, some-times, it seems like yesterday."

Rees looked at the old man, his face crumpled into lines of regret, and said carefully, "Did you never consider marrying Olive?"

Mr. Gray flicked a glance at Rees. "I wanted to. But I was married myself when Phinney died. And after my wife and daughter passed on . . ." He shrugged. "Olive refused me. No reason." The hurt, even after all these years, was raw in his voice. "I assumed that, after marrying Phinney, no other man could equal him."

"But . . ." Rees started to point out that Olive had found someone to father Maggie, but he refrained. Why cause Mr. Gray more pain, especially now, years later? "Did Phinney know Maggie was Olive's?" Rees asked.

Mr. Gray shook his head. "I don't think so. He never said anything. Of course, by then, he was often lost in opium dreams."

They both lapsed into silence. Rees was saddened by the long-ago grief and regret. "One final question," he said at last. Mr. Gray was leaning his head in his hands, clearly tiring. "Did Silas know Maggie was Olive's daughter?"

"Doubt it." Mr. Gray shrugged. "Maybe he would have been kinder."

Rees pursed his lips, skeptical. "I'll return this to the wall upstairs," he said, waving the silhouette.

"No, don't," Mr. Gray said, stretching out his hand for the framed item. "I'd like to look at it." Rees put it in his hand. As he walked to the front door, Mr. Gray bent over the framed picture, his expression pensive. Rees wondered if the old man was remembering those long-ago days of youth.

He grabbed his greatcoat from the hook and went out to his buggy. During his visit, an icy wind had sprung up and a light snow had begun to fall.

His visit had taken longer than Rees expected. Clapping his hands to warm them, he climbed into the buggy seat and started home.

The smell of roasting meat greeted him as he turned into the drive. He hastened to put the gelding into the lean-to and park the buggy.

When he pushed open the door and stepped inside, Nancy ran to him, crying, "Surprise!"

Lydia, wiping her hands upon a rag, approached with a smile. "Simon brought some lamb home from the Bakers yesterday. We thought we would surprise you for dinner." She turned and looked over her shoulder at the iron pot hanging over the fire. "It's almost done."

"The sheep are beginning to give birth," Simon said with an air of importance. Rees hid a smile. "This lamb was not strong. Mr. Baker gave me a share of the meat."

"This is why you wanted me home by dinnertime?" Rees said, looking over Simon's head at Lydia.

"You're like the wind," she said. "When you leave the house, I never know when you'll return."

"You're not calling upon Miss Pike?"

"I am. But you didn't need to arrive home this early for that."

"I set the table," Jerusha announced.

"I see," Rees said, glancing at the mismatched plates. She couldn't decide upon which side the forks went, and at some of the settings the forks were on the left, while at others the forks were on the right. But she was so proud Rees didn't have the heart to correct her. "You did a very good job," he told her.

A few minutes later, Lydia bore the baked meat to the table in triumph. It was a small amount of meat for seven, and so Rees was very careful in its division. He didn't care for the strong flavor of either lamb or mutton, but would never be so rude as to say so. In any case, he made a very good meal on a few slices of the meat and the boiled carrots and potatoes that accompanied it. Not a scrap of the lamb remained when Lydia finally slid the dirty dishes into the steaming water of the dishpan.

Chapter Twenty-five

After dinner, Lydia changed into her best gown, the indigo-dyed dress that was Rees's favorite. Lydia made a bright spot of color standing by the door in her dark blue frock with the burgundy cloak over it.

"I'll drive you," Rees said. "I need to speak to Mr. Randall anyway."

"Miss Pike lives on the eastern outskirts of Dover Springs," Lydia said, smoothing her black gloves over her fingers. "I don't want to visit with her for more than an hour or so; I can't conceive what we shall find to discuss. And I know you. When you're deep in conversation, you forget everything else and lose all track of time."

Rees, who viewed the prospect of his confinement at the cabin with no buggy or horse almost with terror, said firmly, "I'll drive you and return in an hour."

Lydia looked at him, her expression skeptical. "Very well," she said. But she did not sound happy.

Half an hour later, they reached the fine gray stone house at the end of a circular drive. Although bare snowy fields lay to one side, the estate was an uneasy combination of town house and gentleman's farm. Rees suspected not very much farming went on here, although that might change once Miss Pike and Reverend Vermette married.

Rees pulled up at the steps and assisted Lydia to the ground. He watched her ascend the stone steps. Once she'd entered the fine building, Rees drove away, back to town and the Ram's Head.

He allowed the ostler to put the horse into the stable; the snow was falling faster and harder now and to Rees the air felt much colder. He went into the inn. Although a few tables in the common room were filled, most were empty; it was between dinner and supper and the falling snow discouraged casual tipplers from visiting. Rees approached Mr. Randall, who was playing checkers with Caleb Griffin, Maartje's husband.

The old man noticed Rees's approach and jumped several of his opponent's pieces, clearing the board. "That's enough for me," said Griffin, rising to his feet. "I believe a fresh victim is approaching and anyway, I should get home."

As Mr. Randall began laying the disks upon the board, he said without looking up, "Care for a game of draughts, Mr. Rees?"

"No, thank you, Mr. Randall," Rees said. "Mr. Gray suggested I talk to you. About Olive Tucker."

Now Mr. Randall looked up at Rees. "Olive? I thought you were concerned about Maggie Whitney?"

"I am," Rees said.

The old man scrutinized Rees with clever blue eyes. "I find this last game has left me thirsty," Mr. Randall said. "Shall we move to a table to talk?"

"Gladly," Rees said.

With a groan, Mr. Randall struggled to his feet and paused for a moment, stretching out his legs. "My knees fail me," he said to Rees. "Don't get old, lad." Rees laughed a little ruefully; no one had called him lad for many years. Mr. Randall gestured to a table and they sat down. Mr. Randall's daughter ran over with two beakers of ale. "So, what do you want to know, Mr. Rees?"

"Who murdered Maggie Whitney?"

"I can't help you with that," Mr. Randall said with a smile. "You're not interested in who murdered Silas?"

"I am. But Maggie was first."

Mr. Randall nodded. "I see. What else?"

"Well, I doubt the motive is money. Maggie lived in a shack on only a few acres. I thought Silas might have killed her for them, but I haven't heard of anyone else who wanted that pitifully small farm."

"I think your assumption is faulty, Mr. Rees. The small size of that property doesn't mean there isn't someone who wanted it. My nephew, Caleb Griffin, wouldn't have his farm without the assistance of my old friend Elias Gray. He might have coveted Phinney's farm otherwise. There is nothing so small that someone does not envy the possessor for it."

Rees nodded. "Yes, that is true. Sadly. But in this case, I believe the reason for Maggie's murder is something else. Frequently the past haunts the future. So I began to wonder about her parents." Rees paused, knowing he was about to step into speculation territory now. "Mr. Gray confirmed several suppositions for me. Olive Tucker was Maggie's mother, was she not?"

Mr. Randall looked to the side, thinking. When he turned his rheumy eyes back to his companion, he said, "I can promise you, Maggie's parentage has nothing to do with her murder." Rees didn't argue but he didn't agree. The silence lengthened uncomfortably. Finally Mr. Randall said, "Phinney told me Olive was Maggie's mother. I always wondered if he'd imagined it. He'd been sick a long time and the medicine sometimes gave him strange dreams."

Rees nodded thoughtfully. Phinney would have known.

Although Olive might have been able to avoid the village and hide her pregnancy from others, her swelling belly would have been obvious to her husband. "And Maggie's father? It wasn't Phinney? You're sure?"

"Absolutely. He'd been ill for far too long to father any child. He gave Maggie his name, that's all."

"Do you know who fathered her?"

"No. You must understand, Olive spent a lot of time away from the cabin."

"Doing what?"

"I don't know that either. But I suspect she was bartering food for opium with the British. She could have been hung for treason by the Patriots. But I think we understand why she did what she did." Mr. Randall's gray eyebrows rose meaningfully.

Rees tried to interpret the insinuation. "Are you suggesting Olive offered her favors to a British soldier?" He shook his head in disbelief. Nothing he'd heard about Olive suggested she was anything but a virtuous woman.

"Of course not. I'm just saying, well, I doubt we'll ever know who fathered Maggie."

Rees sagged with disappointment. "Mr. Gray thought you might know. He said your wife regularly called upon Olive."

"Yes, she did, God rest her soul. She believed charity to the less fortunate was a duty. But she stopped calling on Phinney about then. Too dangerous, with the British everywhere. And she never said anything about a pregnancy." Rees eyed Mr. Randall in surprise. A pregnancy seemed like it should be big news. After a moment, the old man continued. "Those were dark times, when Phinney died. Still a young man and in such terrible pain."

"And the war coming," Rees murmured.

Mr. Randall nodded. "Those red-coated vermin lived in our

houses, ate our food, and would shoot you just as easily as looking at you."

"I remember," Rees said. "The British were in Maine, too."

"Trying to keep the inn going was such a struggle." Owen
shook his head, intent upon his memory. "All the officers billeted
in my best rooms . . . but you don't want to hear about that. We
were all short of food, whiskey, medicines. Phinney dying—
although he didn't finally leave us for five more years—made life
very difficult for Olive. We were all desperate."

The two men sat in silence, recalling the past. Finally Rees
said, "Tell me about Elias Gray."

"We were three: Elias, Phinney, and me. Elias's wife died
young, taking their baby with her."

"Could he have fathered Maggie?" Rees asked.

Mr. Randall laughed. "Of course not. Elias wasn't interested
in Olive. I would have known."

"He never remarried," Rees pointed out. He remembered Mr.
Gray's assertion that he'd asked Olive to marry him and she'd
refused. Rees contemplated the old man. Clearly Owen Randall
did not know as much as he thought he did. But he knew something, of that Rees was certain.

"Don't jump to conclusions, Mr. Rees," Mr. Randall said.
Leaning forward with an appearance of sincerity, he added, "I'm
going to tell you something Silas did not want widely known.
He paid the taxes on that farm. The entire amount."

"No, he didn't," Rees responded disbelievingly. "When Maggie died, Silas put those children out."

"I was here when they came searching for you," Mr. Randall
said. He thumped his finger forcefully upon the table. "But Silas would have allowed them back. I am certain of it. I believe
you are misconstruing his motives."

Rees said. "You talked to him, didn't you?"

"Yes. He would never have expelled those children permanently from his home," Mr. Randall argued. "Although Maggie was not his niece, he cared for her."

"So why did he go to the farm immediately after her death?" Rees demanded. "I saw him, Mr. Randall. He'd already put some of her poor sticks of furniture into his wagon."

"I don't know," Mr. Randall said. "But he assured me he would have allowed those children back into their home. Their disappearance surprised him."

"I believe you are too much influenced by your friendship with Mr. Silas Tucker," Rees said in annoyance. Mr. Randall shook his head, a fleeting smile crossing his face. That expression, odd under the circumstances, brought Rees to a pause. "I saw you at the selectmen's meeting," he said slowly. "You spoke for Maggie. Are you her father, Mr. Randall?"

"No, I am not." Rees watched a mottled flush rise into the old man's neck. "As I have said many times, it should not matter who her father is. She was born and raised in Dover Springs. She owned property, left to her by Olive Tucker. Nothing else should matter."

Rees eyed the man with doubt.

"I assure you," Mr. Randall said, "I am not Maggie's father. If I were, I would have gladly acknowledged her. No, her father was most likely a British soldier. And if that is the scandal you wish talked about, then continue down this path." He jerked upright, his chair falling over behind him, and limped back to his draughts board in the corner.

Rees sat there for a brief time and then rose to his feet and left. Mr. Randall had sounded completely convincing when he denied fathering Maggie, but Rees still wasn't sure he believed him. And then there was the revelation about Silas Tucker. Mr. Randall must have been lying, he must have been. But Rees knew the old man wasn't. Cooper had given Maggie's few pennies back to Rees and said someone had paid the taxes. Such a generous gesture did not fit with Silas as Rees knew him. Could his opinion of the man be so wrong?

Rees hesitated just outside and tried to gather himself. The fat wet flakes of spring snow fell so thickly he could barely see the stables. And the snow was building up. Lydia! Suddenly realizing he'd spent more than an hour with Mr. Randall, Rees hurried through the deepening snow to the outbuildings and the buggy.

The horse had to be hitched again; that took almost twenty minutes. And then the traveling was slow; the snow was already deep upon the road. Another twenty minutes passed before he reached the outskirts of town and began the approach to the Pike house. He saw, coming toward him, a figure wrapped up in a burgundy cloak, whose rapid steps toward Rees revealed a dark blue gown.

Her quick gait through the deepening snow alarmed him; she was angry. He pulled the buggy to a stop. Although he planned to call out, Lydia saw him before he opened his mouth. Her expression was set in a scowl. He jumped down and hurried around the horse to assist her into the seat. Although she accepted his assistance, she neither glanced at nor spoke to him. When he jumped up beside her he burst into apologies. "I'm sorry. I . . ." But she waved his apologies away.

"Please, don't worry. Although I wish you'd come sooner."

Rees waited for a few moments and then said delicately, "Your visit didn't go well?"

"I just have little patience for someone whose selfishness is overlaid by sanctimony."

"You've taken against her," Rees said, selecting his words with care. "To me, she seems pleasant and sincere, if a little condescending."

Lydia paused, considering Rees's statement. "Maybe I am behaving unfairly," she agreed with a sigh. "I've known too many society matrons who pride themselves on their charity."

"What did she say?"

"She talked at length about her upcoming wedding to Reverend Vermette. She is, she says, looking forward to calling upon the poor and needy." A line insinuated itself between Lydia's dark brows. "She wants to be a 'helpmeet' to her husband as he 'prepares souls for salvation.' I can just imagine how the recipients of this largesse will react. And she gave me a pocket Bible. 'To help me on my path to Salvation.'"

Her dry tone startled Rees into a chuckle. "Surely you didn't speak only of Reverend Vermette."

"No. Although she did ask me if I didn't think he was truly kind and good."

Now Rees burst out laughing. "You agreed, of course." He knew Lydia would not have described Vermette in those words.

"Of course." Lydia raised her brows. "We agreed on one point, however. Reverend Vermette is away regularly, traveling to the frontier to minister to those without preachers and churches of their own. He's away now. And I expect she'll be lonely, without the duties of a housewife or such society as she enjoyed in Albany."

Rees wondered if she knew how much her comment about traveling hurt him. His profession as traveling weaver took Rees away from home regularly as well, and although Lydia hadn't seen much of that yet, he worried she would feel as abandoned as David did. "I believe Reverend Vermette said he planned to spend more of his time here after his marriage," Rees said.

Lydia nodded, unaware of the guilt and worry that curled through him. For a few minutes they rode in silence. Then Lydia said, "I hope she doesn't call upon me again. She spoke very harshly about Maggie and the cabin. I've no doubt Miss Pike says nasty things about me to Mrs. Griffin." Giving herself a shake, she turned to Rees. "And how did your errand fare?"

"Well, it seems that Maggie was not Olive Tucker's niece, but her daughter."

"I wondered," Lydia said sadly. Rees glanced at her in surprise. "But it seemed so sordid."

"Yes. The identity of her father is still a mystery. And Mr. Randall swears that Silas Tucker paid the taxes on Maggie's house and would never have evicted Maggie and her children from the property."

Lydia looked at her husband with an expression of total disbelief.

"I know," Rees said. "I can't believe he would be so . . . so altruistic."

"But if Maggie was Olive's daughter, she was a legal resident in Dover Springs then, was she not?" Lydia asked.

"I would certainly think so." Rees threw Lydia a glance in which disgust and resignation were equally mixed. "But no one knows that secret. And who then is Maggie's father? I wish I knew. Because if Phineas had fathered Maggie, the children would not be in danger of warning out."

Chapter Twenty-six

O nce Lydia and Rees reached the cabin there was no more opportunity to talk. Lydia set Jerusha to spinning and then began preparing a light supper. As she peered into the barrels and bags she said, "We'll have to purchase more supplies. That cornmeal you bought is almost gone. We still have some beans, but no bacon. Thanks to Mr. Baker, we still have a little cheese. But we're down to only a small jug of maple syrup."

Rees hesitated. His fund of coins was dropping dangerously low. "Tomorrow," he said, looking out at the white world outside. The whirling snow completely occluded the lean-to, and he thought the snow must now be above his knees. "I wonder if I should harness the horse and fetch Simon." Turning to Jerusha he asked, "He did return to the Baker farm, didn't he?"

Jerusha nodded. "He said they were counting on him."

Rees hesitated a moment and then slung on his greatcoat. If the snow went to his knees, it would surely be higher on Simon; he was just a little boy. "I'm going for him," he said. "He won't be able to come over the hill. The snow is already too deep."

He hurried to the lean-to. Ares resisted every attempt to pull him from the lean-to and tried to bite but finally, panting and angry, Rees managed to propel the gelding into the buggy traces. They started down the drive. The snow drifted to the hubs of the wheels, even as high as they were, and crept well up over the horse's knees. The buggy trundled slowly down the drive, and the gelding was soon panting and blowing with the effort.

Other wheeled traffic had left channels upon the road, and they were able to speed up a little. Rees settled back into the seat, trying to relax. He would have to rely on Ares's senses to keep them on the road and traveling in the proper direction; the white cocoon blinded him to everything surrounding them.

They were almost at the Baker farm when a small black-clad form, tramping determinedly home, appeared suddenly out of the white. "Simon," Rees shouted. "Simon." Ares jerked to a stop and Rees did not fight it. He looped the reins around the front bar and jumped down. Simon stopped, panting. He'd been following a buggy track; the drifting snow on the road's shoulders would reach his chest. Rees grasped the boy by his shoulders and jerked him out of the snow. He carried Simon through the wet and clinging drifts to the buggy and deposited him in the seat. He clambered up beside the boy and took up the reins.

Ares found his path and started home. He traveled more quickly on the journey back to the cabin, although he struggled to pull the buggy up the slope. Rees finally jumped down and, taking the bridle, pulled the horse forward. Without Rees's weight, the buggy moved more easily anyway, and within a few minutes they came to a stop in front of the cabin. Simon jumped down and ran in. Rees unhitched Ares and, leaving the buggy where it was, put the horse into the lean-to. A thorough rubdown, a blanket, and a bucket of oats, and he was settled. Finally Rees struggled through the blizzard to the cabin.

Lydia was waiting for him beside the door; the window was steamed opaque by the water boiling on the hearth. Heedless of the nearby children, she plunged into his arms. Surprised by the tears he saw in her eyes, he squeezed her shoulders before releasing her. "The snow won't last," he predicted. "It isn't cold enough. This is winter's last gasp before warm weather."

She nodded, smiling as she wiped her eyes. "You might not have made it home," she said. "And Simon surely wouldn't have."

Rees nodded and looked over at the boy, still in his coat and sitting wearily at the table drinking coffee.

Rees woke up that night, wondering what had pulled him into consciousness. The fire was banked, the coals throwing a subdued reddish light upon the hearth. He heard nothing from the bedroom save for a soft baby snore. But rain thrummed on the roof and hissed into the fireplace.

Quietly he rolled out of the bed and went to the window. He could see nothing but white. The rain sounded like a fistful of pebbles as it hit the ground, and Rees realized it was a mixture of water and ice. After a moment of staring into the white blankness on the other side of the glass, he returned to bed. But now he couldn't fall asleep. His thoughts focused again upon Maggie Whitney. Why was Mr. Randall so determined to keep the secret of Maggie's birth? Both Olive and Phineas Tucker had passed on and most certainly no longer cared. Rees wasn't sure he believed Mr. Randall's denial about fathering Maggie, and the old man's sudden anger now seemed odd. Mr. Randall's temper had put an abrupt end to the conversation. Could Rees even trust what the innkeeper had said?

And then there was Mr. Randall's revelation about Silas's uncharacteristic burst of altruism. What did Rees know of that man? He was grasping and felt entitled to this tiny farm of ten acres. Yet, according to Mr. Randall, Silas had paid the taxes.

Why would he do that? If the taxes had not been paid, he would have been that much closer to taking possession of the farm.

Rees could understand why Silas Tucker might have murdered Maggie; his reasons were clear and obvious. But then who had murdered him? And why? A falling out between business partners? Or had Silas known something about Maggie's death? Had he tried to blackmail the murderer? That fit exactly into his character. Rees thought again of Silas's tidy house, recalling the disorder around the desk, a disorder not entirely explained by the cold wind whipping through the shattered window. Someone had been looking for something. Had he found it?

So Silas's house, Rees decided, merited another search. He felt like kicking himself; he should have thought of this previously. His delay meant the murderer could already have found whatever he was looking for. And destroyed it.

Rees yawned. Every thought led to more questions. And now he felt sleep reaching out for him once again. He rolled over and closed his eyes. Tomorrow he would return to Silas's house and search, more thoroughly this time.

By dawn the precipitation had changed to all rain, but an icy glaze remained on the diminishing snow. Rees drank his coffee in front of the window. A torrent of muddy water raced down the drive to the main road. But as the morning progressed the rain eased to a fine misty drizzle and finally, mid-day, the sun came out. Despite the amount of snow that had fallen the previous day, enough had melted to reveal great swaths of mud. Rees knew the wagon would be of little use. He would have to walk over the hill that separated Maggie's property from Silas Tucker's.

After dinner, he put on his coat and boots, slapped his hat upon his head, and set out. Almost immediately he ran into trouble. The slurry of snow and mud that coated the downslope of the hill was so liquid and yet so sticky it was like climbing through molasses. Rees walked north across the field, past the bedraggled scarecrow, to a less steep incline, and struggled up to the crest. By then his boots and the bottom of his greatcoat were thoroughly coated with mud.

The slope continued to rise, more gradually now, undulating over a series of crests as far as Rees could see. The individual fields were separated by worm fences. Already panting, Rees plunged into the long climb. An hour later, he crested the final hill and saw Silas's house in the distance, at the top of another rise. A henhouse, a long barn, and a pigsty with a low fence surrounding it sat directly behind the house. With a groan, Rees plodded toward his destination.

He wove his way around the fields and the structures, finally arriving at the back door. It opened directly into the kitchen. The fireplace was swept clean of ashes, and the copper pots hanging on the brick wall sparkled. The long wooden table had been scrubbed white. But mice were beginning to make themselves at home.

He went through the door to the hall and into the office/bedroom on the other side. Snow and rain had swept through the broken window, turning all the papers on the desk and floor to a sodden mass. Rees peered through the window. The snow in the yard out front was melting down to mud. Wagon wheels scored the sludge into a deep grid.

Although Rees spent a good hour searching the desk, he found nothing that could incriminate anyone, certainly nothing that pointed to a murderer. The wet paper on the desk, as far as he could determine, pertained only to rentals. He went through the files in the drawer. Some were out of alphabetical order, at odds with the neat arrangement. Other papers were stuffed carelessly in anywhere, and were ripped and crumpled.

Everything about Silas argued that he had been a thoroughly detailed man, not one to treat his business documents so carelessly. It took no great leap to assume someone else before Rees had searched the drawer.

Rees paused, irresolute, in the middle of the floor. Of course, if Silas had had something that might incriminate Maggie's killer—and possibly his own, although he would not have foreseen that—surely he would have hidden it where it would be hard to find. After a few moments of thought, Rees turned and went up the stairs to the second floor. Several rooms opened off the landing, but all were almost empty. Only one contained any furniture, a bed and an old cornhusk-filled mattress. Mice had been at it; they'd chewed through the ticking and the old brown leaves had fallen to the floor. Rees walked through every room, even kneeling beside a bed and looking underneath it. He saw nothing at all out of the ordinary.

"Damn," he said. He was missing something; he had to be.

The sun was beginning to drop toward the horizon when he left; the western light spilled bloodred upon the remaining film of snow and long shadows stretched east from the house. He paused a moment on the front step, trying to imagine other hiding places. Barn? Henhouse? Of course it would help if he knew what he was searching for.

Crack! A sudden rifle shot echoed over the hilltop. With the instincts of a former soldier, Rees flung himself to the ground. The ball struck the door behind him. He raised his head and looked around. His first glance revealed nothing. He swept his gaze across the yard again and saw movement in the copse of trees on the other side. Someone was shooting at him. He wouldn't be safe here, not against someone with a rifle. Counting the seconds necessary for reloading, he crawled rapidly around to the side of the house and started down the slope. He flung himself behind the henhouse just as another shot split the air, and the ball whined past him.

When Rees peered around the coop's side, he saw a figure moving through evergreens across the yard. Coming toward him. Throwing himself down upon the snow, Rees rolled farther down the slope, toward the pigsty. Involuntarily he hunched his shoulders, expecting a bullet in his back at any second. With the rain and warming temperatures, most of the snow had melted. The spiky tufts of dead vegetation poked into him as he rolled across them. The wet snow soaked his coat and stockings, and he felt a steady trickle down the back of his neck.

He slid to safety behind the pigsty just as another gunshot cracked across the hill. The ball struck the ground nearby. He had to keep moving; he knew that. He hadn't so much as a pocket-knife to defend himself. The shooter need only find him.

Rees looked at the empty snowy expanse behind him. No cover at all, and in the long golden rays of sunshine, he would be clearly visible. But if he could reach the crest of the hill behind him and drop behind it, he would gain a measure of safety. Crouching low, he started to run, slipping over the snow and falling more than once. Another shot, but the bullet hit the snow behind him. He was moving out of range. He took a moment to catch his breath, peering back at the house to see if the shooter was in pursuit. No movement. Rees's heart hammered in his chest and he felt sick with fear. But he made the crest and slid down the side behind it. Stumbling to his feet, he began to run, as fast as the surface beneath his feet would allow. Since the ground sloped down, with only a few rises up, he soon built up a tremendous speed. When he fell, he shot down the hill like a toboggan, fetching up against the scarecrow and flattening it to the ground. He was almost home. Groaning, he sat up. Soaking wet and muddy, and his right leg aching, Rees struggled to his feet and staggered the last few steps to the bottom of the hill. The cabin came into view but it was still a distance away. Rees limped toward it, hurrying as much as his injured leg would allow. Lydia came to the door. When she saw him she uttered a cry of dismay and hurried toward him. "What happened to you?"

"Someone shot at me," Rees said. Lydia clapped her hands over her mouth, the blood draining from her cheeks. "I'm all right," Rees hastened to say. "I fell. That's all." He inhaled deeply and tried to slow his breathing. He put his arms around her and held on tight.

"Oh Will." Involuntary tears of fright gushed from her eyes.

"Clearly," Rees said, "I spooked the murderer."

Lydia nodded and used her apron to wipe her cheeks. "Don't tell the children," she said. "We'll discuss this later."

Chapter Twenty-seven

They went inside, and Rees hurried to stand in front of the fire. Lydia hung Rees's coat to one side; the mud could not be brushed away until it dried. Water ran out of the garment with a steady pattering sound, and soon a pool lay beneath it. Rees's boots, so coated with mud their weight had doubled, were also dispatched to the fireplace. He retired to the bedroom to change to dry breeches and stockings. His shirt was still mostly dry, although the narrow collar was damp. When he limped into the main room, Lydia hurried over with a blanket.

"What happened?" Jerusha asked, her lips trembling.

"Nothing," he said, forcing a smile. "I slipped and fell."

Lydia bit her lip. "Coffee?" Rees hoped Jerusha did not notice the shakiness in Lydia's voice. She poured out a cup of the strong bitter brew and brought it to the table. For a moment Rees just sat there. His large freckled farmer's hands were white with cold and purple from scrapes and bruises picked up on his frenzied trip home. He couldn't stop shivering. Finally, as he began pouring in milk and sugar, she leaned forward and said in a low voice, "Will?"

"I wanted to search Silas's house again." He met Lydia's worried gaze. "I wondered if Silas had gotten ahold of something that identified Maggie's killer. That would make a good reason for murdering him. But, whatever Silas might have had, the killer hasn't found it. That's clear. He returned for a second search, and then he began shooting to make sure I didn't escape with it."

"But now he might believe you found it," Lydia said. "Oh Will." She clasped her hands so tightly together the knuckles went white.

"Yes," Rees said, putting his hand over hers. "So, that means I must find it, and soon. I just wish I knew what it might be."

Furious knocking on the door interrupted him. Jerusha quickly ran over and flung it open. "Constable Cooper," she said. He ruffled her hair and looked over at Rees, his expression both distrustful and anxious.

"What happened?" Rees asked.

"Silas Tucker's house is on fire," Cooper said.

"He's not going with you!" Lydia cried fiercely, jumping to her feet.

But Rees was already rising. He drank the last of his coffee. "How are we getting there? I'm not walking. I injured my leg."

"I rode over," Cooper said. "Wagons and buggies aren't any good in this weather. Is the horse"—he tipped his head in the direction of the lean-to—"broken to the saddle?"

"I don't know," Rees said. "Guess we'll find out." He collected his shoes. They were not as sturdy as his boots, but they were dry and free of mud. Then he stopped and looked at his greatcoat in dismay. Most of the excess water had run out of the wool but it was still damp and muddy.

Cooper turned to Rees with a suspicious stare. "What did you do?"

Rees, who hadn't wanted to confess his earlier visit to Silas's farm, sighed. "I went to the house to search it," he said.

"And you thought you'd set it on fire before you left?" Cooper's voice rose.

"Of course not," Rees snapped. "When I left someone shot at me. He shot at me," he repeated, almost as though he couldn't believe it. "I wondered if Silas had something that identified the killer. If so, it would appear the killer hasn't found it."

"Did *you* find it?" Cooper asked.

"No," Rees said. His suspicions of Cooper roared back. "I don't even know what it would be. But why else would someone try to kill me as I left Tucker's house? And why set fire to it unless he's trying to destroy the evidence?" He paused and watched the constable fit the pieces together.

"Of course. Silas saw a way to make a few shillings. Stupid greedy fool," Cooper muttered with a nod. "Come on."

Rees stood up. The injury to his right leg, which seemed to center upon the knee, had stiffened while he sat. Waves of pain radiated to ankle and thigh. He paused, waiting for the ache to subside, looking thoughtfully at Lydia's cloak and Jerusha's shawl hanging on the pegs. He elected to wear his jacket outside.

As soon as he left the cabin he smelled the fire: thick and choking and much stronger than the smell of wood smoke from the cottage chimney. Cooper nodded at the sky and Rees turned. Smoke had darkened the reddening sky. "Mr. Baker rode into town to tell me," the constable said. After a beat, he added, "No matter what you think of me, I take my position seriously. I want to find this killer, or killers."

Rees nodded but said nothing. He couldn't promise a trust he didn't feel.

"And you seem to have some facility for unraveling these knots," Cooper went on.

Ah, flattery. Rees didn't take it seriously. "Let me fetch the horse," he said and limped away.

Since Rees owned no saddle here, he threw a blanket over Ares's back and awkwardly, with the aid of the fence, pulled himself up. As a boy he'd frequently ridden in such a manner, but he now found the climb up much more difficult. Gripping the horse's broad sides proved challenging with a sore and weakened leg. Especially when Ares, although comfortable with the bridle, sidled skittishly when he felt the weight upon his back. Rees suspected the horse had been broken to riding once, but it had been a long time ago. He spent the first third of the ride struggling to control Ares until, finally, the horse settled.

By the time they rode up Silas's lane the house was a flaming ruin, a bright ball against the darkening sky. Smoke carried the stink of burning into the air and, as they neared the blaze, the snap of embers and crash of falling beams grew louder. The Bakers were already there, standing in the yard and staring at the fire in dismay. They carried buckets but Mr. Baker, gesturing with the wooden pail, said, "It was already too far gone when we arrived." Cooper jumped down and ran over. Rees remained mounted for a moment longer. His body remembered the crack of gunfire and trembling spread out from the pit of his stomach to his hands and legs.

"Coming?" Cooper shouted at him.

Rees would never reveal his fear; he jumped down without thought and thudded to the ground with a shudder of pain. His leg buckled, but he grabbed the stirrup and did not fall.

Cooper approached the fire as close as he dared. It was impossible to see now where the fire had begun.

After one glance at the ruin, Rees left the cluster of men and walked in the opposite direction, to the copse of trees in front of the house. It was only a narrow band of evergreens with a scattering of oak and elm; Rees could see another open field just beyond the trees. He eyed the furrowed ground with its slick covering of snow and selected a thick branch to use for support. He picked his way through the trunks to the other side, following a path already inscribed by another's footsteps. Something, maybe the rifle barrel, had been used for support and the track of the left foot pressed more deeply into the snow than the right.

Rees broke through the trees onto the field. The lines of Silas Tucker's plowing remained faintly visible through the snow. Under his feet, the thin stripes from buggy wheels, still crisp and new, dug deep through the snow to the mud below. That meant a man of some consequence; a poor man might own a horse, but not a buggy. Horse apples, one pile so fresh it probably dated from just a few hours ago, dotted the strip by the trees. Someone had driven up here, hidden his buggy behind the trees, and watched Rees as he went into the dwelling. Then this person had moved into the trees and fired upon Rees when he came out of the house.

But there was no way of telling who that man might be. Or if he were the same man who'd shot and killed Silas, although Rees would lay money on that.

"What did you find?" Cooper asked, suddenly appearing through the trees. The quick glance he shot at Rees was wary. Rees gestured at the tracks around him.

"Someone saw me go inside," he said. Cooper looked at the ravaged snow and nodded.

"Same one who killed both Silas Tucker and Maggie?"

"Probably," Rees said. "But Maggie wasn't shot. We need to find the place where she was attacked.

"We've looked everywhere," Cooper said in frustration. "Even in the meetinghouse."

They started the walk back to the burning house. Cooper plodded along, swearing under his breath. But Rees, although disappointed by the lack of a definitive identification, was not as downcast as Cooper.

He still thought Maggie was the key, just as she'd always been.

By the time Cooper and Rees arrived back at the yard the Bakers had left, and indeed it was now almost too dark to see. The blaze was beginning to diminish, the embers glowing red like the eyes of some wicked being snared in the blackened stubs of wooden beams. Only the foundation, the stones stained with soot, remained whole. "I wonder what Silas might have found," Cooper muttered.

"Did he have any close friends? Someone that might have hidden a package for him?" Rees asked.

"You saw him at the meeting with the selectmen," Cooper said with a shake of his head. "Maggie was the closest thing to family he had, and you saw how he treated her and the children."

"Perhaps Owen Randall?" Rees suggested. "They seemed to be friendly."

"They were?" Cooper looked startled. "I'll ask him. Of course he probably won't tell me anything. The selectmen think they own the town."

Rees hesitated, reluctant to ask the question he felt must be asked. "Cooper. Where did you meet Maggie?"

Although Rees thought for a moment that the constable would not answer, Cooper said abruptly, "My wife was living with her parents then. Maggie and I met in my house at the back of the shop. Once or twice we went to the shop, after hours." He sighed. "I should have married Maggie Whitney. I was a coward.

I allowed my father-in-law to frighten me. Now I am wed to Genevieve for good or ill, and I regret it."

Rees clapped the constable on the back with wordless sympathy.

Rees rode back to the cabin on horseback. It was painful. He no longer rode astride very often, especially without benefit of a saddle, and he hurt. Muscles unaccustomed to this position complained in bands of fire and he thought he might be rubbing up some blisters in his nether regions. Dismounting with a groan at the foot of the drive, he walked the horse up the slope to the lean-to and put him inside. He limped into the cottage. Lydia was serving supper to the children, including Simon, who'd returned from the Baker farm. Baked beans and salt pork, now rather crusty from reheating, and biscuits soaked in milk.

Rees waddled to the rocking chair in front of the fire and gingerly lowered himself into the chair. "Rough ride?" Lydia asked, approaching with a bowl of beans.

"I'm not a boy anymore," Rees admitted with a rueful smile.

"What happened?"

"The house is gone," Rees said. "Whatever Silas had was destroyed." He sighed. "The cleansing power of fire."

Lydia nodded. "Like Dugard." During Rees's search for a friend's murderer at home in Dugard last year, one of the suspects had been put in jail for his own protection. The murderer had burned down the jail in an attempt to kill, not just destroy evidence. Lydia put her hand upon his. "I'm sorry. But your investigation isn't over." She glanced at the children. Rees followed her gaze. Jerusha and Nancy so fair, their light hair curling around their faces. Simon, white skinned, but with hair almost as dark as Joseph's and those astonishing gray eyes. And then there was Judah, fair skinned and brown haired. "Who is Judah's father?"

"Do you believe Mrs. Baker?" Rees asked in a soft voice. "She accused Maggie of picking up men."

Lydia hesitated, her face wrinkled with thought. "No," she said at last in a very low voice. "I don't. Think about it. The constable fathered both Jerusha and Nancy, and when Maggie knew she was expecting the older girl, she married Mr. Whitney to give her a name. She tried to maintain a certain respectability."

"The man who fathered Simon cared enough to give Maggie a valuable teething stick," Rees said, following her thoughts.

"And the silver dollars." She paused. "Let's talk to Mouse. It's been several days since we visited her anyway, and . . ."

A shrill scream interrupted her and she moved quickly to separate Judah and Nancy.

Rees remained seated for a few seconds more and then rose to fetch the Bible from the shelf. He sat down in the rocking chair to read it by the flickering light of the flames burning on the hearth.

He looked for Maggie's untutored printing several pages in. He skipped the entries for Jerusha and Simon. Nancy's birthdate was given as summer (Independence Day?) 1791. He looked at her, carding wool at Lydia's feet; she would be five this summer. Although Maggie had wet-nursed Maartje's baby after Simon's birth, the Griffin baby's death had removed the contraceptive effect and Maggie's relationship with Cooper had resulted in another pregnancy.

And finally Judah, born May 1794. Maggie had been employed as a wet nurse after his birth, but the length of time between children also hinted at an enforced chastity.

Rees flipped forward to the Tucker page and the list of deaths. Olive's death was entered, in Maggie's crude hand, as May 1793. Rees had been in Pittsburgh that year, caught in the turmoil now referred to as the Whiskey Rebellion. And Maggie, clearly, had been busy caring for her mother as well as for her children.

He looked at the notations for Olive's siblings: "gone west" was repeated several times. And throughout the Bible there were comments written in Olive's carefully schooled hand in the margins. "This is truth," read one.

"Did you find anything useful?" Lydia asked.

"Not really," Rees said. Slamming the Bible shut, he dropped it onto the mantel.

Sleep did not come easily that night. He thrashed about, his busy thoughts keeping him from relaxing. He was almost convinced the Reverend Vermette was Judah's father. But, if so, where had he and Maggie gone to meet? Rees had searched the church and Mr. Randall's daughter had sworn no one could creep into the inn without being seen.

"Can't sleep?" Lydia asked, turning to face him.

"No." Rees sighed. "I think I must search the Reverend Vermette's bedchamber at the Ram's Head. His betrothal to Miss Pike is recent and, if he and Maggie were meeting, they must have gone somewhere. And Maggie's cloak still has not been found."

"Perhaps Reverend Vermette cleaned the attic in the log meetinghouse very carefully," Lydia suggested. "That's why you saw nothing. But Maartje might have seen Maggie and the Reverend." Her words trailed away.

"Perhaps," Rees agreed. "I think I'll take another look at the meetinghouse, too. Just to be thorough."

"We should talk to Maartje," Lydia said, adding, "She is probably still home with the new baby. Miss Pike told me she'd delivered."

"Yes," Rees agreed. "And I must speak to Mouse again, as you suggested."

"I miss her," Lydia said.

Rees nodded. "And she knew Maggie, at least a little, and she's the only one I trust to tell the truth. Everyone else, Cooper, Vermette, even Owen Randall, have lied to me."

"Good," Lydia said, beginning to sound drowsy. "I want to see her again."

Rees nodded and yawned. Now, with a plan, the activity in his mind was easing and he thought he could finally sleep.

First thing the next morning he hitched Ares to the buggy. Although the rain had stopped the previous day, the warmer temperatures had continued melting the snow. Ares plodded through the mud with his head hanging low, conveying without words his distaste for these conditions.

Constable Cooper was not in his shop but at the tavern eating breakfast. With the departure of Cooper's wife, Rees suspected the constable spent most of his time now at the Ram's Head. Mr. Randall sat at the checkerboard, as usual, playing one of his innumerable games. And no doubt listening to all that went on behind him.

Cooper was tucking into a bowl of stew when Rees approached. With a much put upon sigh, he put down his slice of bread and pushed away his bowl. "What now?" he asked.

Rees sat down in the chair across from the table. When Mr. Randall's daughter scurried over with a bowl of stew and a

beaker of cider for Rees, he did not protest. He ate a few mouth-
fuls before speaking. Cooper fiddled with his own glass of ale
and began tearing his piece of bread into fragments.

"You know I suspect Reverend Vermette is Judah's father?"

"For a while the pastor visited the farm regularly." Cooper
pushed his glass around the table. "But that doesn't mean he
and Maggie were intimate. Besides, fathering one of her brats
doesn't mean he murdered her."

"But it could. Maybe Maggie threatened to tell Miss Pike."

"And why would Miss Pike care?" Cooper asked with a
nasty grin. "She won. Vermette dropped Maggie for Miss Pike.
And for her daddy's land and money. That's the way the world
works."

Rees wanted to strike Cooper for his cynicism. "Maybe if
Maggie threatened to tell the selectmen and they assessed Vermette for Judah's maintenance?" Rees said. "I'm sure Miss Pike
wouldn't care for that."

"Maggie would have to prove it first."

"And then there's the shame. . . ."

Cooper rolled his eyes.

Even Rees knew that argument was weak. "Is there anyone
else?" he asked.

"She may have simply picked up a man."

"Do you believe that?" Rees asked quietly. "I didn't know
Maggie. You did. But I don't believe it of her."

Cooper hesitated for a long moment and then slowly shook
his head. "No. I don't. Maggie wasn't like that. She's had some
bad luck with men but . . . she just wanted a home and family."
He looked up, his eyes moist with tears. "I still can't believe she's
gone."

Rees paused for a few beats to allow the other man to

compose himself. "We still have not found Maggie's cloak. Will you accompany me upstairs to search Reverend Vermette's room?"

Cooper scrubbed his arm across his eyes. "All right. I don't believe Vermette is guilty of murder, but I've been surprised before." He swallowed the remainder of his ale in one long draft and stood. "We're going to take a look at the preacher's room," he told Mr. Randall.

"I don't think he'd care for that," Mr. Randall said. Cooper stared at him. Mr. Randall sighed and followed them to the foot of the stairs. "Don't destroy anything," he shouted after them.

Vermette's room was at the very top of the house, at the end of a steep climb to the fourth floor. The sole door was unlocked, and as soon as Rees opened it he understood why. The room was monastic in its simplicity, containing only a bed covered with a quilt, a stand with a jug and ewer, and a chair with a Bible upon the seat. All the pegs were empty except one, from which hung a clean shirt. A canvas valise, much worn, lay upon the floor. Rees recognized it as the one he'd seen in Mr. Gray's house. He stared at it. What had Vermette been doing there? And did Mr. Gray know?

"You see?" Cooper said. "Nothing here."

"I see," Rees said. "Vermette couldn't have brought Maggie here without someone spotting them." And not just Randall would be watching. Rees and Cooper had passed several people on the way up to the fourth floor; the stairs wound through the center of this old building, and there was no way to get through the building unseen.

The constable said nothing, but he threw a smug glance at his companion and chuckled as he clattered down the stairs.

Rees sighed. He would have to question Mr. Gray again. And maybe Mouse had remembered something more. He hoped so. He was beginning to fear everything he thought he knew might be wrong.

Chapter Twenty-eight

The wheels of the buggy got stuck several times in the heavy, wet, melting snow. The muddy surface underneath was no help: just another sticky layer. Rees had to help Ares pull through it, and his boots were quickly soaked. When the slurry of snow and mud caught the wheels for the third time, Lydia jumped down to remove her weight from the buggy. She walked by the side of the road where it was drier. With no weight but the buggy's, Ares succeeded in pulling it free. Rees and Lydia climbed back into their vehicle. The hem of Lydia's dress and cloak were saturated six inches high.

When they reached Mount Unity, later than they expected, they saw the Brethren out in the fields. Long dark furrows sliced the white. They were probably planting peas, usually one of the first crops.

Rees was unsurprised by the length of time he and Lydia had to wait; everyone was busy. Finally one of the Eldresses appeared and brought them upstairs to the apartment. She smiled at them, but tendrils of hair had escaped from her cap and she appeared flustered. She left them alone in the cool hall for some time, finally reappearing with Mouse in tow. Then she ushered them all into the small room at the back and departed. Rees took down three chairs from the pegs on the wall.

"Have you solved the mystery?" Mouse asked. "Oh, I hope so."

"No. But getting closer," Rees said. He watched disappointment dim her excitement.

"But I don't know anything," she said. "I told you everything I heard."

"I'm sure you did," Rees said. "But I am at a standstill. And you are the only one I trust to tell me the truth."

"Let's start at the very beginning," Lydia suggested. "When you and Sister Joan arrived at the cabin. The second time. What did Maggie say when you went in?"

"Nothing," Mouse said. "She was in the bedroom. Sister Joan and I brought the basket in and then I heard Joseph's breathing." Remembered fear brought tears into her eyes. "So I picked him up. And I asked Sister if I could stay a little while."

"Was Maggie already passed out?" Rees asked in confusion. He recalled Mouse describing a conversation with Maggie.

"No. She was talking with Mary Pettit. I couldn't hear what they were saying. But Maggie started crying. And then laughing." Mouse looked at Lydia and Rees in astonishment. "I'd forgotten that."

"Mary Pettit was there?" Rees's voice rose into a shout. Mouse jerked back, startled. Lydia put a hand over Rees's. When he looked at her she widened her eyes and shook her head. Frowning, Rees fell silent.

"What was she doing there?" Lydia asked in a gentle voice.

"Visiting, I suppose." Mouse grimaced in disapproval. "She brought Maggie whiskey. I could smell it on them."

That explained some of the jugs lined up in the cabin, Rees thought.

"Do you know why Maggie was crying?" Lydia asked.

"No. And I couldn't hear what they were saying. Judah and

Nancy were quarreling over a toy. I wasn't paying much attention anyway," she added, lifting her chin defiantly. "I was holding Joseph."

"Did you hear either Maggie or Mary Pettit say anything at all?" Lydia asked.

"As Mrs. Pettit started out the door, Maggie said, 'I'll make him pay.' And they both laughed."

Rees looked at Lydia. "Vermette," he said in a quiet voice.

"Maybe," Lydia said. "We can't be sure of that." She turned back to Mouse.

"Then what happened?"

"I told you. Maggie started talking about a man. Or men." Mouse looked confused. "About love. And she ignored her children. I didn't want to listen." She hesitated a moment. "Will you bring the children next time?"

Lydia and Rees exchanged a glance. He realized with a shock how dependent he'd become upon her opinion. "Maybe," Lydia said.

"If the Elders allow," Rees added.

While Lydia asked after Mouse's health, and how she fared, Rees paced about the room. He was determined to find out what Maggie and Mary Pettit had talked about that day.

As soon as Rees deposited Lydia at the cabin, he headed first for Mr. Gray's. He had no idea where Mary Pettit lived, and anyway, today he wanted to quickly search the log meetinghouse once more. Spring was finally coming. The sun shone from a blue sky and the snow melted with a steady dripping sound. The buggy wheels cut through the slush, throwing spatter in every direction.

The woman who opened Mr. Gray's door was younger than

Maartje Griffin by a few years, and the hair revealed by her cap was flaxen. "Ah, Mr. Rees, I presume," she said, eyeing him with frank interest. "I am Maartje's cousin." She smiled at him flirtatiously.

"How nice to meet you," Rees said. "Is Mr. Gray here?"

She stood away from the door, allowing him to brush past her. "Come inside." She guided him into the kitchen. "Uncle Elias," she bawled. He looked up.

"Mr. Rees," Mr. Gray said with a scowl. "You're like a biting flea. What do you want this time?"

"The key to the meetinghouse," Rees shouted. Mr. Gray looked at his niece, a glance of mingled anger and long-suffering resignation, and she hastily began searching through the litter of crumbs and dirty dishes on the worktable.

"Here it is," the girl said, holding up the massive iron object.

"I'll return it shortly," Rees said, taking it from the young woman.

The back door lock at the meetinghouse proved stiff, but he finally managed to open the door and enter the building. The still air and silence confirmed that he was alone. He walked around quickly, since he expected to find nothing on the ground floor. He circled the pulpit and peered into the small lobby by the back door. Then he braved the narrow twisting staircase to the small loft above, traversing it with especial care. The injury to his right leg had healed somewhat, reminding him of its presence with only an occasional pain, and he didn't want to reinjure it. Once at the top, he peered into each corner and examined every inch of the floor. The attic was even cleaner than it had been during his previous search. He found nothing that indicated any use, not even burn marks from smoking boys. And the floor had been thoroughly scrubbed with vinegar. "Damn," he muttered in frustration.

He descended the stairs once again, pausing by the small side window. Mr. Gray's house and kitchen window were clearly visible. In fact, Rees could see the dim outline of Mr. Gray himself. Now that was interesting. Maybe Lydia was right, and either Mr. Gray or Maartje Griffin had seen Reverend Vermette with Maggie. Rees would ask.

He locked the door behind him and started back to Mr. Gray's house, breaking into a rapid limp as he crossed the muddy ground. He gave a token knock upon the door before entering. Maartje's cousin looked up as Rees entered the kitchen. She had filled the dishpan with steaming water and dirty dishes, but instead of washing them she was indolently swirling her hands through the water. She promptly abandoned her task. "Done already?" she asked, approaching Rees. "Find anything?" Mr. Gray, who'd certainly been watching the church from his window, held out his hand for the key. Rees considered asking if Mr. Gray had seen Reverend Vermette with Maggie, but the presence of Maartje's cousin persuaded him to keep silent.

"I'll call on you again, Mr. Gray," Rees shouted and retreated.

When Rees arrived, Cooper was in his shop, laughing but keeping his apprentices hopping. Rees had grown so accustomed to seeing the constable in the tavern that he was startled to see him working. "Well, Mr. Rees," Cooper said, tossing him a glance. "To what do I owe the honor?"

"Just looking for Mary Pettit's address." Rees inspected Cooper. "You seem merry."

"I received a big order." He pointed to the back window. Rees peered through the wavy glass. Several large wagons, laden with barrels of all sizes, were lined up in the yard. "And my wife is moving back to town. To the house with me."

Rees turned a skeptical look upon the constable. "This may be your last chance," he said.

The smile dropped away from Cooper's face. "I know," he said. "Even her father . . ." He stopped short. Rees wondered if Cooper had been threatened. If so, he didn't seem distressed by it. Instead, he was cheerful and grinning like a fool. "Why do you want that old woman's direction? You can't believe anything she tells you."

"I just want to talk to her for a minute," Rees said, purposely vague. "See how she's doing."

Cooper shook his head at him. "She lives out on the west road. If you reach the Griffin farm you've gone too far. Little shack she rents from Owen Randall." He paused. "I'm telling you, Rees, you can't trust anything she says. I wouldn't believe her if she told me the sky was blue."

"I'll keep that in mind," Rees said. With a quick thank-you, and an instruction to Cooper to work hard, Rees went out and climbed back into his buggy. He picked up a few supplies at the store for Mrs. Pettit, eyeing his dwindling coins in dismay, and began his journey west.

As soon as he saw the shack described by Cooper, Rees realized he'd passed it several times. He just hadn't paid any attention. The structure, the wood weathered a deep grayish brown, seemed ready to collapse. One of the panes in the window by the door was broken and the inside shutter drawn across. A thread of smoke drifted from the chimney.

Rees jumped the stairs to the porch and pounded on the door. No one came. He was just ready to turn away when the door opened and Mary Pettit peered out. "Mr. Rees," she said in astonishment. Rees offered her the basket. She looked inside. "No whiskey?"

"No." Rees inspected the woman before him. The whites of

her eyes were yellow and the body under the rags looked swollen. "I need to speak to you for a minute."

Mary looked at him uncertainly, and then she inspected the empty road outside. "You'd better come inside," she said, opening the door a fraction.

Rees pushed past her into the shadowy interior. A scanty fire burned on the hearth, and the smell of woodsmoke combined with the stink of old sweat and stale whiskey. Water dripped from the leaky roof into a pail. A pallet consisting mainly of rags had been drawn up to the hearth. "Do you have any food?"

"Yes." She smiled at him. "You just brought it." With a sigh, she added, "Ask your questions."

"Just before Maggie was murdered," Rees said, "you visited her. Why?" Mary clutched her hands tightly together and pressed them into her chest. Her hesitation told Rees she did not want to answer. "Why, Mary?"

"We were friends. I delivered all her babies."

"What did you talk about?"

"Nothing much." Her gaze slid to a point over his left shoulder.

"Maggie was overheard crying and laughing. Clearly, you told her something important." Rees fixed a stern glare upon the woman. She looked aside, the draperies shrouding her quivering as she trembled beneath them. "Mary," Rees said in a soft voice, "someone murdered Maggie. The woman you claim was a friend. She was begging for money to pay her taxes. You told her something."

Mary did not speak for a long moment. "You must understand," she said at last, "that . . ." Her eyes shifted from side to side. "Mr. Randall owns this house. The selectmen decide who receives help and who doesn't. Maggie's children have you and your wife to look after them. I have no one. My daughter is

barely able to support herself and all my boys have moved away."
Rees looked at the woman shivering before him. "If I anger the
selectmen, I'll have to leave Dover Springs, and my daughter
and grandson live here."

"I appreciate the situation," he said. "I won't tell anyone anything you confide to me. But I need to know. Maggie was murdered. Do you want to allow her killer to go free?" The silence
went on for so long he thought she would not respond.

"Maggie was pregnant again," she said at last.

Rees gaped at her. Then he nodded; of course she was. "Do
you know who the father was?" She began to shake her head, her
eyes shifting to the side, and Rees knew she was preparing to lie.
"Don't," he said sternly. "Don't you dare lie to me."

"She was seeing Reverend Vermette," Mary said, in such a
quiet voice Rees could barely hear her. "I assume he . . ." Her
words ran down.

Pity washed over Rees and he fumbled in his purse for a
few pennies. They would not last long. "Get soup," he said.
"Not whiskey." She nodded, but Rees had the strong feeling she
was not listening. She looked terrified, and Rees wondered if
she'd told him everything.

"Don't worry," Rees said. "I'll tell no one that we've spoken."
Mary rolled her eyes at him, looking like a frightened animal.

Rees went outside. He gathered some of the deadfalls and
stacked the wood on her porch as another thank-you for the
information. Then he climbed into the buggy and headed home,
his mind churning. He was eager for supper.

Chapter Twenty-nine

Thursday morning, after a breakfast of eggs and johnnycake sweetened with molasses, Rees and Lydia set out for the Griffin farm. They left Jerusha in charge and busy washing dishes. As they went out the door, Rees heard the girl say in exactly the same tone as Lydia, "Nancy, there is a basket of wool that needs to be carded."

Lydia caught his grin and said, "Jerusha needed a woman's hand." She sighed, and Rees wondered if he would be able to tear Lydia away from these children when it was time to leave. For that matter, the thought of abandoning these children to the cruel mercy of Dover Springs sent a shiver through him as well. He would have to ensure their safety with the Shakers before leaving.

As soon as the buggy started down the drive, Rees knew this journey would take longer than usual. The slurry of mud clutched at the wheels and held them back. Rees allowed Ares to go at his own pace and turned to Lydia to share his experience with Mary Pettit. Lydia listened in silence, lines appearing and disappearing in her forehead as she reacted to his report.

"Hmm," she said when he finished and looked at her expectantly.

"What? You don't think Mary was telling the truth?"

"No, not entirely anyway." Lydia's brow furrowed. "I can believe she's scared. The Reverend Vermette is an important man. I also believe Maggie was pregnant. But I don't think Mary told you what they really discussed."

"Why not?" Rees recalled the woman's trembling. "She seemed genuine to me."

"Maggie would have known she was pregnant. Any woman would, especially after having had so many children already. She wouldn't have needed someone else to tell her." Lydia turned to Rees. "I think Mary told Maggie something, but it wasn't that she was pregnant."

Rees regarded his wife. "You may be right." He recalled his sense that Mary had not told him everything. "I'll have to speak with her again."

Shortly afterward, they passed the shack by the road and Rees pointed it out to her. Lydia gazed at it. "It looks abandoned," she said. Rees threw a quick look at the house. Not even a thread of smoke came from the chimney, and the wood he'd collected yesterday had not been used.

"Yes, it does," he agreed. "Maybe she is in town." He hoped she'd taken the pennies and gone to the Ram's Head.

It took over an hour to reach the Griffin farm. By the time they pulled up to the house, mud crusted Ares's legs right up to his belly. Caleb Griffin's buggy still sat before the porch, and as Rees tethered the gelding to the rail, he wondered if Mr. Griffin was around. Lydia jumped down and they went up the front steps. Maartje's cousin opened the door to Rees's knock. She glanced at Lydia but concentrated the full power of her smile upon Rees.

"We've come to call upon Mrs. Griffin," Rees said.

"She's busy," she began. But Lydia pushed past her and went into the small room to the left of the hall. Maartje Griffin was spinning, one foot rocking the cradle every now and again to keep the baby inside from waking. Rees paused in the door as Lydia hurried forward.

"What is it?" she asked, looking at the baby.

"A baby boy," Maartje replied, peering into the small red face. "We're calling him Jacob, after my uncle's father."

"When was he born?" Lydia asked, bending over the cradle. "Oh, he is so beautiful."

Maartje smiled, radiant with happiness. "Two days ago, after I left my uncle's. My husband set out for the midwife immediately, but I knew they wouldn't be home in time. Fortunately, my maid's mother lives nearby, and she delivered Jacob."

Rees, whose patience had evaporated, said, "Jacob is a beautiful boy. Mrs. Griffin, I wondered . . ." Lydia shot him a quelling look.

"I know you didn't come to ask about the baby," Maartje said. "More questions?"

"I wondered, since you spent a great deal of time with your uncle, if you ever noticed Reverend Vermette and Maggie Whitney going into the log meetinghouse?"

She stared at him for a moment, a faint pink crawling into her cheeks. "How did you . . . ? But I don't want to . . ." Her eyes slipped away from Rees's and he saw her struggle. Coming to a decision, she said, "Yes, I saw them. Many times."

Rees exhaled his breath very slowly.

"Do you think he murdered Maggie Whitney?" Maartje asked.

When Rees didn't answer, Lydia said, "It is one possibility."

Maartje was silent a moment and then she said, "I can't blame him for it. She was a wicked, wicked woman."

"I know you grieve still over the death of your baby girl," Lydia said with warm sympathy.

"Not just that." Maartje tossed her head. "Maggie was a harlot and a thief. I told you about the silver dollar." She nodded vehemently in emphasis. "I daresay she was not able to steal enough money for her taxes. She tried to extort money from my uncle."

"Your uncle?" Lydia repeated.

"Why would she apply to your uncle?" Rees asked.

"I don't know." The flush in her cheeks darkened. "But I heard her. I distinctly heard her telling him he owed her."

"When was this?" Rees asked, trying to fit this new fact into his head. Could Mr. Gray be Judah's father? Couldn't be. Mr. Gray was sixty at least and Judah barely two. Maggie would have been twenty-three or -four, no more.

"What did he say?" Lydia asked.

"No." Maartje looked at her in surprise. "No, of course. I'll wager Maggie went around to many men asking for money. She . . . she . . ." Tears filled her eyes. Rees watched her in consternation. Lydia put her hand upon Maartje's wrist. Rees withdrew to the door to wait out the emotional scene.

Maartje quickly mastered herself and Lydia, with a quick glance at Rees, said, "I'll come again, I promise, to see how you and Jacob are faring." Rees helped her into her cloak. She linked her arm with his, and they went through the door into the cold outside.

"So Maartje did see the pastor and Maggie together," Rees said as they descended the stairs. That was the answer he had been anticipating.

"Is that enough proof?"

"Maybe," Rees said. Mrs. Griffin's account was just what he'd expected, so why wasn't he happier about it? "I must speak to the constable."

Lydia nodded, her gaze snared by the buds upon the trees and shrubs. The melting snow and mud were harbingers of spring. "My bees will be waking soon," she said. "They'll need me. I want to go home."

Rees nodded. "I miss my loom. I have trouble thinking without it."

She unfolded his hand and looked at the calluses on his palms: calluses from holding the reins and chopping wood. "You've been working hard anyway," she said.

On the way home, Rees took a detour to the log meetinghouse. He hadn't been sure Vermette was in town, but he noticed as he went past that the front door was unlocked and flung wide to the air. He pulled into the yard. He asked Lydia to remain in the buggy while he went inside to investigate. Sunlight streamed through the windows and glowed upon the cross under the central window over the altar.

Rees paused inside the lobby, listening. He knew someone was here, a vibration in the air betrayed another presence, but he saw no one. He began walking down the central aisle, his footsteps echoing in the silence.

Reverend Vermette popped abruptly through the door to the stairs. Rees wondered what had attracted the pastor upstairs, to the gallery. When he saw Rees walking down the aisle the pastor stopped short. "Back from circuit?" Rees asked.

"Preparing for services on Sunday," the pastor replied brusquely. Rees interpreted Vermette's belligerence as a guilty conscience.

"I'm glad to see you. I have a question. Did Maggie Whitney approach you for money?"

"Why would you think so?" Vermette's eyes twitched away from Rees, looking everywhere but at his visitor.

"Did you give her any?"

"Of course not." Realizing he'd been trapped into telling the truth, Vermette glared.

Rees glowered back. "You know, don't you, that you are Judah's father?"

"I'm not . . . we . . ." A mottled flush rose into his neck.

"You were seen coming into this meetinghouse with Maggie many times."

"I never brought her here," he declared.

"Miss Pike isn't here, so at least tell the truth to me," Rees said. "You and Maggie formed a bond when you were counseling her aunt. You maybe even made plans to marry."

"How do you know that?" Vermette collapsed into the front pew.

"And then you met Miss Pike, the affluent Miss Pike. By then Maggie was pregnant again. Is that why you strangled her and threw her into the grave?"

Vermette stared at Rees for a moment and then leaped over the few feet separating them, his arms flailing. Taken completely by surprise, Rees took several blows before the simmering beast within him rose and he reacted with a strike of his own. Taller and heavier, and well used to fist fighting, Rees's punch struck home and Vermette went down.

Rees flashed back to his battle with his brother-in-law, Sam Prentiss. For a moment Rees smelled blood and his heart began to pound. He couldn't catch his breath. Then, with a shudder, he returned to the present.

That brief hesitation gave Vermette enough time to jump to his feet and run. Rees heard the back door slam and, a few minutes later, the sound of horse hooves. He realized then that his nose was bleeding, dripping onto his unbuttoned greatcoat to the linen vest and shirt below. He pinched his nostrils together to stem the flow and headed toward the staircase. He wanted to know what Vermette had been doing upstairs.

He traversed the narrow tower to the loft above. But although he searched every inch of the loft and the nave below it again, remembering with every moment the touch of Vermette's hands on his shoulders when he'd almost fallen, he found nothing. Finally he gave up and returned to his buggy.

"What happened?" Lydia breathed when she saw his swollen nose and the blood on his shirt and vest.

"Reverend Vermette hit me."

"He's smaller and weaker than you are." He saw the fear in her eyes, that he might have hurt Reverend Vermette as he had Sam Prentiss.

"I didn't attack him," he said, his tone sharp with impatience. "He hit me first."

"Oh Will," she said, laying her hand upon his face, "you must learn to turn the other cheek. Your temper gets you into trouble." Rees had never found that doctrine a successful one, but he didn't want to worry her.

"I know I must learn to tame the beast," he admitted, taking up the reins and urging Ares into motion.

"I need to lay a cold compress on your nose," Lydia said, shaking her head at him.

"My nose isn't bleeding anymore." His words came out slurred.

"Your nose is swollen." Lydia leaned forward to examine the injury. "Why did Reverend Vermette hit you?"

"I asked him if Judah was his child, and he came at me. I hit him only once and he ran."

"Do you think he murdered Maggie?" Lydia asked.

Rees sighed. "Probably."

"What a pity," Lydia said.

They soon arrived in front of the cabin. Rees threw the horse blanket over the gelding and followed his wife inside. She had already put a roll of linen in a basin of cold water.

"Take off your coat," she said. As Rees hung his coat upon a peg by the door, he thought again of Maggie's cloak. Where was it? "Change to a clean shirt and I'll soak this one, otherwise the blood will stain." Rees nodded and did as he was told. When he returned to the main room, Lydia put his stained shirt in a basin of cold water and pressed Rees into a seat at the table. A cold damp rag went on his bruised nose and another pad upon the back of his neck.

Forced into inactivity, Rees's thoughts darted from Reverend Vermette to Owen Randall to Silas Tucker. Silas's unexpected generosity in paying Maggie's taxes remained surprising. How Rees missed his loom! In previous such situations, he would sit down to weave and the turbulence in his mind would smooth out. Without it, his thoughts moved like lightning, fast and uncontrolled. He rose to circle the tiny cabin. Lydia scolded him and ordered him back to his chair. He obeyed but stood up again so many times Lydia finally lost patience and told him to stop.

"I'll chop some wood," he said and left the cabin for the back of the lean-to. His previous chopping had left a good supply, but Rees needed to think. He picked up the axe in his right hand and, holding a log with his left hand, swung. The log split in half. He swung again and the half split into quarters. He fell into a rhythm, swinging the axe into the logs, the crack of impact punctuating every stroke. He knew people had lied to him. What was Mary Pettit keeping back?

And suddenly he understood something completely unrelated. Throwing down the axe, he ran into the cabin. Lydia looked up, alarmed. "What's the matter?" she asked.

"If Silas had evidence indicating who Maggie's killer was, he must have hidden his proof here," Rees said. "And then paid the taxes on this house. He knew as long as the children lived here, no one would be able to come in and search."

"That's why he put the children out, for privacy?"

"Yes. Oh, I have no doubt he would have ejected them later, when it suited him." Rees's words trailed away as he glanced around him. There were so few hiding places here, and Silas had had very little time.

"It must be in the bedroom," Lydia said, dropping Rees's shirt into the basin. "I would have found something hidden in this room."

"But I searched the bedroom," Rees protested weakly, dropping into step behind his wife.

"But not for this," she pointed out. Four pairs of eyes stared at Rees and Lydia as the children turned to watch.

Working in silence, Rees and Lydia went over everything in the fusty room. Rees lifted the corncob mattress while Lydia took down the clothing from the pegs. She turned out every pocket, finally coming upon a small Bible. "Will," she said, her voice trembling with excitement. "Look at this."

He glanced at the little Bible. "I saw that before." It was not the large family Bible, but the most common sort of cheap Bible, sized to fit in a pocket and often given out by preachers so the members of their flock could pray anywhere.

"Look at the inscription," she urged him.

Rees took the Bible and flipped open the front cover. Dark brown stains, both mud and blood, occluded the dedication and the signature, but when Rees held the book up to the light he could read it. "To M, the companion of my soul. Abner Vermette."

"He must have given this to Maggie," Rees said. "I know he

and Miss Pike have been handing out these Bibles to likely congregants."

"So Silas knew Reverend Vermette had motive to murder Maggie," Lydia said with a nod. "But how did he find the Bible?"

"I'll wager he found it in the grave," Rees said. He thought back to his arrival in the churchyard the day he examined Maggie's body. "Silas had left by the time I arrived. The Bible probably fell in the grave when Vermette threw her body down." Rees clenched the Bible tightly, angry at Silas once again. "And instead of saying anything, Silas took the Bible, no doubt intending to use it as leverage against the minister." He looked down at Lydia. "I must take this to the constable right away."

Chapter Thirty

By the time he reached town, Rees's nose was swollen and sore, but the bleeding had stopped completely. He did not remember that today was Friday until he found the square congested with wagons and horses. Although not the type of market held on Saturdays during the summer, the local farmers came into town at week's end to pick up supplies. And also socialize. When he went into the tavern he saw it was crowded as well.

Cooper waved him over and pointed to the seat across the table. "What happened to your nose? Did that fiery redheaded wife of yours lose patience with you at last?"

"Vermette hit me."

"Vermette?" Cooper couldn't hide his surprise. "He's the most peaceful man I know."

"I asked him if Maggie had approached him for money. He admitted she had. Then I accused him of fathering Judah and strangling Maggie because of it."

"You didn't." Leaning forward, Cooper thumped the table. "Have you lost your wits?"

"Mrs. Griffin said she saw Maggie and Vermette together."

Cooper jerked, startled. "She did? What did he say?"

"That's when he punched me."

"Some men would say you deserved it," Cooper said with a chuckle.

Rees brushed away the comment. "Look at this," he said, tossing the Bible onto the table. "This is important. Silas hid it in Maggie's cottage." Cooper looked up at Rees and then at the book. He picked it up and examined it.

"I'll wager that's Maggie's blood. Look at the inscription," Rees urged him.

Cooper did as he was told. His eyes widened but he shook his head. "This isn't enough to even cause suspicion," he said. "We have no proof this is Maggie's blood."

"Mud and blood?" Rees leaned forward. "It was taken from the grave, Cooper, and Silas was murdered for it."

"We have no proof of that either," Cooper said. Disappointment silenced Rees and he collapsed into the seat next to the constable.

Cooper eyed Rees's expression. "Oh, all right. The Bible does tie everything together, but remember, fathering a bastard or two does not make a man a murderer."

Rees sighed, wondering if Cooper saw any difference between the treatment of Reverend Vermette and of Maggie. Dover Springs had pilloried her over her out-of-wedlock children and she'd been given no chance at all to defend herself. But no one would blame the pastor. "So he escapes justice," Rees said in a bitter tone.

"I'll talk to Reverend Vermette and Miss Pike," the constable said at last. "That's the most I can do. I can't arrest a minister on this, especially when he is engaged to wed the daughter of one of the wealthiest men in town. Not without a credible eyewitness or a confession. That's the law."

"What will it take?" Rees asked angrily. "The entire town watching Vermette hold a gun to my head?" Realizing that every man in the tavern was watching him, Rees jumped to his feet and stamped out. He drove home in a temper.

"I don't know what else to do," Rees confessed to Lydia that night. The children had been put to bed, and Rees and Lydia sat at the table.

"Don't be discouraged," she said, putting a hand over his. "You'll . . ." They both heard the hoofbeats at the same time.

"What's that?" Lydia looked at Rees with wide eyes. "Not Mouse again, not after she promised."

He rose to his feet. The sound of horse hooves had stopped, but no one came to the door and knocked. He used his sleeve to scrub a hole in the moisture covering the window. He could see nothing. Adrenaline burned down his back and his stomach tightened. This was no casual visitor. Rees wanted to swear and pound the wall: his rifle was out in the lean-to. He had not thought he would need it in a houseful of children.

With a crack that echoed from the surrounding hill, a gun was fired and a ball thudded into the door. Rees jumped away from the wall, his heartbeat hammering in his chest. Was it someone who wanted to silence him forever? Or just warn him? He flung the door open. While the shooter reloaded, Rees would have a few seconds to run to the lean-to and get his rifle. Crouching low, he sprinted. It was even darker in the lean-to, but he had learned long ago how to load his rifle under any conditions. When he peered around the wall, he saw nothing. The horse and rider had retreated, down the slope of the drive into the concealing darkness of the road.

This time when he heard the echoing thud of hooves coming up the drive, he raced outside and lifted the rifle to his shoulder. Cooper and his rawboned horse appeared out of the darkness.

"Jesus," Rees gasped. "I almost shot you. Why didn't you come inside before?"

"Before? I just arrived." Cooper dismounted as Rees stared at him in horror. "But there was someone else here. He galloped off down the road as I came up to the drive. Why?"

"Nothing," Rees lied, the gun dropping from his trembling hand. He bent down and retrieved it. "Nothing at all. But I hope you have good news for me. This needs to be resolved." Before the killer threatened Lydia and these children again.

Cooper came in, nodding politely to Lydia.

"Would you like something to eat?" she asked him. "I fear we have nothing to drink."

"No thank you," he replied, although Rees felt certain he would have accepted whiskey. Rees gestured to the table, and they sat.

"I spoke to the Reverend and Miss Pike," Cooper said with a grimace. "He swears he never experienced sexual congress with Maggie."

"Then he's a liar," Rees said. "Maggie was pregnant again."

"But he admits he and Maggie had formed a connection and were discussing marriage when he met his dear Miss Pike."

"Poor Maggie," Lydia said in a low voice. For a moment, both Rees and Cooper were silent. Rees recalled Randall's daughter describing Maggie's despair and wondered if Vermette had just told her he planned to marry Miss Pike. Maggie must have already known she was pregnant. Still, despite her disappointments and personal sorrow, she hadn't given up her quest to secure the future of the cottage and protect her children. Rees admired her for that.

"And the Bible?" Rees asked.

"He said it didn't belong to him. Miss Pike claims to have given several away in town, all signed by the Reverend, of course." Cooper shrugged.

"You believe him?" Rees asked, wondering if he was attaching too much importance to the bloodstained Bible.

"You don't, I see," Cooper replied with a mocking smile. Rees bit the inside of his lip so he would not shout at the constable.

"He didn't sign mine," Lydia said, holding out the Bible given her by Miss Pike. Cooper shrugged. The fire snapped, sending a shower of glittering sparks up the chimney and illuminating her hair, touching it with gold. Rees knew he couldn't take even the slightest chance of losing her. The murderer had to be publicly identified, and quickly.

"So if Vermette is not the murderer, then who do you think it is?" Rees asked.

"I don't know." Cooper sounded glum. "We may never solve Maggie's murder." His mouth curled in distaste. "As I left, Vermette and Miss Pike were swearing undying love for one another. Disgusting."

"I'll walk you out," Rees said. A plan was beginning to form in his mind, but he didn't dare share it with anyone. At least not yet. And especially not with Lydia. He knew she would not agree.

"I'm sorry," Cooper said, rising to his feet. Rees nodded brusquely and followed the constable into the cold air.

"Tomorrow morning," Rees said, as soon as the door closed behind him. "I will be in the log meetinghouse praying for guidance. Maybe God can help me find the answer."

Rees slept poorly that night, rifle by his side, waking at every sound. He was glad to see the first gray light of dawn creeping through the windows. After breakfast, and without telling Lydia where he was headed, he went outside and dragged the scarecrow from the field. He put it in the buggy and drove to the log meetinghouse. Then he cut through the shrubbery separating the church from Mr. Gray's house. Rees went up to the front door, but this time he did not knock. With the memory of Vermette's monastic bedchamber in the inn clear in his thoughts, he opened the door as quietly as he could and tiptoed inside. Although Mr. Gray was deaf and most likely would not hear Rees, it was possible the elderly man had visitors. Rees did not want to explain his suspicion that Reverend Vermette had been using Mr. Gray's house for his assignations with Maggie until he was sure it was true. Rees paused on the stairs and listened. He could hear the old man moving about in the kitchen, but Mr. Gray gave no sign of knowing anyone else was in the house. Rees tiptoed upstairs, to the back room with its collection of girlish clothing and toys, and quickly slipped inside. Once the door was closed, Rees paused in the center of the floor and tried to remember this room as he'd first seen it. The canvas valise had been positioned at the foot of the cot.

A woman's voice sounded from the front door and was quickly followed by a heavy slam. Rees waited a few moments and then tiptoed to the landing and peered over the bannister. "How are you, uncle?" the woman asked brightly. Rees thought it might be Maartje. "I've brought my maid to help me today."

"You're late," Mr. Gray snarled in loud reply.

Rees descended the stairs as quietly as he could. When he glanced at the pegs by the door he saw Maartje's gray wool cloak. He slipped out the front door and knocked, as if he'd only just arrived. Maartje opened the door.

"You again," she said with a frown. "My uncle is eating breakfast."

"I need the key to the meetinghouse," Rees said. "I found something that suggests the identity of the murderer, and I must pray to God for guidance."

"I would not have taken you for a churchgoing man," Maartje said, staring at Rees in astonishment. "Come inside." She preceded him into the kitchen.

Rees nodded to the old man. "Good morning, Mr. Gray," he said.

"Here is the key." Maartje lifted it from a hook on the wall. The kitchen already exhibited signs of her work: the dishes were done and drying upon a towel, the spiderwebs were down, and the table was scrubbed. Rees reached out for the key, never removing his gaze from the man seated by the window. He could not conceive of Mr. Gray fathering Judah.

"What is your connection to Maggie Whitney?" he asked loudly. Mr. Gray looked over, his eyes watery. For a moment Rees thought Mr. Gray might speak, but he changed his mind at the last minute.

"I can't hear you," he said. "Speak up." Rees felt certain the old man had heard every word.

"Mr. Rees," Maartje said in annoyance. "Please don't pester my uncle." She looked at the key as though she wished to snatch it from his hand. Rees folded his fingers around it and turned to go.

More mud clung to his boots as he threaded his way through the line of vegetation separating Mr. Gray's home from the meetinghouse, and he suspected they would never be the same. He opened the back door and carried in the scarecrow he had brought from the farm that morning.

After installing the scarecrow in the shadowy pew at the back of the church, so it appeared to be a praying man, Rees drove into town and went into the tavern. As he expected, Cooper was there, and this time seated across the table from Reverend Vermette. By the sudden silence that greeted Rees, he guessed he had been the topic of conversation. Several men were grinning, so whatever the discussion, it did not reflect well upon him.

Cooper motioned him over. "And what are you doing here?"

"Just thought I'd get something to eat and drink before going to the meetinghouse," Rees said, waving at Mr. Randall for an order of cider. Turning his gaze to Vermette he said, "I found something that indicates the identity of the murderer."

"Not that Bible," Vermette sneered.

"No," Rees lied. "Something else. I plan to spend the rest of the day praying for guidance."

Cooper turned to look at Rees in disbelief. "What are you playing at?" he muttered.

Vermette looked incredulous. "I am glad to hear you are a God-fearing man," he said. "I would not have expected . . . I mean . . ."

Rees glanced around him and saw that the men sitting near him were not troubling to hide their interest. Mr. Baker and his son, one of the selectmen, and several regulars: this news would be all over Dover Springs in an hour. Smiling, he drained his glass of cider and left the tavern.

Rees let himself into the meetinghouse once again, carefully leaving the back door open and slightly ajar. Then he and his rifle took up a position in the vestibule, hidden behind the wooden half wall and in clear sight of the scarecrow slumped over the back of the bench in front of it. A lamb to the slaughter.

He heard a clatter outside a little while later but no one came into the building, so Rees settled back against the wooden wall with his rifle across his knees. The effort of waiting, without movement or noise, lulled him into a semi-doze. When the attack came he was unprepared. Footsteps whispered across the wooden floor; Rees didn't recognize the sound at first, and by the time the soft slip of stocking feet connected with the notion of threat, the attacker was well inside and aiming his blunderbuss at the scarecrow. Rees raised himself to his knees and rested the rifle upon the lip of the half wall, but before he fired a shot erupted from the back door.

"Hold it," shouted Cooper.

The blunderbuss went off and the scarecrow's head exploded into a shower of straw. Rees leveled his rifle and shouted, "Stop." Caleb Griffin lowered his weapon. Cooper, holding his rifle up to his shoulder, walked forward.

"Put the blunderbuss onto the pew," the constable ordered. Griffin made as if to comply, but as he turned he hurled the weapon into Cooper's stomach. The constable fell to the floor, gasping. Griffin started running, right past the constable, toward the back door.

"Cooper," Rees cried, running through the gate and sprinting toward the constable.

"I'm fine. Go after Griffin."

Rees leaped over the constable and thundered out the back door. He knew where Griffin must be heading: to Mr. Gray's house. Sure enough, when Rees ran outside, he saw Griffin, struggling through the greening shrubs that separated the properties. Rees broke into a sprint and went down, full length, into the mud. Scrambling to his feet, he adopted a running hop, trying to leap over the slick dirt. His long legs gained more ground than Griffin's. As Caleb tried to make his way through the shrubs, Rees grabbed him. Griffin smacked Rees with all his strength and he went down, but he didn't release his grip on Griffin's coat. The two men fell together and began rolling over and over on the muddy ground, punching and kicking as each tried to gain the advantage.

Panting, Cooper came up to them. "Stop, Caleb," he ordered. "You can't escape now." Winded, Griffin ceased fighting. Rees struggled to his feet and, as Cooper grasped one of Griffin's arms, Rees grabbed the other. "I've got him," Cooper said. "I'll take him to my shop and lock him in."

Rees nodded, panting hard as he tried to catch his breath. "You'll have to tell me how you knew." Cooper jerked Griffin to his feet and dragged him to the front of the meetinghouse.

Rees slowly made his way back inside. He retrieved his rifle and dropped into the pew. His hands were trembling; the rifle slipped from his fingers and clattered against the floor. He hadn't been sure who would appear, and had been more than half certain it would be Reverend Vermette. Now he needed to rethink his interpretation of the facts.

He was still sitting there when Maartje hurried in. She'd tucked her skirts up around her waist, and her clogs and stockings were spattered with mud. "Where is my husband?" she cried. "I heard a shot."

"The constable has him," Rees said. "He tried to kill me."

Maartje stared at him in shock before whirling and running out the door once again.

Rees rose carefully to his feet and began gathering up the scarecrow. The head was gone. That could have been Rees's head. He sat down once again.

Chapter Thirty-one

He finally drove home an hour later. Although he closed the meetinghouse's back door, he did not revisit Mr. Gray's house to return the key. He just couldn't face either Maartje or Mr. Gray again—not yet, anyway.

As Rees removed the scarecrow from the buggy, scattering straw everywhere, Lydia came outside. "Where were you? Why are you covered with mud? What were you doing with the scarecrow? What *happened* to the scarecrow?"

Too unnerved to manufacture a plausible lie, Rees said, "I set it up in the log meetinghouse and told everyone I was praying for God's guidance because I had discovered who the killer was."

She stared at him, the color leeching from her cheeks. "You set yourself up as bait?" Her voice rose to a shriek. Both hands flew up to cover her mouth. "Oh, dear God."

Jerusha appeared at the door, drawn by Lydia's scream. "What's the matter?"

Lydia threw Rees a glance in which both fury and terror were mingled, and he knew he would hear about this again. Then she turned to Jerusha and said with an artificial smile, "Why, nothing. The scarecrow was damaged." Urging the girl ahead of her into the cabin, Lydia directed another furious glare at Rees and disappeared inside. He quickly followed them.

Sleep did not come easily that night. Rees told himself he'd never really been in danger; he could have shot Mr. Griffin before he'd reloaded the blunderbuss. But he couldn't really believe it, and shudders regularly shivered through him. And Lydia would provide no comfort; she was so angry she refused to speak to him and had gone to sleep with her back set solidly against him.

As Rees stared at the patterns cast by the fire on the cabin ceiling he wondered how he could have been so wrong. Maggie's death made sense only if Reverend Vermette had murdered her. But he hadn't. Why would Mr. Griffin kill Maggie? Was he Judah's father? Or perhaps the father of Maggie's unborn child? But no, both Maartje and Mary Pettit had identified Vermette as Maggie's lover. Unless they were both lying? Rees turned over, too irritated with himself to relax. He reminded himself the investigation was over. The killer, Mr. Griffin, had been identified. But *why* had he done it? Silas Tucker had thought Vermette was the killer as well; that's why he'd hidden the pocket Bible in the cottage. But if the inscription was for Maggie, from Reverend Vermette, then Mr. Griffin had no reason to kill her. Rees flopped over again. It made no sense. Unless the M in the Bible's inscription referred to Maartje, and Rees couldn't believe she and Vermette were lovers, not when she'd clearly expressed her dislike for him and his church the first time he'd met her.

Rees ground his teeth in frustration. He was missing something important. He didn't understand why Caleb Griffin had murdered both Maggie Whitney and Silas Tucker.

One of the children turned over in the other room with a muffled cry, startling Rees into alertness. After a moment, he rose to his feet and, wrapping a quilt around himself, went into the bedroom to check on the children. They were tumbled together like puppies, Joseph snuggled up in Jerusha's arms. Rees stared down at them for a long time, wondering what would have become of them without Mouse. They were so vulnerable. He understood now how desperate Maggie had been to keep them safe. People would do anything to protect those they loved. What had Maggie done as her last reckless action? Whatever it was, it had threatened Caleb Griffin and gotten her killed.

What was Mr. Griffin hiding? Rees had to understand.

He returned to the pallet and lay down. Almost everyone in Dover Springs had lied to him, of that he was certain. He needed to clear away all the lies people in Dover Springs had told him and lay bare the truth. Tomorrow he would start by questioning Caleb Griffin.

Constable Cooper arrived first thing Sunday morning. He held his right arm awkwardly and Lydia immediately asked after the injury. "I'm fine," he said, barely acknowledging her. He looked at Rees. "Bad news."

"Griffin escaped," Rees said. He'd wondered if that would happen; for all he knew Griffin and Cooper were cousins. These incestuous small towns!

"He's dead."

"He's . . . what!" Rees gaped at the constable. "Dead? How?" Now Rees might never learn what Griffin knew.

"I had him locked up in my shop, until I had a chance to take him to the jail in Schoharie on Monday. Somebody broke the window and shot him dead." He paused and then added in an aggrieved tone, "So, was he Maggie's killer? Or not?" Rees did not reply. Instead, thinking furiously, he stared over Cooper's head. If Griffin was Maggie's killer, then who had shot him? It had to be someone who shared his secret, and Rees could think of only two people who were that close to Caleb Griffin.

"Rees? Do you hear me, Rees?"

"What?"

"So, is the baby"—his eyes swiveled to Judah—"Griffin's child?"

"I don't know." Rees didn't want to admit that with Griffin's appearance, all his assumptions had been exploded. What was he missing? "I don't think so, but I need to think."

"We all want to know," Lydia said, turning to her husband with a frown of exasperation.

"It's best if I explain once, to everyone all at once," Rees said. "In the meetinghouse."

"Today is Sunday so the meetinghouse is in use. But I'm sure Reverend Vermette will not deny you tomorrow, especially if your solution absolves him," Cooper said in a dry tone.

"Tomorrow morning then? And I need you to perform a service, if you will. Please call on Mrs. Griffin."

"I doubt she'll attend," Cooper said. "She's in mourning, remember."

Darting an anxious look at Lydia, Rees drew Cooper to the side and whispered into his ear.

Cooper nodded and said, "I'll spread the word at the Ram's Head." He paused and then added, "I'll also try to persuade some of the selectmen to attend."

"Until tomorrow then," Rees said. He needed to spend this day in serious thought.

First thing Monday morning, Rees pocketed the small Bible stained with Maggie's blood and put his copies of Olive Tucker's will into the large family Bible. Nerves kept him from eating his breakfast, and his first sips of coffee made his stomach roil. Although certain his resolution of all three deaths was now correct, he knew it was critical he persuade everyone else. There still would be some who would refuse to believe the truth, even though Griffin had been caught trying to kill Rees.

Once the children had finished their breakfasts and Lydia had repeated her instructions to Jerusha for the third time, Rees declared himself ready to leave. Lydia scarcely had time to grab her cloak before he took her arm and propelled her through the door. He had harnessed Ares immediately after breakfast so the horse had, by now, been waiting for almost an hour.

"I don't think we need to hurry quite so much," Lydia said. "Everyone will wait for you. They must."

Rees did not reply. He remained silent all the way to the log church, reviewing the deductions that had led to his final conclusion. There were so many points he wanted to remember.

The meetinghouse was more crowded than he expected. Rees looked around, surprised to see how many had come. Constable Cooper, accompanied by his wife, waited in the front pew. Reverend Vermette and Miss Pike sat behind the constable in the second row. They seemed to have eyes for no one else, staring at one another and sighing like actors in a play. Rees, who thought the emotion on display patently false and inconsiderate of everyone else here, now understood Mr. Cooper's many grimaces and frowns.

Mr. Gray sat across the aisle, accompanied by Maartje and her cousin. The sleeping baby lay in a nest of blankets on the wooden bench beside Maartje, and she peered into the baby's face every few minutes as though assuring herself of Jacob's continued health.

As Lydia found a seat and Rees walked to the front, Mr. Randall entered, his cane beating a counterpoint to his soft limping footsteps. Mr. and Mrs. Baker and their son followed close behind. They took seats behind Mr. Gray and Maartje Griffin. Then Elder Herman, Eldress Agatha, and Mouse appeared at the door. They paused, looking around in trepidation, before finding seats at the back. Elder Herman sat on the opposite side of the aisle from the two Shaker women, and right in front of the four selectmen. These were the men Rees must persuade. Of the four, three sat with crossed arms and hostile postures. Mr. Shaw, Cooper's father-in-law, looked particularly angry.

Rees cleared his throat.

"So, how did you know it was Griffin?" Cooper called out.

"It's a mistake," Mr. Gray bawled, his voice echoing loudly around the hall.

Rees ignored them. "Let's talk about Maggie Whitney for a moment," he said. He waited for the sounds—the scrape of a shoe, a hastily muffled cough—to die down. "I'm sure most of you feel you knew her. Knew her well; that the only secrets she kept were the names of her children's fathers. I began my investigation there."

"Mr. Rees," Cooper said warningly, shifting uncomfortably in his seat.

"Dover Springs is done with secrets," Rees said, so loudly his voice echoed in his own ears. Cooper lowered his eyes as his assembled neighbors turned to stare at him. "Few will be surprised to hear Jerusha Whitney is your child. But you were seeing Genevieve Shaw at the same time. And Maggie had no father, especially not a selectman, to compel you into marriage." Rees rested his eyes upon Cooper's frowning father-in-law. "Fortunately, Roger Whitney wanted to marry her. So she wed him and moved away. Isn't that true?" Rees paused.

No one spoke, although Cooper squirmed and finally nodded. His wife, after one angry glare, lifted her chin and looked straight ahead. The selectmen eyed the constable speculatively, whispering together.

"Mr. Whitney was a sailor, however," Rees continued, "and Maggie found herself a young widow with a baby. So she went to work as a wet nurse. While in Boston, she became pregnant with Simon and returned home. She brought one hundred silver dollars with her."

"Why didn't she use that for her taxes then, huh?" Mr. Baker blurted. "Every year she struggled to pay them."

"She did that, once, and was accused of theft." Rees paused again. The expressions upon the faces of the selectmen did not change, and Maartje shook her head, refusing to believe it.

"She was a thief," Maartje muttered, just loudly enough to be heard.

"Was she? Most of that money is intact, waiting for Simon to reach his majority. I know it must have been difficult to save. When my wife and I first met her children, there was not a scrap of food in the house." Rees brought his judgmental gaze back to Cooper. "With Maggie's return to town, she'd reconnected with Mr. Cooper here, who was living apart from his wife."

"Rees, be quiet now," Cooper shouted.

Rees regarded him in silence for several seconds before speaking again. "By your own admission, you accused Maggie of believing you were a couple. Nancy is the result."

Genevieve's mouth began to tremble. Reverend Vermette turned a sneer upon the constable.

"By then," Rees continued, "Olive Tucker was quite ill, and the recipient of many pastoral visits from Reverend Vermette. And when Mr. Cooper returned to his wife, Maggie formed an attachment to the pastor. He was single and unconnected to any woman. I believe she expected marriage." Now Rees turned his eyes upon the pastor.

"I don't deny that I suffered from lust," Vermette declared in a strong voice. "I confess to that sin." Cooper looked at the minister in dislike, and Rees felt his face twist with disdain.

"You admit to a connection with Maggie then?" Rees asked.

"I wouldn't call it a connection," Vermette began, turning to Miss Pike. She did not look at him.

"You met Maggie in Mr. Gray's house." Rees cut off the Reverend. "Why not use the meetinghouse?"

"When we began—um," Vermette said, dropping his gaze to his hands. "Well, we did use the meetinghouse. But we were almost caught by those boys." He flicked a gaze at Mr. and Mrs. Baker. "We needed more privacy."

"I see. Well, last fall you met another woman, one with status and wealth: Miss Pike. In December you asked for her hand in marriage. When she accepted, you broke it off with Maggie." Rees paused. Quietly the meetinghouse door opened, and Mary Pettit came inside. She sat upon the rearmost log. Rees felt a knot of worry begin to uncoil inside him. "Did you know, Reverend Vermette, that Maggie was carrying your second child?" Vermette's eyes widened and his mouth flapped open.

"Of course not . . . not then." His eyes flashed toward Miss Pike. She was regarding her fiancé in horror.

"I didn't know she was with child. I didn't." Vermette's voice was shaking.

"So, you didn't kill her to protect your engagement to Miss Pike?"

"No! Of course not. Mr. Griffin killed her."

"He did not," Maartje said.

Rees did not look at her. He let the silence lengthen until Vermette shifted uncomfortably in his seat, an expression of sullen shame upon his face. "Are you prepared to swear," Rees said at last, "here in this meetinghouse, under the eyes of God, that you had no part in the murder of Maggie Whitney?"

"I swear." Vermette's voice reverberated from the rafters. "I'm sure any man who enjoyed her favors will tell you she invited such attention."

"No doubt," Rees said. "A young and pretty girl, what else should she desire but a husband of her own?"

Vermette turned a ferocious glare upon Rees. "Why would *I* marry *her*?" he demanded.

"So, why did Mr. Griffin try to kill you, Mr. Rees?" asked a selectman, his voice laden with scorn. "Are we supposed to believe that Mr. Griffin fathered one of Mrs. Whitney's brats, and you knew it?"

"Did your husband stray with Maggie?" Rees asked Maartje.

"No. No. He wouldn't. He didn't," she cried. "If that harlot accused him of it, she was lying." She clutched her hands tightly to her chest.

Rees looked around at all the faces. Most of them, with that human predilection for believing the worst, suspected Griffin was guilty. "I believe you," he told Maartje. "I doubt your husband had any kind of a romantic interest in Maggie Whitney. But he murdered her nonetheless. And Silas Tucker as well. The question is why. I began to wonder if Maggie's death had anything to do with who fathered which of her children. Until she was desperate to pay her taxes, she asked the fathers for nothing." Now Rees looked back at the selectmen, not troubling to hide his disgust. "She knew the selectmen were ready to warn her and her children out, and although she had some defenders they were fewer in number than those who wished to expel her. Silas Tucker was just waiting for a mistake, any mistake, that would give him those few acres he thought should be his. And she didn't have the money for her taxes. Hell, she didn't have money for food. Other than Simon's dollars, which were as likely to land her in jail for theft as not, she had nothing."

"She killed my baby and tried to pay me for it," Maartje said, exhibiting no guilt or remorse for accusing Maggie of theft. "As though that would make it right."

"So, Maggie approached those individuals she thought might give her a few pennies towards the taxes. Mr. Cooper—he was generous." Rees looked over and nodded at the constable. "Reverend Vermette."

"But I had none to give her."

Rees nodded, hearing exactly what he expected. "But you were affianced to someone who did." He looked at Miss Pike. "You, Miss Pike."

Her cheeks flushed red and then the blood drained away, leaving her face the white of porcelain. "Yes, she called upon me. I gave her a tuppence. And then I sent her away." Mutters rumbled through the assemblage. Miss Pike straightened and lifted her chin in defiance.

"Hmm. And so she applied finally to Mr. Gray." Rees paused and then, raising his voice, said harshly, "Don't lie, Mr. Gray. Your own niece overheard you and told my wife. Unless Maartje is lying, but I think in this case she is not. And when Maggie applied to you, she sealed her death warrant."

"Yes, she came to me," Mr. Gray admitted, his eyes lowered and his voice trembling. "But I didn't kill her."

"Elias had nothing to do with this," said Owen Randall, appalled.

"What most of you don't know," Rees said, "is that Silas suspected Caleb Griffin of murdering Maggie. Suspected it and thought he could use his knowledge for gain. And he had proof." He pulled the small Bible from his pocket and held it up. Since he fixed his gaze upon Miss Pike he could see the fear that froze her expression. Rees opened the Bible and read the inscription: "To M, the companion of my soul. Abner Vermette."

"I never . . . I didn't . . ." The Reverend gasped as he tried to find words.

"I know." Rees kept his eyes fixed upon Vermette's fiancée. "Miss Pike is the one who gave away this small Bible. Didn't you, Miss Pike?"

"I gave out many copies, all with the same inscription. Reverend Vermette signed them but yes, I wrote the dedications. I gave that Bible to the Griffins; the M refers to Maartje." She directed a shocked look at Maartje.

"Yes," Rees said. "You and Maartje were united by your dislike of Maggie Whitney."

Maartje stared at him. "Are you mad? I'm not strong enough to subdue Maggie. And I was pregnant."

"I do not doubt you are strong enough," Rees said. "This is what I think happened. Maggie decided to apply to Mr. Gray a second time for the money necessary to pay her taxes. But you met her at the door and refused her entry to his house. In the scuffle her cloak came off. Your husband, who had come to fetch you, struck her. Probably more than once. When she was unconscious, he took her to Mr. Gray's grave and threw her in. He used this Bible to read a passage over her. Then he sang a hymn while that poor young woman, who could still have been saved, lay unconscious on the ground. But you knew that. You knew he had killed her. And you lied over and over to protect him. You lied about seeing Mouse near the graveyard. You knew Reverend Vermette was taking Maggie upstairs to the bedroom in your uncle's house but told me he was taking her to the log meetinghouse. You knew Maggie's cloak could tie her to Mr. Gray and to you and your husband, so you smuggled it home.

You wore it right in front of me, wore it home and hid it so no one would find it." Rees nodded at the constable. He pulled a bundle from under his seat, a bundle that unfolded into Maggie's old blue cloak with the three-cornered tear in the hem.

"Tucked into the baby's cradle," Cooper said.

"Stop it, Mr. Rees," commanded Mr. Gray, staring at the cloak in horror. "Stop it." Tears filled his eyes and ran down his lined cheeks.

"Did you keep silent because of your baby's death?" Mrs. Baker asked, willing to extend compassion. "Was that it?"

"Or because you suspected your husband of sleeping with Maggie?" Cooper asked.

"He would never do that, never," Maartje cried. Her son woke with a start and began to wail. She picked him up and nestled him close, staring over his downy dark head.

"I think you colluded in Maggie's murder simply for financial gain," Rees said. "Mr. Randall told me your uncle Elias Gray gave you the money for your farm. And you told me how much you resented the gift of land your uncle had given to Reverend Vermette for his church. You did not want to share your uncle's estate."

"I won't stay here and listen to this," Maartje said, gathering up the child to her breast. "It's nothing but vile slander." Clutching the baby to her, she ran from the meetinghouse. Her sobbing began before she reached the door.

"Was such cruelty necessary, Mr. Rees?" Mrs. Baker asked. "Her husband is revealed as the murderer, not her. And she is now a widow with young children."

Rees turned his gaze to her and under his stern frown she flinched. "Cruel? You call me cruel? She blamed Maggie for all that was wrong in her life. She could have prevented this tragedy at almost any point, but she chose not to." He looked at

Vermette. "She knew about your association with Maggie, but did not say or do anything to prevent it. And that, despite her friendship with Miss Pike." He glanced at the woman. All her confidence had fled and she was weeping quietly. "Maartje knew her husband was guilty of murder, twice over, and said nothing." He shook his head. "I'm not cruel. She was. And now she will experience life as Maggie did." His prediction was so cold and so accurate it silenced everyone.

"But that doesn't explain why Caleb murdered Maggie," Cooper objected after a lengthy quiet. "Maggie had no claim on Mr. Gray. In fact, if I hadn't seen Caleb blow the head off the scarecrow I wouldn't believe it now. Why did he?"

"The answer lies in Maggie's past."

Mr. Randall stirred and shook his head. "No, Mr. Rees. This isn't necessary."

"Protecting the reputations of some of the men in this town put Maggie and her children under the constant threat of warning out and ultimately cost her her life. Yes, I think this is necessary." He stared at both Mr. Randall and Mr. Gray, not troubling to hide his contempt.

"I don't understand," Mr. Gray said. He looked around in confusion. "I don't understand any of this." In his bewilderment he looked vulnerable and very frail.

"What are we talking about?" Vermette asked. "What does that have to do with Maggie?"

"Most of the people in this town believe Maggie is the child of Olive Tucker's sister."

"Mr. Rees." Mr. Randall stood up, frowning. "What are you trying to accomplish?"

"Would you care to explain?" Rees turned his gaze upon the old man. Anger made his lips tremble and he pressed them together.

Mr. Randall sat down again.

"No? Then I will continue and, unless I am corrected, will assume I know the truth." Rees paused, but no one said anything. "Because Olive's sister was not a resident of Dover Springs, Maggie and her children were not considered residents either." Now Rees stared at the selectmen. "They lived under the constant threat of being warned out, sent to the town where her mother or her father came from. If she had applied for Poor Relief or could not pay her taxes, the council would have expelled her. Is that not true, Mr. Demming?"

Although none of the selectmen spoke, several members of the audience nodded.

"Well, I'm going to tell you who Maggie's mother and father were."

Mr. Randall shifted in his seat, rapping his cane upon the wooden bench. Rees looked at him, but the elderly man folded his lips together, refusing to speak.

"In 1771, the colonies were preparing for war. British soldiers were everywhere. Although I did not grow up here in Dover Springs, I remember that time. Local arms of the Sons of Liberty destroyed the properties and lives of the Loyalists. The Tories reacted in kind. And of course, some people attempted to remain on good terms with both sides. After all, no one knew who would win." Rees hesitated. He was moving into guesswork now.

"What does this have to do with anything?" one of the selectmen snapped.

"Phineas Tucker was ill, very ill, with the disease that would kill him a few years later. Olive was struggling. She had young children and a dying husband. Some of her husband's friends offered what help they could, but it wasn't enough. Phineas was in constant pain and required opium for relief. An expensive medicine."

"We all know this," Mr. Gray said.

"I suspect Olive began trading with the British to survive. I found a list of livestock and their prices in her family Bible."

"She would never do that!" Mr. Gray cried.

"She was desperate and the troops needed to eat. So she sold whatever she could to be able to afford the medicine Phineas required."

"Even if that's true," Cooper said, "who cares now? That was twenty years ago and more."

"That's not the end of the story," Rees said. "I would guess few knew of her secret activities. Olive's husband and his friends were passionate Patriots. But someone else, a Loyalist sympathizer, discovered her secret." Rees looked around but no one spoke. All eyes were fixed upon him.

"Your father visited her regularly," Rees said to Mr. Gray, turning to him suddenly. "You told me that yourself. As did Mr. Randall."

"He was trying to help her," the old man said. But guilty knowledge made his words shake. "Trying to help her and Phinney."

Rees shook his head. "Mr. Randall? You claim to be Phinney's good friend. What do you say?" Mr. Randall stared straight ahead, stone-faced. "I wondered why Maggie applied to you for help," Rees said, turning to Elias Gray. "She went only to those with whom she had some kind of connection. And there was never any suggestion that you fathered any of her children."

Mr. Gray gasped. "Of course not."

"Once I knew Olive Tucker was her mother, I knew Maggie's father must be local. Maggie went to you, Mr. Gray, because you share the same father. You are her half-brother." Rees expected a denial, but Mr. Gray did not speak. Instead, tears filled his eyes.

"How can you possibly know that?" Demming said. Turning

to the other selectmen, he said, "Mr. Rees is making this up from whole cloth."

"Mr. Randall?" Rees looked at the man. He turned his gaze away from Rees and fixed it upon the pulpit, so Rees continued. "Mouse mentioned hearing Maggie refer to her brother as though he were living locally. But Olive did not know where her sons had gone. The entries in the Bible said only 'gone west.' So Maggie must have had another brother."

"Elias Gray is her brother." Mary Pettit rose to her feet. With a rustle, the people shifted around to see her. "Olive confided the father's name when she gave birth to Maggie. I never said anything for all those years. But I knew Maggie was desperate. Pregnant again." Her gaze shifted to Vermette, and then she looked back to Rees. "She was struggling to pull together the money for her taxes and in real danger of losing her farm and being warned out. I thought she had a right to know about her half-brother, so I told her, the day before she was murdered."

Elias Gray bowed his head.

"Your father loved Olive," Mary said, gentling her voice, "and Olive cared for him as well."

"You're going to believe this old squaw?" Demming said, looking around him in disbelief.

"Maggie believed," Rees said. "And Mr. Randall, at least, knows it is true. Isn't it?" He stared challengingly at Owen Randall. The old man sat in silence, with no more reaction than a statue.

"You persuaded Griffin to deal with Maggie by telling him that he and Maartje, who were supposed to inherit Mr. Gray's land, would lose the property to Maggie. Didn't you?"

Still nothing.

"When Silas tried to blackmail him, Griffin killed him, too. But it was you who tried to shoot me and set fire to Silas's house."

"How could he do such a thing?" Cooper protested. "He's lame."

"He left buggy tracks."

"Caleb drives a buggy also."

"Indeed. But I found Mr. Randall's footprints, and the marks of his cane, in the snow," Rees replied, fixing Owen Randall with implacable concentration. "I wondered why the man shooting at me did not pursue me down the hill. And of course, the answer is, you could not. So, since you failed, you sent your cat's-paw after me. Griffin came first to the Whitney farm. But he did not try very hard to kill me, instead shooting a warning shot into the door. Was he beginning to lose his taste for murder? In any case, the arrival of the constable scared him off. My "praying for the Lord's guidance" gave you an opportunity to send him after me again, but this time it was a trap. And when Mr. Cooper took Griffin into custody, you knew you would have to deal with him. Otherwise, he would betray you. You walked down to Cooper's shop and shot your own nephew through the window." Still the old man didn't speak. But Rees, as he looked around, knew he'd succeeded in making his case, at least to Mr. Gray. His face was contorted with suffering

"Maggie told me she was my sister. I sent her away. I didn't want to believe."

"The question remains: why?" Rees continued, keeping his attention upon Mr. Randall. "Why keep the secret of Maggie's parentage? Almost everyone involved is dead."

When Mr. Randall still did not speak, Mr. Gray said, his voice breaking with anguish, "Tell me, Owen, why did you keep this secret from me?"

"And shame you in front of the entire town?" Mr. Randall retorted angrily. "Shame you and Phinney? I value your friendship too much."

"But you told me Phinney knew that Maggie was Olive's child by another man," Rees said. "You said he shared that secret with you."

"I lied. Phinney never knew," Mr. Randall said. "I saw Judge Gray and Olive together. Both married. And her wed to Phinney. She didn't deserve him."

"You told me Phinney, your close friend, begged you to look after Olive and Maggie." Rees's voice quivered with outrage. "This is how you do it, by collaborating in the death of Olive's daughter?"

"Well, I didn't know the whole truth, did I? Maybe Olive offered herself to the judge. Maybe she sold herself to British soldiers. She was desperate, after all. I didn't know. But Judge Gray was a great man, well respected by all. I wasn't going to tarnish his reputation. Or dishonor Phinney's memory and embarrass Elias. And my nephew and Maartje, well, they deserved to inherit Elias's property. As for Maggie, I did what I could; I spoke for her at the selectmen's meetings."

Rees looked back at the four selectmen. Although Cooper's father-in-law was regarding Mr. Randall in revulsion, the other three town fathers were shaking their heads. They refused to believe. But Mr. Gray, he accepted the truth. Tears ran freely down his cheeks. He lifted one blue-veined hand to wipe his eyes.

"She applied to you for money so she could pay the property taxes. But you sent her away," Rees said, pitying the old man in spite of himself.

Mr. Gray nodded. "I didn't believe her then. Didn't want to." Using the heels of his hands, he scrubbed at his wet eyes.

"Then?" This time Rees paused to allow Mr. Gray a moment to speak.

"I . . . thought about it. After, you see. I remembered certain things I had overheard. And there was Olive's silhouette on the wall of my father's room. I realized . . ." He swallowed painfully. "I realized Maggie might be speaking the truth."

"And you began to think you might give her some money?" Rees suggested. Mr. Gray nodded.

"Yes. I even thought of amending my will. Those children are my nieces and nephews." Even now the wonder of it filled his voice. "But I said nothing to Maartje."

"She knew," Maartje's cousin said loudly, her sweet high voice cutting through the air like a knife. "She overheard your conversation with Maggie. And she was furious about it. She felt you owed her. Because she took care of you, you see." Mr. Gray turned to her.

"I'm sorry," he said, ashamed. "Maartje was always my favorite. I'm sorry for that now. I wronged you as well as Maggie."

Rees, drained into exhaustion, lowered himself into the front pew next to Lydia. After a minute of appalled silence, people began to prepare to leave. No one approached him. He hadn't expected it. Telling the truth, especially when it revealed long-buried secrets, made him unpopular. He remembered hearing a story about a female fortune-teller named Cassandra. Nobody listened to her or believed her and she was hated when her predictions came true. He knew how she must have felt.

In the pew behind Rees, Reverend Vermette turned to Miss Pike and reached out for her. They rose together and started toward the doors, arm in arm.

"So they will wed after all," Lydia said, joining Rees in the front.

He nodded.

"And what of Mr. Randall?" Lydia said, turning around to look at the old man. Rees followed her gaze. Mr. Randall was threatening the constable with his cane as he attempted to take

Mr. Randall into custody. Cooper met Rees's eyes and saluted him with a quick wave.

"Mr. Randall will be lucky to escape hanging," Rees murmured, "not the least because he made fools of everyone. His fellow selectmen, once they accept Mr. Randall's confession as true, won't forget that slight."

By now most of the audience had hurried out. Mary Pettit approached Rees, her steps hesitant. Rees stood up. "Thank you," he said. "You told the truth."

Mary paused a few feet away. "Maggie was my friend. Anyway, I'm dying. No one can hurt me anymore." She attempted a small smile and turned to go, her gait slow and unsteady.

"Wait." Rees pulled his last handful of coppers from his pocket and offered them to her. Mary accepted them with a bow of thanks.

"I give her no more than a month or two," Lydia murmured as the old woman made her careful way to the door. "But that impulsive generosity of yours will keep her fed for a little while."

"Mr. Rees?" Elder Herman said from behind Rees. He moved around to face the Elder. Mouse, her eyes downcast and her hand held protectively over her mouth, stood a few steps to the Elder's side.

"I am so grateful to you both," she said. "You've cleared my name. Thank you for that."

From her tone, Rees suddenly experienced an unwelcome suspicion that something unfortunate had happened and the Shakers were keeping it from him and Lydia. "What do you mean?" he asked. "Tell me, Mouse." She threw a glance at Elder Herman. Rees looked at the Elder, who was watching Mouse with sadness. "What have you done?" Rees asked.

Herman sighed. "Sister Hannah will be transferred to another community now that the murderer has been found and our Sister cleared of all wrongdoing."

"Away from here?" Rees asked.

"Away from Joseph?" Lydia's voice rose. "But she loves Joseph."

"Yes," the Elder said. "It is felt by the Ministry that she should not obtain her heart's desire through an act of wrongdoing. She attempted to steal those children twice."

"She probably saved Joseph's life," Lydia argued. "And the other children . . . they needed our care."

Elder Herman inclined his head in a tacit acknowledgment of her point. "You may very well be correct. And those of us who know our Sister"—he looked at Mouse with sympathy—"know she acted only from the very best and most loving of intentions. But this was not her decision to make. And she disobeyed a direct order. I instructed her to leave those children alone and she took a buggy and went after them a second time. And then, after I gave my promise to the constable, she didn't remain at Mount Unity."

"Oh, Mouse," Lydia said, reaching out to take Mouse's hand.

"I know." The Elder bowed his head a moment. He didn't want to take this step any more than Mouse did, but he had to follow the Shaker way. "Sister Hannah understands."

Mouse nodded. "It's all right, Lydia. I do understand. Watch over Joseph for me, please." Lydia nodded, unable to speak, and the two women bowed their heads together in silent grief.

"And what of the children?" The Elder asked Rees. "When will you bring them to us?"

Lydia looked up, her tear-filled eyes flashing. "Wait," she said to Rees, so vehemently he paused. She stared at him, her fierce gaze warning him to promise nothing.

"There are some . . . knots still to be worked smooth," he said. "Simon is the heir to both Maggie's and Silas Tucker's farms. I will have to see about a contract."

Elder Herman nodded. "Very well. I look forward to speaking with you again." He looked at Mouse, who slowly and reluctantly pulled herself from Lydia's comforting embrace.

"Remember," she said to Lydia. "Take care of him for me. You promised."

Rees put his hand upon Lydia's arm and slowly drew her away. Mouse looked at Lydia once more, her gaze full of meaning, and then she turned and meekly followed Elder Herman down the aisle.

"We have to keep Joseph," Lydia said.

"What!"

Lydia offered Rees a slight smile. "Mouse just asked me to raise him and I promised I would. And I will."

"But Lydia," Rees began. She did not argue, but she looked at him with an unyielding expression. He knew this was a battle he could not win.

"And the other children?" he asked, already resigned to something different than leaving them with the Shakers.

"We'll see."

When he followed his wife into the cabin, all the children but Joseph were seated around the table. Joseph was lying on the floor playing with Judah's wooden cart and horse, thumping them both relentlessly upon the floorboards. Jerusha and Simon looked at Rees anxiously.

Rees sat down. "We know the identity of the man responsible for your mother's death," he said. He paused, but neither of the two older children asked who the murderer was.

Instead Jerusha asked, "What will happen to us?"

"Are we being sent to the Shakers?" Simon asked, clutching his hands anxiously together.

"Yes," Rees said. "For the time being. And you," he spoke to Simon as though he were another adult, "will want to learn all they have to teach you. When you reach your majority, you will inherit this farm and this money." He pushed the bag of silver dollars across the table. "This was given to your mother by your father."

Simon opened the bag and looked at it. With the air of a man of business, he pulled out a coin and shot it across to Rees. "For your expenses," he said. Rees almost sent it back to the boy but didn't. His pockets were empty.

"Thank you," he said. "This will pay for the journey home."

"The farm," Lydia said, looking around her, at the rough cottage, "was left to you by your grandmother Olive."

"She wasn't our grandmother," Jerusha began, jumping to her feet.

"She was," Rees said. "Maggie was her daughter. Olive had her reasons for not telling the truth." Looking puzzled by the mysteries of the adult world, Jerusha sat back down.

"An agreement with Elder Herman will be drawn up," Rees continued. "You won't have to join that community unless you wish to. But, until you are old enough to farm it yourself, the Shakers at Mount Unity will make sure no one takes any of this from you. They are the only ones I trust. And this property will be waiting for you."

Simon remained silent for a long moment. "And my brothers and sisters will go with me?"

"All but Joseph," Rees said. "Miss Lydia promised Mouse that we would take Joseph and raise him." Lydia looked at Rees and smiled at him.

"And me," Jerusha said. "I'm going with you." Both Rees and Lydia stared at the child in surprise. "You can't go without me. You can't. You'll need my help with the baby."

"I do believe I can manage Joseph," Lydia replied with a smile.

"Not Joseph. The baby that's coming. Your baby."

Rees turned to gape at Lydia, surprise, joy, and fear all running through him. "Baby? We're having a baby? Why didn't you tell me?"

A betraying tide of scarlet swept up her neck and into her cheeks. "I was going to," she whispered. "I just, well . . . there never seemed to be a good time."

Rees sat back in his chair, stunned. He didn't know which of his emotions was uppermost. Joy? Fear? Elation? All three. "When is the baby due?"

"Fall. September, I think."

"I know you'll need me," Jerusha said, her saucy confidence overlaying the fear that they would not want her. When she looked up at Lydia, the yearning for a mother shone so nakedly from her eyes Rees felt a lump form in his throat.

"But what about us?" Simon asked.

"Don't leave us," Nancy said, clutching Jerusha's skirt with one grubby hand.

Jerusha looked from her siblings to Lydia and back again. "Can't you take us all? Please." Lydia gazed at Rees, her mouth trembling and tears hovering in her eyes.

Rees swallowed. He knew Lydia's heart was breaking; he felt the same.

Jerusha clutched her hands together in an agony of hope and stared at him pleadingly. He looked at Lydia and, although her hands were not clasped in prayer, her expression was no less beseeching.

He sighed. "Oh, very well," he said gruffly, just as though he was angry and unwilling to adopt them. "It will be a tight trip to Maine. I'm warning you." But he was glad. He'd been given another chance to be a better father.

He wondered how David would react to this suddenly enlarged family.

Author's Note

How much of the information about the Poor Relief Laws and warning out is true? Unfortunately, all of it. Many town selectmen did exactly as described: decided which people would receive help and which would not. Many people who'd spent their entire lives in a town would be warned out, to travel the roads searching for shelter and food. Or, sometimes, they would be transported to the town of their births, where they knew no one and had no home and no way of earning a living. Pregnant paupers were particularly at risk, since the town fathers would not want a child born who might later have a claim to financial help.

Children were apprenticed out at the age of twelve or thirteen. Orphans could be given out as apprentices as young as six, although usually the new masters expected some remuneration, because children this young couldn't work as hard as adults. Masters were expected to educate their charges as well as feed and clothe them, but abuse was rampant. Contemporary accounts do mention some cases where the children were removed due to abuse so extreme neighbors complained.

Finally, a word on language. This was a much more formal age than our own. Surnames were used in preference to first names, except for children. Parents were not called Mommy or Dad but the more formal Mother or Father. One account I read described a wife who referred to her husband as Mister their entire married life. However, I have chosen to use a lot of first names, especially in the case of families, where calling multiple characters by the same last name might result in confusion.

I also use a somewhat formal writing style, perhaps not as formal as Tobias Smollett or Jane Austen, but more formal than most of us contemporary readers are used to. I apologize for any anachronisms. Sometimes they do creep in, but usually I have chosen to use a word familiar to my readers instead of the one accurate to the period, just for the sake of clarity.

Eleanor Kuhns